C.3

22.99

P9-CAO-604

TALES OF THE CITY

TALES OF THE CITY

St. Mary's Bar & Slipshod Watchman

Huck Fairman

For Pam & Lexie

ACKNOWLEDGEMENTS

I would like to thank Ann Hayes, Leita Hamill, Lee Gardner, and my wife, Pamela McPartland-Fairman, for their patient and insightful help in shaping and editing these two stories.

I would like to thank Mara Arakaki for her cover design and art work.

In *St. Mary's Bar*, excerpted lyrics from the song, 'Fair Ireland,' are used with permission from Alfred Publishing Co., Inc. 2006

In *Slipshod Watchman*, lines from Yevtushenko's poem, 'Colours' are used with permission from Penguin Group, London. 2006

Copyright © 2007 by Huck Fairman.
Cover Design by Mara Rubia Arakaki

Library of Congress Control Number: 2006908303
ISBN: Hardcover   978-1-4257-3402-2
                 Softcover   978-1-4257-3401-5

All rights reserved. No part of this book may be reproduced or transmitted in any form
or by any means, electronic or mechanical, including photocopying, recording, or by
any information storage and retrieval system, without permission in writing from the
copyright owner.

This is a work of fiction. Names, characters, places and incidents either are the product of
the author's imagination or are used fictitiously, and any resemblance to any actual persons,
living or dead, events, or locales is entirely coincidental.

This book was printed in the United States of America.

To order additional copies of this book, contact:
Xlibris Corporation
1-888-795-4274
www.Xlibris.com
Orders@Xlibris.com
31014

ST. MARY'S BAR

NEW YORK CITY

Mid 1990's

FRIENDS AND LOVERS

TERRY . . . painter, art appraiser, gallery owner with wife, Viv, father of two

VIVIAN . . . painter, gallery owner with husband, Terry, mother of two

PETER . . . graphic designer, amateur painter, lives with Sam

SAM . . . graphic artist, amateur singer, lives with Peter

LOU . . . computer salesman, close friend of Errol, boyfriend of Irene

JOSEPH . . . college professor, novelist, magazine editor, husband of Bonnie, father of Noah

CHRISTINE . . . journalist, novelist, lives with Daniel

FIN . . . journalist

ERROL . . . school teacher, aspiring playwright, husband of Leslie, father of Molly and Lilly

DANIEL . . . poet, living with Christine

LESLIE . . . Errol's wife, mother of two, Molly and Lilly

BONNIE . . . Joseph's wife, mother of Noah

IRENE . . . Lou's girlfriend

I.

The Round Table

Squinting Terry pauses in his telling, surveys the scene, takes in the faces arrayed around the table. Friends of a sort. Odd sorts mostly. Artists chasing self-expression, at the margins sadly . . . So what then are these evenings? Freakin' feel-good sessions?

His eyes fall to his drink, from which he plucks the red cocktail cherry. Turning it slowly, he considers its bright, acrylic sheen, then brings it to his lips and bites it cleanly from the stem. Wedging it to one side, he throws down the dregs of his Manhattan and savors the bitters. The faces come back into focus as he positions his incisors and cleaves the cherry, his tongue feeling for the meager pulp.

Across the table Louie's watching, telling himself that 'Terry the Teach' loves this, holdin' forth. "Il padrone," he whispers to himself. Like the professor, he thinks, glancing at Joseph. The two of 'em serious, privy to the way things work, they'd have us believe. Where would we be without 'em, the self-anointed, lifting us from these mean streets? . . . Basta! . . .

The group, Terry sees, is ready, primed for the finale. Peter, Sam, Christine, frowning Louie—What's with him?—and punctilious Joseph. Each with his own discontent. But then who isn't battered by the struggle, drowned in the clamor?

Carefully, deeply, Terry inhales, clears his throat, picks up the story: the museum, elbowing its way onto the map, hired him as an art consultant to evaluate the authenticity of a painting. But the directors dismissed his first misgivings, that the background figures were not rendered in the artist's style. They simply repeated that the provenance was certified, that other experts had signed off on it.

"Christ!" he'd muttered—wondering if it wasn't bowling balls and box cutters, he heard, bashing, slashing at his reputation—why then had they come to him? Standard procedure, they replied, to assure the integrity of the process. Whose bloody integrity? he'd wondered.

He had returned to the painting. The pigmentation had seemed plausible. The other chemical tests he did were inconclusive. But removing the frame and backing—again he clears his throat, replaying the moment—he found, analyzing a sliver of the canvas's back fold, that it was . . . a fake.

"All right!" cries Peter above other cheers and laughter rimming the table. Peter is tickled, and appalled, by the deception and cover up in the hallowed world of art. His black eyes gleam uncertainly.

Terry holds up a hand for quiet, his full, mauve lips worming in consternation. His large, brown eyes, watching amid the folds, seem to swallow the light, before, with a silent sigh, he presses on, "But once again they dismissed it, saying I was mistaken, perhaps didn't have the necessary expertise . . . What? *Their* unexpurgated expertise?" Irritated, he swipes at the remaining wandering strands of dark hair atop his large, pale crown. His pained expression wordlessly impugns their fraud. Reliving the rebuff, the humiliation, inflames the Dureresque winter hues of his face, and watching him, his audience cannot but share the sting.

"So," he shrugs, looking over at the crowded bar, "they went ahead and bought it." His gaze falls to the table and his empty glass, at which he unhappily stares, before lifting his heavy eyes. "Last week, however, I got a call from an art historian, over from Delft, who had been allowed to see the painting. He'd caught wind of my investigation and examined the canvas . . . There was no other conclusion possible, he agreed . . . It's a scam, a repro . . . The museum will not be hanging it."

For a moment the others waver, until snorts and shouts ignite a rising laughter, briefly crescendoing, quickly subsiding. "But why, Terry, why?" calls puzzled Peter, a painter in his spare time, "why would someone with talent turn to that?"

Terry's dark gaze rolls his way. "Money, Peter."

Peter groans, slapping his thighs and anxiously squeezing them, while next to him, Sam, his girlfriend and live-in roommate, presses the point, "But why would he not simply do his own work?"

Once more Terry's heavy eyes grope for his inquisitor. "Most likely the counterfeiter is Eastern European, or Russian, and there's not much of a market for their original work."

"He could support himself like you do, like Peter and I do," Sam grouses with little sympathy, "like we all have to."

Inclining his head Terry lowers his voice. "It's not easy to find a job that pays a living wage." Against the back of his neck a faint current riles the hairs—his wife's breath. Vivian has heard the story, several times, and expels her impatience with a sigh. Terry reaches back to gently stroke her leg, only to encounter her hands carefully cupping his.

To Terry's right, Peter continues turning the story in his mind. "How desperate that poor Ivan musta been," he mumbles, slowly shaking his head. "Almost seems a shame he was caught." Then Peter mentally kicks himself: damn it! The wrong way to kowtow to big T, big Buddha. Guess I'd better not pop the question tonight . . . But when, old goat? When the hell are you going to take my work, give me a show? My stuff is as good as that scungilli you hang. Better! Better than your stuff, the both of you. What you guys know is how to squeeze those johns of yours. As for that guy, whoever he is, in his underground studio . . . what balls! And what a jerk, to screw up on the canvas of all things . . .

For months Peter has been edging toward asking Terry to hang his paintings in the gallery the couple runs, and now he expels an inner cry: let's do it, Terry! Let's do it to it, for Mother Mary! . . . As the ensuing silence washes emptily through his brain, he knows, however, that above all he wants to avoid the definitive no, the thin thread of hope being severed.

It is on these winter Wednesday nights that this group and several straggling late-comers gather here at the round table in St. Mary's Bar, as they've dubbed it, to drink and talk. From Lower Manhattan's brick buildings and brown tenements they come, from Bowery and Chrystie, from east on Houston and west of Hudson, from down Second and up Sixth, on foot, on buses, on horseback, assback, in trains or cabs, pilgrims bundled against the cold, minds pawing toward its light. With its narrow face unproclaimed by any sign, and its large iron-framed window dimly lit by three neon beer logos, the bar stares obliquely out on the street, so plain that it's all but unnoticed by passersby. Yet it fills with stout knights and their ladies in their twenties, thirties, and forties and rings with their congealed excitement.

Still seeking reactions to his story, Terry's restless eyes falter over Peter, hunched down and mumbling. He wonders about him, why he doesn't push himself beyond his Rothko-like planes of color, stroked in his apartment year after year, like salve to an unhealing wound. It's not that there isn't something to them—some are of rich Etruscan shades—but they are neither sufficiently innovative nor alive to sell. They don't stir the acquisitive juices . . . So why doesn't he wrench something else, something new, from his narrow life? . . . But then, few do . . . few do . . . Terry's now-slitted eyes fall to his hand on the table, frozen by dissatisfaction with his own paintings.

Vivian leans forward gently upon his shoulder, her mind floating up and out of the bar, though her large oval eyes and African features do not move. She thinks of their two young children home in their apartment with a teenage babysitter from the apartment below—the former, she hopes, and not the latter, sleeping. Slowly she surveys the faces before her, some shadowed, some lemoned by the bar's yellow light. She would like to try to paint these faces, these friends, of a sort, in half-circle before her, turned this way or that—a pallid plane of profiles, eyes, bodies, all adrift, like the pale, plucked chickens nesting on ice at Meyerbaum's Market.

Her thoughts swing southward, skimming aqua skies and soft Caribbean clouds to her childhood home in Antigua and her stone-faced, stone-hearted mother, about whom she has long felt, at best, ambivalence. Her mother, in whom she began life and from whom she has never ceased parting, like continental drift, she thinks, from embryonic Gondwanaland. Oh yes, Mother felt her life was hard, never rising to the levels she envisioned for herself. But why then—along an endless, fluttering ribbon of questions—did she burden herself with four children? She was not stupid. She would have foreseen how that would obligate, subjugate . . . Did she, in some period of weakness, fall sway to wifely duty misconceived? . . . Certainly it was not maternal compulsion . . . And why did she allow that schooner-man, that all-but-unknown sailor, to become my father? He with his windy comin's and goin's on that big boat ending only with his disappearin' altogether.

Likely it was Mother's own bitter self which pushed her into the corner. Deep down, Viv shudders, aware of her own tinctures of bitterness. Yet without it all being like that, I might never have fled up here . . . might never have reached out to painting, never've met Terry . . . never've had dear Lizabeth and little William. Sometime we'll fly back down again, t' introduce 'em to their grandmother . . . Won't that be somethin', t' see d' expressions all around . . . Only hope the sun down there c'n smooth over all d' wounds.

Across the table, Joseph, age forty-three, serious, graying, features oddly disjointed, had been talking to Christine next to him—a decade younger, and beautiful, he is thinking. A bloody flower pushed up through the rubble. He had wanted to ask her about submitting something to the Baruch College literary magazine he edits, but her attention had been drawn off by Terry's

16

story. Now, when she half-turns back, he tries, "Christine, you interested in sending us something?"

Christine looks over, her short blond hair an indistinct brightness floating above her black sweater. She notices, with her eyelevel now slightly above his, that she can read something unmistakably anxious, darkly bitten, in Joseph, pressing him down, pinching his lips, all but closing his eyes. And yes, something, she hears, is choking the flow. Frustration maybe, for she knows a bit of his story and knows the struggle of writing. And though he's recently sold a novel, because it was, well, a baldly commercial effort, he seems restive, touchy. Yes, all the too-familiar symptoms . . .

When their eyes meet, he sees that hers are now watching him carefully, coolly. Judging him no doubt . . . Judas! Is there nothing to unlock the possibilities of friendship? Nothing to connect us around this table and the interests we share? . . . Evidently not. The chemistry is missing, or wrong, or some fractured thing . . . freezing me out, beyond the circle of her cares.

Christine has guessed something of his thoughts, the tenor of them, if not the details, and she looks down, to spare them both. There was a time in her life, several years ago, when she was similarly gripped by frustration, loss, and her inability to quite find the right path.

Left by hers now, Joseph's eyes briefly sweep the table. Yet he feels her preference for others gnawing at him. A judgment, a relegating, in the way she listens to and watches . . . Errol, say, who will eventually straggle in . . . What makes him so God-favored? His innocence? His probably futile struggle to get a play produced? Joseph feels his stomach roll and roil, so that he must cough and swallow its bitter bile. Contributing to the distancing, no doubt, is his so-called success. No longer do the others ask about the magazine or his manuscripts and battles lost and won. Instead they turn their halting inquiries to Errol, plying, commiserating with, finding solace in troubles worse than their own.

Looking up again, Christine remembers his question and tells him that yes, she could submit some chapters from a new manuscript. Joseph feels his chin affirming with short, quick chops. "Fine, good, good. Love to, love to see them." Yet inwardly he winces, wiping his brow, remembering he'd shown no such enthusiasm over her first novel, which he'd been unable to finish, eventually hiding it out of sight under other unfinished books. Tipping his head and stein back for a long swallow, he confesses that he's come to enjoy gazing at her, however simple and mindless. Superficial, sure; unfair, of course, to one of the few noble souls he knows, but it's damn near slid into obsession . . . Jesus! Sometimes wonder why else I'm here. Again he coughs and shakes himself. Get a grip!

Watching him, Christine adds that she'll send the chapters over to his office, and as Joseph nods uncomfortably, she reminds herself that she likes him, his old-world seriousness, his sinewy tenacity, his face from Krakow or Brno—a pale medieval knight, scarred by life's encounters. She admires what he's achieved, with his magazine and his writing. Not easy on top of a full teaching load and family.

Distracted by these thoughts, their glances drift across the other faces, until a frigid draft, sweeping in from the nearby door, steals their breaths and augurs another arrival. Head swiveling, Terry trumpets, "Fin! . . . Good man! Glad you made it. Glad you could fit us in."

"Mista Fin-n!" brays Louie, ahead of other flocking greetings. "Sir Lance-a-lot! Our wick-dippin' lover boy," he sneers under his breath before belching into the din.

Finian Waite, mid-thirties, wrapped against the cold in scarf and pea jacket—an image torn from a Jack London paperback—stops behind Christine and Lou who are twisting around to see him. Fin gives Lou a heavy, hearty cuff on the shoulder which sends Lou tipping nearly into Christine's lap.

"Louie!" she cries, "Not here! Not now!"

"Go for it, Lou!" cries Peter. "Snatch those golden threads."

"Hey watch it, cowboy," growls Lou Fin-ward as he slowly rights himself, apologizing to Christine. Eyes alight, she pats his shoulder, wondering at these ancient male rituals.

Silently Sam and Viv watch Fin's turning face catching the light. Sam sings his name to herself, fond of its syllables: Fin, Fin, Finian. Come, come, come again; Fin, Fin, Finnegan. While across the table, Viv, studying the soft contours couching his ancient-seeming, glittering eyes, is thinking, nonetheless, childe.

Unwrapping the scarf from around his dimpled chin and longish brown hair, Fin unveils a devil-eyed liveliness which some enjoy but which others feel veers too frequently into irreverence and sarcasm. Scanning the crew, he offers, "C'n I get any of you rumguzzlers another round while I'm up?"

Terry alone accepts his offer, scudding his empty cocktail glass across the wooden table. "Manhattan, straight up, Fin. Thanks."

Stretching unsteadily over Lou for the glass, Fin warbles, "Good man, Terr. Screw the Zeitgeist. Hold with the eternal verities." And he raises the Grail high before returning it to eyelevel and sniffing its contents, then gagging. "What *is* this stuff, Terr? Something for the out-of-body rush?" He throws down a lingering drop, then hastily exhales, "Wow-ee! . . . Industrial strength!"

"What's the matter, old man?" sniggers Lou. "Too tart for that cherry-pickin' tongue?"

"Olé!" bursts Sam, revved by Louie's energy, not his derision. "A toast, Finnegan," she sings out, lifting her goblet, "a toast to us all! To our fellowship!" Cries and gurgling levity, midst fleeting doubts, run round the table, save from Terry, who suddenly disenchanted, stretches forward to hand Fin a crumpled five.

Taking the bill, Fin spins about, holding it to the wind, and sidesteps over to the bar, gliding past heads and backs of patrons chatting, swigging. Find the boozers in the best bars, he sings to himself, hear the rhymers in the dives. Come let us all go, down to desolation row. Finding a space, he leans in to order, wondering at the same time how he might engage the elusive maiden, the genuine Christine, in conversation tonight—she, an uptown girl with a downtown sensibility, a vessel of mystery, to be gazed at, wondered at, imagined, embellished. He pictures her long, slender waist, pictures everything as some internal back-up choir croons: cryin' t' get to heaven, before they say no more.

Seeing the bartender waiting, he sings out his order, "One Wicked Ale and a Manhattan straight up." The bartender sings back, "I'll take Manhattan . . . Brooklyn and the Bronx . . ."

Fin's eyes bounce along the line of faces, then back to the table of friends, visible through the haze and milling bodies. How small and vulnerable they appear, heads and arms frail as marionettes, as insects wiggling, swilling . . . Yet stuff that frailty! The irrepressible life force wriggles on. Crush the hind legs, and the fore legs claw the air.

In the course of collecting his drinks and tipping the singing bartender, he allows his gaze to ascend the shelves of liquor and glasses, up to the top where a small, dusty fresco of Mary, mother of it all, holding the still innocent controversy in her lap, stares serenely out through the yellow haze. Somewhere in his pinwheeling mind, Fin blows her a kiss.

At the table, he stretches across to hand Terry his Manhattan and change, then pulls a chair around between Christine and Lou. As she's again talking with Joseph, he turns to Lou. "So Louie, my man, what's the internet joke-of-the-week? What's new in computers that I can't live without?" But listening to Terry expand on details of art sleuthing, Lou shushes and waves him away. Fin's eyes fall to his Wicked Ale which he hoists for a good, full swallow. Ahhh, soldier . . .

Emboldened, he turns back to Christine still inclined in conversation with Joseph. Can't let another evening slip by, he chides, as she's hinted she'll soon bring her knight to the table—Danny . . . Danny boy, the pipes, the pipes are calling—That'll shut down the fantasies. Are not the epistles the true wives of the apostles?

But now Lou, feeling more amenable, swings around to find him. "So, Don Juan, what were you askin'? . . . Hey man, you look wiped . . . Those long jousting nights hammerin' your days? Sorry I haven't read your latest."

Rolling his head—Lou's always just a little off—Fin considers the limitations of these glancing connections. Lou's not a bad dude, but the walls are quickly reached. I mean, what really do we give each other, besides some mild comradeship? Propinquity possibly . . . or mild encouragement in our work . . . Shouldn't disparage, though. We do our best, we males, the best we know how . . . Wonder, though, if I can goose him a little. "Lou, when are we gonna see those stories? The ones you keep mentioning, your portraits from the South Bronx?"

"What?" grumbles Lou unhappily looking away.

For several moments the two watch the others, until Lou, nosing toward Christine, whispers to Fin, "I thought it was tonight she was bringing her honcho."

"D' poetical dude?" wonders Fin, eyebrows arching, framing his view. "Maybe she decided to have mercy on the unsuspecting grinch."

"Mensch, is what I hear," amends Lou.

Fin shrugs disinterestedly. "Unseen is unreal."

"She was smart not to shove him in Joseph's face," Lou speculates, eyes running over her north to south.

Fin leans toward him. "Why? They don't need Joseph's rag. It's he who needs them—her in particular. What she symbolizes."

"Symbolizes? . . . And what's that?"

Fin gazes at her, trying to reign in straying thoughts. "The independent woman, alone and unbowed."

"Really?" Raising an eyebrow, Lou looks over again at the two conversing. "But she's not alone."

Fin stops glancing around and stares into Christine's hair a yard or so in front of him, into which he'd like to sink his face, and concedes, "No, but that's her rep." And yet, it's now to Joseph that his thoughts for some reason swerve. Earnest, driven Joseph, deeply ensconced professor, savant, author—our King Author—holding the realm together, a struggling, burdened husband, yet somehow turning out the stuff. As Fin tips down another swallow, he finds his mind asking itself: and you, Sir Type-alot, what can you claim? . . . Caught in the maw of a marble-eyed coelacanth, sucking you into its tunnels black as nothing . . .

From across the table, a rolling, phlegmy throat-clearing suppresses conversation and draws all eyes to Peter. "Hey, paisanos . . . got a little announcement, something to tickle your testicles—Sorry, ladies . . . . Sam, here, is giving a recital this coming weekend."

Murmurs of surprise and excitement wash through the group. Vivian, her attention called back to them, leans toward Sam. "Why congratulations, girl! What is it you'll be singing?"

With her brown hair swinging just above her shoulders, Sam's pleasant features smile through shyness. Uneasy with so many watching, she hides in Vivian's bottomless pupils. "Two Puccini arias, Viv, and an Irish song. Hope you'll come."

"Oh, don't worry Sam, I'll be there . . . Sounds like a lot to prepare," fears Viv, eyes round with concern.

Lou—Louis, Louie, Luigi—sitting next to Viv, his pale, puffed, unshaven face contrasting her smooth brown one—asks Sam, "Yo, girlie, where and when is d' gig?" Originally from the South Bronx, the final and forgotten child of a Russian mother and Italian father, Lou digs the little riffs of street talk that filled his early ears, and which he claims he'll someday set down on paper.

"No gig, Louie. It's really only for my teacher, but he said I could invite a few friends. Sunday at three, M&M Studio, Broadway at Spring." Straightening her back, steeling her sense of self, she surveys the faces watching. In them, she reads sincerity mixed with surprise—in all save Peter, her Peter, her Little Lord Fauntleroy, shining with false goodwill. Oh, he acts the act, talks the talk, but behind that, holds himself apart—he, who prods her to adore his paintings, refuses to applaud her singing progress. And how pathologically he avoids the C-word, with jittery derision, keeping everything light, undefined . . . *un*committed. All questions about their future are dodged. They're the only un-analyzed couple she knows. God, half of her friends are in therapy, and while she understands the crazy, matriarchal family he comes from, the oppressive older sisters, his teary, manipulative mother, in league against him and his sweet, defenseless father . . . still, I mean, the man's recently pushed into his forties, for God's sake.

Next to her, Peter sees that her soft brown eyes have glazed over, in the way they do when she's thinking unhappy thoughts. "Motherhumper," he mutters to stir himself. Better say something. "Ah folks," he calls out, "if

I may have your attention once more . . . first, I want to say to those who haven't heard Sam here, this is a lady with a real voice . . . and I've heard a few in my day . . . and second, by way of celebration, I've brought, for the discerning members here, something to mark the occasion." His smiling eyes fall to his shirt pocket, from which he draws two fat cigars. "Like Sam here, the real thing." He displays the two over the table for inspection. "As close to a Havana as one is likely to get, short of the real deal. So how 'bout it folks?" His eyes widen in anticipation of both positive and negative reactions. Placing the cigars down, like two legs, he struts them smartly back and forth, before repeating his offer, primarily to the men in the circle. When there is no clamor to accept, he seeks Christine's dulling eyes. "Christine, my dear, I know of your appetite for things cylindrical. What d'ya say?"

Christine, familiar with Peter's taunts, humors him, "Why Pietro, you flatter me. But why waste their oral charms on the unappreciative? When clearly they better suit your sensibilities."

Peter waggles his eyebrows up and down Groucho-style, though his eyes avoid hers. Turning, he holds a cigar out for Lou, intoning, "Luigi, uno sigaro?" Then gestures to Fin and Terry to take one. "Needn't fear depriving anyone, gents, I've got plenty," and he pats his other pocket.

To rescue Peter from his limb, Fin leans forward to accept, and Terry follows. Lou indicates he will too, groaning and leaning to Peter who fishes out another. "Atta boy, Luigi. Hey, you know, life is short."

"Yours will be nasty, stinking, and short, if you light up those things," warns Christine, bright-eyed, yet serious-faced. "Cabish, Pietro?"

"But they're fresh . . . and sweet . . . and wholesome," protests their purveyor, taken aback. "Try one, Chris. Share the magic. You'll never know, unless you do. Por favore," he implores, his eyes crinkling to enlist Christine, but her warning has already had its effect. Fin, despite placing his squarely between his canines and chomping down, clearly has no intention of lighting up, while Terry stores his away in his shirt pocket, and Louie uneasily parks his behind an ear. Peter's cheeks twitch as he tries to hold his smile.

The arrangement between Christine and Joseph has been concluded. Fin, gazing past Joseph's shoulder, encounters Sam's pensive stare. A silence settles over the group.

"Errol coming tonight?" asks Fin to no one in particular. Several affirming murmurs eddy above the circle. "Said he was," mumbles Lou. "I mean I called over, 'Yo Er-rol, you comin' to the soirée?' And he, ever locked in his earnest self, says, 'Yes, I am, Louis. As I always do.'"

Eyes consider Louie's rendering. It's common, if sketchy, knowledge among the group that Errol's life is not easy, that money and family strains weigh upon his ability to rip from himself the plays he envisions—this though he does not discuss the details with anyone but Lou.

Under lingering reflections, the members carefully sip and study their drinks.

Lou, however, feels uncomfortable leaving it there. He, like several of the others, is drawn to Errol's nature: Yo, Errol, a good man, a sweet man, a natural man, uncorrupted by the city's cynicism and self-absorption, despite being dogged by a kind of tragedy. Picturing his friend, Lou asks, "Pietro, you got more 'gars for our tardy friend?"

Peter, whose thoughts have fallen back to his paintings, distractedly taps his pocket once more. But Fin, hoping to flush out a little of the back-and-forth that frequently animates the group, calls out to Sam, "Hey Sam-u-elle, speakin' of Irish songs, I heard one at the office today, the likes of which aren't broadcast much anymore: . . . *'it's long memories and short tempers . . . that have cursed poor Ire-land . . .'*"

Finding Fin, Sam tries to recall the faintly familiar tune from beneath continuing annoyance with Peter. At the same time she wonders if there is some reason why Fin has mentioned this song. As its phrases slowly resurface, she repeats to herself there's something she likes about Fin, beyond his face, into which she gazes as she softly sings,

> *". . . from Boston . . . we send more gun-ns, and tell them they can win . . . then we turn back to our green be-er . . . and to McNamara's band . . . It's true friends with false perceptions that have cursed poor Ire-land . . ."*

Fin finds pleasure in the mix of sweet sounds and sad truths, as does Vivian who murmurs, "Oh yes, another poor, bedeviled island."

But Lou scorns, "Whose molasses is that shit?"

Peter, eager to curry Sam's favor, quickly supplies the answer, "Peter, Paul, and Mary, Louie. Fin probably knows them from the days of singing 'Puff the Magic Dragon' with nanny."

"Ooh, the man's tongue is spicy tonight!" rags Louie, gassed by Peter's ribbing. Peter's face broadens into an Italianate Cheshire grin. "Trouble is," carps Louie changing his tone, "that's that sixties shit, folksie-feely stuff. Harmony, messages, and crap. Stuff that was run outta the South Bronx early, thank d' Lord. I mean we had good rock 'n' roll back then. What'd we need with that syrupy shit?"

"They're lovely songs, poignant songs, with graceful harmonies," Sam reflects for herself, unconcerned with Lou's jiving. And Vivian agrees, "They are . . . I sometimes wonder where they've all gone."

"Gone to bone yards, every one," croons Fin.

Louie, a finger poking down his throat, affects a dry retching. But Viv smiles sadly. "Yes buried and forgotten . . . Marley recast them, giving them new life and rhythm, but now he's gone too."

"They come out of sad lives, sad situations," Sam reflects.

"Yeah," jazzes Louie, "back when there was only your Hi-Fi, your TV, and your rad-i-o. But *now* we've got dis good electronic shit: your Walkman and your VCR, your CD and your Mac, your satellite and your dish—Hey! Ain't we cookin'!"

"All right Mr. D.J.," cheers Fin. "He not busy sowin' scorn, is busy fryin'."

"What? You always playin' with the man's words, but his stuff is dead 'n' gone," jabs Louie, half-smiling, half-annoyed at Fin for jumping his riff. Fin smiles at Louie's indignation, studying him as Louie's strainin' to get back to his riff. "Hey, listen folks . . . young people dese days have a lot more styles 'n' stuff to choose from than that old shit. No more soppy ballads, no more just chillin' on the stoops, in d' alleys 'n' arcades. Dey kin pitch for dollars Michael Jordan style, or dey kin soar with coke, dive with liquor, float with ecstasy, yeah! Dey kin spike, bike, or mic . . . or march. Yeah! They kin shake with hip-hop, be-bop, or swing. They kin hack or jack or pack. No need to cry for them."

"Don't cry for me, Pa, I'm only sigh-in'," finishes Fin.

"Enough of that shit!" cries Lou, irritated. "What do you know about that life?"

Eyes jump his way at his sharp, angry tone and find him wound up, loaded. "Yo, bleeding hearts of the world, what do you know of real difficulties 'n' dyin'? You with your cushy lives. What do you know of the temptations that stalk the streets? For you, evil is Stephen King, or some airport pot-boiler. Well shit on that, I say. Shit on all of it!" Memories of two high school buddies who punched out early in the South Bronx gang wars crunch through him. He sees their limp bodies lyin' in the street, two piles of rags, and his eyes fall into blankness. Most around the table haven't quite followed and look at Lou hoping for an explanation. But he is sucking air for his kicked out lungs and is beginning to peel back through his riff, thinking: maybe, jus' maybe, in there somewhere, is a little light.

Fin has watched him closely, trying to understand where Louie's coming from and imagine Louie's own disappointment in not portraying that lost life. Louie, in fact, reminds him of a chained bear he saw once uptown in the Russian circus, a great confused, caged beast up on hind legs, arms flailing from a long, shoulder-less, sack-of-a-body and head rolling, roaring ineffectually.

But Joseph, engaged by no such image, is frowning heavily, thinking of all the work he must do later, and Peter's eyes have closed, while Terry is suppressing a yawn, his forearm thrown like a gray salmon across his mouth. Only Vivian feels she's caught something of Louie's thrust, the serious side, that opportunity for some remains limited. Wonder if anyone here besides Terry recognizes that? she asks herself. "Lou, I know you're not just jawin' . . ."

"No, Viv, not jawin' at all."

"Yeah okay, and you hit several things right—one bein' that the world has changed. It's all rush 'n' money now. No time for ballads, little time for listenin', less for carin', none for helpin'."

"Hey that's crap, cause we got rap," chants a recovered Lou, his lips protruding. "The new protest. And we've got posses, where marchers used to tramp. Yo, d' times dey done changed, man. Jumped you there, Fin."

But it's Sam who jumps back, "You're right, you two, whether we like it or not, whether we even recognize it, times have changed, and so has the music."

"Not entirely," opposes Joseph. "Popular taste has—" His search wrinkles his forehead; his eyes waver through distant pages—"Balkanized," he settles for and shrugs. "Dial through the bands, and you can hear pretty much everything."

"But the old songs were melodic," mourns Sam. "You could sing them. There will always be a place for them . . ." Softly she sings,

"*. . . They weave tales of wit and ma-gic . . . and their songs are strong and free . . . but they fail to hear each other, pris-on-ers of his-to-ry . . .*" Now she stares down at the table to shield her gathering emotion.

Fin, to tie it up, chants low, "*. . . and we're left with re-tri-bu-tion . . . it's the cycle of the damned . . .*"

"The damned?" mutters Lou. "Damn right! Life twists some of us around real good. Fuckin' stacked deck."

Terry shifts his gaze away from the table to the line of people at the bar. He feels the urge to flee this cant, these too-easy generalizations and wonders if the group is losing its honesty and clarity . . . Maybe should stay home 'n' read, read to the kids. Yet when his attention slides over the faces again, he feels a grudging acceptance of them trickle back. Who is not filled with hope and imperfection? He inhales, lifting his eyes, and in doing so, notices standing behind Lou a motionless figure. Blinking, he discovers Errol, just arrived, face ashen, eyes dark and stricken. "Errol . . . my man! . . ."

Sam, Christine, then several others turn to look, calling his name, even as they begin to discern his distress. Lou, his back to Errol and turning only slightly, lightly pokes, "Yo dude, thought maybe you got stuck watchin' Xena or Buffy."

Instinctively Errol leans into a shadow near the wall.

"What, Errol?" calls Sam. "What's wrong?"

With difficulty Errol raises his eyes to take in those at the table. His mouth opens slightly, to speak, but then falls shut, and his gaze with it, allowing the others to see that his usually pleasant, pale face is creased and despairing, mirrored by the worn raincoat drooping from his shoulders.

"Tell us," urges Christine.

He breathes, and without looking up, begins, "Something happened in my building a little while ago, to a neighbor—is why I'm late." He stops, biting into the side of his lower lip.

"God," sighs Lou, "from the way you look, old fug, I thought you were gonna say something happened to Leslie or one of the kids."

Errol shivers and runs a hand through his thinning, reddish-blond hair. His cheek quivers as he shakes his head, "No . . . not to us."

"Well sit your sorry ass down and tell us what happened," Lou urges, rising and pulling out the last chair. "Come on, Sir Errol," he encourages softly, along with several others. But seeing that Errol is caught in a trance, Lou steps over and guides him into it.

"Get you a beer?" Fin asks pushing up.

Working an arm out of his coat, Errol searches uncertainly for Fin, thinking Fin must hear this, but also deeply wanting a beer. When their eyes meet, Errol nods, and Fin swings his gaze over to the others, silently requesting that they wait until he returns, before he hurries away. But Sam cannot restrain herself from pressing Errol to explain.

Glancing after Fin, Errol seems to withdraw into himself, before again shaking his head. His eyes run over the table, bumping over initials, hearts, and crests gouged by others through the decades. Like them, he can't keep it bottled up. ". . . I was, uh, in my apartment, getting ready to head over here . . . when suddenly there was—I don't know—banging, shouting. I wasn't really paying much attention. You know, sorta half-listening . . . Then comes a sharp crack, high-pitched, muffled, toy-like, followed by a barrage, like firecrackers, bleeding together, just outside, down the hall from our door."

"Shots?" checks Lou, not sure he's heard correctly. "Gun shots?"

For a second, Errol hangs frozen, until uncomfortably he seals his pale lips and runs his eyes over the faces before nodding to Lou. "Then more shouting . . . Leslie, in the kids' room, starts yellin,' 'What's that? What's that noise? What's goin' on?'"

"'Don't know,'" I call. I tell her to stay put, close the door. She slams it like a shot. I nearly jump out of my skin . . . 'n' move away from the front door, wonderin' what the hell *is* goin' on . . . Listenin', I make out voices calling, ordering—I don't know—next comes sounds of wood splintering, a door bust open, heavy footsteps runnin'. The floor under me is shaking."

Now as curious as he is wary, Errol studies the faces, faces caught unsuspecting, mouths parted as if clocked by a cudgel. With his own mouth dry, he can't swallow and eyes the other drinks.

Fin returns, placing a stein down in front of him. Errol encloses it with two shaking hands and brings it to his lips, eagerly sucking the foam. Fin moves around to his chair, asking, "What'd I miss?"

"Cops, sounds like," Louie tells him. "In his building. Gunshots."

Frowning, Fin slowly lowers himself into his seat as Errol, pausing for breath, stares into the stein, at the bubbles rising, foaming, forming, fomenting. Fermenting things are bound to burst. The immutable laws. For every action, reaction . . . He brings the stein up again for another brief, precious sip, before finding the others. "Now I hear voices shoutin', keyed up. Leslie's still callin' through the door, 'Phone the police! For God sakes, phone the police!'" I'm staring at the door. 'The police,' I yell as loud as I dare, 'are right outside!'"

"Was it the police?" asks Terry hesitantly.

Errol wipes foam from his cheek and meets Terry's eyes, pursing his lips, affirming unhappily. He feels it all rush back: edging to the door, listening, turning the knob, cracking it. "Voices, rapid-fire, rising, ringing from the next apartment." He looks down, sucks in an urgent gulp. "Stuck my head out. Nearly choked on something searing . . . gunpowder, I guess. Had to blink my eyes clear. Didn't know what to think. Half-frozen, half-mesmerized, I couldn't tell what was goin' on. The guy whose apartment it is, is no criminal, unless I'm way off . . . I looked down at the other two doors on the floor, but no one's stuck his head out. I began to think: 'What the hell do I do? What if it's drug dealers, or something . . . masquerading as cops?'

. . . "Leanin' out more, I see shadows on the door crouching, moving quickly back and forth, up and down, swinging night sticks, rainin' blows . . . I start urgin' myself to close the door . . . 'cept I know this guy, Clayton. See him all the time, say hello. He's friendly, works in a camera store on Broadway. Does photography. Seen him takin' shots in the neighborhood . . . Clayton Kenny, maybe thirty, black guy, decent . . . So what's *this*? What's goin' on? . . ." Errol again shakes his head staring at the table, bent by remorse over his own fear, when really, he himself was never in danger.

No one moves, watching, imagining, trying to piece it together. But needing to go on, get it all out, Errol raises his head. "So I'm wonderin' what to do? . . . Call the precinct? . . . I'm sorta leaning out of the apartment, when a wedge of four guys in street clothes, cops I guess, size of Big Ten tackles, come flyin' out of his apartment, draggin' him. He's—they've got him under his arms; he's handcuffed behind his back; he's being pulled along; his legs aren't under him; he's not walking; they're dragging him . . . and he's got nothing on, not a stitch. The cops, seein' me, start yellin': 'Back in your apartment!'

"I try to tell 'em I know this guy, my neighbor.

"'In your apartment, buddy boy!' they cry. Clayton sees me. One eye's half-closed, from a blow looks like; one cheek is red, purple—a welt or something . . . He exclaims, 'I didn't do nothin'; I was makin' my supper.'

"A couple of the cops coming along behind tell him to shut up, and glare at me. 'Inside, Bubba, or you're comin' with us!' I try to get one more glance at him, but he's gone, thudding down the stairs, groans trailing up. On the lower floors I hear doors opening, voices, cops yellin', doors banging shut. I consider going over to look into his place, but I can hear other cops still inside. I stand there . . . like some dumb fuck, stunned."

Around the table, the others sit like stone. Not a whisper, till Lou leans over and checks, "Hey, really—you know this guy?" Errol's eyes nearly close, before they slide to Lou. "Yeah . . . not well, but we've talked, you know . . . He lives right there."

"So what did the cops want with him?" Christine wonders, turning to Terry.

But at a loss, Terry feels a frown rumple his face. "Could be anything . . ."

Fin, who had been imagining the brutality of it, offers, "Maybe a street crimes unit, working from a profile . . ."

"Yeah," scorns Viv, "and we know *what* the profiles are." Her words curl with angry Caribbean lilt. Glancing at her, the others find their tongues have grown thick imagining her indignation. Only Peter manages, "They have a warrant for him?"

All eyes reach back to Errol. "Not that I ever saw . . . but . . . I mean I still can't imagine he's involved in anything . . . What would he be doin'? . . ."

"You never know," mumbles Terry, thinking of the times he's been fooled. "One thing I've learned: you never really know."

"It's not a matter of *what's* doin'," snaps Viv, "but *who's* doin'. It's always the same people they're bustin': people of African descent, Caribbean people, Hispanic people."

Peter clears his throat as if to scoff, 'I wonder why?' But most eyes slide over for confirmation to Terry, who, head bowed, groans, "'Fraid so."

"Damn right, 'fraid so!" cries Viv. "*We've* been stopped, Terry and I!" Her eyes bite bitterly some distant point, before she turns her frown on Terry.

"Yeah," he acknowledges, face puffy, eyes clouded and conflicted. "They were fairly restrained, but still . . ."

"But still nothin'!" Viv cries again. "There was no God-damned reason, other than my skin. It was so outrageous . . . so bloody, fucking irritating!"

The others don't quite know where to look, other than into their drinks. Some steal glances at her. The group seems to freeze; time stops, until Lou again, out of the side of his mouth, mutters to Errol, "So what happened to him?"

Errol stares down into his near-empty beer. Remembrance brings remorse, he recalls from somewhere. "They took him off . . . Thought of calling down to the precinct, but I mean . . . the cops can be, you know, so unhelpful, so curt, so disinterested . . . On the other hand . . . well . . . I decided I'd better go down there, t' see if I could see him, and tell them that he's a neighbor, has a job and has always been . . . peaceful, law-abiding, so far as I know." God, he hears himself silently uttering, it's so unnerving. "Suddenly you don't know what's what. What's up, what's down, what's safe, what's right."

"So d' you go?" presses Louie, anxious for him.

Errol's body sags. "Yeah . . ." In glimpses from the dark streets, he relives the walk down to the precinct: Down through Little Italy into Chinatown and east on Canal, weaving through sparse sidewalk traffic. In the low evening light, everything takes on the black-and-white graininess of old movies, save for the aromas of Chinese food reaching into his empty stomach: egg rolls, spareribs, General's chicken. Nose up, inhaling, eyes half-closed, he side-swipes someone, a small Chinese woman laden with shopping bags and trailing two tiny children. She sends him a cat-like hiss and a string of sharp Chinese rebukes. The two tiny faces float by, upturned, taking him in with expressionless wonder.

He goes on, turns south on Elizabeth, and finds the precinct, a modest, unimposing building. Stepping up and in, he discovers it's unexpectedly confined, but almost cheery, as if a stage set, with a small desk near the door, a strange miniature courtroom off to the right, and a few bright corridors leading away behind.

"Sittin' at the desk," Errol resumes, drawing in a breath, "a young cop 's talkin' on the phone. Personal business, sounds like. No one else's around really, so I stand there quiet, tryin' to collect my thoughts, till he gets off.

"'Help you?' he asks, not unfriendly. We stare at each other. Something's goin' on behind his eyes. I tell him I'm seeking information.

"'Bout what?'" he asks, eyes closing a little.

"'About a neighbor, who was arrested . . .' Now I see the cop's smile fade." Errol surveys the faces of the wide-eyed knights and ladies bowed over the table, waiting.

"'Yeah, well who are *you*?' the cop asks, his voice tightening.

"'A friend, neighbor.' The cop's chin drops, taking his eyes down with it. 'Fraid we don't give out information to just anyone. It's gotta be family, attorney, guardian or somethin'.

"Course I know so little about Kenny. I mean I have no idea whether he has family around here, a lawyer or what. Feel a little foolish, but now the cop begins reciting by rote, 'He's entitled to three calls. Most of the time, they call family.'

"Not knowing which way to go, I explain the guy was dragged off pretty rough, with no clothes on.

"The cop puts on a skeptical smile, implyin' I don't know the full story. I tell him that I was right there, saw it.

"'Everything?' he grunts, workin' his jaw.

"Of course not, I'm thinking. But what I did see was not right. 'A dozen plain-clothes types. Heard 'em bust in, 'n' then whistle him right out of there, nothin' on.'

"The cop stares at me, like he's wishin' I wasn't there. But he doesn't say a thing.

"'Musta been a struggle,' I tell him. 'Looked like the guy took some blows to the head; his face was all puffed up, discolored. Cheek 'n' mouth swollen . . . Will somebody take a look at him?'

"Still the cop doesn't budge, then glances out the front door, like he's wishin' I was headin' there. I'm wonderin' what to do. I try askin' him if Kenny's okay. Now something snaps; all signs of patience vanish. He starts actin' like a cop, askin' me if I didn't catch what he said. I tell him that it seemed like my neighbor was wrongfully arrested. He doesn't like that; his eyes close down t' slits. I ask him if it's possible to talk to Clayton. His head starts shakin' like he can't believe. I press him: What would *he* do, if some neighbor of his was arrested wrongfully? But he's not listenin', instead pushin' himself up till we're standin' eye-to-eye. "'Look,' he starts in again, 'if you're not related, if you're not the representin' attorney, you have no reason to be here. You get it? You get what I'm sayin'?'"

Errol breathes, again reading the faces ringing the circle. They're listening, trying to understand, while in his own head things are pumping and pulsating, but he manages to clamp a lid, drop his voice, and ask, "So what am I supposed to do? . . . A guy, my neighbor, is hustled off, mistakenly, I'm thinkin', and I want to find out why, what happened, and this guy won't tell me. There's somethin' wrong there."

Terry meets his plaintive gaze. "Unfortunately, that's the way it is too often. Wrong, stupid, piled high with procedure."

"You can't get information about somebody?" wails Sam in disbelief.

Terry inhales through his teeth and explains they have rules they've got to go by. "When it suits them," rasps Vivian, leaning forward and slapping the table with her palm. Terry avoids turning back to her, but his head bobs: true, true. Maybe not always, he's thinking, but too much, way too much.

Errol's wondering if any of them would've done what he did for a neighbor, for a black man. Or am I a chump? . . . Huh? Am I? . . . Maybe . . . maybe some would take up the gauntlet, but . . . He wipes his eyes, takes a last swig. "The cop begins sayin' that maybe this neighbor doesn't want my help. Maybe the family doesn't. Maybe they don't want people nosin' into their business."

"'Okay . . .' So I ask, 'Maybe you can just tell me if he's restin' okay, not hurt, and if he's got somethin' to put on.' So what does the cop do? Turns and calls back behind him. Another burly, Sumo-type waddles forward. The first guy tells him I'm a little thick in the head. Annoyed, I say, 'At least it's with gray matter and not department-issue styrofoam.' The big guy silently jeers, but he wants to get things over and done, so he asks who I am. I tell him I'm the guy's brother. The first cop sneers, wipes his face—irritated, pissed. 'Come on, pal,' he warns, 'stop pullin' our chains. Why don't you go on home and call his people or somethin'.'

"I tell 'em the guy works in a photo store, does photography—a decent guy, who could lose his job.

"The second cop, Mr. Sumo, now steps around to the front of the desk, arms folded across his chest, like he's part-uncle, part-primate, privy to the God's truth, and he tells me that most people have no *idea* what their neighbors are doin'.

"I tell 'em I know the guy a little, have a feeling for . . . for what kind of a guy he is. A photographer, no criminal."

"'Sure . . .' they nod, shakin' their heads, snortin', scoffin'. I mean their view of the world is so jaundiced, so fucked. 'We could tell you stories,' they start spoutin'. Well, I mean, what are you going to say to them? They don't want to hear. You can't tell 'em anything . . . So I try once more, just to shake 'em up, tell 'em that the mayor himself is a regular customer in Kenny's store. Knows him . . . That stops 'em both . . . for about a second. Then they turn away, sputtering and swearing.

"I say sorry and ask 'em if I can leave Mr. Kenny a note. The first guy starts foamin' at the mouth: 'We're not your fuckin' UPS!' But maybe the big one sees it as closure and lends me a pad and pen. I tell Clayton I came by, to see how he is, and that I'd try to find a lawyer tomorrow . . . I put it on the front desk. But of course I don't know whether they ever gave it to him.

"I happen to see now, leanin' against a wall behind them, two other cops, one of whom is black. They're sort of watchin' disinterestedly. I try to read the black guy's reaction, but what's he gonna do?

"Now the big guy, maybe aware of this, says that if it's some mistake, then it'll get straightened out. 'So there's nothin' to worry about, because eventually he'll get released . . . if there's some mistake.'"

Errol rubs his temple, kneading it deep, then lifts his aching eyes and resumes spooling out the story, "By now the first cop's had enough. I'm trying to thinka something, but I see the big boy's also had it. He leans right in my face, askin' if I need help findin' the door. I see his hands are flexin'. He must be 250 at least." Errol closes his eyes. Lou whispers, "It's okay, my man, it's okay. We'll figure it out." He pats his friend's shoulder, but Errol just stares at the table. Then slowly, like a sleep-deprived cobra, his head starts weaving side to side, until his mouth drops open, and he exhales before he gathers himself. "But seein' I wasn't gonna get any more from New York's finest, I say goodnight—which they neglect to return . . . But still . . . I don't feel good about leavin'."

"What are you gonna do? Take on the whole squad?" nudges Louie.

Errol is not consoled, and the expressions of those around the table are uneasy. Terry and Joseph try to cheer the group by promising to telephone two lawyers they know in the morning. Peter, huffing and anxious to insert something, blurts, "Of course cops are not infallible, but then, who among us is?"

Listening, head down, eyes closed, Errol feels compelled to respond, "Yeah, Peter, but as I said, I never saw signs of anything. I mean he talks like he's college-educated, middle class, you know, a regular guy, works regular hours. He's not some junkie or somethin'."

"Any signs," muses Peter, "of a lady friend?"

"What the hell's the point of that?" cries Sam.

Unruffled, Peter stares at Errol. "I don't know, sometimes it can tell you something, depending."

"Yeah," snorts Sam, "like anybody'd have a clue about me from meeting you, Lord Eversneer."

Turning his head away from her, he rolls his eyes, but the others are waiting for Errol as he squeezes his brain for anything that might help. "Fact is, I see him once, maybe twice, a week . . ."

Joseph sniffs sharply, clearing his nasal passages. "It's possible, as Terry said, this may have nothing to do with him. May simply be mistaken identity, or a clerical error. God knows it happens often enough at school where I spend hours in the dungeons chasing screw-ups by the staff and students."

"There's another problem, however," Terry reminds them, resurrecting the issue of the gun, broached by Errol's report of a single first shot. Errol's face grows hot and still. "Yeah, one crack," he recalls, "then a barrage, a string of them. Made me jump. Everything changed, grew eerie . . ."

"Twilight Zone, man," hisses Lou.

But Errol doesn't hear, feeling the shots hammering him into the floor.

"So the question is: what set it off?" infers Terry, but Viv immediately jeers, "What d'ya mean? Happens all the time!" And she scowls at having to explain. "Business as usual."

"Maybe, but something started it," persists Terry. "The question is what?"

As no one around the table can say, Errol reruns the sequence, "First I remember the bangin' 'n' shoutin'. Police, it sounded like, announcin' themselves, poundin' 'n' cryin' out like a buncha yahoos."

"But how did it escalate from there?" Christine wonders. "You said Clayton claimed he was making supper."

Dispirited, lost, Errol gazes back, imagining Clayton by himself in front of his stove, as he himself frequently is. "Maybe he froze with the banging at his door . . . thinkin' what the hell is that? What in God's name do I do?"

"Turn me to fuckin' jelly," confesses Louie.

"If he did freeze, and didn't answer," suggests Fin, "maybe the cops got itchy."

"Do we know," asks Sam warily, "if he had a gun?"

Most turn to Errol, who under the pressure, exclaims, "God! I don't know!"

Terry feels compelled to kind of set parameters, "I'd say generally the police won't shoot first, unless there's a threat. I mean they're trained."

"Oh yeah!," groans Viv, choking down incredulity. "We've all seen in the papers how well they're trained."

"And from what I've read," adds Christine, "those two heavily reported cases are just the tip of the iceberg." She's trying to imagine how she would react and whether or not Kenny had a reasonable chance to respond. Across the table Terry's picturing cops keyed up, frustrated, facing the unpredictable. They meet a little uncertainty, a little resistance, some flicker of something, a blink, a jerk, and they blow. "Happens like a shot," he murmurs. "It's a harsh, different world, where you never know what's coming 'round the corner."

"And they're often dealing with people out of control," adds Peter. "People who don't give two hoots about the law."

"Oh come on, Peter," scoffs Lou, "like the cops do. Blowin' away that unarmed African guy, or reaming that other guy up the kazoo."

"From what I read," Peter doggedly replies, "in the first case it was a mistake; in the second, the cop cracked. The neighbors said he'd been a choir boy up till then . . . So, who among us can claim we'd never crack?" As a silence falls over them, most consider this, before eyes slide back to Terry, the resident expert and keeper of the code. His consulting on cases of forged or stolen artwork periodically brings him in contact with detectives. But Terry, feeling the pressure, tucks his chin and sucks in a lung-full. "To be fair, there are thousands of cops, all types . . . Some really shouldn't be there, but then there are decent guys, who, having to make split-second, life-'n'-death decisions, sometimes make mistakes."

The others in the circle try to picture this, eyes half-closed, partly attending to their drinks, while the bar noise flows over them. But Vivian, irritated by what she feels is Terry's glossing, shakes herself and challenges his assessment, "Mistakes? Is that what we're really talking about?"

Terry reflects, then nods thoughtfully, supportively. Yet he feels he needs to address the unanswered question. "On the other hand, if there *was* a gun, I can understand the cops going berserk . . . But then, what were they doing there in the first place?"

"Damned right!" snaps Viv. "What were they doin'?"

"Gotta be mistaken identity," Joseph breathes.

"Yeah!" cry Lou and Sam.

Still intent on maintaining objectivity, however, Terry reminds them, "Maybe it was; maybe that's where it all started, but then the gun—if there was one—raises a second issue. I mean one shot changes everything; with it all snowballs out of control, off the map."

But Viv's still not happy. "Is it really so complicated? I mean the cops are supposed to be protectin' people, all the people. Not just their own kind."

"Sometimes that gets lost," acknowledges Terry feeling stretched between truths.

"There's somethin' else, too, that gets lost," adds Peter, "because it's not P.C."

"Oh boy, here it comes," moans Viv, reaching her limit.

Peter's eyes grow hooded in his effort to ignore her. "It's not through some conspiracy that some groups are receivin' special attention from the police . . ."

"Oh come on, Peter," calls Lou, "you never heard of racial profiling?"

From behind an uneasy smile Peter slowly swings his attention to Lou. "You're not going to tell me most of the boys in the clink here don't deserve to be there. I mean some groups just happen to be committing a disproportionate amount of the street crime. And let's not forget it's their neighbors who are calling for more police protection. And one other thing: while it's fine for us to sit here making judgements, how many of us would give up our cushy jobs to go out into the streets and alleys and risk our lives like the police do? . . . I know I'm happy to have others do it for me. And I'd bet a box of cigars that if some of us did do it, we'd grow just as wary and cynical."

"Nonsense. We're not sadists!" barks Sam sharply. "And why are you defending cops now, when most of the time you're ridiculing them?"

"Trying to be fair," replies Peter, outwardly cool. "Trying not to let emotion take over."

"Oh right!" snarls Sam. "Mr. Cool, when he's out in public. Mr. Rant-'n'-Rave at home."

Vivian's begun wondering why she needs to come to these Wednesday nights just to listen to this cant and ignorance, and Joseph is squirming under the rising voices. Fin, studying Peter, muses, "You pulling out the old Dirty Harry theme: have to break the law to preserve it?"

"Or Vietnam, man," croons Lou, "where they tell you you gotta destroy the country to save it."

Terry now feels the need to dampen the emotions. "To be fair, I think most cops try to be professional."

Viv grimaces, snapping her head around toward the door. "I'll tell you what would make them professional," she growls, "is if they would have to read their own damn histories, those Irish and Italian cops. Then they'd see who were the petty criminals a few generations back, and they'd be reminded who was at the bottom of the social heap, and how many years it took *them* to rise—the ones, that is, who aren't *still* scrapin' around in ignorance and hate."

Terry agrees, "Yup, no question, it takes time." Each focuses in on the other's agitated gaze, and both seem ready, in the implicit way of close couples, to accept the better part of the other's point. But Peter now breaks in, his voice flat and strained, "Cops don't make or break communities. Parts of the Italian community have been—still are—up against it with the cops, but the rest went about their business, kept their families together, educated them, made a living."

"Sellin' drugs in the inner city, runnin' prostitutes and protection, strong-arming the unions," accuses Viv. "Tell me about it, that famous Italian morality."

As tension streaks through the faces around the table, Peter frowns and nods, "Sure, some, but most were law-abiding."

"So what's your point, Peter?" croaks Lou unhappily.

"That scapegoatin' the cops won't solve things."

"But here, in this case," interjects Christine, "the cops are the issue. Sounds like the police badly mistreated a man."

"Nobody knows for sure," corrects Peter.

"Like you'd be happy to be dragged off like that?" taunts Lou.

"Of course not, if I'd done nothing," Peter tells him.

"He was makin' supper, when they came through his door," Sam heavily reminds him.

"Possibly he fired a gun," Terry reluctantly repeats.

"Maybe we've heard enough of all of this," exhales Viv.

Twisting around to see her, Terry finds her furrowed frown and concedes, "Probably that's right . . . enough for now."

But in the quiet that follows Errol cannot restrain the images from flowing back: the hefty white sheriffs dragging the thin black man away; the thumping of bare feet down the stairs; swords clanging over clattering voices, distressed, unintelligible—the overwhelming sense that something was wrong, way wrong. Errol wipes his moist brow and breathes, "Watching them take him away, I felt myself grow cold . . . like ice; then I was sweatin', like some . . . daunting inferno." Unable to quite understand it, but thinking guilt figures in there somewhere, he slowly, despondently runs a hand over his prickling scalp.

Around the circle the members watch, murmuring their respective states of mind, until Errol, now working his suddenly aching neck, expels one final thought, "I was thinkin' . . . maybe a couple of us could go down there, to the station, to tell 'em again, more forcefully, we think there's been some mistake."

This catches most by surprise and sends eyes peering carefully for reactions. But Christine, wanting to support Errol, volunteers, "I'll go," and Lou and Fin—for Errol and the novelty—chime in 'Amen,' followed by Sam. Peter though, about to disparage the idea, instead mutters in frustration, "Naïve crew," and his mouth twitches as he glares resentfully down at the table. Terry, too, has doubts, fearing that challenging the department will only set them to digging in their heels. "Might be better," he proposes, "to use the excuse of bringing him some clothes or a blanket. Then maybe ask them if he's okay . . . and mention you think there's been some mistake."

"What if they say buzz off?" worries Lou. "What if they claim it's none of our frickin' business?"

"As long as you keep it simple, I don't think they'll object. Just say you want to make sure the guy's warm. Then ask if he's been arraigned. That may give us an idea whether they think they've got a case."

"Sounds good, man," Lou breathes, his fears for the moment soothed. "Let's do it to it."

Sensitive to possible objections or conflicts, Errol repeats, "We don't all have to go . . ." For a beat uncertainty stills the group, until he tells them, "But I'm goin' . . . and those who want to come . . . well, I think we should go do it now."

"I'm ready!" exclaims Sam, ahead of several others.

As they begin to push up, Louie looks over at Errol. "Hey cheer up, man. You got your posse, your wights 'n' wenches." But Errol, staring at the table, seems dazed by the prospect of returning. A vise seems to clamp his head. What is this? Fear of facing the black knights again?

"Unfortunately *we* can't go," Terry announces, with some discomfort, as he moves around to collect his coat. "Our baby-sitter can't stay late. In fact we should be home now." As Vivian stands, she raises her eyebrows to him, releasing him if he wants to go. But he's reluctant to send Viv home by herself and is wary of getting into a squabble down there. She too, aside from the sitter problem, has no desire to confront cops. Too bloody angry, from when they stopped us. Might start hollerin'—not to mention I'm doubtful the visit will do any good, the damage being already done. The gesture is really for the people here, some feel-better thing, in place of meaningful change. No, the underlying issues aren't gonna go away tonight, not if the high profile cases haven't chased 'em.

Looking over, Lou asks, "Joseph, how about you?"

As Joseph is up pulling on his coat, he appears glum and unexcited by the prospect. "I've got work, for my students, the magazine . . ." The burden drives his shoulders downward.

"Come on, man, it's gonna be quick," Lou promises.

". . . Not to mention some other stuff I'm contracted to do." Head bowed, Joseph shoulders deeper into his coat, shifting his feet nervously, wiping his nose. "On the other hand . . . if I believe in any of this, as I say I do . . . then I've got to go."

"At-ta-boy," encourages Lou.

"At-ta-boy," mimics Fin. "At-ti-*ca*!"

Lou picks it up, "At-ti-*ca*, At-ti-*ca*!" The two brandish fists in the air. "At-ti-*ca*!" Viv, watching, finds her doubts about them confirmed. But Sam, observing Joseph, tries to ease the burden. "Everybody's got their work, Joseph, you know?" And as he turns, Joseph acknowledges this reluctantly, reaching for his briefcase. Peter, also turning, confides to Sam, "You don't need me. You got your escort."

"Peter?" cries Sam. "*I want* to *go*!"

"Good. Go . . . Don't let me hold you up. But for me it's been a long day, and we've got that presentation tomorrow. And, as you say, the cops and I have no particular affinity. Finicky Fin, or some other knight errant, will escort you home."

Sam glances at him, eyes smarting with disappointment and anger. Her lips puff out as she spits, "But then when do you *ever* extend yourself for anyone?" Feeling pent up fury rising through her, she hisses, "Egotistical bastard!"

Peter feels a chill blow through his thoughts. "Don't push it, old girl."

"Don't give me your 'old girl' shit!"

Head tilted toward her, eyes narrowed, he stares hard. "The reason you're goin' down there, I hope you know, is to stroke that little do-gooder self-image you have, the PC liberal. And the reason it needs polishing is that you only pull it out once a year. So who are you kidding?"

"Least I'm willing to do something for someone," she snaps as she pulls away, swinging her coat around her shoulders. It's been two years since they met, when she joined the design firm he works for, and where they spend much of the day together, but at this moment, each wonders if they've reached some fork in the road. Defiant, a little hurt, she avoids looking at him as one-by-one the others work into their heavy coats and shoulder up their staffs and sacks.

II.

The Keep

Outside, where the temperature has dropped, and the wind whips east along unsheltering Houston, Viv and Sam lean into an earnest hug. Next to them, Terry thrusts out his plump hand with a gaunt grunt to Joseph, "Good luck." But Joseph manages to corral only the middle three fingers, giving them an unintentional yank. Terry winces—his painting hand—and withdraws it tenderly, his eyes and mouth flapping with hurt. Fumbling for a 'Sorry,' Joseph garbles instead, "Ss-talk t'yatomorrow," and spins away seeking anyone heading downtown.

Rocking and flexing his fingers as he turns, Terry spies Errol and slides over to find his friend's skittish eyes, but Errol is curled deep in his collars against the cold, against memory and apprehension. Behind the two, Christine feels something poke into her cheek. Recoiling, she discovers Peter wheeling away, wearing the dull glow of a vengeful smile. Protest puckers her lips. "Piss off, Peter!" But her words are swept up by the pale fist of the wind.

Joining hands, Terry and Viv now swing west and bow their heads against the blustering gale, while unnoticed by them, Peter steps deftly in behind to avail himself of their windbreak. The remaining six fold together, amid clucks and cries, and shuffle toward the curb, where two or three hands, pried from pockets, are thrust up for a cab and wobble in widening gyres until two cabs, running west, swerve across lanes, scattering scavenging crows and traffic, and screech to a halt. Deferring to the women, the men hold the doors, then push in at their heels. Sliding after Sam, Errol leans forward to give the driver directions, only to come eye-to-eye with the dark, impenetrable gaze of a turbaned Sikh peering back at him without expression. For the second time this evening, Errol experiences a tremor of disorientation, encountering a sensibility, like the cops', wholly disinterested in him as a person. Somewhere in his tumbling mind the names Japhet and Jodhpur resound for reasons he can't identify. Uncomfortably he recites the addresses. The Sikh turns away.

Behind Errol comes Lou folding and twisting into the small cave that is the back seat. Wedged next to the other door, Sam breathes in relief at escaping Peter and the penetrating chill. Enough of those oppressive opinions, she silently rejoices, although at some point, she knows, they'll have to be confronted. To soothe herself, she sings under her breath, "*. . . it's old hatreds, and young victims . . . which have cursed poor Ire-land . . .*"

Errol half-turns to her, wanting to join in, but the damp cold sunk in his chest convulses into violent coughing, and wrenching himself away, he crumples down, burrowing into the footwell, muffling his mouth. The hacking wracks his body dislodging his confidence. What is this? What am I doing, dragging these people down here?

In the second cab, Christine, Fin, and Joseph, in the flickering alternation of street light and darkness, also try to figure out just what it is they're doing. Sifting back through police encounters she's had or heard of, Christine recalls that in most there was a distance, or divide, no matter what the situation. Terse, reluctant, impatient, bored, the cops seemed eager only to cut short the contact. What is that? The job? The training, culture, types? What?

Joseph, bent in his seat, stares out the window, trying to latch onto the details of the old buildings streaking by. Brick and block, cement and stone blur in the darkly violet haze. Textures and hints of color bleed together in the facades and floors, in the steps and stacks, the columns, volumes, and reams all piled shoulder-to-shoulder, floor-to-ceiling, building-to-building, block upon block, all to be shaped, composed, analyzed, and corrected by him. A spasm shakes him, his arms uncoil defensively, thumping the door and Christine. He apologizes, and wonders if it is avoidance . . . or Christine, that draws him on this fool's chase.

Fin is picturing his trips a few years ago to Riker's Island Prison to interview young men for an article, some of whom were boyish, or loutish; one was quick and bright, another irremediably dim. How had they all collected there? The culture of their peers? Not a one with a live-in dad? Where could, and would their lives go? What could they do in their middle years? If they last that long . . . Dichotomies, inequities—all the clichés rush in, chasing him to the brighter auras of Christine and Sam, images of Heaven over Hell, aware that neither is pure or simple.

In the first cab, Sam is shouldered against her door by Errol as the driver swerves and brakes. Apologizing, Errol explains that he needs to dash upstairs to his apartment for clothes and a blanket for Clayton. Lou pushes out ahead of his friend who scrambles by. Sam watches Errol hunch and hurry through his building's double doors. To the side she notices the unlighted windows of a failed Italian restaurant watching her with a cold, pearly stare. The half-length white curtains have curled and yellowed. Restaurants, she tells herself, are a crapshoot, like men.

Soon Errol returns half-jogging, arms wrapped around two bundles, and squeezes in next to Lou. In the instant he pulls the door shut, the tires spit and squeal sending the two cabs slithering on.

At the corner of Elizabeth and Canal, all unfold back out onto the sidewalk, gazing around like daytime tourists at the Chinese signs and facades. Gathering, they follow Errol the short distance to the precinct entrance, and there huddle to decide who will speak and what will be said. It's begun to snow, and their heads bow together away from the prying flakes.

Swallowing his own hesitation Errol proposes, "Uh, since he's my neighbor, maybe I should start." While this makes sense to most, Christine recounts that in her experience the police are generally more helpful to women—even the women cops. "A testosterone thing," chimes Fin.

"As you would know, Dr. All-Around-Town, Sir Gal-ahad," rags Louie.

"The main thing is to be cool," advises Joseph. "If they sense we're not serious . . ."

"If dey catch any at-ti-tude whatsoever . . ." drawls Lou.

"We'll lose any hope of learning anything," closes Joseph.

Reading the faces, Errol detects a whiff of doubt and wonders again if it's his own fear. But encountering Christine's clear gaze, he finds the encouragement he needs, and turns to lead them through the door.

Inside Errol and Christine stop at the small front desk, as the others file choir-like in behind. The officer at the desk—not the earlier one—glances up blinking as he watches the four awkwardly side-step in. What's this, carolers? he wonders, frowning, as his gaze loops back to Errol—recalling something about a guy earlier—before his restless eyes slip to Christine. "Yes ma'am, can I help you?"

Christine flicks a glance at Errol, whose eyes are oscillating under the stress of trying to read the officer and avoid signs of another quick dismissal.

"Something, ma'am, we can do for you?"

Christine matches his artificial smile. "We have a question or two."

Carefully the officer inhales. "Okay, well, shoot."

Errol jumps a little. He cannot help but notice that while the officer sounds polite, there is an undercurrent of weariness and disinterest, and as Christine also notices this, she sticks to bare-bones, "But first we'd like to drop some clothes and a blanket off for someone who was arrested."

The officer glances down at various papers before him. "And who was this?"

Christine defers to Errol, who straightens with dignity as he recites once more, "Clayton Kenny, neighbor, 121 Broome Street, Sir!"

Slowly rotating his head, loosening his neck, the officer surveys Errol, Battery to Broadway. "You were in before . . ." Errol nods as he raises the bundles and asks, "What should I do with these?"

Unhurriedly shifting his gaze to them, the officer mutters, "I'll take 'em," whereupon Errol places them on the desk and waits as the cop searches for a pad. But growing concern presses Errol to ask, "Will he get them soon? He was dragged away without a stitch on, and it's damned cold out there."

The officer nods minimally and without affect, but Christine inquires anxiously, "Sir, can you tell us how he is?"

Whether the policeman ignores her, or is just preoccupied, is impossible for her to judge, but with his attention focused on his scrupulous lettering of the form, silence frames the faint scratching of his pen. Finally, with one hand, he pushes the bundle to the side and calls out behind, "Hey, Malory."

Emerging from a back room, a well-fed, ruddy-faced, older officer from the Dark Ages scuffs forward. The desk officer addresses him without looking up, "These people brought some clothes for one-a the collars. You take a look?"

Malory casts a mild, bleary-eyed glance over the group as he begins to pull out the clothing. From behind Errol, Lou calls out to the desk officer, "Uh, Sarge, any word on this guy, our neighbor, Mr. Kenny?"

The desk officer peers past Christine to Lou. "You with this crew?

"You bet. Like I said, neighbor and tax-payin' citizen of New York, New York," sings Lou pushing it a little. "The people who pay your sal-a-ry."

The officer's eyes slide away without acknowledgement, to scope out the others. "All of yous is neighbors?"

"I live across the hall," explains Errol. "They're from the neighborhood, generally." The desk officer tilts his head and raises an eyebrow, not without a twitch of amusement. "I was askin' them." Errol swings a leg back to clear the sight lines.

"That's right, Officer. We're all neighbors and friends," Joseph coolly confirms. The officer's small dark eyes pulse like a cursor over Joseph, Fin, Lou, and Sam, all of whom do their best to stare steadfastly back. Now two more officers amble forward. The desk officer exhales and finds Christine again. "One of yous, this fellow here, was in before. Didn't he tell you the story?"

"He did," Christine concedes, "but since we know that Mr. Kenny was taken out of his apartment without any of his clothes on, we want to make sure he's warm—until he's released." To which Joseph adds, "And we'd like to know how he is."

"And yo, we have reason to believe that not only was this seizin' wrong," raps Lou rhythmically, "but our man was treated . . ." (he considers a half-dozen zingers) "like somethin' excreted . . . that is, poorly, a touch poorly."

The desk officer studies him for a moment, then murmurs, "Well, a poet. We have ourselves a poet." Lou shrugs off the compliment.

The younger and shorter of the two newly arrived cops, a clean-cut patrolman in his twenties, asks the desk officer, "What's this, Paddy? Jehovah Witnesses? The precinct's already got a Bible. Better hide your billfold."

Standing closest to this fellow, Sam is amused by these signs of life. "Don't worry, Lieutenant," she reassures him, "we're not looking for money. We *can* offer salvation, however, for a little info." While his eyes narrow, then brighten slyly, he's not about to play her game. Now the desk officer raises his voice for the four behind, "Uh, listen up folks, we, uh, told your friend here, that the person he was askin' about is okay, and we don't have any indication that there was any mistake."

"Can you tell us what he was arrested for?" presses Joseph.

"Why they just happened to come bustin' through his door," adds Lou upping the ante, "and drag him off without allowing him even to put on his skivvies. It's winter you know. How about a little CPR, courtesy, professionalism, respect? Your department motto so nicely decoratin' all your motor vehicles, Sir!"

The desk officer scopes the crew, chewing his lip, then nods knowingly. "All this will be addressed by his lawyer, or if he don't have one, then the court will appoint him one for his arraignment," to which the fourth officer, red-cheeked and paunchy, adds, "Hey folks, this is a busy place. You people need to talk to the community relations person, who'll be in, in the morning, regular business hours."

Fin turns to him. "Busy place? Looked to us like the city morgue, the castle keep, dead to the world, when we first came through the door. As for our friend, it's a long cold night to be spending in the clink, naked and for no reason."

The paunchy officer's disenchanted eyes seek the desk officer, who slowly brings his hand to his brow and reflects, "Well, let's see now, a comedian *and* a poet—one talented group you've got here." Lifting his chin, a faint, sardonic smile spreading up from his mouth, he throws it back to his older colleague to make another pitch, and Paunchy takes the plunge, "People, this department doesn't arrest people for no reason, and believe me, it don't take its business lightly."

"Yo my man, tight with you on that one, bro," sounds Lou. "Guess you can understand our concern."

The desk officer's eyes snap toward Lou, thinking maybe this has gone far enough. Slowly he pushes himself up. "Listen folks, I've told you everything you need to know. Now I want you all to go home and let us do our business." He punctuates this with a too-broad, pre-fab smile.

Sam turns to the young cop and tells him, "If it were Donald Trump who'd been arrested, you guys would be tripping over yourselves to help."

The officer averts his face to hide his reaction to her droll assertion, then corrects her, "The only thing that would get The Donald down here is if he was gonna buy the place."

"But why treat our friend with any less dignity?" Sam pesters, growing serious. The young cop tilts his head and lifts his eyebrows, as if to say, hey, I thought you was smart. "Listen, Miss, let's be clear. Things don't happen for no reason."

"One man's reason is another man's treason," sings Fin, to which Sam elaborates, "That's what we want to know, the reason."

The young cop studies her. He likes her and wants to enlighten her. "The world's full of reasons, Miss. For instance, there must be some reason, difficult as it is to detect, that places a nice young lady like you down here with a crew like this."

"Which crew is that?" inquires Christine, eyes lightly smarting as she challenges the young cop, and Sam playfully mooches, "Hey, you cops aren't *all* so bad," while Louie cries, "Don't diss my friends, Sirrah. They're as good and honest as the day is long." The rapid fire wipes the young cop's easy smile off his face at the same time Sam is stretching a false one across hers. Christine tries to refocus the exchange, turning back to the desk officer, "We're serious. We're here because we're concerned about our neighbor."

Growing impatient, the officer has begun to slowly rub his hands together in a ruminative, faintly menacing manner. Next to him, aware of the growing tension, Malory puts down his pocket pad and tries to smooth things, "Listen people, you know how many individuals are pulled in here each 'n' every day? And all of 'em, I swear, has friends 'n' relations who swear, who cross themselves, cross their hearts, their swords, their chopsticks, whatever, that their perp is innocent . . . Why, listenin' to all ah ya, a person might think there's no crime whatsoever in the five boroughs; that it's all in the heads of the police, to keep ourselves occupied . . . Well, listen Miss, and everyone, don't you swallow a word of it. Ask the good people in any neighborhood."

Sam frowns. "But what reason could you possibly have for draggin' someone off with no clothes on, on a cold night like this?"

"You were there, lady?" challenges the desk officer, and the young officer adds, "We follow procedures, Miss. We don't just ad lib, you know. And among the rules is keeping a lid on the discussion of cases."

"But on big cases, your people are out there briefing the cameras," Fin points out. "Why is this so different?"

The young officer seems about to reply, but then defers to the desk officer who has lowered his chin to contain his annoyance. "Uhh . . . Folks . . . time to go. Like we said, try back tomorrow." Carefully he moves around the desk as he remembers hearing about the arrest: when the unit went out to pick up this guy—their guy, sounds like—he took a pop at 'em, with an unregistered gun no less. Not out of the ordinary, but it always pisses the boys off when that happens. Now these people are down here squawking, when they have no idea. In fact I see one of 'em is still at it—Joseph insisting, "Can you at least tell us what the charge is?"

But having circled the desk, the desk officer is determined not to get into anything. Summoning a little necessary anger, he sharply warns them, "Folks! You gonna move along now? Or do you need us to show you the door?"

Sam and Joseph, believing that their point's been made, turn to leave, but Christine stands firm, meeting the officer's eye. "Aren't you supposed to be serving the public? We're only seeking information about our neighbor. Why is that such a problem?" The desk officer's sight goes dark for a moment as he pinches his sinuses. What's she want? "I explained, Miss. You hard of hearin'?"

"What's the problem in responding to our concerns?" she repeats.

". . . One last time," he breathes. "Lotta people come through here, lotta people just like you. If we attend to 'em all, we can't do our job. People just can't come in and write their own tickets, 'n' waste our time. We're not in the public relations business, nor are we in a position to judge who or what's legitimate or not. That's for the courts. Now please, go back home or wherever you came from."

"I'm sure, officer, that if you had some friend . . ."

"Don't start!" the desk officer commands, his voice spiking. But Louie, too, is caught up. "But our guy was treated unfairly, like an animal!"

"Enough!" decrees the officer. "Enough! . . . Since you're obviously not hearin' what we're sayin', I'm gonna hafta escort all of yous outta here right now." The three other cops begin urging the group toward the door. As she begins shuffling behind Lou, Sam half-turns back to the young officer at her shoulder. "Our guy is no criminal. We don't understand why he was treated like one."

The young cop leans close to her ear. "What would you say, dear, if I told you a little birdie was chirpin' about some guy, a guy who could be your guy—some character who had an illegal, unregistered handgun? . . . And when a few officers come to his door, he takes a whack at 'em."

Sam is first surprised, then skeptical. "No . . . I don't believe it."

"Of course you don't, dear, 'cause you don't pack a gun. But maybe you heard a lotta people out there do."

Fin, having heard, asks, "That true? About the little bird?"

The cop shrugs. "Birds can't talk, can they, sport? So maybe what you heard was just a little somethin' in the wind. Nothin' that you'd wanta quote anybody on."

Sam mumbles, "Well, if true, that's not good . . ."

The officer forces a smile. "That's right, you got it now." His hefty colleague, next to him, adds, "I suspect none of you'd like to be in a situation where someone's takin' a shot at you, while you're caught out in no-man's-land."

Joseph overhears. "Who was shot at?" But the two cops are mum, leaving Fin to tell him, "There's an assertion that Mr. Kenny took a shot at the cops." Joseph wonders if this is a red herring, the truth, or something in between. He turns back to the two cops. "You guys know whether he called a lawyer or not?"

Faces deadpan, they shake their heads.

As the six begin to file out the front door, the desk cop sends a parting message, "You see, the facts of a case often get misconstrued by a suspect, to help himself—by the defense, by the press, by people in a community . . . so you see, you have to be careful before jumpin' to conclusions."

Errol, the last to leave, turns to protest. "But I saw the guy dragged off, out of the building, without any clothes on. There's no cause for that."

Slowly, heavily, the desk officer shakes his head. "Like I said, you gotta be careful how you interpret things. Did you see what happened prior to that?"

". . . Not everything, but . . ."

The cop tilts his head as if to say, see? Then bows in absolution. "Good night, gentlemen, ladies."

Sidestepping out the door, Errol calls back, "But no one should be treated that way."

The young officer leans out. "Hey, that's why we have courts of law, to resolve disputes."

"This was no dispute, this was an outrage!" Errol cries, though the last word is half-swallowed as he watches the precinct door slowly close.

Outside on the sidewalk, the snowflakes are falling thickly as the six stand at odd angles, glancing back. "Hey," growls Lou, "was that the bum's rush, or what? We shouldn't have to take shit; we've got rights . . . to be in there, to seek information . . . don't we?"

"Congress shall make no laws" recites Fin firmly, "to abridge the rights of dudes and knaves to gather information."

"Amen," sings Sam, but the others, seeking Errol, discover him agitated and crestfallen. Glancing around, discovering their concern, he lowers his eyes, aching and stinging, and presses them, sending red suns coruscating across the front lobes of his brain. "I'm sure they screwed up and are making *him* pay."

"I'll call a lawyer I know," Joseph repeats. "He handles these cases."

"What I don't understand is why they're so unfriendly, so unhelpful, almost adversarial from the outset," complains Christine. "It's so primitive, so punitive."

"It's perspective," offers Fin. "Them against the world, the misunderstood, the last bastion of the Law."

"Which they bend to suit themselves," grumbles Sam.

Under the falling snow, eyes edge from the other's face down to the disappearing sidewalk. Unexpectedly and with sudden heat, Joseph asserts, "This kind of thing has been going on for years, decades, centuries . . . because the victims have no clout, allowing the mayors and police to turn a blind eye." His brow darkens; his mouth re-opens but then falls shut. His features sag under the recognition that there's little that can be done tonight, and probably into the foreseeable future. Next to him, Errol is feeling uncomfortable leaving things like this, but tries to buck them up, "Guys . . . I appreciate everyone comin' down . . . Maybe the higher-ups will hear about it . . . and do something."

"Don't bet on it," mumbles Lou, while Sam grumbles, "The whole thing was so stupid and unnecessary."

"So fucked, in my opinion," mutters Lou.

"Unfortunately bureaucracies, kingdoms, empires, and democracies," notes Joseph, "all become corroded and unable or unwilling to maintain the laws that made them vital."

"All right, professor," mocks Lou.

Displeased, Joseph glances at him thinking Lou's sarcasm is not unlike that of the cops. Maybe the differences are really a question of where we're standing, or where we've fallen. Exhaling this futility, he tries to dismiss it for the moment, as best he can. "I've gotta get back . . . to do some work, but I'll make that call in the morning . . . Think we can get a cab around here?"

"Up on Canal," Errol tells him. "I'm gonna walk home."

"Share a cab with us, Errol," Christine urges, having watched him closely.

Glum with replaying it all, he half-turns not sure where. "Thanks, but I need the walk."

Lou gives him a whack on the shoulder. "Oh, come on . . . It's not like your man's dead. How long can they keep him? And anyway, his lawyer will make 'em pay big time." But this doesn't console Errol. Sam steps over to fondly embrace him, and Christine follows. To each woman, however, he manages only a dispirited hug and hollow smile, which he then sends on to the men. "Thanks, guys."

Eyes bump around the group, trying to read what's what, as faces appear caught between bewilderment and resignation. Errol throws a hand briefly up into the white air, calling, "Good night." Then thrusting his hand back into his pocket, he steers himself around and heads up to the corner. Lou watches for a second, then groans, "I'll walk the dude home, the dumb fuck." And he runs after him. The others watch until the snow shutters their eyes. Lowering their heads, they too begin kicking through the snow toward Canal.

III.

Hearth

In their darkened bedroom, Terry and Viv lie awake next to each other, staring up at the ceiling. Neither has slept, although Terry's eyes are shutting as his thoughts spin off toward the cusp.

"B-loody police!" sputters Vivian into the stillness. "Never admit a damned thing, even when the facts are lined up against them. Culpability is for civilians . . . Hope to God he squeezes the city good, to pay for this outrage . . . though it'll probably drag on for years 'n' ruin his life."

"Mm," lows Terry in accord, gently exhaling empathic exasperation between his lips. He knows, however, the case for police abuse will not be easy to make, particularly if there was a gun. But now, from an upper corner of his mind, a painting diagonally descends, its streaks of color coalescing into form: pea-green drips framing a pale plaster wall, sea-green drops splattering a clay-brown floor, a stripped walnut table displaying a ceramic bowl of spiraling blue and white arms—suggestions of, records of, motion in stillness, reality in two dimensions—antinomies of perception. From the medium flows the form and function. Once more from that corner comes apparent movement: a pea-green, paint-spattered hand, straining for the bowl, trailing its plaster-encrusted, deeply-gashed forearm dotted with plum-colored bruises. The materials of creation: flesh and emotion, yearning and design, paint and its application, canvases to fill . . . The vocabulary of our medium. Connections to consider, if you can remember till morning, old man.

"If I keep thinkin' about this too much," Viv grumbles, "I'll never sleep . . . It brings back all the indignation from our incident . . . Now I'm hot 'n' sweaty . . . Have t' throw off the comforter, on a cold night like this."

"This is ten times the affront," Terry murmurs.

"Mmm . . . But why, tell me why so many white people are like that?" she wails, her tone constricted and high. "What's wrong with 'em?"

"Don't know . . ." Terry sighs, his attention drifting off again. He has his theories, but he's not going there tonight, not to that lawless frontier.

"I'm not so sure about these Wednesday nights anymore," she breathes, picturing the bar. "Errol, Sam . . . Christine, maybe . . . but some of the others . . . Not sure I want to hear their naïve opinions anymore."

"No-o," acknowledges Terry faintly, sensing sleep creeping close. "Not all so bad . . . harmless . . ." Where the painting was, now floats a great, gossamer bubble, shimmering, beckoning, lifting him weightlessly away. Time was when he had little interest in sleep. Now he finds himself eyeing it, inclining toward it, intermittently through the day, imagining its release, its Vermeer window light, its intimate faces.

"Peter at least," Viv is brooding, "you know what he thinks, not that I want to hear it . . . but the others, I don't know. Don't trust 'em . . ."

But Terry doesn't respond. She rolls her head toward the breathing barrow next to her. Husband, she thinks, even you spend too much time tryin' to understand and befriend those detectives you work with. Do your work, deal with them when you have to, but otherwise leave 'em be. They don't care nothin' for you. Fact is, it's probably worse, probably nothing but sneering contempt. She leans closer, straining to see his eyes, now closed, and realizes that she doesn't need to tell him. Probably he knows, probably he takes it 'n' shrugs it off, the way men do.

*　　*　　*

Silently, sullenly, Sam and Fin stare out from their cab as it sleds, lazily fish-tailing through the snow-quilted, narrow streets. Their heavy eyes run over the newly frosted stoops and rails and briefly follow the few pedestrians, heads bowed, shoulders whitened and folded as they zig after prior footprints denting the ankle-high accumulations. The city is shutting down beneath the white curtain billowing through the neighborhoods.

The thoughts of the two are drawn away from the snowscape, however, back to images from the police station and their own renderings of Errol's darker story. In her mind, Sam hears again the sharp crack of gunfire that Errol described and feels it sucking her breath away. Recoiling, she presses against her seat, avoiding the beefy bodies battering the door, bursting into someone's quiet home. Pursing her lips, she sips the icy air.

Fin, to her left, is watching, through Errol's spellbound eyes, his neighbor—Kenny, was it?—dragged off, within arm's reach, between hulking cops. Kenny, dazed, head limp, no longer protesting, unable to get his bare feet under him, rushed, hurried, hauled, through the hallway, past Errol's widening, cringing eyes that shutter closed so that he only hears feet and bones thudding down the stone stairs—doors squeaking, slamming, before all are gone out into the freezing night. Fin attempts to put himself in Kenny's place, but his thumping heart resists.

Seeking something to distract herself, Sam feels her mind filling with un-recognizable darting images, soon discerned as anger emanating from and directed at Peter, indistinct memories swelling and pressuring her skull, until she gasps, "That bastard! The selfish bastard! Caring only for himself." Why had she not noticed? In fact she had, but his humor and agility at dodging issues had enabled him to dance around confrontations over their year of living together. She had discovered variations of his behavior erupting unexpectedly in his mother and sisters, dismaying her, horrifying her, in their cruel, unheeding needling of his elderly father. At home, she had questioned Peter about it, but he refused to acknowledge or deal, and so, for most of their year, they skirted, skipped past issues, attitudes, crises, before tonight's abrupt, naked differences cracked open . . .

Looking over at Fin staring out the other window, his head nodding with the motion of the cab, she thinks there is something she likes about him, though she fears it may be no more than his boyish liveliness playing in his features, or his interest in and appreciation of her singing, or his trying to somehow take stock of the city in his columns, or maybe . . . simply his looks. She weakly tries, and fails, to tease these tangles apart. Unmistakably, though, there is some rapport, despite his reputation of dangling several women—some recognition lurking in his accepting eyes. "Fin . . ." she breathes. He looks over. "That guy'll get out, right? Once the cops admit their mistake."

Meeting her gaze knocks her question clean out of his mind. In the dark of the cab, her mahogany hair, curving like a seashell, frames a face that somehow knows him. How is that possible? No intimate conversations have ever passed between them. From where does it come? It is as if he is looking into a mirror, a mirrored sensibility. That which he is thinking, he suspects she is.

In the midst of these wonderings, her question resurfaces, and he nods faintly. "He should be released . . . but then it sounds as if he should never have been arrested—certainly not in that way—in the first place." Distantly an interior voice reminds him how little he knows of the facts, such as they are. Any one of several scenarios may have unfolded, or maybe no single truth is possible, only perceptions. He's read articles about the police, about the difficulties of the job, the inadequate training, about how they—our modern-day knights, but no less human than the rest of us—are thrust into impossible moments. Yet somehow these generalities seldom adequately illumine, or excuse, a particular incident.

Sam has turned back to her window, but her thoughts hang back with her image of Errol, and she wonders about his life. Lightly she elbows Fin. "Why did Errol take it so personally, as if it had happened to him?"

Her concern meanders along the muddy riverbank of his mind, past shattered limbs, broken beavers, splintered halberds. "Maybe, Sam, because it was just outside his castle, his home. It could have been him, and his family . . . Or maybe it was the brutality, or the injustice . . . I don't know. The cops are so difficult to read, wrapped in their layers of idealism and power . . . frustration, cynicism, and a desire to serve. Going into it, many want to make a difference . . . going in . . ."

Sam's eyes nearly close under the weight of this. Ahead she searches to see if a cop stands duty at the corner, or sheltered in a doorway. But not a soul is visible. All doorways, steps, and stoops are empty and white. Curtains of snow, swaying out from the cross street, drift across their path. She succumbs to this emptiness, slumping back into the seat. "Fin . . . I've seen Errol fidgeting at the bar, on other nights, shifting nervously . . . preoccupied, as if something's eating him. Do you have any idea? I mean I've wondered if he's depressed or suffering from . . . something."

Fin, also dazed by the unstaunchable snowfall, shakes his head. He attempts to picture Errol at the bar, but instead catches sight of a shadowy figure outside the cab, striding along the sidewalk in their direction, a fellow encased in a long, gray greatcoat and black boots, holding his Napoleonic head erect, shoulders back, gliding unaffected by the storm. Fin tries to find the face behind the snow-domed cars, but can only see a high, pale brow rising into straight, dark hair, webbed with a net of white. Retreat from Moscow? Yet Nappy copped a sled; it was Pierre and Karatayev who walked. Mind over body. Fin swivels for a clearer glimpse, but the other is gone, behind the drifts, street lamps, and thickening flakes.

Sam, he hears, is asking, "What's the story with Errol's wife?"

Fin swings back to find her, the Madonna, haloed by the passing street lights. He wonders what exactly her interest is, closing his eyes for a moment, admitting that if he knows little of Errol, how much less about his wife? And still less of Kenny. He likes Errol, as they all do, and involuntarily he inhales.

"Errol's a private dude. Lou's the only one he really talks to . . . But from the few comments I've heard, the marriage sounds a little shaky."

"If he's a city elementary school teacher, how much can he be pulling in?" she crabs with surprising sharpness. "How can you raise a family on that?"

Taken aback by her sudden veering, Fin pauses, reaching for what he knows, "His wife works . . . doing something . . . I forget what . . ."

"You ever seen one of his plays?" she asks him, looking over through curiosity and mild disparagement. When Fin shakes his head, she jeers, "Some friend." Ruefully he nods, before turning and studying her. "And you? Have you seen any?"

"No . . ." Heavily her head rolls back toward her window, bowed by restlessness and by admitting she's no less derelict. Her sinking mood presses her again into the seat where she slumps smarting and feeling snared.

Too harsh, he sees. "Sorry. Didn't mean to *j'accuse* you. Just curious." Yet she seems not to hear, continuing to stare out her side. He nudges her shoulder with his. "Hey, even Lou's never mentioned a word about his plays."

In the dark of the quietly rumbling cab, she looks over, and they take in each other, warily. She wonders what really what might be shared. What would be different? Would the hints of sensitivity evaporate with inevitable contention, or be rubbed away by buffeting reality? Peter at least is a known quantity, mostly. Should I blame him for his family's genes? "The fault, dear Finnegan, lies in our little maps, where sympathy's not included." Yet, she thinks, we each bring other things, too. She's read a few of Fin's pieces, in which he's tried to present things a little differently. Suppose there's some worth in that, but other attempts of his strained, fizzled. How deep does his concern go? Do our public postures really take the form of . . . What was it? . . . Personal something . . . Luck is what I need. Luck. Surprise me, Fin, surprise me.

Watching her alabaster face—Lady of the Lake—he sees that her eyes alone seem alive, yet heavy with moisture barely contained by her lashes—her forty lashes . . . How familiar, how compelling . . . Do we not imbue women with that goodness of our earliest days, our mother's gaze? Perfect, patient peace. The lucky among us. And though other realities soon stalk us, the emotions do not entirely forget that past, and hope. Nor can I deny there is some affinity, which does not come every day. I wonder if her faint smile acknowledges this. Alas our daily lives too often lead us away, take us off, never to know what might have been. Should I lean and kiss her? Lip to lip, body tracing body? Something stirs, plummets, shakes body 'n' soul. But I cannot forget that it is, and has been, Peter to whom she has tied herself, and who has filled her with life.

Disappointment darkens her face, and she looks away, then unexpectedly begins again: "It's funny . . . that though we come regularly to the bar, only Errol and Lou seem to have what you'd call a friendship." She turns back, and her eyes rush over his face, wondering, until flashes from the early days with Peter blot her sight—Peter, her wunderkind, knowing and showing her things she'd never dreamt of, showing her a new life, a new way of being, teaching her passion and unbridled sex, things she'd only heard about, read about, things she didn't think were done. These memories can still throb in her, can still excite . . . At first it had turned her inside out. He seemed to have entered and taken up residence in the middle of her . . . though recently, less and less.

Her eyes tumble to the rubber mat in the footwell. "I wonder why Peter, for one, bothers to come to our gatherings," she muses, her voice thick and slow. "He doesn't give two shits about most of you . . . you, Terry, Lou. And poor Kenny even less . . . He sorta admires Joseph, for some reason, although not as much as Joseph admires himself."

"N-o," disputes Fin. "Joseph's not so bad. You read his novel?"

She sends him a groan, then grimace. "You kidding? More detective trash, another who-done-it? Who cares about guns 'n' guts?"

"It's not bad, of its type. It offers some psychology . . ." he counters emptily, his conviction evicted. But her thoughts have moved on, and she asks him idly, "You see him wooing Christine?"

"Wooing? . . . I thought he was enlisting her for the magazine."

She sends over another dubious look, shaking her head and laughing a little. "Maybe it's a survival advantage, men being oblivious. Never have to pause to think about others." Fin recoils at the underlying bitterness, countering to himself that nature doesn't deal in morality. He turns to look out at the buildings altered by snow. It takes him a moment to gain his bearings. No one's out; all buried or driven inside. An empty theatrical set, he imagines, or desolate headlands in an ice age mountainscape across which the occasional hunter, or small band, trots tracking the last hope for food—hunters who may in an instant become the hunted. Even now, in these streets, the odd murder happens. Some poor unsuspecting soul . . ."Maybe," he breathes, half speaking to her, "we men are only tuned for the hunt, or battle, evolved to confront the saber-tooth tiger, the last auroc . . . the charging horde."

Her eyelids droop. "Yeah, that's it." Resignation sags in her cheek. "Except I can name ten women I'd feel safer with than any of you guys. And they can write rings around you all, Gunga Din."

Eyebrows rising, he searches for her eyes again, but she has turned away. He tries to understand her mood, her anger, her hurt . . . what she needs . . . Gentle-ness. "Sam, I like you; I get a kick out of you—sometimes literally. But we should become friends."

She's not sure she's heard right and twists her neck around, squinting, replaying what seems both more and less than what she might have hoped for. She finds he's watching, a tentative light in his eyes, suggesting, she thinks, hesitancy. Of course. What else? She reflects for a minute, then observes, "While you've learned a bit about my situation, Fin, you've told me nothing about yours."

His eyes scan the street ahead, where trash cans and hydrants have turned into gnomes. Where to start? "It's nothing too complicated . . ."

"What are you trying to do with your life?" she interjects with terse incomprehension. "Where is it you think you're going?"

His eyes fall to his knees. What is it she doesn't understand? Is the journalist's life too open-ended for her? Arbitrarily he begins, "For now I'm quite happy to be able to do my column, do a little reporting for the paper . . . blend the streams, the real, the ideal, the personal, the social . . . perception and expectation . . . I feel lucky."

"Does it have any effect . . . any benefit?" she quizzes impatiently.

He glances over to find her gaze grown hard, and he wonders if she fears his work may be less than it appears, as occasionally he does. Again he tries, blindly, "I get to talk to a lot of people, interesting people, hear their thoughts, reflect, reassess . . . imagine."

"But who reads it?"

Again the practical, which he, too, must regularly accommodate. The issue is not new, indeed is one, he suspects, that many like him must address. "I figure that on a good week, maybe . . . six people read the column. The reporting has its built-in constituency of course, depending. But sometimes I wonder if I'm just . . ."

"Jerking off."

Not expecting this, he blinks. A smile covers his chagrin. "You pick that up from Peter?"

She stares ahead unhappily. "Probably, but could be any of you."

". . . So bad? . . . Lumping us all together? Like the cops and we do to each other?"

Her cheek creases with disapproval, rejecting his feigned innocence and inaccurate analogy, "Come on, which guy can you recommend? Can you name even one?"

"Have to confess, haven't given it much thought. Maybe I should."

"Don't bother. It's not worth it."

He feels unsettled, and distanced, by her tone, and bitterness. What brings it on? Sensing this, she softens. "I read a couple of your pieces a while back. One on the Bowery I liked, but some other thing on 'beauty' I thought was pure bs, another male crock."

"It's always gratifying to feel understood," he breathes, releasing some mild disgruntlement. "Some women liked it, they told me," although right now he can't place names or even faces to those opinions.

"I understood all right," she smiles disparagingly. "I might have read more of your pieces, but Peter steals the paper to wipe off his brushes, once he's read the few pages that interest him."

Fin shakes his head as his eyes lift and gaze into the blank, gray ceiling. Exhaling, he observes, "The fate of the written word in our time: ornamenting the cleaning cloths of a preoccupied citizenry."

She expels her annoyance. "Yeah well, I read what I find that's worth my time, which is usually *not* the logorrhea in your newspaper." He looks at her, studying her profile, which he likes, but wonders at her anger. How deep, and how far back does it reach? She offers no explanation, instead slowly folding her arms, closing her lips, and sitting, once again, perfectly still.

Arriving at her building their cab pulls over, but in braking, it skids on an icy patch and bangs heavily against the curb and then into the parked car ahead. The two passengers, amid cries of "Whoa!" and "What the . . . ?" are slung sideways, then jammed forward into the partition. The driver has braced himself with the wheel, but the two friends have nothing to grip. Fin has flung an arm around Sam to hold her back, thrusting his other arm forward, but the double impact throws them off balance to the side, then hard ahead. For a dazed moment, they feel welded, joined, pancaked into the other's heaving body.

*   *   *

Two figures, heads bowed against the storm, silently kick through drifts heaping up over forgotten objects. At mid-block, they halt, peer about, and turn toward the snow-covered steps of a brownstone where they begin feeling their way up. Arriving on the landing, both twist unsteadily to find the other through the gusting gale. Christine and Joseph shared a cab to her corner and now try to balance the desire to gracefully say goodnight with that to get warm and dry. Across the street and down the block, the ghostly light, carried in the swirling, fluttering flakes, hovers between the known world and an imaginary one, entrancing both, even as they search for some conclusion about the evening. Her thoughts feel blown back to the central event, Kenny's arrest and their reactions, while Joseph's thoughts stagger in attempting to make sense of the precinct confrontation, before lurching ahead to the hours of work he needs to complete and then circling back to Christine—not as infatuation, he tells himself, but as colleague and someone to discuss the thoughts and emotions of writing—as his good wife, Bonnie, did for years, but which has fallen off, as things do—some of it onto their son, most into a void. Renewal, he thinks, is what he needs. Rebirth, an infusion of something. Maybe it's not that we age or lose hope as much as it is that we grow tired, ground down by frustration and repetition—like the cops. Glancing at Christine, he fumbles for some conclusion: "The law, like our own behaviors, needs constant vigilance. I'm sure the cops believe their behavior was justified. Every action, every point of view, has its rationale."

"Yes," she allows. The ineluctable subjectivity of the rational . . . Our ardent self-assertion, our egoism, that drives and colors so much. Our indefatigable ability to excuse our endless errors. All this descends upon her mind incessantly, like the snow, like the millions of flakes forming one pattern, then another, until truth is blurred and buried. Are the cops cynical or worn down? Does the lowest among them corrupt the rest? Is their insensitivity defensive or intentionally offensive? Like the accumulations building on the sidewalks, these questions fall more quickly than her mental shoveling can clear. Through the blanketing white, she seeks Joseph's face. "Joseph, will you call me tomorrow," she asks, "after talking to the lawyer?"

"First thing," he reassures her, though he recognizes that something is gripping him, has a hold of his brain, and he searches her face. He wants to get beyond these exchanges, and he attempts to begin by meeting her eyes, but she is pulling at her scarf to better shield herself. Frustrated, he tries, "You interested . . . in getting a coffee somewhere? Chat a bit?"

The moaning wind and movement of her scarf around her ears smother his hesitant words. She looks to see if he's said something, but finds only his pained expression, behind which he is waiting to see if she's heard.

"Good night, Joseph. I'll get the chapters to you."

He searches for hints of what happened, why she's ignored his invitation. She appears to be waiting for something from him. His mouth opens to ask again, then resets, "Well, another time . . ."

"What?" she calls, beginning to turn.

"Thanks," he swallows, before spitting out a desperate variation, "let's talk about writing sometime. What do you think?"

"Yes," she smiles as she waves, before groaning and casting an unhappy glance up at the snow. She steers herself around and up the final step to the door, her hand wriggling into a pocket for her key. Shielding his eyes with a hand, he tries to follow her as she seems to disappear into the white. Searching, waving away the snow, he urgently tries to find her, but she's no longer there. All he can make out is her front door slowly closing. His frustration presses suddenly heavier upon his shoulders and heart. A weariness begins to fill him, as if it were the snow, the great white father reminding and admonishing. Yet he recognizes this feeling for the self-pity it is, and he scolds himself. He listens for it to come again, but there is only the wind. He'd better get himself home before he freezes and is buried on these steps. Jamming his hands into his coat pockets, he jerks himself around and carefully edges sideways back down, following their now faint footprints. He should have kept the cab, he groans. How many blocks to push through? Eight, nine? An anguished cry rises. His. It seems to precede him, echoing down the block. He listens. But again hears only the wind, the moaning younger brother of the snow, together swarming through the night.

*   *   *

Pushing up Elizabeth Street, Errol and Lou lean into gusts, steer around snow-heaped trash cans, duck under avalanches plunging down from the roofs. The wind, vertical then horizontal, drives the flakes through the seams and holes in their coats, freezing flesh, compelling the two to slap, then beat, the numbing patches with palms, then fists.

"Fricking freezing!" Lou shouts, his words instantly absorbed in the wind.

Errol's thinking he's some sort of idiot for wearing only his raincoat. And of course Leslie will skewer him for going out at all, after the incident—perfectly happy, as she is, to deny him his evening, despite her religious observance of her weekly escapades, sometimes twice weekly—out for dancing lessons with her girlfriends, or so she says. Who she's so eagerly dancing with I have no idea. God surely knows more about her outside life than I do.

He searches up into the sky, but the snowflakes lunge at his eyeballs. Attempting to blink them clear, he notices a white cloud hovering not far above. A fog? A lake? A sword rising from its mists? . . . He thrusts an arm up, trying to punch into it, but it withdraws, rising as it seems to expand. He blinks again; it recedes farther, merging into the greater whiteness. Mentally he whacks himself, 'You imbecile!' and expels a breath heavy with disgust. Their trip to the goddamned precinct had no effect at all. What am I? Misfortune's fool? What was I dreamin'?

Lou swerves closer, "Yo, Errol, know what I'm thinkin'?"

Errol turns his head, swiping the snow off his nose.

Lou pulls his coat collar tighter, "I'm thinkin' I finally found a way, a framework, for my stories, to write 'em up."

". . . Your South Bronx stories?"

"Yeah, I'm thinkin' put in the whole crew, the whole crazy mix: the neighborhood, the boys, their families, even somma d' cops . . . It hit me at the precinct. The different cultures, a thousand views and tales, true to life, like it was . . . Wouldn't be no New Yorker magazine shit. Raw, in your face, the world I knew. Call it 'Confessions from The Street' or 'Where Hell Froze Over' . . . Whaddya think?"

"Sounds good. Sell it to Joseph's magazine."

"He doesn't pay shit . . . . I'm thinkin' book, movie, interviews, maybe Oprah and stuff."

"Like that Irish guy, Frank McSnow."

Lou's mouth twists with disgust. "I'm serious."

"You know he was just a teacher, in the public schools."

"Then there's hope for you," gibes Lou.

"And you too. You were exposed to education."

"Ever the wise ass, the secret wise ass. If only people knew. So what do you think?"

"Try it. What you got to lose? Besides Irene."

"Why? She likes books."

"Cause you won't have time for her. And you won't have any money either. Broke, like me."

". . . No? . . . I was thinkin' you could help."

"Ohh, I see . . . you dream up the tales. I have to make 'em work."

"Well, you're the writer . . ."

"Yeah, rolling in dough, a play in every playhouse. And I know, you'll take all the credit. But hey, no problem." Errol can see it all, having heard these schemes before. Like the others, he's sure this one will melt away with the snow.

"No way. We'll split the profits, everything. Really . . . You know, Errol, I told you a bunch o' those guys I grew up with are dead now, history."

"You told me . . . You know it's been done, don't cha? Ten ways from Sunday. Ancient history . . . What're you gonna bring that's new?"

Finally irritated, Lou asks, "What's with you? You sure put that Kenny guy out of your mind quick."

"I was trying to, until you keep shoving him back in my face."

"Sure," Lou grumbles, then groans, but he wants to get back to his idea. "Okay . . . well listen, you know I been wonderin' 'bout somma those guys, wonderin' what it's like to be dead, to that degree."

"To what degree? What the hell you talkin' about?"

"Dead for a long time."

"Dead is dead."

"You ever think about that?"

"All the time." But Errol concedes to himself it's mostly intellectual. The real thing, the thing itself, would be dumb, boring . . . fucking uninteresting.

". . . What's it like, you think?"

"Like nothing, like empty."

"They say some people come back from there, with wild tales, light, conversations with family . . . colors and clouds 'n' stuff—not that I totally believe it."

"Lou . . . I've never been dead . . ."

"Never had memories of your life flash by like a movie?"

"My life was never a movie."

Lou glances at him trying to read his mood. Errol's face, tipped eye-deep in his coat, shows only his brow pinched and pale, and Lou realizes his friend's thoughts must be elsewhere, probably back railin' against the cops. "Hey . . . you think Kenny believed he was looking at death?"

Errol jumps a little. "What the fuck, Lou? What are you doin', buggin' me? Cut it out, will ya!"

"He musta been, huh? I mean all those shots rainin' through the door . . ."

Errol feels his mind career down a stair. He draws in a chest-full of the bitter air. Damn me . . . He glances over at Lou wondering what he does with his smarts sometimes. But then the images of Kenny-being-dragged return, elbowing everything aside. He shakes his head, careful to keep his chin covered. "Can't believe the way they treated him. And if he'd a been in front of his door, if he hadn't dived down or somethin', he'd been peg board, swiss cheese, pizza—some Expressionist paint job, spatterin' everything, floor to ceiling." Errol again inhales the cold air—too cold and damp—and coughs. The trek is requiring increasingly heavy breathing, something close to wheezing, from them both. Conversation is shoved to the back-burner. Fortunately, Errol sees they've got only another block. Ask Lou up for a beer? Or is that riskin' a run-in with the dancin' queen of the night? Treat him to one of her tirades. Man! . . . What's goin' on, and what am I doin' . . . in this crazy vale of frozen tears? Tears from the fuckin' centuries, pourin' down on me.

*　　*　　*

Metallic clink and clank from the radiators and their disparaging hissing greet Christine as she steps into her apartment and closes the door. For a moment she stands in the dark listening for sounds of Daniel, but detects none. She flicks on the light and sees neither his great coat nor his tall black boots. As she eases out of her own coat, trying to contain the shaken snow to a small woven rug, she is disappointed that he's not returned, to hug and to listen to her account of the evening's extraordinary events. For though she feels she shouldn't label it so, it was an adventure to her—as certainly as it was not for Clayton and Errol. Fleeting images from Errol's recounting beat at her inner ear, exacting a muffled cry. She wraps her arms, grabbing opposite shoulders, and in frustration twists herself around fretfully. But her arms fall limp to her sides, in disappointment, then rise anxiously again, lifting her hands up over her eyes and brow. Blurred figures sweep behind her sight, figures bent in receiving pain and delivering pain. She leans over to begin pulling off her boots, tapping their snow onto the rug. Errol's face returns, wavering and shadowed in the bar, relating haltingly his experience. It was for him, as well as for Kenny, that she went to the precinct. The puffy, unhappy faces of the cops warned of their impatience, before their cries and commands burst out, and their dark, beady eyes, like little night sticks, prodded the friends toward the door. She tries to picture Kenny's jail cell but can manage only TV's sanitized sets. She attempts to imagine what Kenny must have experienced but can conjure only a few, fleeting fragments, admitting she has no idea. Yet those fragments lodge in her chest like shards of glass, so that she dares not move. Her heart thumps, from fear, empathy, anger; her temples squeeze. The brutality of it. Our still-animal anima.

Re-wrapping her arms around herself, she walks into her small kitchen to make tea. She runs water into the electric kettle, clicks it on, reaches for a teabag. Shouldn't our civilization do better? . . . Or is this simply where we are, the stage we're at? Forty, fifty years ago things were worse. What now to reasonably expect? Because we know more doesn't mean our actions entirely reflect it. Yet a community ought to do better, and some do . . . But violence is everywhere, streaming into our homes, our eyes, through all the media, holding up a mirror.

Maybe write a piece, she thinks, on this and what people see ahead. She wonders if she could get in to interview the top cop, the Mayor or appropriate deputy, minority leaders, and maybe an officer from a street crimes unit. See if anything fits together.

Her water is boiling. The kettle clicks off. She pours, flops in her teabag, stirs in a spoonful of honey. In its first sip of warm sweetness she experiences the equivalent of simple peace.

She goes into their small bedroom and begins to pull off her partially wet clothes, into which snow somehow seeped. She swings her robe around her shoulders. Joseph wants something from her. Something collegial, and, she senses, something more, which is slightly disappointing. But also reality. How thin the layer. Errol, in contrast, seems truly an innocent, or maybe it's that he's preoccupied, or overwhelmed—while Daniel, I assume, is truthful with me, though I know he thinks of other women—they're in his poems—their stories, their misconnections, their minor tragedies. I've said nothing, as we both come with prior lives. The city serves them up, the possibilities. While I have no reason to doubt him, the histories of writers and poets are not reassuring.

Wrapped in her bathrobe, she returns to the kitchen and dials Dan's office number. No answer; must be on his way. She pictures him striding in his gray greatcoat; imagines herself being out in the storm again. If one is dressed, it's glorious, to be surrounded, embraced, buffeted. The miracles of snow and cities and consciousness. Another sip; the tea is cooler now. She stares into it, glances at the microwave, stirs the tea slowly, watching its amber strands.

IV.

The Witching Hour

Under the falling snow Sam and Fin tent heads together for a goodnight kiss. But dampness seeping into Sam's shoe pulls her attention down to her aching arch half-buried in a small drift, and Fin's lips connect not with her cheek but her snowy crown. "Ffuff," he blows, clearing his mouth of flakes and hair.

She looks up, jarred by the bump and the chill, to find Fin feeling his lip, watching her strangely. "Sorry . . ." she cedes, weakly laughing. Their eyes meet, but her thoughts carom upward, to her apartment above on the top floor, and glancing there, through the descending snow, she finds her hopes pelted by the heavy flakes. She closes her eyes, only to see Peter's friar-like face looming, watching, a near-perfect oval framed by his black hair, which, with detail fading, becomes a noose. "Fin . . . I can't go upstairs, into screaming recriminations . . ." She shivers and searches desperately down the block. "I need a drink, first." She eyes Fin's waiting face. "Wanna get a drink?"

Fin studies her, wary of her reasons and the wisdom of this. "Well . . . uh . . . if you wanna, Juana."

She tries to read Fin's interest through the rush of her own thoughts, wondering if he will want to listen, when his shifting expressions suggest a pelagic mind. But what am I thinking? Which guy does want to listen to a woman's troubles, for very long? So, what to do? . . . But then, what choice, really? "I wanna."

Agreeing on a nearby bar, they swing around and head off, weaving between the snow mounds. Yet what fills her mind's eye is her memory of their apartment ceiling, Peter's Sistine Chapel, his most lively achievement, ranging across the expanse of their largest room, diagonally dividing it into noon and night, its two triangular planes adorned with great vege-tals and ani-mals, as Peter calls them, all parading from sunlight into moonlight. Giant-sized green and yellow squash march shoulder-to-shoulder with red and orange peppers and gnarled olive trees whose serpentine branches bow heavy with midnight fruit. Fat ani-mals, two great gray geese waddle in the flow, followed by a balletic brother pig, squinting through disgruntled piggy eyes—Peter's scorning eyes, Sam has secretly thought, eyes that reveal his need to oink his edicts and acerbic notions. Other ani-mals and reptiles plod and slither in a line stretching to the horizon, but Sam's attention falls to her frozen feet.

Fortunately the bar is close and still open on this unlikely evening. Inside, they stamp their shoes, brush the snow from each other, and wander over to the bar stools where they hike themselves up. She curls her feet to warm them, cracking toes and icicles. Nearby, pale patrons, faces wreathed in dark hair and dark clothes, murmur motionlessly. Sam asks the Dostoyevskian barkeep for a Black Russian, Fin, a Wild Turkey on the rocks—for the name. Eagerly they sip down the warmth, feeling it seep to the extremities, as their minds fall pleasantly free.

Glancing into his face, as her fingers flex and piano along the bar and then rise to push her damp hair from her eyes, she assesses Fin's readiness, and when she has his gaze, she confides with a sigh, "Tired, Fin . . . tired of Peter's inflexibility and narrowness, the tension and the fights . . ."

He hears and slowly nods, imagining how this must be so.

"He doesn't want relationships with an equal . . . He doesn't really see the value of friendships. He has little compassion for others. Certainly not Kenny." Like the sinking moon, her head descends barward as she stares into her dark drink.

Fin asks her if she thinks Peter was playing the devil's advocate tonight. She shakes her head. "No, that was him." She pictures Peter's mother and the three sisters grim staring at her, whispering in league against her. Revulsion erases those faces, feature by feature.

"On the other hand, Sam," Fin earnestly reminds her, "he's obviously attached to you. I thought there were many signs tonight."

Her body slumps a little. "Cares? . . . I suppose, in the sense that who else is there? I'm the sole source, outside of himself, of what he feels he needs."

". . . Isn't that true, to one extent or another, for all of us?" he tries.

Sam sends him a heavy-lidded look. "I thought you considered yourself a romantic—one of the last."

Fin tips his head, conceding, "In moments of weakness."

"What Peter wants is someone next door, not in-house."

"A question of space?" Fin asks.

"No-o, come on . . . People are here to be useful to him. Much as his mother and sisters believe."

"What about confronting him?" he asks. "Unstunting him?"

"No way. Not open. Locked into his way of doing things . . . I think we're both concluding that maybe it was a mistake."

Fin's wincing eyebrows confine his sight to his drink, which he savors with an extended sip, until his gaze wanders over to the bartender, leaning perfectly still over the bar, staring out at the snow. Most bartenders, Fin reflects, are in perpetual motion, ever busy—no end of puttering—a way, he supposes, of dealing with being ever on display. But this one, God bless him, is bent upon his elbow, Russian mustache drooping, staring out, lost in reverie, his inky hair as lightless as a crypt. Y-van, Fin nearly calls. "You know, Sam, though it's from a distance, I like Peter."

"You don't know him. You two aren't close. He's not close with any guy."

"Lotta guys 're like that. But Peter's funny . . . wry . . . a character, and I like his paintings."

She blinks, looking away to hide her feelings. "Yeah . . . I like him too, on occasion . . . He can be fun . . . funny . . . affectionate, loving . . ." She imagines his laugh, hears his caustic asides at work. "He's like no one else, Fin, and he's a good lover . . . It's been gratifying to share our interest in design and graphic arts . . . There are times when I adore him." She clears her eyelashes of moisture, product of the happymoments. She wonders if she could simply sidestep the pain.

From the corner of his eye, Fin takes this in, finding her feeling affecting, down-eyed lady of the snowlands. He imagines this weight attached to her heart, slowing it down, down.

"I've tried, God knows," she breathes. "But he's destructive . . . of us, of himself, of his work. He's destroyed some of his best paintings . . . which was heart-breaking. They were so beautiful." She looks away. "And he's indifferent to my music, probably because it's not his . . . Do you know what that's like, that disinterest toward what I pour so much into?"

Nodding, Fin tells himself he knows something of it, as the two women he's dating show little real interest in his word-whittling, beyond some calculation of his minor celebrity. He likes them, but probably all of them know it's not for keeps.

Staring ahead, picturing Peter, her voice wavers, "I love him . . . but he makes it impossible."

Again Fin tries, "What about sayin' just that to him?"

A moment and a long sip are needed to refill her composure. "Tried that . . . He just scoffs, walks off, changes the subject . . . It's his way or the highway . . . Routine rules. It's what he can deal with, how he manages life, with its disappointments. He's tormented by the fact he isn't the painter he'd like to be, can't get the recognition, can't get a show. And maybe to deal with that, he measures out the rest in teaspoons, figuring how little he needs to give to work, friends, me—stirring in his spite . . . It's his painting, and secret mourning, that claim his devotion."

Fin takes in a slow, full one and holds it in his cheeks. Sad . . . He swallows. Swallows fill the night sky. Capistrano, Hotel California. "Never easy, is it."

"But why? . . . Why is it so hard? How is it some people get along?"

"Luck," Fin mumbles, feeling a light helplessness. "The throw of the dice . . . Or, I read somewhere, good sex."

"We had that, I thought."

Fin turns his mind to those tricky scales. Who can keep a balance through time?—that other, consummate Iago.

Sipping, both fall silent, recalling contention, disappointment, pain. At length Fin ventures, "Someone told me it's all in the phrasing, in finding the right way to say things, so that it's palatable to the other. Maybe you can find that right way."

"I've tried . . ."

He sends a doubting frown her way. ". . . What about throwing yourself on his sympathy, or threatening to move out?"

She laughs bitterly. "That the '*right way*' you learned, Fin? Don't go getting married too soon . . ." She shakes her head. "Peter knows all the tricks. And if he ever gave in, even to some degree, he'd never let me forget it. He'd be pecking at me all the time." Glancing at Fin, she allows him to see the hopelessness she feels. He swings a hand up and rests it on her shoulder, lightly. She sniffs back the effluence as he studies her, rotating his glass uneasily, trying to understand the ways Peter is important to her. Couples build up histories, layers, invisible to the outside world. Again he pictures the two women he's been dating—how different they are, how different he is with each . . . How odd, it sometimes seems, that he can care for both, and no doubt others. Uncensored animal affection, light yet, for a time, sufficient, sharing an instant rapport, like the hugging toddlers he passes in a schoolyard.

For all ages love comes in through the eyes, welcomed by that gatekeeper, need, later reconfigured by reality, and sometimes understanding.

"At the moment, I'm feeling I've had it," she murmurs softly but heavily. "Tonight was humiliating, the way he was deliberately baiting me . . ."

Surprised, he wonders, "You sure that's what he was doing?"

"Yes."

"But he announced your recital, and he seemed excited and happy for you."

"'Seemed.' He was trying to appease me, throw a sop at this trifle I pursue, whereas his paintings are worthy, serious, or so he'd like them to be perceived . . . You can't know his real feelings, unless he chooses to let you. Even now, only when we are alone do the real ones surface, sometimes." Her mind wanders away, her eyes bumping over items and shapes along the bar. "Listen, Fin, I was wondering . . . I mean I can't go back to the apartment tonight . . . I was wondering if I could crash at your place tonight. You have a couch, right?"

Surprised, he studies her. "Peter would love that. He's already a little funny about our rapport or whatever."

"He knows we come from similar backgrounds, share outlooks, maybe. His family's working class. He's the family star, the only one who went to college . . . but he's sensitive about those things . . ."

"Then why would you . . . ?"

"Because I can't face going up there. And because maybe not doing so just might wake him up . . ."

Fin, not without some sexual attraction to her, tells himself that this could be dicey. Shouldn't even begin, signor . . ."But I don't want to make things worse."

"It's not for you to make better or worse!"

Surprised at her sharp reply, he looks carefully as she waits. To the extent that any of us know each other, how do we? . . . Intuition? Vibes? . . . Through a cocktail glass darkly? . . . Is need mother to our intentions? "Well . . ." he begins, not knowing where he'll end. ". . . I guess . . . you're welcome to my sofa."

She stares into the bar's mirror behind the liquors, where she can make out the fuzzy image of their two heads. Too bad Peter can't see this. Not that that would change him. The mold is permanent. "Thanks," she breathes, thinking she'd like to see Peter's face when she doesn't show. So pleased with his own opinions, with the way he's arranged his life, so cock-sure . . . Well arrange this! I know, and he knows I know, it's all defense. But tell me Peter, how far do you get by always playing defense?

*   *   *

A cone of light cuts the darkness in the corner of a long living room. A man bends over papers piled on a table, rubbing his eyes and brow before leaning closer to read the one before him, once more. But the words shimmy in and out of focus, rising, then falling away as from a great height. His eyelids quiver and re-close. Ohh . . . to be in bed, releasing the world, free to gambol after my own inclinations. He finds some intellectual relief in the recognition that his wife and son are sleeping, off in strange lands of queens and ogres and wish fulfillment—that other, often better mode of being. On occasion he has watched them sleeping, their faces peaceful and smooth, wondering in which rooms they are wandering, wondering if he appears in their dreams, as they do in his.

Joseph wipes his chin, tries the paragraph a final time, but his brain bunches. What's the subject here? What's this kid trying to say? Is it him or me? He stares at the words, which do not cohere. The thinking is scattered, indecipherable, sprinkled with clichés. Joseph checks the student's name, and the pale outline of the young man's milky face gradually surfaces, before sinking back away. Joseph's eyes drop shut; his attention flees, escaping up near the ceiling, circling silently on muffled wings.

His agent left him a message today. The screenplay's first scenes are due next week. Joseph has nothing on paper. He presses his palms to his eyes. Fireworks silently erupt across the dark dome of his mind. His agent's words follow on luminous tickertape: "Joseph, Joseph, finally we have a foot in the door. Let's not screw it up! This is it—everything we've hoped for."

Is it? . . . He doesn't really know why he's doing it—other than momentum. And money. He wrenches himself up out of his chair and staggers away through the dark, to the kitchen to make coffee. He clicks on the Krupp's, half-fills the reservoir, measures the scoops. The yellow walls carousel around him . . . Yea, though I walk through the valley of the shadow of death, I fear no evil . . . But ohh, the future. What good will come? How will we manage to live in other than our current hand-to-mouth mode? The walls of our existence circle closer, constricting choice, narrowing paths. How will we lift our lives? What am I doing? . . . What happened tonight? Should not have gone to the bar. Or made a fool of myself with Christine. Our efforts on behalf of that poor fellow were a waste. What possibly could we have done? . . . And yet, once we heard the story . . . we were compelled . . . I feel for him, but should have known that Mark is the man to call, in the morning. Lawyers know how to navigate the corridors, sling the jargon. Useful, billable knowledge . . . whereas mine is at best a chimera. He thinks of Bonnie again, sleeping, dressing, stepping out from the shower. We've both aged, sharing physical indignity. It's bitter-sweet, sometimes humorous, usually disheartening, gazing at our sagging bodies. This is us? . . . And yet, we adjust. What if we went the other way, came into the world wrinkled, creaky, and went out in swaddling clothes, without language, without experience, without world-weariness? . . . Helpless, hapless, dependent either way. Things circle back. Poor Kenny, to have part of his life, and dignity, stolen, ripped from him, by agents of the city, of its citizens, of us. Are we not responsible? How is it there can be such abysmal behavior, with all we know? The Founding Fathers understood the only way, the only hope, was to check and balance. Check and balance. Does it exist in the city? . . . Outside of us?

As for the money from the book, and the unwritten screenplay, all is already gone, spirited into electronic accounts, for Noah's college, our retirement. Leaving us to continue to crawl through our existence. Noah, at least, is thankful for his education, and more excited than many of my students. I try to implant joy and a sense of the richness in them—but into too many deaf ears. The lower end of the bell curve. Is this missionary work? Performed by one who is not a believer?

*   *   *

Pounding interrupts Vivian. She'd been off in a dream, dealing with the kids. But now she's in the kitchen where this thumping is jiggling pictures on the walls, rattling glasses, dishes, sending tremors through the floor. Concerned, wondering where the kids are, she moves out into the living room, and finds the hammering growing louder, closer. She stares at the front door, which appears to be receiving the blows. "Who is it?" she calls, waits . . . No answer.

Faces come to her, not warm, welcoming faces but cold ones, dangerous, looking to do her hurt, take her away, take them all away. The pounding intensifies. She calls out again, cries out, really, but the percussion only deepens into a whumpf, whumpf, whumpf now shuddering against the front door. She can see the door's belly beginning to sag. White lines begin running down the panels. The hinges and screws are starting to pull from the frame. Concern careens into desperation, claws into panic, catches at her throat . . . She looks around not knowing what to do. Whoever it is will be inside in another second.

Head throbbing, she bolts back through the apartment to the kids' room, considers the fire escape, but the window gate is locked, and there's no time to get the key. She runs to the closet, slips in, sliding past hanging clothes and dolls lying with stuffed animals on the floor, trying not to disturb them, then reaches back, pulls the door partly closed, sinks into a corner.

Heavy footsteps—booted, thudding—are coming down the hall, shaking the floor. They're entering her bedroom, circling, then out into the hall again, scuffing closer, louder. Now they're entering the kids' room; they scrape and slow, approach the closet. Shrieks fill her head, alarms sound, scream, and somewhere, over the noise, she makes out the click of a trigger, hears it cock. Hears, almost sees, a finger squeezing, emitting a distant squeak, the last sound she will hear before . . . A roar explodes unleashing a force. She feels hurled from a blinding flash . . .

She is . . . sitting up somewhere . . . breathing rapidly yet not deeply enough, sweating, trembling. But awake, alive. The featureless faces in her mind have fled to the edges, peering back at her before they dissolve. She shakes her head, wipes her eyes. All is dark. Where in the lightless universe is she? . . . She can feel something next to her warm, faintly rising and falling . . . Terry. She leans, to rest her head on him, stretch her arms around, embrace him, but stops, not wanting to wake him. Her head and shoulders hang in an arc over him as she listens, relieved to hear her own heart racing, her breathing rushing in and out.

*   *   *

Lou's shower is running, as he's pulling off his wet socks, pants and shirt. The bathroom is beginning to steam up as he sets his phone down by the sink, then begins to gyrate out of his u-trou.

Finally someone answers. He calls into the receiver, "Yo, Reenie, how ya doin'? Gotcha on speaker phone, babe."

"Where you been?" asks irked Irene, his girlfriend in her east 30's apartment. "I was callin' all evening."

"Come on, Reenie. It's Wednesday night. We were at the bar," he reminds her, now shaking his hips so his white jockeys slip down his legs. Exposed to the mirror, he studies himself: the ample tumtum, the formerly fleet, taut legs, the twiggy arms. Only his shoulders, he thinks, suggest the youthful physique of his twenties, now ten years back through a growing haze. "It was quite a night." Glancing at the shower, he steps clear of his undies and checks the equipment. "You wanta come down, Reenie? Junior here is thinkin' of you."

"Nah, you come up. I don't do well in snow."

He glances out the bathroom window. Still blanketing. Remembers the long, muffled hike back with Errol, where he tried to relieve his buddy of the burden, "Come on, old man, you did what you could. You think he'd do the same for you?"

But Errol didn't respond, ducking his head down, trying to wriggle further into his raincoat, away from the furious flow.

"Come on, man, Joseph or Terry will call in the A.M. Get someone. Don't drive yourself into a funk. Enjoy the snow. Ya never know which 'll be the last big snow in our lifetime. Unless biotech figures out how to keep us each humming for another fifty to a hundred years. Can you imagine? . . . What the fuck would we do with all that time? . . . Hey, they'd have to put on one of your plays somewhere. Right? They'd need material, just to keep us entertained."

But glancing over, Lou saw that Errol didn't appear to have heard. "Go mope, then," he grunted.

Lou raises his voice, calling to Irene, "It's still comin' down pretty good. I don't think I'm gonna make it up."

"So why d'ya ask me to come down?"

"I figured you could grab a cab up there—Park or Lex."

"I'm ready for bed," she sighs, releasing the day's stresses.

"Me too, babe." He checks to see if there's any action in the mirror. Maybe, with a little attention. "We had quite an adventure, at the bar."

"That why you're late?"

"Yeah, Errol comes in with a story about a neighbor in his building arrested and dragged off by the police, for no reason."

"Come on. There *had* to be some reason . . ."

"No, we think they blew it. Somehow got the wrong address. Dragged this guy off with no clothes on. Errol thinks he's innocent."

"Errol's innocent."

"Yeah . . . but the cops weren't too helpful. We went down to the precinct. They're sittin' around doin' nothin', and they won't tell us a thing."

"They're not supposed to."

"Wha? What do you know? This is not some police state, where only cops got rights. You hearda habeas corpus?"

". . . My girl friend 's having a party Saturday. You want to come?"

"Irene?! I'm talkin' . . . tellin' you something. What's with this chirping about a party?"

"Yeah, I know habeas corpus. You gotta have a body, right?"

"You can't just hold a man . . ."

"Or a woman . . ."

"Without reason, without bringing him to trial."

"So . . . ?"

". . . . My shower's almost ready."

"What happened to the man?"

"Which man?"

"The one that was arrested, genius. Did Errol get him out?"

"No, Errol can't do that. We're gonna get some lawyer."

"So why d'you go down to the precinct?"

"I don't know . . . Listen, sure you don't want to come down?"

"I'm practically in bed. We've got some big client comin' in tomorrow, another corporate take-over. My boss is hopped up, says everything's gotta be perfect."

"Good luck."

"Yeah, what do you know, smart mouth?"

"I know my little man's ready for you."

"What do I want with a little man?"

In any case Lou finds it's a lie. The little man looks like he's thinkin' sleep.

"Tomorrow night," she offers. "The little man going to be in?"

"Depends . . ."

"I thought he had a thing for me."

"We'll see. Guess I'll go take my shower, and you get some rest . . . I may be dreamin' of this woman in our group, a writer and real knockout."

"Yeah, and I'll be dreamin' of my boss. Loaded, houses in Greenwich, the Hamptons, and not bad lookin' either. Recently divorced. Promised us big bonuses, if we do good."

"Thanks, Reenie. Sweet dreams to you."

"What's good for the goose . . . And who opened his big mouth anyway? And one more thing, if you got a problem Lou, step up, my man, step up."

"Yo, goodnight." He blows her a kiss as he lifts junior into the saluting position. But junior is tuckered out, like his boss. Lou reaches over and clicks off the phone, sighing, "Well buddy, no action tonight. Sorry."

No problem, whispers junior, eyeing the shower.

*　　*　　*

Errol stands in the snow, staring at the empty, silent street. Then pushes west into the oncoming storm. The flakes pile persistently upon his head and flow about him as inescapably as the evening's earlier trials: the gunshots, the dragging away, the bar, the precinct, Lou bugging him . . . all so futile . . . Though I have no real connection with Kenny, though I'm not his keeper . . . still I feel I shoulda done more . . . But what?

The wind and snow are freezing his neck and head even as his body sweats from the walk and anxiety. He shivers at the interface: body, wind, and ice—frozen legs and frozen sidewalk. Conditions: ex-treme . . .

He looks around and rolls his shoulders, trying to alleviate the growing discomfort . . . What is it that plagues me? The injustice . . . my own weakness . . . or my unborn little plays? Those pale, tepid manipulations . . . whereas the real human story unfolds painfully in full color: humiliation—bright white, electric pink; frigidity—cobalt blue and silver; brutality—black and thickly flowing red.

Does anything I've written mean shit? Deep inside, I fear the answer . . .

The faces of little Molly and Lilly shine through the night, as do those at school, my pupils, my charges, with bright, upturned eyes. May their possibilities blossom, somehow, despite my fears that their paths are already narrowed, confined. I try to give them something, but it's not enough. Not enough time or know-how or insight. In my awkwardness, in my inadequacy, it feels too often that I'm going through motions. It's not really me . . . and though I love dear Moll and Lill, I end up not spending enough time with them either. Their dad. Yet there is a certain sweetness between us. Somehow they seem to understand, and accept—Lilly anyway—my limitations.

No one's on the street, not a cab now in sight. The snow has brought all to a halt. North up West Broadway only a few lighted windows, most are dark . . . What to do? . . . Stop . . . stretch out both wings, tilt back my head, allow the flakes to land and build, on forehead, feathers, lashes, all slowly freezing . . . The rest will follow, and I will become a snowman . . . a simple snowman, having landed somehow in the wrong time and place. Yet here I might decorate, might beautify, this corner, might unleash smiles, brighten eyes, turn heads, for as long as the cold spell lasts.

He feels his frozen thumb and finger slide together, hears them snap, hears the sound leap weakly away and echo for a split second before it joins the gently burying stream flowing down upon him.

V.

Dawn

Dim daylight hangs by the windows, paled by the snowscape. Fin stirs out of a blank sleep, cracks an eyelid; finds Dawn, not rosy-fingered, but gray, arctic-hearted. He shuts his eyes, draws in a fresh, cool lungful, recalls the odd evening, glimpsing its dank dungeons and red-eyed moments. A snowcloud, he sees, hangs over the snowslow city defusing into dawnlight . . . Yet hours to dream, ours to dream . . . Why is it that people, communities, don't act kinder, exchange less bitter bicker, batter, and bite? Why don't we bash guns back into butter? . . . Slowly Fin is tip-toeing toward sleep, with Organ Morgan, Sinbad the sailor and . . .

A faint tremor stirs the bed, near his feet, a tremor not his. Fin awakes. Mouse, or rat? . . . He curls his toes, clamps his breathing, waits. After a moment, the tremor returns, closer, stronger. He gets ready to spring. Something is pulling at the covers. In a flash, he rolls, throwing the covers off, ready to grapple or dash.

"Oh Fin . . ." whispers Sam, trying not to gaze at the ghostly male body unveiled before her. "Sorry, didn't mean to wake you, but I'm freezing."

He watches as she, wearing her turtleneck shirt from last night and panties, reaches to reinstate the covers he has whipped off, imploring, "Move over. Let me in." Only as he, habitual sleeper in the buff, pulls the covers back over himself, does he remember (a) his modesty, and (b) the doubtful wisdom of naked proximity to a lightly clad siren, someone else's siren.

But she, trembling noticeably, does not wait upon ceremony, and as he sidewinds leeward, she hastily slips in. "Ohh, warm, so warm. God, there's no heat in your living room."

"I keep it off, otherwise it's a bloody oven during the day."

"Well it's ice in there now . . . This is better. Go back to sleep. Sorry . . ."

She turns away from him, trying to lie still, shutting eyes and thoughts so that both may sleep. And he, smelling her faint perfume and warm, natural aroma, tightens his eyes, turning too, thinking sleep is best. And briefly somnolence prevails. But at some point, she stirs, nestling instinctively toward the greater heat. Closer still is warmer still. And then she is slowly rolling, bringing her hand to rest upon his bare hip, from where it inevitably slips downward, inducing a sharp inhaling, his, and a quick retreat, hers. Yet in time she wiggles closer again, inadvertently tipping him, precariously balanced, over onto his back where she begins inching up, ever so slowly, his warm ladder of ribs, now expanding and contracting with increasing scope and rapidity. From such beginnings, poised upon such a precipice, each is instinctively aware, there is no going back.

*　　*　　*

Elsewhere, too, daylight insinuates itself into dreams. Snaking through dark curtains, it wakes as it slithers. Peter's eyes snap open, leaving behind the husks of dreams. His breath catches on a vague presentiment of something amiss. And yet, as he rolls onto his side, he tells himself that he feels good, rested. Throwing his legs out, rubbing his eyes, he thinks: excellent, up early, do some painting, go up to the office before the rush.

Carefully he pushes up, so as not to disturb Sam and walks quietly to the window, straightening his pjs. His head pokes through the curtains, where he finds the snow's tailing off, only a few flakes scalloping down. Peering down at the street, however—whoa! Holy Mother—he discovers the transformation. A world white and pristine, smoothly carpeting everything knee-deep and more. Nothing's moving: no tracks, no trucks, no plows . . . And the office? Will anybody be able to get there? Must assume the presentation will be put off. Hey Sam, he thinks, get a load of this. Turning, he looks back at the bed, but something's wrong. Sam's side is smooth, unrumpled. His heart misses a beat. Where is she? Sleepin' out on the chaise? . . . He heads out to the big room, brain brewing, thoughts stewing, grabbing his bathrobe from its hook . . . Shit . . . not here either . . . He surveys the place. No sign . . . Never made it back . . . The little . . . Bet I know where she stayed . . . His eyes run over his ani-mals, who shrink from his ire. His chin falls, digging into his chest.

Pressing his eyelids closed, rubbing them, he staggers in a circle. Putta! . . . Then stops and twists back, staring across the room toward the kitchen, thinking: well . . . so this is it . . . no reconciliation this time. Fury, he feels, is bending things, iron things. Heavily he moves across the room, picking out her belongings, squeezing them, compacting them, throwing them down, trampling them. No! No way back! Out! Outta here . . . Heave the song books, the Cuisinart crap, her Laura Ashley collection. Get them out, gone. All!

Half-seeing, he stalks through the loft, recalling that some had predicted this, that WASPs, wrapped in their false smiles, focus their eyes and hearts up the social ladder—ice filling their veins. He lifts an antique wooden armchair of hers, lifts it high above his head and brings it down full force, again and again, until its spindle arms and legs crack, splinter, then splatter out across the floor.

Enough of this hysteric, he scorns, searching for the small table of hers. Finding it, he raises it too and smashes it into the floor, splitting its veneer, spilling out, scattering its contents. Then to the bedroom and her great grandmother's bureau. Reaching for its back edge, he pulls it over with one great cry. The drawers slide forward and out, crashing and clattering. Jewelry, perfume bottles, framed pictures, tiny sculptures all cascade to the floor and shatter, scattering silver slivers.

Wound too tight, like the cops, he mutters to himself, moving on around the place. Surprised she's not more sympathetic toward them. What I need is someone who doesn't spend the day yipping and yapping, who thinks before she barks or bites. Suppose this is the end of the group, too, for me. She'll be down there, spinning her version. But she has a rude awakening if she thinks he's her man. What then? She'll be stuck. She needs someone to believe those crocodile tears. Well, screw her . . . Fuck'em all.

A plan takes shape. Sweep and pile her stuff by the door, to pack or heave. Set a deadline. Then dig out my boots, hike up through the snow to work—plenty to do, before the others straggle in. And tonight? . . . Following the storm, the clearing sky will stretch cool and crisp, and I'll roll out my easel, free, free at last . . . to paint in peace.

*   *   *

Six-thirty releases the faint pulse of salsa from a radio alarm: "Come daddy, dance daddy, wake me to the music . . ." Through the dark, Vivian's fingers feel for the button and tap it off. Never enough sleep, always need more . . . but wait . . . the snow . . . maybe the snow will shut the schools . . . and we can rest.

"You awake?" Terry's voice scratches through the dark. They probe back and forth, asking if the other slept, wondering if there's school, thinking they should listen to the radio for school closings. Vivian feels last night's images descend upon her: Errol's agonizing story, the frigid hump home, the sweat-wrenching dream. If I'd been dressed warm, might've enjoyed the walk, like Terry, polar bear that he is, inhaling, snorting, having sloughed off Errol's story, which smacked me up against the differences once more . . . Surprised I slept at all . . . What sustains the hate in those cops? Some primitive need to feel superior? Don't they know we all come from the same place? Or maybe it's power. Rise up on the backs of others. Even some of Terry's family sling their looks at me, feelin' superior. Don't even want to know. Terry too, avoids them, the entire thing . . . Orphaned people, the two of us. Me, triply so. ". . . Terr?"

"Yes?"

"I felt the cops' hate last night, in how they mistreated Kenny . . . Didn't like it."

"No . . . me neither . . . But gotta remember things die slowly, and some things *are* better. Less of it now. Change starts with the children."

"But too many of the parents are passin' it on . . ."

"Fewer now. The schools are helping. A lot of things are."

"Why couldn't I live a thousand years from now?"

Terry's hand burrows under the covers for hers and grips it tight. "There'll be other problems . . . if anyone's here at all . . ."

*　　*　　*

Joseph's bed is rocking; his head, cheek to pillow, is reeling. He opens an eye, to find his son's face looming close, nose snorting and snuffing, the smell of eggs on his breath. "Noah . . . what?"

"No school, Pop. The snow's totally awesome. Everything's shut. Dy-no-mite! Outta-sight!"

Joseph shuts his eyes. What hour, which day? . . . He remembers he fell into bed around five. Can it be seven already? Mere minutes . . . Now it turns out there was no need to get through all those papers . . . Godsgift . . . Close an eye for a moment. Later, into the office to catch up . . . Oh? But Kenny . . . gotta make that call . . . The cops' bull-headedness . . . Wonder if Mark will bother coming in. Could call him at home, but don't know where . . . A person's freedom shouldn't depend on these threads.

"Pop, all right if I go up to the park? I wanna try my snowboard."

What? Noah thinks he's 15 or something, at age 10. Both he and his snowboard are easy pickings. Why didn't Bonnie say something. "No, Noah, someone needs to go with you."

"You Pop, you."

Joseph opens his eyes to read Noah, how serious he is, but the kid's gone, calling out to his mom that Pop and he are going. Joseph moans. Can't. Need to work, though it will lead to screaming protests, headaches. Bonnie comes hurrying into the room. "Joseph, you're taking him?"

Joseph groans. "No, I've got work, at the office."

"So where did he get his idea?"

Another heavy groan. "Plus I've gotta find a lawyer for this guy."

"What guy?"

Joseph pulls himself up into a sitting position. Rest is over, face it. "Some neighbor, of one of the guys last night."

"What's wrong with him, this guy? And why is it your business?"

Planting his hands, Joseph swings his legs out of the bed. "Because no one else knew a lawyer, and Mark does this sort of thing."

Bonnie's eyes widen, then close down, tired-looking, as she thinks of Noah's letdown. "Like you need more things to do. You don't have time for your business now, not to mention your son, your family."

"Please . . ." implores Joseph. "Is there coffee? Then I'll think."

"What time did you come to bed last night? I heard you come in."

Joseph shakes his head. "I don't know . . ."

"You're not the only one here, you know, with things to do," she tells him.

"I know . . . I know . . . but . . ." Thinking of all the work he must do, he feels he's sinking back down into the mattress, away, into sleep.

"Joseph? . . . What's the matter with you? Did you catch something last night, at the bar? . . . I don't like you going out on nights like that."

He wakes with a start. "What?"

"Didn't you hear me?"

"What? . . . *Eloi, Eloi, lama sabachthani?*" That plaintive cry, beyond all understanding.

"What? What is this you're talkin'? Don't start with that stuff. Get up. Take a shower. You need one. Then come; I have coffee, eggs. We need to talk."

From out in the hall, he hears Noah calling, "Come on Pop. Tell Mom we're going—what you said. Come on, Pop, get up!"

Joseph's mind flattens under the pressures. The walls around him flow in one continuous plane. Oh God, the screenplay . . . Just get something down on paper. They'll change it anyway. Last night glows distantly like stations along a subway line, oases of light and life: the bar, the cops, her stoop in the storm, her scarf-covered face, an image from the '40's—then pushing back through the shin-deep snow, his feet wet and freezing—the fear of becoming frozen, snow-bound, buried beneath the mounting piles . . .

*   *   *

Tying his tie, Lou waits for Irene to pick up.

"Morning, Louie."

"Hey babe, you goin' in?" His voice rasps with early-morning frogginess.

"Almost out the door."

"How they expect you to be on time today?"

"Dunno. They do. Can I call ya? You going in?"

"Yeah, as if anybody's gonna be buyin' today." Lou works at a retail computer shop, Cybersite. He's been thinkin' he should really do his own dot.com, although deciding exactly what to sell has not been so simple. In his deep sales voice he asks, "Dinner tonight, Reenie baby?"

"Oh I don't know now, Lou. Let me call you. I've gotta go."

"Is that a yes or no?"

". . . Let me call you. By-ye." She hangs up.

Irritation buzzes his brain. Nobody can give you an answer in this city, as far back as I can remember. Everyone's so caught up in their own stuff, they don't listen worth shit. Back in The Bronx, he remembers his frustration in trying to get some skenk to spill about a friend who'd been blown away— remembers askin' his pop why he was always beatin' him. What'd I do, Pop? What? . . . Nothing came back but glower in Pop's eyes.

Last night the cops, now Irene. Poor guy last night. Some cops are just nut-jobs hoofing around with a badge. He looks in the mirror, straightens his tie. Not bad when he's cleaned up, has his business face on. Could sell pretty much anything . . . Imagines pounding at his front door. Cops pushin' through, callin': 'Hands up buddy.'

What'd I do? What's the problem?

Shut up and turn around. Spread eagle, wiseguy. Your fuckin' old man sent us down here. Said you was fuckin' up. Ain't doin' shit with your career.

My old man's dead ten years. You got the wrong goddamn address, shit-for-brains.

Listen bud, you want this stick up your rectum?

What's that? Department protocol?

* * *

From far away, a voice is calling. Errol tries to lift his head, but something's weighing it down . . . pillows, piled on him like a snowdrift. The voice comes calling again. Rolling his head, neck aching, he squints out from under and spies a woman's legs, in shiny pantyhose. Leslie. He feels the spasm of a stretch. His hand on which he was sleeping is prickling, stinging, not responding.

"Errol!" bursts her exasperation, reaching him under the lifted pillow. "Listen, I've got to go in to work, despite the snow. But the schools are closed, so you've got the girls. You hear me? They're having their breakfast . . . I have my class tonight. I'll call you."

He knows he should reply, but can't think what to say, or why. His head slowly sinks back to the sheet warm and faintly moist. The pillows fall snuggly down again, like a great snow hat, yet he can still make out the faint rustle of her pantyhose. Checkin' herself in the mirror, Morgan Le Fay—her morning ritual—turning side-to-side, reaching for her purse, striding away, in those high-heeled stilettos, her dancing shoes.

So . . . no school, huh? The three of us left—Molly, Lilly, 'n' me. Now he hears the high-pitched goodbyes at the front door, hears the door ka—thump shut, feels the faint tremor. Then silence. If he could just get a half-hour more . . . Eyes close. Deep breath, cool air, peace.

"Da-ad," comes Molly's soft but not-to-be-denied voice, "will you take us outside, to play in the snow?"

"Wha?" croaks his voice, as hopes begin to crumble.

"Da-ad . . . Would you get up. The other kids are already out."

He knows, knows it's over. They will not leave until he's up. His mind rolls back to last night, then flees the other way, digging frantically into a mountain of snow.

"Da-ad . . ."

"Wha? . . . Okay, okay . . . I'm comin'." Doesn't want to disappoint them, hurt them, though he could use the sleep. He pushes up, trying to free his right foot from the sheets. But it's tangled. Wildly he kicks and shakes until all the sheets and blankets are vanquished, slumped in a pile on the floor. His two daughters stare wide-eyed at him as he sucks in oxygen. He wishes he could please them more frequently, provide more things for them, the endless things little girls seem to want.

Molly turns away. He meets little Lilly's frozen gaze. Standing with her hands behind her, she seems sad for him. "Dad . . . what was that noise last night? In the hall?"

He opens his arms, inviting her to come for a hug. But she hangs back, concerned. He pushes himself up unsteadily, reaching for the bureau to support himself, trying to think, trying to remember. "Noise? . . ." He realizes he needs to think of something. "Maybe, Lil, it was someone trying to fix their door . . ."

She appears doubtful. "Why did Mommy have us climb under the bed?"

". . . Did she? . . . I don't know. Was it fun?"

Her eyes seem ready to spill tears. "I didn't want to. I was scared."

Slowly he moves toward her, hands out. Molly now reappears in the doorway behind Lilly. "It was a gun, Dad. Someone was shooting."

Errol stops, not sure what to say, feeling himself swaying. He reaches out again, to the wall, again to steady himself. He looks at Molly, then Lilly. His mind's still slow, blurred. "Was it, Moll?" He finds it sad, beyond describing, that Molly can announce this, that this has become a reality just outside their door. Fortunately she can't yet fathom the implications.

Half-turning away from him, her face remains distorted with disenchantment, he sees. Her mother's child. "How soon can we go?" she asks, annoyed.

He looks at her. He attempts to leap past the suspicion that there is little rapport between them, sadly. "I'd like to have breakfast first," he breathes.

"We've already had breakfast," spouts Lilly.

"We're ready to go," reminds Molly, in case he didn't get the message.

"Well good. I'd still like a hug," he tells them both.

Molly twists her mouth. "I'll pour your cereal." And she disappears from the doorway.

He peers down at little Lilly, and opens his arms a second time. She hesitates, then seems to glide to him. He picks her up, so light, so small. A tiny yet complete creature. He brings his cheek against her hair, feels tiny cool lips kiss his ear.

Slowly setting her back on the floor, he tells her he'll be in as soon as he washes up. But now, from behind her back, she brings out a small pink paper bag and holds it up happily for him. He takes it and peers inside. "What's this?"

"For you," she whispers in her tiny voice. So endearing, he thinks, as he takes out a folded butterfly that probably Molly has cut and she has colored. "Ohh, very pretty, very nice. A butterfly . . . for me?"

She nods sweetly.

"And what else, Lilly?" He peers in. "Ooh, money. Where did you find this?" He takes out a twenty and looks at her. She smiles munificently. He looks in once more, and retrieves a lipstick, Leslie's, his driver's license, his apartment keys, a pair of Molly's socks, a tiny doll, a juice box. "Very interesting, Lilly. Where did you get these things?"

She smiles bashfully and shakes her head.

"Well, Lil, this juice box needs to go back in the kitchen, and some of these other things are really Mommy's and Daddy's."

"I know . . ."

He bends to hug her, then repeats that she should take the juice box back to the kitchen, and he'll be right in. She scoots off, her pink pants and blue turtleneck flashing as she disappears around the corner. He calls after her to get their snowsuits on, before his mind wobbles ahead to the day. Call Terry . . . try to fit in some work on the play . . . While he was sleeping warm in his bed, he realizes Clayton was lying in a cell . . . Maybe he got the blanket and clothes.

A short time later, as he is shoveling down his last spoonful of corn flakes, and chasing it with lukewarm coffee, he hears the girls exchanging instructions as they wiggle into their snow gear. Gauging that he's got a few moments, he edges out into the hall, listens again, hears the same steady murmuring, then tiptoes to the front door, opens it, and slips out and down to Kenny's door. Yellow police tape crisscrosses the entrance. Half of the door hangs from its lower hinge, crushed, splintered. He leans forward, peers in. Everything's turned upside down, like a tornado buzzed through; the far wall is chewed, as if by a pickaxe. He finds the love-seat Clayton must have dived behind, its seat-back punctured with patterns of small black holes, bleeding stuffing. The floor is littered with papers: newspapers, photo magazines, Clayton's prints, and photo supplies. His camera bag and paraphernalia are strewn about. The cops must have been searching for drugs, in their considerate way. The lawyer's gotta see this. Errol imagines the fusillade coming through the door and walls, plaster and sheet rock spitting, bullets pinging, dust rising, the noise deafening. He turns away, clamping his hands to his ears.

He stumbles back to his apartment and into the kitchen, where he snatches up the phone and dials Terry's office number. Reaching only the machine, he implores: "Get a lawyer down here. See what they did, Terry, how they trashed it, totally destroyed the place. And for what?! This on top of the way they treated him? . . . I mean it's just insanity! . . . I mean *just total insanity!*"

*   *   *

Eggs sizzle in a frying pan. The seductive aromas of frying butter and brewing coffee distract Christine from choosing chapters for Joseph. Seated at their small kitchen table, she attempts to scan her pages, but her attention is tugged toward the stove, and though she has wrapped herself in a thick cardigan sweater over her pjs, chill drafts reach her neck and ankles, as steam from her coffee lightly coats her cheek—replaying last night's mix of sweat and freeze. Indeed all of last night's images lurk just behind her thoughts.

Daniel, at the stove, stares down at three fried eggs, chin on his chest, hands clamped in his pits. Slowly releasing one hand, he reaches for the salt seller, sprinkles more of the white crystals, picks up the pepper mill, grinds the corns onto the yokes, takes a pinch of thyme, another of marjoram, rubs them over the pulsating surfaces. What else? Savory? The herbal scents summon landscapes and villages of the Luberon, from their trip last summer.

Christine finds it disappointing that next to last night's cops and storm her pages exert little power. The angry red faces, punctuated by piercing eyes and lines deeply gouged in their puffy features bull their way back into her vision, and chase away her words. She feels the chill white swirl of the storm and imagines Daniel fighting through its blustering surges, head down partly averted, great coat impervious, boots flashing, tramping for nearly an hour, block after block, eschewing cabs, caught between fascination and discomfort. This morning in bed, he said he had needed it, the muscling, the struggling and straining against the wind and pelting snow. "You had your confrontation last night, your brush with another reality. That encounter with nature was mine, shouldering into it, feeling the physicality of it, fighting through the gusts."

She doesn't believe their experiences were equivalent, but she thinks she knows what he was getting at, in facing it down, having the courage, the determination to fight back. Men need that physicality. Maybe we all do, in one way or another. But now her concern shifts to another issue. "Dan . . . what do you think *we* would have done?"

"About what?"

"If a neighbor of ours was dragged off like that?"

His mind, focused on the storm and eggs, stutters to frame her question. ". . . What? . . . By the . . . by the cops?"

"Yes."

". . . It depends, doesn't it," he begins, attempting to piece it together, "on the circumstances."

"If the circumstances were unclear." She feels a faint stab of impatience at his hesitation, with his not engaging; he must realize what she's asking.

". . . I guess I would have attempted to find out what those circumstances were." His eyes fall back to the spitting, sputtering eggs, whose browning edges are jiggling like nervous lips. He smiles . . . But her question—What does she want him to say? He suspects she has her own answer, but wants him to arrive at something close. Yet doesn't everything depend on the circumstances, on how the cops behaved, on who the neighbor was? A waft from the buttery eggs and herbs calls him away.

She is thinking the circumstances in last night's case *were* clear. The police broke into someone's home, probably mistakenly, perpetrating (yes) a humiliating miscarriage of justice. "Okay, what if the police had come here, pounding furiously on the door, then bursting in?"

He looks over. Their eyes meet as he feels himself falter over this extreme improbability. He would have simply answered the door. She, however, is remembering that it *did* happen, that banging and bursting in. And there seemed to be no time for rational response. Suddenly the police were in, going berserk. She feels her lips working against each other, rubbing, slightly sticky. Dan's not helping.

In fact he's frowning. "But what are the chances of that happening? . . . And if it did, we could have asked the police to speak to our neighbors, people we know, who would vouch for us."

"This fellow tried to speak to Errol as the cops whisked him away, but they wouldn't let him, shooing Errol back into his apartment. Once they had an idea of who they wanted, it seems they didn't bother checking anything."

Dan nods and looks back at the sputtering eggs. From somewhere in the pan he hears a pop, feels a tiny burning on his wrist, and rubs it with his other hand, easing the sensation. He looks at the spot. Nothing's visible. He rubs it again, erasing it from his mind. He wonders how much race had to do with the way the guy was treated.

Unhappily she waits for a response until impatience shoves her back to her own thoughts. "I find it hard to believe, after all the publicity in the other cases, that still the cops behave this way. Hasn't someone read them the law?"

Stretched once more between her question and his cooking, he tries to assess both. The eggs are almost done; her agitation is simmering. Staring into the pan, he asks, "Want yours over easy?"

Disappointed, she stares at the table, attempting to explain to herself, before sighing and nodding. He flips the eggs, then touches the tiny burn on his wrist. It seems to pulsate, then fade. Is that a function of the nerves in his wrist, repeating their little alerts, or is it a second spatter? Butterfat and butterburn, catch a culprit, rub a wrist.

She is concluding that her timing was ill-advised. After all, what should she expect from a poet, a night owl, in the morning? "Dan, whatever the circumstances, it's no way to treat people."

"No, it isn't," he agrees thoughtfully, then notes that in another few seconds the eggs'll be done. "Was there some reason for it, do you suppose, or is it just the way they operate? It's conceivable that some provocation could explain it—not justify it, but explain it."

"The cops are the city's representatives of the law, the people's. They are who the average citizen comes in contact with, and as such should act respectfully and certainly lawfully."

He admires her but also feels sorry for her, that she sticks to her guns, her idealistic views where the ideals have been worn away. "Few people would disagree, Chris, but cops are people too, year after year thrust into difficult circumstances . . . What can we reasonably expect?"

"What? Why not? We're not asking perfection. Just restraint, and lawful behavior."

Glancing over at her, he finds her mouth closed, her expression pinched, unhappy. But now he needs two plates on which to dish out the eggs. Reaching high to a shelf, he lifts two from a stack and brings them down to the stove and there spatulas out her egg with quick movements. He then steps over to serve her. Softly she thanks him. He returns to the stove where again with quick movements he serves his eggs and turns back to the table. Before sitting, he pours her the fresh coffee and retrieves his cup. She has placed her chapters on the floor.

Settling in his chair, he eagerly slices his eggs and inhales their flavors. She takes a first taste. "Mm, good . . . Thank you." He finds her eyes and smiles. He knows her thoughts linger on the incident. She does not let go of things easily.

"Dan . . ." she begins, looking at her plate, then at him, "I don't think we can begin to imagine what it must be like for African-Americans."

Chewing and carefully tasting, he agrees, nodding but not meeting her gaze. Her eyes run over the small table, the eggs and flecks of herbs and pepper. The two of them, she thinks, educated, fortunate, should be able to reach some conclusion or lesson from last night's events, but it's proving to be elusive.

The toaster pops up. Hastily he rises, noting and enjoying the effort his muscles must make. He likes to feel them work, given that he spends so much of the day sitting. He swings about to the counter for the butter. He recognizes that he enjoys these little moments and movements: cooking, brewing the coffee, chatting sleepily together, all in stirring contrast to fighting the storm last night. It's contrasts that enliven, shake and awaken—are probably required, as mammals do little more than they must . . . and yet some are driven . . . by compulsion, energy, inspiration, as, last night, each was.

She is wondering why this incident doesn't evoke more indignation from him. He's sensitive to social things, as a poet. Why is it he doesn't seem outraged? Haven't I painted the picture starkly enough?

As he brings the toast to the table, he sees that she is dissatisfied with their exchange, or more specifically, his response. Sitting down, he apologizes, "Sorry I haven't shared your anger. I guess I have to confess it seems . . . a little remote and . . . I don't know, some of those other well-known cases were a lot worse."

She reaches for a piece of toast and takes a tentative bite, chewing it as she reflects, nodding reluctantly.

"What about writing something?" he asks.

Avoiding his eyes she tells him, "I've been considering it, if I can get to some people who can do something. No point in just adding to the speculation and hand-wringing." Now she looks over at him, seeking his reaction. With a faint bow of his head, he acknowledges her point. She is picturing the young policeman at the precinct, wondering if he'd be willing to talk, generally, if not in specifics. She hears Dan inhale. "How different are our modes of working," he reflects. "Yours is reaching out, mine mostly interior—taking us to quite different spheres in our work-a-day lives."

She looks over trying to see how he means this, then observes, "We live in both spheres, no? Moving in and out of both."

"Yes," he agrees, "but largely reside in one or the other."

". . . I wonder if the cops ever imagine the lives of the people they deal with."

"I'd be surprised," he says softly, reaching for a piece of toast. "I find it difficult, almost impossible, myself to imagine lives of people quite different. How could I imagine that guy's life?"

"It's not so different," she contends. "And you're constantly in the heads of the people in your poems."

"But I choose them, from among the few I know, and then imagine much of the rest, as you do in your fiction."

She presses and stretches her lips in reflection. He knows what she is thinking: he's being literal and contrary. My fault, she concedes, slowly moistening her lower lip, for bringing it up over breakfast.

*   *   *

Pinning the phone between shoulder and neck, Sam listens while she tugs up her pants, a stream of oaths clogging her mind over the difficulty of this maneuver and over the fact that no one in her office is answering. With a final yank, she succeeds in jerking the pants over her hips and widening her stance to hold them as she leans to hang up. "For Pete's sake!" she exhales. No one's made it into the office. They'll have to push the presentation after lunch, or cancel . . . And Peter's probably stuck at home, charged, nervous, full of venom.

A few feet away, around the corner in his tiny kitchen, Fin is pouring Sam a mug of coffee and checking the bagel in his toaster-oven. He pulls the toaster door open, releasing a small cloud of smoke, and scoots out the charred halves onto the counter with dancing fingers and painful protests, "Ooh! . . . Out, out, ow. Ouch!"

Sam peeks around, then slides into view, pulling the turtleneck down over her head. "What's the noise, chef? What's burning?"

Fin's eyes leap frantically between the disappearing bra, the steaming mug of coffee, the cream cheese melting on the toaster, which he swipes off. "Shit . . . Interested in cream cheese soufflé?"

"Easy, Jean-Claude." She sings, "Don't burn for me Argen-tin-a. My roommate . . . has al-ready done that."

Fin finds her gaze, wondering if she is now remorseful about their liaison, their sleeping together. Her eyes are as dark and clear as the coffee he has handed her, while he, underneath, feels drained, worried.

She sips, then exhales, "Yeow! The impressario of Espresso. Got milk?"

He spins to the fridge for a quart, and, after she's sipped again, plops in several drops while reaching for a plate to serve his blackened offering.

"Cool, dude. Charred bagel. Crunchy," comes her lilting laugh.

"House specialty," he croaks.

She laughs again silently, eyeing the smoking rings.

He too stares down at them, wondering if they're chewable, then looks up at her, remembering that other things may be burning. "You gonna be all right, at home? . . . What are you going to do?" Nervously he begins applying a smear of runny cream cheese to each half, then pushes the plate her way.

She stares at the carbon-crusted things. "Try one, I guess," she mumbles, before taking a tentative bite. It hurts her tooth. She sloshes it down with coffee and speaks out of one corner, "Never had rock bagel before."

He half-turns, not sure where, pursued by vague lamentations.

"I have no choice, but to go home," she says, to his hanging question. "Have to change for work."

He cannot suppress a wince. "What are you going to tell your roomie?"

"That you seduced me against my will."

An anxious smile pulses in his cheeks. Despite her humor, he's apprehensive. "Guess I'll be avoiding St. Mary's on Wednesday nights."

"No need. He'll find some excuse not to go. Basically he hates confrontations, particularly with larger males."

"Does he know any 'wise guys'?"

"He loves to hear Italians stereotyped."

"Oh, but has no problem laying it on others," Fin softly scoffs.

"What are *you* worried about? It's *me* he's going to kill . . . Besides, you got what you wanted."

Fin wonders if this is true. He tries to read her. ". . . Well . . . sure you should go home?"

"Can't afford to lose my job."

He understands but tries to imagine just how angry Peter may get and whether he'll take it out on her physically. She too becomes still, imagining the same. "No . . . what he'll do—most likely already has—is move all my stuff out into the hall, and have the locks changed. He told me he did that with one of my predecessors."

". . . If there's anything I can do . . . the couch is here . . ."

She throws a preoccupied glance out at it, then sends him a sardonic nod, before her thoughts turn serious. "Didn't think it'd be '*police abuse*' that would end it. Neither of us is what you'd call political. I don't even hate the mayor."

He watches her, noting how hawk-like her eyes become while frowning. A raptor. Our doubleness. He reaches forward for her free hand and squeezes it gently, reassuringly, feeling warmth for her, remembering last night, which was much better than he would have guessed. He feels a softness, if not outright love—maybe it is love—at least something one wants to protect from winter winds. He looks at her burnt bagel and fingers round the coffee mug and her dimpled face.

"Will you call later?" he asks. "Let me know?"

She nods. "You got any storage space?" Though her cheeks and brow are lustrous, her eyes are darkly heavy.

"A little," he murmurs, wondering if in fact he has any—wondering too about the attraction, and hesitancy he feels. There is something very human about her, with her variable emotions right at the surface. He wants to embrace them, and her . . . yet is wary, of her volatility. One imagines, hopes for, a certain harmony, along with something that stirs, reaches deep—even as one is aware of one's own short-comings . . . How does one align these desires and offerings? Or do we just try to get what we can . . . what presents itself?

Sam shakes her head, as if to say she doesn't understand quite how to order her own issues. She looks around the tiny kitchen and feels faintly depressed. The romanticism of these small kitchens and apartments, these limited dwellings, is wearing off. It's a sharp drop from her mother's comfortable, if narrow, life style. She thinks of Peter's paintings, how much he puts into them, and how little recognition he is likely to receive. Is it a tragedy? Or is it a reflection of flaws and limitations? Out of a sigh, she mumbles, "The stupid thing is . . . I love him, the idiot."

VI.

Work

As Joseph holds the phone away from his ear, waiting for someone to pick up, glimpses of his well-wrapped, snugly-booted, morning trek through the white drifts and un-shoveled walks tramp through his mind. The air was crisp, the city just beginning to stir, and he felt surprisingly fresh, given the little sleep the night afforded him. Ahead, he remembers he's promised to take Noah snowboarding in Central Park, and he hopes this unexpected energy won't desert him. But as he continues to listen for an answer, he feels that and other commitments tightening around his head. Mark must have a machine on his line, he mutters to himself, though none has announced itself. About to hang up, he hears a receiver grabbed, bobbled, a "Hello!" cried frantically into it. Joseph straightens up. Instead of a secretary telling him that his quarry is in a meeting, he hears the very voice he is seeking. "Mark? You're in?"

"Yes, just fought my way through. Who's this?"

"Joseph."

A brief, unguarded moan follows, conveying too clearly Mark's disappointment. But then he is recovering, pulling out his professional bonhomie and transitioning into stock observations about the storm. Not appeased, Joseph cuts him off and sketches Kenny's story, but as he launches into his request, he detects creaks and groans emanating from the other end: "Um . . . uhh . . . Joseph, Joseph . . . Listen, sorry . . . can't, really can't . . . You know I'd love to; I know I told you I do *pro bono* from time to time, but right now it's out of the question. We're totally maxed out on a major, major case." Feeling his anxious throat drying up, Mark gulps a swig of coffee, then loudly clears it. Joseph tilts the receiver away, returning it only in time to catch, ". . . and one of our partners just split and is suing us, the scumbag . . . So you see . . . we're up against it. Normally, I'd love to, but . . . Listen, let me give you the name of a guy."

"What?"

"Quite competent actually . . ."

"Competent? . . . Wait . . ." Joseph hears pages being rapidly shuffled before Mark finds his referral. "Here . . . really, more than adequate, a bit of a character but experienced . . . Got a pen?"

Joseph feels hope crumbling, hears himself protesting, "Mark, we need someone with a little clout." Sensing futility however, he growls, "Is this the thanks I get after all the work I've brought you?"

But Mark is reading off a name and number, blurts an apology, and clicks onto another line. Joseph sits stunned. For some moments he doesn't move, until with resignation, he stares down at the number he's written and stiffly dials it. Once more the phone rings and rings, until a half-asleep someone picks up, then drops the receiver, retrieves it and groans, "Hello . . . Who's this? . . . What time is it? . . . Whoa-o . . . would ya look at the snowwww!"

Joseph hangs up, irritation wailing through the corridors of his mind. Wait till Mark discovers I'm yanking my magazine business. Maybe not a lotta money, but steady, easy income—now for someone else's pockets. He'll wish he'd been a little more . . . circumspect . . . It's not me who suffers, but that poor guy shivering in a cell.

Clasping his forehead to brake the dizzy whirring, Joseph feels fatigue and the weight of frustration, sloshing heavily like ice water in his brain. He stares down at his list on a notepad and wonders which task he should tackle first: the magazine, his students' papers, next week's assignments . . . or the screenplay . . . always the screenplay . . . With surprising fury, he crumples the note, rolls it into a ball between his palms, and fires it to first base—somewhere out the open office door, where it lands and skids lightly across the hall floor.

About to choose, he notices a shadow in the hall stoop to pick up the wad. A large hirsute figure then straightens and faces him. A sasquatch, draped in winter layers, holds out its gloved palm, offering to return the crumpled note. Joseph looks more closely, within a wrapped scarf, under a knitted hat. ". . . Christine?"

The figure scuffs forward into his office, still proffering the paper. Joseph squints to reassure himself it is her, before he launches up and around his desk with long strides and swinging arms, sweeping toward her. In her other hand she holds up a shipping envelope. "Chapters for you, Joseph."

Intending to take her hands warmly, to even possibly embrace her, he instead finds himself grasping the envelope, exclaiming his excitement, his appreciation, his eagerness to plumb its delights.

Still she holds out the wadded note, which he finally snatches, pockets, and offers to help her with her coat. It's unnecessary, she says, beginning to turn and tug her way out. But almost immediately she gets hung up in a sleeve. Unbidden, Joseph gently reaches over to hold the bunching fur so that she can free her arm. Mildly amused, faintly embarrassed, she explains, "My father's raccoon. The lining is worn and separating. I really only wear it when it snows."

He almost laughs, at the sight, and idea. Yet he appreciates it too. "An artifact from another era." Happiness begins to seep back in. "Allow me, Christine, to extend the courtesy of the academy." Decorously he bows, with amusement, then pivots to hang up the heavy coat—bleed it more aptly, he thinks—then slides the institutional armchair over to her—"Lady, prithee"—into which she, after peeling additional layers, sinks. With another bow, he swings back around his desk, keeping his eyes on her as he lowers himself straight-backed onto his chair, weight upon his toes.

An awkward pause follows. They have never spoken outside the bar and last night, and so she seizes upon the question of the lawyer. Lowering his eyes which narrow with chagrin, Joseph summarizes the dead end with Mark.

Another silence follows, until she remembers, "Terry . . . What about Terry? Shall we call him?"

"I guess . . ." He buries his face in his phone book, and holds it there as he dials. Peering up, he catches a glimpse of her attentive, high-cheeked attractiveness, but on the phone he reaches only a machine and leaves his news.

She sees a shadow pass across his face, and, to disperse it, she muses that Terry and Viv must be out playing in the snow with their kids. "Probably," allows Joseph, moistening his lips and telling her of his plans with Noah later.

"What fun. And how old is he now?" Christine asks, her hand fidgeting under her sweater for a warmer spot. She had forgotten Noah's existence.

"Ten . . . Good kid, really . . . Maybe too trusting for the city." Joseph's thoughts dive through diffuse images of Noah's future, then bank steeply toward reflections on writing he might share with her.

The notion of having a child has given her pause however. Images of friends' children click like slides through her inner eye. Dan has never mentioned the subject. How could they work it? Write and rear? She's seen the struggle: women mostly, with more compassion and patience. She looks at Joseph, trying to imagine what kind of father he is, and wondering if he feels his life is cramped by fatherhood. Enriched too . . . how could it not be? . . . In contrast, her life sometimes feels castaway . . . Yet all modes of living are mixed—the old trade-offs. What astonishes is the variety, if you look.

Joseph is watching her and asks how she feels her novel is coming. She finds herself surprised and pleased that she can report that it's coming along, that she's reasonably encouraged—before she turns the question back to him, asking if he's begun something new.

A strange smile spreads up into his cheeks as he tells her that he has not, that frankly he hasn't had the time.

For a moment she feels a squirm of discomfort with her relative freedom, though she recognizes they have both made choices. But there must be other factors too. He looks carefully at her. "Maybe in another year or two, I'll start one." She sees that he is studying her, perhaps to understand the differences between them. But then, she notices, his attention falls inward. "Next time, I'll write something more personal. Not another detective story, though it brought in some money . . . but a story of teachers and students—the intersection of timing and levels of development, of paths and expectations . . ."

She waits to see if there will be more, but now he is motioning to her pages.

"I look forward to reading this."

"It, too, is different," she tells him. "As I am different than I was, in doing the first one . . . Daniel, for one, has influenced me . . ."

Joseph nods, attempting to picture the influence of a poet on her writing—its rhythms, its economy, its harmony . . . Or does one fall back too quickly into habit, and self, and what is known? . . . And how much does her attractiveness contribute to her views? Her style? . . . And then he remembers Mr. Kenny. They both do.

"Are there other lawyers we might call?" she asks. His eyebrows rise, trying to summon other names, unsuccessfully. He inhales, thinks. "The ACLU?"

She feels her brow bunch under the shadow of past experiences with them. Impossible phone system; bureaucratic, not receptive, could never get through to a lawyer. She reminds herself to call Dan's friend at *The Times* later, see if he's interested, see if he wants to take up the story.

Joseph recognizes that he'd rather return to the subject of writing, but as he is considering where to begin, his phone rings, stirring them both out of their reflections. Picking up, he finds it's Terry, at the gallery, who tells him that he's just spoken to his lawyer who's agreed to assist Kenny. But before Joseph can respond or tell Christine, Terry hurries into apology, explaining that he needs to return a host of other calls and will get back later. Dazed and disappointed at being cut short again, Joseph slowly hangs up, feeling tugged between relief and vague emptiness. Pushing the phone away, he tells Christine, "Terry's found a lawyer."

Her eyebrows rise, as her features brighten, more than her mood. Both of them sit silently, between slim elation and unspecified discouragement.

*   *   *

Listening for sounds, she hears none, and so quietly approaches her apartment door and inserts the key. It still works—no locksmith yet. She turns it and pushes in. Silence. He's not here. Must've gone up to the office. The choices aren't many with him. He likes going in early, puttering around alone.

"Peter?" she calls, just in case. Nothing but an echo. Ahead on the front table lies a hand-written note. She looks away, then forces her eyes back slowly, and edges over. Leaning minimally, fingers trembling, she lifts it gingerly.

> Sam, it would be best if you collect your belongings and move out as soon as possible. P.

Predictably curt. Her chest tightens. She spits, "Screw you! You started it; you move!" But then she allows: not that I wouldn't mind, if I could find a decent, affordable place . . . But where . . . ?

Disbelief ripples outward, surrounding her with concentric walls of concern. The veiled threat of the note, his white face lined by anger, his pale, trembling hands . . . But why? Why me? You're the one who pissed people off; you're the one who spews out noxious notions. Why should I pay?

Yet reluctantly she knows there are other considerations. And given an alternative, she wouldn't want this place. Turning slowly, gazing around at the apartment, she discovers not far from the door that he has already piled some of her belongings: her mother's chairs, the coffee table, lamps. Stepping closer, she sees that things are not piled neatly but are smashed, shattered. Her breath leaves her as her chest is squeezed and, like a net, darkness drops. A cry escapes; she covers her eyes and mouth, pressing both, fleeing away inside. Moments, maybe minutes, pass . . . before she finds herself swaying slowly, squatting down, reaching for a fragment of a leg, an arm, a drawer, a vase—examining by touch, her vision blurred. Mother's heirlooms . . . Grandmom's . . . irreplaceable. Utter, utter bastard! She runs her fingers over the pieces. Above and peering down over her, the two, Mom and Grandmom, hover bent, stunned, unable to comprehend. What kind of man was this?

And then she remembers, oh no, not the bureau too! Lifted by fear, by accelerating horror, she rises and runs into the bedroom. There on the far wall, it lies, pulled over onto its drawers. All its possessions, vases, picture frames, statues, bottles, jewelry, strewn over the dark wood floor . . . Fragments of glass catch the window light. A piercing wail fills the room.

Sometime later, she is in the shower, breathing with rapid, shallow breaths. The water temperature is scalding, yet she holds herself to its needles. She was unable to bend down to begin reclaiming. He did it. He can sweep it up—what he destroyed.

In the nearly empty, lurching subway, she braces and re-tightens her grip, her mind shooting ahead and behind, like the passing tunnel lights. On one such glide into the past, her thoughts return to the apartment, soar through its rooms, settle over, circle down onto the destruction. Now her body is trembling with rage; she is cursing silently, threatening: he will pay, he will pay . . . Images of them screaming at each other blur into smears of white and red. What would follow? Kicks, blows? . . . And where will she go? Some tiny space, some closet in a depressing, distant borough. She has never foreseen living like that . . .

The train lurches. Her hand tightens around the stainless steel bar whose bone-numbing cold courses through her. Another anguished cry is joined by the high-pitched subway horn, reaching through the tunnels.

The office elevator door opens. She steps warily into the reception area. Lights are on, but no one's around. To avoid him, to avoid the fury, she takes the long way, pushing through the back doors into Design. She can see Marjorie crossing over to the copy center. If she encounters him, she'll flee to the restrooms.

Reaching her desk, she sinks into her chair, sighing wearily, keeping her eyes down. Her voice mail is blinking. At first hesitating, she picks up the receiver, punches in her code. It's Don, informing her that the client can make it, but the presentation is pushed back to one. She pulls out her outline. She needs to memorize the color-selection details, to have them at her fingertips. Slipping into the edges of her mind come his eyes, sending a jolt through her. Her gaze snaps to the periphery. No one's there. But now his eyes loom darkly in her mind, unreadable and cold as a leopard's eyes. She remembers the bar last night, the knights and ladies around the table in pale yellow haze, glancing, listening, laughing—until Errol came, with his story.

* * *

Snow pile to snow pile, his two snow bunnies leap and land, with the spasmodic suddenness, with the lightness and impossible spring of grasshoppers, Molly and Lilly, amusing their dad, pleasing him that he's out here with them. Napoleonic energy, he thinks. What would the world be like if many adults had that? If we were wrapped in childhood absorption, enthralled by each new detail. The tools of genius. Never walk when they can run, no qualms about grabbing what they want. The mindset of child-men, and successful playwrights, who feel the world is theirs.

The three make their way along the narrow, snow-covered strip of Sarah Delano Roosevelt Park, into the playgrounds and out, over the lumps that are bushes, benches, and drifts. And where is Clayton now? Down a tunnel of bad dreams? One lined by the unsympathetic faces of law and order whose cold stares are ready to convict all who pass.

Ahead, on the corner of Hester, he sees a phone booth and wonders if it works, wonders if he could reach Terry. Hurrying, he catches up to his daughters, bends over their sweetly puffing faces encircled in bright, pillowy hoods. Their eyes dance away from his. "Girls, I have to use the phone there, on the corner. I want you to stay here, in sight. Hear me?"

Their eyes hide in their corners.

"I'm serious. You move very far and we're going back to the apartment."

They twirl away. Glancing about he sees no one near, no one to bother them. He crosses the street, and checking back, sees his daughters watching him, eyes dark and round, breaths pumping out whitish wisps. Turning he inserts his coins and dials. Terry picks up. "Terr, it's Errol," he blurts and explains he's at a pay phone. Terry rushes through: he got Errol's message about Kenny's apartment and has enlisted the support of his lawyer to pursue the case—except that the lawyer just phoned back saying that Kenny's no longer at the precinct.

"Where is he?" cries Errol.

"Must be down at Central Booking, or a hospital, the lawyer's guessing. The precinct claims they don't know."

"Oh come on! How can they not know? Give us a break! What the hell is that all about?"

"A cover up, playing for time, is my friend's guess."

"Jeeze . . ." moans Errol, head and spirits falling.

"You said there were signs of blows or something?" Terry checks. "A welt?"

"I think so. It was so quick, as they dragged him away. But someone must have belted him good." Errol finds himself recoiling backward against the booth, which shudders, rattling the door.

"Well, he has a right to see a lawyer, so it's a question of finding him," Terry reiterates to calm them both. Errol tries to draw in his squeezed-out breath, then remembers his daughters. He glances out, eyes lunging, searching. A passing gust shakes the booth, sucking out the air he just inhaled. Not far from where they were, Lilly is up a climber, while Molly, on the ground, is shaking out a mitten. But now Errol notices another figure a few yards from them, slowly approaching. Molly also notices now and glances across the street to her dad. Errol feels his mouth opening to call. Instead he cries into the phone, "Later, Terry!" and drops the receiver.

The figure, draped in a heavy black coat with large while splotches, is now only a few steps from Molly, and the two kids are looking at him uncertainly. His head is largely covered by a black knitted hat pulled down over his brow and ears.

Errol sprints across the street, hurdling the low snow-bank. "Hey!" he shouts sharply. The man rotates his head turret-like toward him. Errol surges past him, reaching out for his daughter who eagerly extends both arms. He swings her onto his hip, before glancing up at Lilly still at the top of the climber . . . then turns with a deliberate, hostile glare toward the stranger.

The man wavers, then halts. He attempts a smile, broad but somehow distorted, displaying yellowed, uneven teeth. Errol begins noticing other details: under the other's odd, heavy coat, glow shiny black, water-proof overalls puffing over the tops of heavy brown, unlaced boots. His skin is almost translucent, save for his chin etched by a thin line of dark stubble.

He appears to be in his forties, and Errol wonders if he's homeless. Now the other's forced smile fades, and, in a strange, high-pitched voice he asks, "These your daughters?"

Errol feels his arms and body trembling. Calm yourself, he counsels. Maybe just turn and walk away. But unintentionally he nods, minimally.

The man wipes his nose and glances for a moment away. "Pretty . . . and so young . . . It's not safe, you know, to leave kids out alone . . ."

Errol feels fists forming, chest tightening. He hears Lilly climbing down behind him. The fellow inhales; his thick coat appears to inflate, then deflate into near emptiness. Shuffling his feet, he partly turns away. "Well . . . you take care . . ." And he begins to move off.

Lilly steps behind Errol and playfully pulls Molly's leg, eliciting a moan, "Lil-ly, sto-p . . ." Errol reaches behind for Lilly's hand and pulls her around and close. The man, they see, pauses and looks back with a baleful expression. Errol feels himself matching it, trembling, his own anger at the surface, ready to pitch out. The park grows darker. He feels Molly squirming, and he puts her down. Lilly is tugging at his hand, wanting to go east, away from the figure moving slowly west.

Errol, with a final glance after the fellow, turns and allows his daughters to pull him across the narrow park. Vaguely ahead, he searches for another phone with which to call the police. But what would he say?

As they skirt several snow-mounded benches, Errol glances back once more and sees the man now standing by an old gray van, its front door open, its motor puffing a thin stream of exhaust. He is staring after them. Errol feels himself bristle, before he once more is tugged east. Reaching the curb, they pass a parking sign, and veering slightly, he raises a hand and slaps it hard with his heavy, padded glove. His daughters stare up at him. For a moment the sign vibrates loudly in the cold air.

*   *   *

At his gallery desk Terry picks up the ringing phone, suspecting it's Viv—quickly confirmed by a seamless discharge of exasperation: "The kids are all wound up, spinning from room to room, up in the window frames, crying out about the snow, 'Momma, look at all the snow! Let's go out!' They've left trails of toys, food, clothes, and crayons everywhere. The place is a sty. I've gotta get them out of here, before we all go nuts. I'm takin' 'em to the park, Washington Square. Let 'em play and chill . . ." Terry hears her sigh, then laugh. "We'll stay until they're froze, and then I'm bringin' 'em to the gallery."

Well aware this is a warning, not a request, Terry soothes, "Fine, good . . . bring 'em down . . ." Discreetly he sighs: yes, let 'em have a good romp in the snow. Wish I could. "When they get here, I'll set 'em up with their easels, or clay. But better bring in something to eat."

"Yes, Terry."

"Sorry." But he knows that once she arrives, Viv will inevitably drift away from the kids and pull out her painting, leaving him to deal. Last night she mentioned wanting to paint something about the bar, the shadowed faces, the haze, the uncertain eyes . . . Could be striking . . . though it's not what draws me to the easel . . . . Yet variety is essential, right? Carefully laying the phone back in its cradle, he runs his fingers lightly over his moist forehead and tries to clear his mind for work. The police, he's concluded, will maintain their blamelessness, until the system convulses and spits that Kenny fellow out, leaving him to pick up the pieces . . . But where is he? Just hope they haven't done a real number on him.

Terry pushes himself up and moves heavily over to the shelf on which are stacked the bios of his client painters. He needs to update two for an upcoming hanging, but his mind wobbles between concerns. He takes the bios down and stares at the accompanying glossy photos of their work. Somehow the photos have more life than the paintings—a heresy he dares acknowledge only to himself.

*   *   *

Fin tightropes the footwide snowpath down Centre Street's sidewalk, mulling the news from Terry, that Kenny's been taken off somewhere. Fin responded by volunteering to walk down to Central Booking to see if he can uncover the cover-up. What would the cops have likely done with Kenny? Beat him up, then carried him off to the hospital? Not exactly the way to win public acclaim.

Ahead he spies another soul out on this crisp, crusted day making his way north, head-down along the same narrow path. Little John vs. Robin? Where's my stout staff? Who will give way, allow the other to pass? The approaching figure doesn't bother to look up until the last moment, when each steps right into deeper snow, and Fin throws a curious glance. Wrapped in scarf, hood, and parka, dark feminine eyes stare out from a snow pale face, then flick away. Fin kicks himself. What's wrong with you? Timid Tommy, reluctant, downright silly on these empty, downtown streets. Uptown with the crowds, sure, it's something else, but here . . . And who knows . . . she might have been my Guinevere.

As for Sam, where is she now? Howling and howled at by Peter. Fin wonders what she took away from their night together. In the morning, the day ahead dominated. Yet in him something lingers, some emotional tie or attachment, some memory of her softness. He recognizes that he's lucky he has the freedom to reflect, while she was drawn pall mall up to her office and uncertainty. He pictures his women friends, each with something endearing. Wouldn't mind an evening with Christine. More than an evening. But who knows? Unlikely in any case. He loves them all. How could you not? Yet he feels sorry for them too, that men are what they get. Some guys are okay, and to a degree the sexes complement, but still, women deserve more. Children may be some recompense, but double-edged, it seems. As for himself . . . he hasn't managed yet to get it right after all these years.

Inside Central Booking it's unusually quiet, as the snow has put a crimp on crime too. Where usually it feels like a subway station at rush hour, today it's empty, echo-y, as he walks to the front desk. Manning it is a woman, a civilian, looking cold despite a heavy gray sweater and steaming tea. He tells her he's from The Voice, shows his press I.D., says he want to find out about someone arrested last night. She nods and picks up her phone. He can just make out her murmuring, "There's a reporter here, for info." He wonders if 'info' is the tip-off for the run-around. She looks up without expression and tells him someone will be right with him. He thanks her, but she's already turned to other business, and so he edges away, taking in the few who wander across the marble floor. A minute stretches into five, then ten, as he scrutinizes the few cops, detectives, lawyers, and their clients. The officers, bundled up in their furry, flap-down hats and bulging coats lose a lot of dignity in staying warm. Three young men hand-cuffed together, being led to an elevator, don't glance around with any curiosity, keeping their faces blank, their eyes narrowly forward. Their captors, two plain-clothes officers, pay equally little attention to them, nodding to colleagues as they pass. The numbers, Fin concludes, overwhelm, leaving everyone just trying to get through. If it was ever high-minded for cops, it's long since worn away. Just one long grind. Added to it are the differences between cultures—each all but opaque to the others. Fin has written reports on innovations: smaller schools, smaller classrooms, neighborhood policing, rehab, helping the families, but while they work here and there, somehow they don't replicate or spread. He fears that for some change will take generations.

Now he notices a short, graying officer approaching, wearing his blues, neck warmed by a black turtle-neck, a fellow maybe forty, possibly fifty, with gray stubble softening him, but aging him. Raising Fin in his sights, he gives him the once-over, but his poker face reveals nothing, as he checks, "The Voice?"

Fin shows him his card. Motioning, the guy has him follow, pushing through a door into a corridor running between small cubicles, one of which he ushers Fin toward. "Coffee?" he asks as Fin steps past him.

"Sure," says Fin, thinking it'll give him a minute to think, strategize. The cop, most likely, is here to keep him at bay. The tiny plastic-paneled cubicle is filled by a gray metal desk, gray file cabinet, and three metal chairs. Not exactly homey, but matching up nicely with the fellow's grizzled growth.

Back with the coffees and Half & Half containers, the officer drops into his chair, urging Fin to "Take a load off." Fin sits. The other, tearing and pouring his Half & Half, asks, "So what is it?"·

Fin notices that the officer has placed on his desk a sheaf of papers— arrest sheets, he gathers. He tells him he wants to find out about a case, where it is and so forth, and he states Kenny's name and address. The fellow leafs through the sheets, pausing at several, scanning them, then moving on, until he completes the search, unsuccessfully. "Sorry, guess we haven't received it yet from the station house." He displays a veteran's blank look. Fin wonders, as he prepares his own coffee, how long it takes to perfect this. It's going to be a challenge to get anything out of him, but then, in a sudden reversal, Fin feels sorry for the guy, caught in a job like this. Hating it maybe, counting the days. But then, why did he choose it? Could he have done something else? . . . You never know what deposits people where they are. Chemistry, culture, genetics, education, luck? . . . Who you know. Fin inhales carefully, then tells the other, "The precinct said they sent it down."

The officer nods with resignation and looks heavy-eyed through the collection once more. "Maybe I missed it." But the result is the same. They look at each other. Fin selects from his interview repertory the calm, rational option. "If the precinct isn't holding him, and he isn't here . . . where is he?"

The cop swipes at his nose, briefly glancing away, then opens his mouth, as if to free some fly or bird. His eyes, gray and a little watery, swing back to Fin, then past him. "In transit maybe." But he sees Fin isn't buying it, anymore than he is himself. "Maybe he has special needs."

"Meaning?" Fin finds himself wondering if the guy is as alienated as he looks, from his life . . . work, friends . . . He's not completely there. Where would he rather be? With the wife? At the corner bar?

"Maybe he took sick, caught a flu, or something," the cop speculates, with limp conviction, his cheek creasing under the story he must sell. Fin concedes it's well-acted, almost convincing, but in no hurry, he allows the officer a moment to reconsider. No luck. And so Fin ups the ante a little: "The word is, he was dragged out of his apartment without a stitch on. Took some blows, didn't look too good. On top of which, it turns out it was the wrong address, wrong guy." Fin waits a beat, but the cop shows nothing, doesn't even blink. Fin prods, "So, uh, where might they have taken him? This wrong guy?"

The officer, Fin has by now gathered, is not slow, but wary. Dress him in a suit, hire a personal trainer, and he could sit on a board, or behind some mahogany desk. And yet here there's something sad, missing, something caught-out about him.

He, in turn, studies Fin, thinking he's not the worst, not the usual prima donna. Nonetheless he chooses the innocent, uninformed role, shaking his head, eyes falling to his desk. "Don't know. Could be anywhere, depending."

Fin's disappointed, believing the fellow could give him something, at least the options. But he chooses to keep the ball rolling, maybe heat it up a little. "Well . . . what is it they usually do with guys like that? The wrong guys, guys they've beat up and pulled naked into a snowstorm, for no reason?"

"Musta been a reason," the cop mutters thickly. Fin can't tell whether he believes this or is just mouthing. The guy's eyes wander distractedly, then come back to Fin, narrowing on him. "The precinct give you anything?"

Fin studies him, considering whether to take a chance with 'Yes,' but then falls back on the verifiable "Not really . . ."

The other inhales and expels mild relief. Part of him feels sorry for Fin. "Well, I don't know what to tell you. The paperwork will show up eventually. You wanta come back?"

"Can you call Bellevue for me? Find out if he's there? That's where the department takes them, right? If they need medical treatment."

"It is, but only family members or attorneys are given the info."

They look at each other. Fin tries to imagine where the cop lives, Pelham? Maspeth? Tries to guess what he does off-duty, what his wife must be like, and his family, assuming. The guy doesn't carry the usual attitude, be it defensive or offensive. He seems like he just woke up one day and found himself in uniform. Or maybe he's just tired today, from shoveling snow, or couldn't get home last night. Fin rummages for a question. "In your experience, how long does it typically take to get some screw-up like this straightened out, and the guy released?"

The officer tilts his head, in reflection, and brings a hand across his cheek, pursing and relaxing his lips. Signs of life, signs of possibly venturing off the beaten track? "Not long . . . Justice takes a little time . . . to check everything."

"Doesn't it seem a trifle out-of-date to be still treating people this way? A trifle insensitive."

"Insensitive? . . . Who? The criminals?"

Fin waits patiently, tilting his head a bit.

The cops concedes Fin's point with a pout. "Maybe, but when cops go bad, they pay, the city pays. But who pays the victims for the crimes against them? The bad guys have no money. You wouldn't want the city to be without cops, would you?"

Fin smiles thinly.

"I'm sure, you being a newspaperman, you know a number of cops have paid dearly over the last decade or so."

"Of course . . . It's tough, sad . . . but it doesn't help to have these incidents keep popping up. They send a bad feeling."

The officer studies Fin, his eyes once again closing a little under the weight of a distant thought. "But it's a small number, compared to the crime stats . . . Look, you and I can philosophize all we want, till we're blue in the face, but unfortunately I don't have any information to give you."

"Why do you suppose the department isn't making information available?"

The officer pauses, thinking he's spent enough time on this. His jaw drops a little, as if he's waiting for something. "Come on, you know how big this department is. I don't have to explain to you, do I? Sure it's not perfect. What do you want me to say?"

"Problem is, that when mistakes like this are made, people suffer, big time. Lives get derailed."

"Hey, I'm sorry for the guy." The cop looks at Fin, his head tilted down ruefully by some memory. "But I'm sorrier for the guys who lose their lives, leaving widows and children . . . in the course of keeping the city safe."

"I'm sorry too . . . At least most of the guys who do that get caught."

"Often, not always. But that don't bring the boys back, and now not the women officers either."

Fin nods as he studies him, wondering if he was ever out there in the streets, ever made an arrest . . ."So, as for this . . . you've got nothing for me. This is just another unavoidable screw-up. Somebody gets hurt; the city pays; taxes go up; things go on." The cop doesn't seem to react. Apparently he's content to leave it at that, or won't, or can't offer more, and so Fin slowly pushes himself up. "Well, thank you for your time."

The cop also stands, but as Fin begins to turn away, the fellow clears his throat to add, "You know . . . if the city wanted to pay cops a decent salary, so they wouldn't have to take second jobs, you might get better, more motivated people on the force."

Fin turns back to him and nods that he understands. "I hear you . . . Problem is: firemen feel the same; so do teachers, the MTA, Sanitation, pretty much everyone. Yet who wants to cough up more taxes to pay for it all?"

"So we live in the house we built," the cop sighs. His eyes drift away. "All of us together . . ."

Fin waits, watching for the other's attention to return, before suggesting, "But everyone could do a little better, right? With a little more attention paid here and there."

"You're young yet," the other tells him.

"You don't agree?" Fin asks.

"If only it were that simple. That's what you could write, that would be useful, so that people understand, that things just aren't that simple."

"I can write that," Fin allows, "just as it's been written that some changes and improvements *have* been made, in the face of opposition, so that *some* complicated things *are* better now."

The cop watches him, a reply forming in his mind, but then decides to leave it there, unspoken. His face, which for a moment looked alert and ready, slowly falls slack. Its melancholy strikes Fin, and hangs in his vision as he swings around, slides out of the cubicle, and moves back toward the door.

*   *   *

Typing at her desk, a new client's requirements for an office re-modeling, Sam becomes aware of someone at her back. Apprehension rushes through her. Warily, she twists around to find, as her premonition warned, Peter standing there, his unhappy eyes, dark and shadowed, glaring down at her.

Thoughts and images flash in her mind. She looks away, draws in a breath, gathers herself, and pushes up, feeling her face contort with anger. Glimpses of her destroyed belongings in the apartment seem to bulge before her. She can hear the glass shattering, feel the wood splintering. "All I can say to you, Peter, is fuck you!"

His eyes snap shut, snap open. His face grows dark. His hand is moving, rising from his side. He is swinging and catches her with his open palm across her cheek and nose. Her head is whipped back. Her body follows, recoiling away. She sees the ceiling lights slowly rotating as pain spikes out from her nose and cheekbone. But she pulls herself upright and comes at him, arms wind-milling. He throws up his forearms to ward her off, looking for an opening, and finding one, he jabs in his right fist, all his weight behind it, reaching and cracking into her jaw. The heavy thud resounds through her skull, a jarring shiver reverberates down her spine. She falls backward, sprawling onto her desk. Bone-deep pain and disorientation cloud her sight. Unable to move, she feels pinned, stunned. Time stops. Somewhere above her she catches sight of his breathing, hateful face glowering at her. Now he is stepping forward kicking at her legs, trying to get them out from under her. With a cry she half-rolls away and slides to the floor heavily onto her hip. With the little breath she has, she screeches, "You bloody bastard!"

Behind Peter, drawn by the commotion, Marjorie leans in and discovers Sam on her side on the floor. "Sam? . . ." Then recognizes Peter leaning over her, his arm cocked ready to deliver another blow. Marjorie is stunned. "What the . . . ? Peter, don't!"

"Call the police!" cries Sam through her aching, fiery jaw which feels as if it's been dislocated. With another glance at each, Marjorie darts off.

Peter slowly straightens, breathing and beginning to assemble his side of the story. She started it, going off with that slime, in front of the whole group, sleeping with him . . . the slut.

Sam's eyes fall away from him to the floor, as she protectively pulls in her legs. She feels herself straining to draw in an adequate breath past the pain in her jaw which feels as if it may overwhelm her. Her brain buzzes, then blanks for a moment, then tumbles through images and words. She tells herself that she's not surprised he resorted to violence; she'll tell the cops, show them the apartment, get a restraining order, send him home to Momma and the sisters. But now the pain, white hot, wraps around her jaw, up into her cheek; her forehead is pounding; her entire skull throbs. The dim office is falling away; things are growing dark, punctuated by lightning strikes of pain, blinding her. She feels she is falling, slipping down, letting go.

*   *   *

Errol stands over a pot of nearly-boiling, tomatoey-orange vegetable soup whose first bubbles slowly rise from the surface and pop, leaving faint, slowly-receding rings. Down the short hall from the kitchen, in their room, his daughters are quietly murmuring as they peel out of their cold, damp snowsuits. Errol feels that his existence has grown as thin and impermanent as the bubbles. While he is happy to be here, close to but not petitioned by his daughters, other things gnaw at him, down deep. The Kenny thing sits in his chest, its weight increasing with each revisiting. Someone should be attending to Kenny, doing something, getting it cleared up, and that someone is probably himself. But he seems stuck, trapped, helpless. Behind this, in some dark, more interior space, lie his own concerns: his plays sitting in different states of conception and completion, in the drawers of his desk—Is he writing only for those drawers? And his marriage, worn thin, hangs by a thread, while his girls and students should all be receiving a greater effort to teach and awaken. All these problems moan in the murk of doubt and helplessness. No one else can, or will, do anything about them. No one else can wrestle with their unruliness . . . How to make the plays more compelling, when he himself has little of that in him? Sometimes he wonders what point, when there is already so much out there. Only gems are worth it, but he hardly has time to polish his little stones, while the current one he's been working on is so buffeted by one distraction or another that its pages accumulate imperceptibly, like the dust on his desk, and he's forgotten its beginning or where he hopes to take it. He had hoped to finish it last Spring; now it's looking like next.

Is this his fate? His life? Floating along, treading water, as the girls are rapidly growing, and Leslie is following her own path. He barely keeps the family account out of the red, while in the outside world around them everything is accelerating. Recently he realized, with a dazed dullness, that more of his life lies behind him now than ahead. Yet he feels an increasing detachment . . . from everything . . . and has no idea how to correct it.

He listens to the girls, their contented chattering punctuated by occasional bursts of excitement or disagreement. Lilly is more like him, Molly like Leslie, having plans, an agenda, whatever the costs, while little Lilly follows or sneakily tries to work her way around obstacles, without anyone noticing, ever concerned with maintaining her balance in the multiple, unrelenting currents.

Before him the orange-red liquid reaches full boil. He turns it off and calls to his daughters, "Lunch girls, lunch is ready." His gaze returns to the three grilled cheese sandwiches in a pan. What should he do? Time is what he needs, yet has no prospect of finding it . . . as hopeless as the thing with Leslie. Sex stopped some time ago. He has nothing to offer another woman, nor could he bear to expose Lilly and Moll to the recriminations of divorce.

The girls bounce in. Molly, sliding into her seat, warns, "The grilled cheeses look ready, Dad." Little Lilly hugs his leg as she passes, leaving a faint heat imprint of her sweet affection. His hand reaches for her and just trails over her hair as she darts off to her seat.

He wonders how to regain momentum with the current play, a drama pitting neighborhood support for a community garden on an empty lot against a developer looking to evict them and build. Enliven and deepen the characters, infuse the dialogue with life . . . but life from where? . . . If only some producer would option it . . . cheap. But even that would require time he doesn't have.

"Dad, the sandwiches are burning," calls Molly staring at the stove with concern. Errol jumps and hurriedly spatulas out the sandwiches onto plates. The phone rings. He passes the girls their sandwiches, before he picks up the receiver, cradling it on his shoulder as he retrieves the ketchup from the fridge—wondering if it's Leslie checking up on him. "Hello."

"Yo, Rip Van Winkle, where you been?"

"Lou."

"Tried you earlier but you musta been sleepin' in."

"Took the girls to a park, for the snow."

"Good daddy. At least someone's enjoying it. Not a singletary customer seen in these parts."

"Any news on Clayton?" Errol asks, serving the girls their soup.

"I was callin' you, to find out. You talk to Il padrone?"

"While ago. The cops took Kenny off somewhere . . . Playin' dumb, said they don't know where. Just hope they haven't you know . . ."

"Yeah, done a number, a second number. So, ah, still not admitting a thing?"

"'Fraid not."

"Well . . . So. You got the girls?"

"Leslie's workin'."

"I think I'll join your humpin' teacher's union."

"Yeah . . ."

"You're still glum."

". . . I guess . . ."

"Cheer up. It coulda been you last night."

Errols feels a familiar thump inside. Maybe he's been breathing the fumes from the stove. He reaches and slides up one of the small kitchen windows.

"D-ad!" cries Molly unhappily. "It's cold."

He closes it with a rough swipe. "What? . . ."

"What what? . . . What's your problem, old man? D'you mind if I asskiss?"

Errol inhales deeply. Yes, he thinks, what is my problem? . . . Any number of things. But Lou doesn't really want to hear. He glances over and sees his daughters eating happily. The basic needs at least. Some parts of life, he consoles himself, are simple.

"Errol? . . . You there? . . . Maybe I'll talk to you later, when you don't have your girls. Okay? . . . Take it easy, dude."

". . . Sure, Lou. You too, take it easy."

There's resentment in there somewhere, both feel and hear in the other as they hang up.

"Fuck me," mutters Lou to himself. "What am I gonna do? You married that woman, had those kids. Deal with it, dude."

Errol finds that his mind has gone blank again. Jesus, Lou can turn on a dime. Wish I could. Now . . . what was it I was thinkin'?

*   *   *

From Central Booking, Fin headed south to Foley Square and then on to City Hall Park, to get out into some open space, take a walk, gain a sense of the snowfall, and maybe this police thing. He passes two bundles of men, heads wrapped in hats 'n' scarves, shoveling the walks where the tractors can't reach—doing the bidding of Tammany Hall. Few others are out. Not many city dwellers brave old Motha Nature, he thinks. City-zens see her as the great, unpredictable Nuisance, ever dumping the unwanted, be it snow, heat, or rain on them at the wrong time. Never the right time. Further south, he sees the towers of Wall Street, silver and gold against the blue sky, and staring at them, he wonders if they're open today, open for business. The sun flares off the bright surfaces so that Fin must close his eyes and turn away, trying to draw in a breath of the crystal air. With more oxygen in the system, he attempts to weigh what happened last night: cops crash a door, probably the wrong door, burst in, trash man and home, then try to blanket it, hush the whole thing. And now a guy is lost, lost to the world. Los desaparecidos, one C. Kenny, right here in River City, with a capital A, double P, L, E . . . . And while one poor dude is getting chewed, not so many blocks away many men are making millions pursuing the holy dollar . . . The post-modern world, where there is no one truth, where each constituency has its Christ, where no one is wrong, where complexity is suspect, where pols pander after polls, and you need only energize your base to gain legitimacy. Where debate spurns argument in favor of staying on message, and the television age has broadened access and reduced discourse to Pre-Enlightenment levels. Continue like this, and we're going down. The other cultures will sweep right by us, if we don't all go down together.

Fin snaps up his collar, feeling anger at the short-sightedness of it all, at the stupidity. He glares around, to vent and clear his mind . . . No kids down here. He pictures the inflexible mask that is the public face of the police commissioner. A charmer at home, no doubt. Hair slicked down by gun-metal mousse. Hug this. Nice day at the office, dear?

In time he makes his way north again, up Park Row, across Chatham Square, and, on a whim, veers west to Elizabeth Street. Although he hasn't decided whether he's going up to the office, or to Errol's Broome Street building, he thinks either way he'll pass the precinct again. Peek in maybe, see if any of the men in blue wanta unburden themselves.

The temperature has risen somewhat. He feels comfortable kicking through the drifts and narrow paths. In Chinatown, portions of the sidewalk have been cleared by the more industrious supers. The Chinese, he sees, glancing around, exhibit little wonder toward, indeed interest in, the snow, as they go about their business, impervious, heads down, without expression. Yet through the millennia, their artists have painted Nature big, while man is but a smudge on the landscape.

As he approaches the precinct across the street, he sees what appears to be an unmarked police car swerve into the curb and slide to a stop, its aluminum hubcaps banging dully. Two officers, in street clothes, push out of the front seat, and one hurries to open his back door.

At the same time behind him, Fin becomes aware of voices coming up the street. Glancing back, he sees maybe a dozen young Chinese men walking quickly, some in sinister black and yellow dragon jackets, others in bright ski parkas, all clamoring like geese, staccato voices honking, arms punching the air, gesticulating, as they break into a trot.

He turns back in time to see that a single Chinese man, long-haired, and entirely in black, has climbed out of the back seat and stands between the cops, his hands cuffed in front. The two cops, now aware of the approaching band, take their man's arms to rush him toward the front door. The young man, also glancing down the street, now tries to jerk free, writhing wildly, attempting to pull away, but the two cops lift him off the pavement and ram him through the door, in past two other patrolmen who appear in the entrance.

The approaching gang reaches the precinct's front door but stops short of entering. Several harass and taunt the two officers before more cops push out, and a sergeant tries to engage and calm the group, asking who speaks for them. But all the young men continue to jeer and shout, in English and in Chinese. The sergeant raises his hands as he tries to call out above the clamor, but the young men lift their voices, chanting slogans which Fin, coming abreast of the station house and half-crossing the street, cannot make out.

Just then the precinct's door is drawn sharply back and the long-haired prisoner bursts out, still handcuffed. He lowers his head, avoiding the grasps of the several officers, and bulls forward through his own crowd of supporters, heading toward the street in desperate flight, exhorted on by the young men who try to wall off the police from following.

So fast do the escaping man's spinning legs carry him, so intent is his effort to flee, that he runs blindly into Fin who has moved just outside the crowd. In the last instant before collision, the prisoner thrusts his cuffed hands at Fin, catching him in the jaw and knocking him violently back. But Fin, to protect himself and ward off the man, has also thrust out his hands and manages to snag the other's jacket. The conflicting forces, of head-long flight and desperate defense, send them gyrating wildly, reeling and teetering, as Fin's greater mass offsets the other's momentum. Around they go, once, twice, nearly three times until they fly apart and sprawl headlong across the snow-covered pavement. Before the prisoner can collect himself, four policemen are on him, having broken through the crowd. Several of the man's supporters try to reach in and wrestle him free, but by now there are more cops than supporters, and a number of those supporters become prisoners themselves, cuffed and hauled inside.

The cops yank the prisoner to his feet, then lug him back into the station house. Fin, head ringing from the blow to his chin, slowly sits up, checks himself and staggers to his feet, brushing the snow off his front as he tests his uncertain balance. Almost as quickly as the confrontation exploded, it has ended. The band of supporters has dissolved, its free members scattering back down Elizabeth Street, bobbing and weaving like sparrows. Those arrested have disappeared inside, followed by most of the cops. Alone, two officers remain outside gazing around and conferring on the scrap. The few onlookers, mostly Chinese, watch without comment or visible reaction.

Only now does one of the original arresting detectives come back outside. He was among the several who re-captured the long-haired prisoner, and he remembered there was some guy who tackled the escapee. The detective, in the commotion, never got a real look at the fellow, nor did any of the other officers, but now he stops in the street where the guy brought down the prisoner, where the snow has been kicked and gouged, and searches north and south along the sidewalks and doorways, but he cannot find anyone who might have stuck his neck out to help them. Up at the corner with Canal, Fin, chin down, striding fast, swings west and is gone.

VII.

Late Day

Winding along paths others have broken through knee-deep, sidewalk drifts, Christine approaches Errol's Broome Street building, extending her arms, soaring over icy patches, a hairy, brown Egret, then gliding back to terra concreta and craning her head skyward, toward the-somewhere-above she's heading. The building appears to stream beneath the blue dome that is both tangible and intangible—a paradox that squeezes her brain as she wobbles and slows, spreading her arms again, for balance, and briefly closing her eyes. She imagines being up there in the sky, above other buildings, where she once lived, and senses intimations of nostalgia and apprehension circling warily. When she re-opens her eyes, she sees ahead the front door—through which ghosts of plain-clothes cops are rushing a shimmering brown shadow through the nighttime glow into a waiting patrol car. She imagines the cops' large, meaty hands clutching Kenny's arms, feels their thumbs digging in, sees them prying his head down through the cellar door, as it were.

Mind a-swim with cries of imagined pain, she pushes past the outer door, pauses to regain her breath, then steps over to read the tenant directory. C. Kenny, fifth floor, E. Pendragon, fifth floor. She buzzes. A little girl's voice answers, "Hel . . . hello . . . Who . . . who is it?"

Christine leans to the speaker. "A friend of your daddy . . . Christine."

A pause, as whispered consultations follow until finally the entry buzzer sounds, and she shoulders in. Finding no elevator, Christine heads for the stairs, debating, then deciding against shedding her boots and coat. The five story climb has her soon huffing, puffing, and pulling herself up the last lunge where she discovers two, rosy young faces peering wide-eyed from their doorway. Pausing, gasping, she manages to throw out a "Hi . . ." with her panting smile.

Over his daughters, shrinking back from the great raccoon, comes Errol's head, a faintly carroty jack-in-the-box. His hands clamp their shoulders against retreat as he greets Christine and introduces his girls. But the approach of the great, swaying coat is too much, and the girls squeal and duck away, disappearing into the apartment. Stepping back, Errol welcomes her in, experiencing from the distant past a whiff of graciousness.

Stopping just inside and beginning to gently stamp her boots and unbutton the coat, Christine asks Errol if he's heard news of Kenny. His mouth stretches wide as he jams his hands into his jeans' pockets and haltingly tells her the bad news, that Kenny has disappeared. Their eyes meet with shared dismay, until he remembers his hosting duties and, pulling his hands out again, takes her heavy coat to hang it on a hook in the hall, then leads her into the kitchen, offering her tea, coffee, or a cup of vegetable soup.

Finding herself touched by the unexpected hospitality, she accepts, "A tea, maybe. Thank you." Looking around, she discovers the girls returned, peeking in from the doorway, which stirs her once more—this tableau of father and daughters so excited and alive amid modest circumstances. Other details now begin to emerge: the worn, dated furnishings; Errol lighting the burner with a match; his less-than-stylish, baggy bluejeans and dark blue T-shirt, all of which take her back to the working-class brownstone apartment of a baby sitter she had as a child, with its indelible cooking smells in the basement kitchen, its earthy colors, the simple lifestyle—all permanently imprinted. A brief lament sinks through her from this world of warm, innocent essentials, long gone. Her gaze follows Errol as he fills the teapot with tap water and carries it to the burner. She waits for him to finish, before asking, "Do you think . . . we might take a peek at Clayton's apartment?"

Several concerns burrow in his brow, the first of which is that he assumes the police will, at some point, return. Yet he realizes that he would welcome another witness to the destruction he discovered, and would find relief in someone sharing the horror he witnessed. "Okay . . . but maybe we should do that first."

She indicates she's ready, and so he turns off the gas and faces his daughters, explaining to them that he's going briefly out into the hall and wants them to stay put in the apartment. Their wide-eyed stares betray their uneasiness.

Errol leads Christine into the hall, where they listen, and hearing nothing, move quietly to Kenny's. She lifts her camera out of her bag. The door is open, though still crisscrossed by the yellow police tape, and both peer in through the frame. The extent of destruction sucks her breath away, as Errol points to the bullet holes in the far wall. Stunned by seeing how close Kenny came to death, she reaches for the frame to steady herself. From there, through half-closed eyes, she surveys the entire room, then raises her camera and methodically clicks off a panorama of shots, before turning to Errol and asking, despite the police tape, "Think we could go in?"

Glancing down the hall, he shrugs. "I suppose . . ."

She peers in once more, before pushing down the tape and stepping over, while he checks the hall again before following. Separately, and sliding carefully around items so as not to disturb them, they circle the room, bending, looking. She takes close-ups of the bullet holes in the wall and love-seat and of his desk with its drawers out and the contents strewn across the floor. Through growing repugnance she exhales, "Was all this necessary?"

Errol groans in agreement, repeating to himself the possibility that this could have been his place. But then, as they work back toward the door, they hear heavy footsteps out in the hall coming rapidly their way, grinding grit into the floor. Christine slips her camera back into her bag as both recognize escape undetected is impossible. Straightening and composing themselves, they wait motionlessly just inside the doorway, eyes fastening on details.

Two detectives, a smooth-faced Hispanic, and a heavy-set Irish type, both squeezed into heavy coats open over chinos and cheap sports jackets, stop short as they peer in past the tape. The Irish fellow's head cocks to the side toward Errol and Christine, who twist around to face him. "What? . . . Who are you?" he snaps, his face growing pink. "What are you doin' in here? Can't you read?"

Playing dumb, Errol asks, "Read what?"

The cop stretches his cheek into a derisive smile as he steps over the tape into the apartment, glancing from them to the surprising destruction. His partner follows, giving the visitors a cautious once-over.

"I live across the hall," Errol tells them. "Just lookin'."

"Well beat it, buddy. Both of yous. You could get arrested for this."

Errol and Christine retreat back over the tape as the sputtering detective surveys the apartment, uttering a short, low whistle. Just outside the apartment but leaning in a bit, Errol asks, "You guys know what happened in here?"

"Keep your nose t' your own business," the Irish one warns as he takes out a pad and pen from his coat pocket.

"I live here, man," Errol replies sharply.

The Hispanic is more conciliatory. "A fellow was arrested."

Errol tries to catch his eye, "I know the guy who lives here. What happened?" But the Hispanic turns away offering nothing more as he unfolds a report form. His partner gives no indication of having heard at all.

"Looks like there was a shooting," Errol probes again. Now the heavy-set detective turns and, taking several quick steps to the door, grabs it with both hands and tries to muscle it closed in their faces, but the door, warped and jammed on shattered pieces, won't budge. He leans into it, emitting squeaks of futile exertion, until giving up, he curses and kicks the door hard and low, then turns to them, growling, "Listen, scram! Get your faces outta here! Now!"

Errol stares darkly back, feeling he's well within his rights and aware of his own mounting frustration. The detective scowls and takes a step toward Errol, his face rippling with irritation, but his partner calls, "Hey Mike, come on. Let's go, let's get it done." He motions with his form, "They're waitin' for us."

Grumbling Mike snorts as he turns. "If they're in such a rush, let 'em do their own dirty work!" But catching himself, he looks dourly over at Errol and motions for him to beat it, outta here. But neither of the onlookers moves.

Expelling another oath, Mike pulls out a cell phone. "I'm calling a car to deal with these two."

"Come on, Mike. You know the story here," the other cautions.

"What's the story?" Errol asks the Hispanic.

"Nothin'. We've got work to do. Come on, go back to your apartment; don't bug us."

Errol moves away, thinking he's got a pretty good idea of the destruction, and Christine's taken her pictures. No point in pushing things with these two. Footsteps, however, are heard again echoing up the stairs. Fearing more cops, Christine and Errol retreat another few feet and look, only to discover that the figure pulling himself up the last step, bent and inhaling deeply, is Fin, halting and staring down the hall at them. His recent Elizabeth Street collision has clattered through his mind as he climbed, and only now, as he stands breathing heavily, does it begin to release its hold on him. Errol and Christine call out their greetings, which slowly reel him in. Errol, closest, extends a hand, then pulls him into an embrace—two veterans of a shared injustice—and unexpectedly Christine follows, spreading her arms. Dazed Fin leans into her embrace, averting his sore chin despite thinking he should savor this, maybe even kiss her. But his jaw loudly warns him away.

Errol motions to the open doorway, and Fin, reluctantly releasing her, slides over to peer in. The two cops lean over their pads scribbling, and as with his friends, the extent of the wreckage shocks Fin, squeezing his recovered breath back out. But he manages to pull from his pocket a compact camera and flashes off several shots.

Wincing Mike yanks himself around and up, spitting onto the floor, his red face puffed with anger. "Hey! That's it! Enough!" Throwing down his pen and pad, he again takes out his cell phone and pokes angrily at the keys. "Who can fuckin' concentrate with these faggots flashing around?" The other detective, Angie, rises too, glancing at his riled partner and the three, and he reaches out in an effort to restrain Mike, but one hand is not enough, slipping off Mike's shoulder then wandering across his own forehead, where it attempts to smooth away the deepening lines of anxiety.

Mike reaches someone on his phone. "Hi, it's Raney. Listen, we got a small situation here. Coupla hippy-dippy wise-asses in the crime scene. Went through the tape . . . How about sendin' a car over? . . . No, but you know . . . It's just we can't do what we've gotta do with these flits gawkin' 'round. Okay?"

Just as he clicks off, Fin presses another flash. Mike reacts like a bull to a cape, all but throwing himself at Fin, restrained only by the police tape, and by being briefly blinded. "Hey!" he screams, head swinging, eyes shuttering, "Where the . . . What in the hell are you doin'?"

Fin falls back a step, surprised at the vehemence and stunned by what seems a replay of his recent street encounter. His mind flails for some response. "Hey, Press, officer . . ."

"Yeah well obstructing police business is what you're doin'. You're going into the station." The detective thrashes at the police tape and gets one leg over, before his shoulders are clamped from behind by Angie. Fin, frozen by the prospect of a second grappling, stares at the wild-eyed, blustering detective, then searches behind for his two friends and sanity. Angie, this time, is successful in restraining Mike, pulling him back to the middle of the room with a lock on his upper arm. "Easy, man. Come on, stop. Cool it." But Mike calls back to Fin, "Okay, meathead, let's have the camera!" Fin, still dazed by all of this, manages to pocket his camera, and with the other hand, pull out his I.D. and hold it up. But Mike twists himself free and reaches over the tape to swat the card out of Fin's hand, sending it spinning along the hall floor.

"We're in a public place!" cries Christine, stepping up behind Fin.

"Hey, what're you doin'?" joins Errol, also coming forward and bending to retrieve the card, then pushing it back into Fin's hand.

The detective's eyes rake all three. "I'm gonna have all three of yous locked up. You wait. You just stay right where you are. You'll see. You'll see a lot more than you bargained for."

"We're not allowed to be in the hall?" Christine challenges.

"In which Nazi-Commie-fascist country did they find *you*?" cries Errol.

"You keep spoutin' off, Carrot-top," sneers Mike jerking himself away, "and we'll see who's laughin' at the end of the day."

Just now Molly sticks her head out of the apartment behind them and calls, "Da-ad, Mo-om's on the phone."

Errol's eyes cloud as they fall. Resignation thicken his features as he mechanically turns away back toward his girls, where he hesitates and nearly reverses himself, before pushing on into his apartment.

Sneering Mike scowls after him and at the other two. "Go on, beat it!" he jeers. "Go on back to mommy, with your buddy, before you get in trouble." Then he spins angrily around and returns to his work.

Christine motions for Fin to retreat a little down the hall, where she confides that Errol and she were in the apartment and took some pictures. Fin feels his head throbbing from this second confrontation. Half-peering back toward Clayton's door, testing his painful jaw, he growls, "Rancid little piece of bacon that Mike is."

On his kitchen phone Errol is trying to calm Leslie who's agitated at finding the two girls alone. "I was just out in the hall, Leslie, don't blow it out of proportion!"

"Don't give me that 'just' business! Look what happened last night. And now Molly told me she was scared."

"Of what? I was right there."

"And who was the woman in the apartment? In front of the girls? How can you do that? Bringing strange women into the apartment? What the hell do you think you're doing?"

As Errol feels his own anger rising, he lowers his voice, "Leslie . . . she's one of our Wednesday night group, a writer, here to see Clayton's apartment, so don't go . . ."

"I don't care who she is! She shouldn't be in there!"

"She's not, now. She's out in the hall with Fin. I didn't know she was coming. She just showed up."

"I don't want you bringin' people in when I'm not there!"

Seeing no end to this, Errol snaps, "I gotta go."

"Listen, I'd leave work if I could. And I may yet. I don't want her back in that apartment."

"Fine. See ya." Hanging up, he thinks maybe some of those characters in the old plays weren't so over-the-edge: Goneril, Regan, Lady Mac B., and he flexes his arm as if shaking a spear at the phone, then presses his two palms up over his eyes, summoning darkness and a proscenium arch through which he escapes up into the sky above the streets, heading south and west past Tintagel and Lands End. But his fantasy fades as he swivels his head around, to find his girls standing behind him. "You two okay?" he asks pausing, looking down, trying to gauge. "There's nothing to be worried about," he reassures them. They try to smile.

Making an effort to understand their fears, he bends and attentively looks into their troubled eyes. "Moll, Lill, don't worry. I'm right here . . . Now what'd you tell Mom?"

"Nothin'" mutters Molly.

"I mean about the woman outside." He motions toward the hall.

Molly looks away, then bravely back. "She came to visit."

"And she's tall, and pretty," Lilly adds.

Errol looks from one to the other, wondering if that was the extent of it.

"Well, okay . . . I'm just going out into the hall again, for a few minutes. You can peek out and watch if you want, but I need you to stay in the apartment, okay . . . . You hear? . . . What do you guys want to do? Hmm?"

The two girls avoid his eyes. Reluctantly little Lilly looks back down the hall, and whispers, "Play in our room . . ."

Errol softens now and pushes out a sympathetic smile. "That's good. I'm not going anywhere. Like I said, I'll be right here, right outside."

Together they turn away from him and drag themselves toward their room, and Errol watches for a moment, feeling his heart go with them, before pulling himself up and heading back to the hall. As he steps out of the apartment, additional footsteps are heard coming up the stairs, sending tremors through the floor. Three uniformed patrolmen pop into view and stride heavily past Errol in his doorway, examining him leerily, and then Christine and Fin a few steps beyond. Looking back, the first patrolman asks Fin, "What's the problem here?"

Fin shakes his head, 'Nothing,' then holds up his press card. "Just taking a look."

The patrolman gives him an unhappy once-over before moving on to Kenny's doorway where he leans in. "Hey. What's doin'?"

Mad Mike comes to the door, writing up his report. "We arrive to find two of these jack-offs in here, inside the tape."

"Which? This guy?" asks the patrolman, tipping his head toward Fin.

The detective frowns and points instead to Errol who is coming slowly forward. "That guy . . . and this one." He nods toward Christine.

She addresses the patrolman. "This fellow lives here, officer, and I'm a friend. We were just looking, wondering why the apartment was turned upside-down."

"And then this wiseass begins takin' pictures," says Mike nodding at Fin. The patrolman's gaze pans reluctantly away from Christine to Fin. Fin feels himself growing impatient. "I was in the hall, Officer. I don't see the problem with that." Mike dourly shakes his head. "Some day someone's gonna show you the problem with that mouth of yours."

"Impressive, Officer, turning the tables. The higher-ups could use someone with your abilities," compliments Fin. But Mike ignores him and tells the patrolman, "I want 'em all outta here." With that he pulls himself around and disappears back into the apartment.

The patrolman, his eyes dull with distaste, now turns to Fin. "Listen. This is a crime scene. We can't have people contaminating it. The detectives can't do their work if people are in the way."

"We were careful not to disturb anything," asserts Christine.

Disenchantment slowly fills the patrolman's face at what he feels was a dishonest assertion. "Fact is, Miss, you were *in* the apartment, and it don't help us if people go in and walk over things, which may be evidence. You don't know what's important and what's not. The detectives need space and peace to perform their duties, so please, how about we clear the hall."

"Do you know what happened here, Officer?" Christine asks.

Wearily he shakes his head and looks heavy-lidded over at his two fellow officers who return his cheerless expression.

"Well I'll summarize for you," Christine tells him and quickly does so as her listeners stare back with displeasure. When she's finished, the first cop redirects the discussion back to where he believes it should be. "I'm afraid the only issue here, at the moment, lady, is vacatin' the hall."

Once again, however, footsteps are heard tramping up the stairs, this time belonging to a tall, balding male in a dark-blue ski parka and red headband. Christine recognizes him. "Tom," she calls, then identifies him to Fin and the patrolman. "A reporter from *The Times.*"

"I don't understand," the patrolman exclaims. "What's this, a convention? What's the big deal?"

Tom pulls out his own I.D. as he moves past the other two policemen and shakes hands with Christine, inquiring about Dan. She replies that Dan's well, and introduces Fin and Errol. Both newspapermen have the sense they've heard the other's name, yet can't place where, before Tom turns business-like toward the apartment door and the first patrolman. "Just want to take a look,

Officer." Although the officer doesn't immediately hinder him, he's glancing around for some means to do so. As Tom peers in, the patrolman rips off an extra strand of yellow tape to move back the line, telling him, "I'm gonna hafta move you all now. The detectives need to be able to concentrate."

Taking a hard look around, Tom tries to commit to memory as many details as possible, though his view is partially blocked by mad Mike who has risen once more to stand in the way. Retreating, Tom turns to the patrolman. "Can you tell me what happened? Why the door was battered in, the apartment ransacked?"

"'Fraid I can't." For a beat or so, they exchange skeptical stares, until Tom turns and moves back to Christine and Fin. Errol, edging closer, offers to fill him in and runs through it loud enough for the patrolmen to hear. Christine adds a few details of the department's lack of cooperation, and under her breath mentions the photos they grabbed. The patrolman, however, feels that the issue of the police lines was conveniently skirted by Errol, and approaching Tom, he explains, "Uh, we were summoned here because these people was interfering with the detectives' investigation. Two of these people crossed our lines. And I'm sure a reporter from a paper like yours can appreciate the problems with that—contaminating a crime scene, for one."

Tom has taken out a small pad on which he rapidly scribbles notes, while Errol steps closer to the cop to demand, "But why is the department stonewalling us? We've been trying to find out about my neighbor, who we think was beaten, and they won't tell us a thing. I saw them drag him away with no clothes on, out into the cold. What about that, Officer? Why aren't you concerned with that man's condition and that man's rights?"

Glancing at him, the officer addresses the four generally, "I don't know anything about all that. What I do know is that I'm going to clear this hall. Now you gonna go peaceably, or are we gonna hafta move you all?"

"I live here, God damn it!" Errol shouts, finally pushed to his limit. "This is my fuckin' apartment! This hall is my hall! I have every right to be here!"

"Not down here you don't." The patrolman glances at Fin, Tom, and Christine. "Can you get your friend here to move? Before we have to move him."

But Errol cries out again, "I've taken enough shit from you idiots. You don't know the first thing about people's rights, or the bill of rights, or anything! All you are are the dumb-fuck-messengers!"

With this the patrolman motions for his two fellows to join him squeezing past the others and begin moving Errol back, but Errol plants his feet and locks hands with the leader. The two other cops reach for his head to pry him

120

away. Fin feels he's witnessing a repeat of the street episode and tries to edge in to restrain Errol, calling, "Whoa, Errol, come on, take it easy!" Above the flailing arms, the lead patrolman warns, "Hey, buddy, if you really wanna join your neighbor downtown, we can arrange it for you."

"This is where I live! What the hell are *you* guys doin' here?" wails Errol, trying to fend off the three. Fin attempts to reach past one cop to calm Errol, but in doing so bumps the cop's shoulder. Feeling this and seeing an arm coming, the policeman swings around and lands a punch heavily on Fin's lip. Fin's head snaps back once more as his arms fly out against the wall. Bending quickly, Christine manages to get a shoulder under his arm and break his fall. A slice has been opened on his upper lip, and blood begins to ooze down into his mouth.

In the same instant, the patrolman's warning and the sight of Fin being rocked back converge in Errol's mind, releasing doubt and discouragement. Hesitating, he is turned by the cops and shoved bodily back toward his door where he discovers his daughters peeking out. This drains away any remaining combativeness as one final push sends him into the doorframe. Lilly screams, "Daddy! Pick me up," and he quickly stoops to lift her.

Glances at the little girls halt the keyed-up cops who then swing back for the others. Tom and Christine are helping to steady Fin who is holding his mouth and chin. Christine addresses the cop who punched him, "That wasn't necessary. He was trying to restrain his friend."

Eyes narrowing uncomfortably, the cop feels unjustly accused, but he's not happy at having to swing at the guy. He nods with some contrition and asks Fin, "You all right?"

Fin, with an additional ache now throbbing through his jaw and skull, nods uncertainly. He tips his head left and right, then shakes it carefully, testing that things are functioning. With a sleeve, he begins stanching the flow of blood from his lip, until Christine pushes a scarf she's pulled from around her neck into his hand, and he presses it against the cut.

The Hispanic detective now peers out from Kenny's apartment to see what the little girl's screams were about, and to tell the patrolmen they're nearly finished.

At this point, above the voices, one more, lighter set of footsteps is heard climbing slowly, and everyone looks back to discover a black man despondently pulling himself up the last step. Though youngish, he is bent by fatigue and draped in a bum's collection of rags and odd garments. Discovering his audience, he stops and stares back. Recognizing him, Errol cries, "Clayton!" But no one moves, other than Clayton, partially straightening, breathing heavily. After a moment he resumes dragging himself homeward, feet and limbs constrained by pain, head bowed by fatigue. Through his exhaustion, he tries to make sense of the scene before him. Errol, he recognizes and sends him a brief, detached glance as he passes. He ignores the patrolmen, who make room for him, and now eyes the Hispanic detective as he arrives at his door.

Only at this point do those watching in the low hall light notice the details of his bruised, puffed face. Black threads bisect stitched-up yellowed patches in his cheek and eyebrow. The clothes he wears are cheap, lace-less running shoes, women's loose, yellow flowered pajama pants, a tattered blanket wrapped around his shoulders, over a cheap white summer blouse. No sign of Errol's things.

Clayton turns his head a little to take in the Hispanic detective. His lack of sleep and aching head make clarity difficult as he attempts to read the face before him, but then he tells himself he doesn't care who it is or what he's thinking. Glancing past this detective, he finds another coming slowly forward, scribbling something on a pad. That cops are still in his place he cannot believe, sinking his spirits further—where hitting bottom, they begin to rebound, in the form of anger. He remembers men of uncertain identity bursting through the door last night, pummeling him after he had thrown down his gun, scudding it across the floor toward them. Now, oh boy, would he like to wade into this faceless detective, hammer him to a pulp, as they tried to do to him last night, three or four on him at once, punching, kicking, even after he was motionless on the floor. But he knows he's in no shape, and there are too many. Stow your anger, he tells himself. Don't do or say nothin', because once it starts, it'll all come rainin' down, fast and furious. And who knows where *that'll* end. Too many of 'em. No . . . let the lawyer deal with it. That's his business.

The Hispanic has watched him closely, expecting an outburst, but Clayton just stares now past both detectives, into his apartment, where the destruction is more wanton, more depressing, more inexcusable than he remembered. As he stares, he feels his anger revving up again. Just wish I had something to take out these guys with. The utter disarray, the ruin of so much, cause his chest to contract, emitting faint gasps, as his eyes run over the devastation, item by item.

Mike moves past him, clamping his clipboard and papers under his arm, as Angie checks, "All set?" Mike nods, moving into the hall, but there he turns and without expression looks back at Clayton still staring into his apartment. Angie takes a penknife from a belt pocket and proceeds to cut down the yellow tape with several vigorous slashes, then gathers it up, puts his knife away and turns to follow Mike. But Mike has been watching Clayton and now calls to him, "Hey bud, go ahead and sock it to the city, you hear? Be sure you make 'em pay good for this. Have your lawyer send 'em a nice fat bill."

Clayton half-hears but has no interest in responding to whatever the cop is saying. He is staring into his apartment, feeling a rush of hopelessness. Mike turns down the hall and with Angie walks past the patrolmen and onlookers, giving the latter a cold, thin stare, challenging them to sound off. Seeing Fin's fat bloodied lip, he smiles. But no one says a thing.

Concluding that nothing more is needed, the three patrolmen follow, sending glances at Fin's face and nodding to Tom and Christine.

For a moment the onlookers stare after the cops, until Errol, still holding Lilly in his arms, slowly redirects his attention around, past Fin, to Clayton leaning against his door. Errol feels someone press against his leg. Molly peers up to ask, "Dad, what happened? Why were the policemen here?" Errol's eyes brush over Christine, Fin, and Tom before falling back to Molly. When he hesitates, Lilly asserts what she can, "Policemen wear blue." Errol touches her cheek with his, as he searches for an answer to Molly's question. Seeing his difficulty, Christine bends to Molly. "They were here to make sure everyone was all right."

Molly stares unhappily up at Christine, then asks her dad, "Why were you shouting, Dad?" Errol gently touches the top of her head. "Because someone messed up, messed up Mr. Kenny's apartment."

"Why?" she asks.

Aware of the confused press of feelings, he shakes his head slowly and carefully puts Lilly down next to Moll. Looking at Fin, he asks, "You all right? We've got some first aid inside."

Embarrassed, Fin mumbles he's okay.

Errol now looks down at the girls, feeling shaken, and though the heat from the struggle with the cops has dissipated, it has left anger curling around edges, particularly the exposure of his daughters to violence, and Clayton's sad situation. As this runs through his mind, he attempts to inhale and discover some sense of what should be done, but instead he coughs, groans, and twists away. But then a clear priority presents itself, and swinging back, he bends to his daughters. "Could I ask you girls . . . to stay here for a minute? I wanta go see how Mr. Kenny's doing."

Fright fills the little faces, and they face each other, their mouths parted in mute apprehension, their eyes closing down. Errol squats down, gently holding their shoulders. "I'm just going right down there. You can watch. I'll be right there and am coming right back. Just gonna see how our neighbor is. You guys keep Christine company, so she doesn't worry."

Christine puts out her hand. Lilly takes it, but Molly doesn't. Seeing that he'd better take his chance while he can, Errol turns once more and moves down the hall to Clayton's door. Tom follows slowly at a distance. Clayton has made his way into the center of his living room and is staring around at his belongings on the floor. Errol pauses at the entrance, before calling, "Clayton?"

He doesn't respond.

Tom stops at the point where he can see in over Errol's shoulders, as Errol tries again, calling to Clayton, but again there's no reply. Tom now steps around and forward, glancing at Errol, before addressing Kenny, "Sir, I'm from *The New York Times*. Sometime, if you're interested, when you're ready, I'd love to get your story on this."

Clayton takes this in by stages, before he looks back at them, his eyes moving over the faces, coming to rest on Errol's. They look at each other. Clayton can't help but mutter to himself: Who do the cops come after? *Not* the strange white man on the floor, but the black man.

Errol, held by the other's stare, tries to imagine all that fuels it . . . At the same time he wants to tell him he's there to help, and that in fact they have a lawyer for him, if needed. ". . . Clayton, this is a god-damned travesty of justice . . ."

Clayton tilts his head, as possible responses occur to him, but he feels no particular need to voice them. Although Errol sees this, he presses doggedly ahead, "I . . . we all went down to the precinct last night, after the arrest. But they wouldn't let us talk to you. We brought you some clothes . . . but obviously . . ."

With his skull still ringing painfully, Clayton stares at him wondering if there is anything he wants to hear from this man, or anyone. No, not really.

Errol wavers, then stumbles on, "You . . . you have a lawyer? . . . Because if not, we found one . . . a lawyer who handles these . . ."

Clayton becomes aware of annoyance. He hasn't asked for anything. He half-faces away, murmuring, "Of course . . . course I've got one."

Errol nods as if confirming this to himself, then looks over at Tom, silently soliciting the next step. Tom addresses Clayton, "I can tell you we'll report this. It'll be in the paper; it won't go unnoticed."

Clayton looks over at him . . . But who will it serve? . . . Should I check with my lawyer first? . . . And really, why should I help white publications sell copies with my story? Not to mention that they'll want me to replay the whole thing . . . when all I'm really interested in is restitution. For some reason 'money rag' sounds in his head, and though he feels it's strained, even silly, still he smiles faintly to himself, shaking his head. What he really wants, right now, is to say nothing. Nothing to anybody. What he wants is to let the whole thing drain away, wants to sweep it away . . . Sure I'm angry. Who wouldn't be? Sure I'd like to pop those cops, but making the system pay will be much more satisfying. Anger feeds on itself. Seen it my whole life. I mean look at those fucking cops.

He turns away from the men at his door. Maybe what I need to do first is deal with the practical: a shower . . . see what's left to wear . . . and where the hell am I gonna sleep? Here? . . . This place disgusts me now . . . and yet, where else am I gonna go? . . . See if I can find my sister's number . . . What did they do to my bedroom? My clothes? . . . Soil everything? He begins picking his way back to his bedroom. Hope they didn't destroy the fucking shower. Guess I should make a general inventory. Call it in to Mr. B., Henry Bade, Esquire. He bade me be quiet. Okay, so be it . . . These cases, he told me, aren't resolved quickly. Warned me the city will try to out-wait us, try to postpone, present excuses . . . I'll need patience, persistence. He'll be sending one of his investigators down. Better not touch a thing.

Clayton puts the white people at his door out of his mind. Slowly he moves into the short hall which leads to his bedroom and bath, to see what was destroyed. Motherfuckers. Left nothing untouched . . . Send them a bill. Fuckin' right I will.

When the two see Clayton disappear into his back room, they return slowly back to the others, where little Lilly stretches out her arms a second time and Errol again lifts her up. Uncertain what's next, the adults glance uneasily at one another. Is that it? Is the episode, so far as they're concerned, closed?

Christine reminds them they need to inform Terry that Kenny has a lawyer, while Tom, eager to get back to his computer and write up the story, takes this opportunity to break away. Thanking all and shaking Christine's hand, he leaves them, striding crisply off. Watching him reach the stairs and drop out of sight, the others are struck by his efficiency.

Errol, inhaling through pinched despondency, finds Christine and Fin and urges them to come inside and use the phone—aware of a mild lift at defying Leslie. In the kitchen, he again dials Terry and Viv. Waiting, the other two gaze around and find the young girls now peering in from the hall. Christine asks them if they got outside to play in the snow, but the girls avoid her question as they stare at their dad. Fin pulls out his camera and catches them with a flash, which sends them backing away, caught between fun and fear.

At the gallery, it's Viv who picks up Errol's call and who receives his news, "Viv, Clayton's out. He's been released."

It takes her breath away. ". . . Out? . . . Well thank God . . . Finally . . . Is he all right?"

Errol vacillates over how to put it. "Well . . . uh, his face is banged up . . . He seemed pretty bummed. The cops really did a number on his place, not to mention on him . . . And they sent him home in women's clothes . . ."

". . . Women's?" she wails. "Those bastards, those racist bastards!"

Errol hears Terry come over to ask her about it. Apparently too furious, or distraught, to talk further, she hands him the phone, and Errol runs through it again: the detectives, the apartment, and Clayton himself. Terry groans, biting back his own anger, as Errol fills in details. Near the end of the account, Terry realizes he needs to inform the lawyer, Arnie, and begs off, promising to call back later.

Slowly replacing the receiver, Errol turns to Christine and Fin, feeling as if he's floating off somewhere, away from the here-and-now. To lesser extents, the other two share this, as their grip on what's right feels shaken and shattered. For Kenny's release and return home, they're happy; that his place has been thoroughly ransacked, and that employees of the city have done this, they're bewildered; that he is distraught, they can understand; that there seems little they can do, indeed that Clayton displayed no interest in communicating with them, leaves them . . . at sea.

"So, well . . . what now?" breathes Errol.

All three pick at the question.

Errol recognizes that part of his own discomfort arises from Clayton's withholding any sign of recognition, and while he understands the probable cause—the man's world has been tossed upside down, leaving him sore, wiped, angry—he wonders if his own efforts were wrong-headed, pointless . . . in vain? . . . Don't think we did it for our own purposes; shouldn't have been any big deal, between neighbors. Didn't think I was lookin' for a thanks . . . Yet obviously I'm missing something.

Christine, gripped by a similar internal debate, guesses at Errol's distress and offers, "Errol, given what he's been through, to expect him to put things aside and return to business as usual, is just not realistic." Uncomfortably Errol nods, not wanting to make his own disappointment the focus. Fin raises another point through his swollen lip: "Ih we wanna wri ih up ih some way, sink he see id as a pwob-wem?"

Errol briefly looks at his injured friend before allowing that he bears some responsibility for Clayton's privacy. "He might . . . I mean, I could understand . . ." But then he imagines the flip side: "On the other hand, the publicity might help his case." By chance glancing at the kitchen entrance, he finds Molly and Lilly watching and reading his concern. He sends them a disconsolate smile, which only Lilly in some measure returns. Molly stands long-faced and unhappy. Errol's thoughts fall back to Clayton. "Most likely, he needs a little time."

This leaves them silent, stalled. Just then, they hear the front door creak open and see the two girls run out to the door, crying "Momma! Momma! . . . Mommie!"

As Christine and Fin turn toward the hallway, they glimpse Errol's features tightening, before the approaching footsteps draw their eyes to the doorway. There, Leslie, still in her coat, holding Molly, Lilly in tow, steps in, registering first surprise and then swallowed annoyance.

Errol, in a flat, withdrawn tone, introduces the visitors, "Leslie, this is Christine and Fin."

Leslie takes in each without welcome or pleasure.

"Les," continues Errol, determined to make his point, "Clayton's home, released. I don't know whether you took a look or not . . ."

"No, I did not. I had to work today, at least until I learned, from Molly, that the police and others were here. I told my boss I had to go home to look after my girls, seeing as I couldn't be sure anyone else was."

Not pleased with her account, Errol looks away, irritation working his jaw, but she takes no notice. Christine and Fin feel uncomfortably caught in the middle and worry they are complicating things. Errol's eyes escape to the ceiling—dully white, cracking, crying for paint. What can you say or do with this woman? As nothing else presents itself, he turns back to Leslie and explains, "Leslie, I was either in the apartment or right outside in the hall . . ."

"You might have made it clear to the girls," she jabs. "You might have let *me* know." But her tense voice suggests this would not have placated her, having little or no interest in the underlying episode.

Christine feels compelled to speak up. "Leslie, I came down here on my own. I wanted to see what the police had done to Clayton's apartment."

Placing Molly down, inhaling with slimly veiled displeasure, Leslie begins taking off her coat. "Somebody else's apartment is not my concern. Errol, however, knows I prefer to be informed of any guests coming here. Indeed I expect that courtesy. Unfortunately I have to work five days a week, no matter the weather,"—a complaint clearly directed against her husband.

Christine sees that Leslie is not disposed to acknowledge anything related to Clayton's plight. She barely acknowledges Fin or her, and it seems likely that the level of anger on display did not originate with this incident. Probably it's best to leave. "Errol, I've got to get back. I'll fill Terry and Viv in on the details." But Errol, caught by other currents, can only vaguely respond, with a twitch of his lower lip, a flick of his eyes.

Fin, feeling similar discomfort, follows suit, "Lie-wise, Err, I mus ge ba d' off-iss." Glancing at Leslie, he finds her draping her coat over a chair, then surveying the unwashed dishes piled around the sink. While his gaze returns to Errol, it is her he now addresses, "D' in-ordan ding, Les-lie, is Claydon's ou. And I'd say widdou Er-ros eff-orss . . . his carin' 'n' concern, 'n' leadashi, he wun' ee . . ."

But Leslie exhibits not the slightest interest—indeed only sour distaste. Refocusing his attention on Errol, Fin finds that his friend's eyes have grown distant, in part, he supposes, from his hope to offer his guests some tea or coffee while together trying to make sense out of the whole thing. But Leslie's arrival has cut that off, cut it right off at the knees.

Christine steps over to Errol to shake hands, enclosing his with both of hers, her smile embracing him with sincere appreciation, and Fin follows, gently cuffing Errol's shoulder and sending him a rueful, fraternal smile. Then both turn away, wave to the girls, call goodbye to Leslie, back turned and silent at the sink, and leave.

Together they swiftly descend the stairs, minds still held by the unexpected turn and tone of events, and in a matter of moments are outside heading west on Broome Street toward the day's last patches of gray light. Their burrowing thoughts replay the wintry moments with Leslie, until Christine can contain it no longer, "Poor Errol . . . to hear that, after all he did."

Under the assault of images and growing pain in his jaw, Fin feels his brain shudder, as both of them are herded along by the crush of memories, wondering how far back these troubles reach—even as the cramping cold sends them working deeper into their coats. Fin's eyes slide her way to read her concern, but her visible distress sends them reeling away to where the buildings, with their patches of snow, seem to mirror her mournful mood. The facades, coated in muddied browns, sooty, peeling beige or creams, rusted reds, are all dimmed by the dying light. A hundred years ago or more, these buildings were new and fashionable, but now, Fin reflects, with few exceptions, they convey neglect, and their architectural flourishes—the towers, parapets, and cupolas that once enlivened them—are now hidden by advertisements, cheap paint, grime, dangling fire escapes, and snow.

Winding along the imperfect path next to him, Christine permits her thoughts to replay the confrontations and gaping rifts back on that top floor, and she supposes that those they witnessed are not alone. In all likelihood, similar stories are being played out behind the neighboring walls, in those lighted spaces that people like herself call home. How many of the residents must be caught up by bad choices, or a lack of choices, or by betrayal or bad luck?

*   *   *

Standing like a statue bowed over the sink, Errol watches the water run over the pot he is slowly scrubbing. Leslie has retreated to their bedroom to change out of her work clothes, and the two girls are in their bedroom playing with dolls and costumes, their soft, high voices a distant balm to Errol's despair. As he scrubs and rinses, he replays the fraying of connections and wonders why so many around him have worn thin. Is it something in him?

Leslie, tugging her bathrobe over her pajamas, is trying to remember what there might be in the house for supper, having resigned herself to its preparation, because getting Errol to turn out even one dish properly is usually a losing proposition. Directions and he just don't work. And now, most likely, he'll be moping over my lack of hospitality to the two barflies he invited in. But he never consulted me, never asked if I'd mind, never considered the girls. What does he expect, an open house? . . . As for that fellow down the hall, who knows what *his* story is. You're tellin' me the cops find their way up to that one apartment by some fluke? Please . . . More likely the guy's past simply caught up with him.

Scraping away the grease from lunch in an iron pan with a brillo pad, Errol gains grim satisfaction in slowly prevailing, leaving faint trails of suds across its surface. The phone rings, and slowly he raises his doleful eyes in its direction. It rings again, and from the bedroom comes Leslie's irritated cry, "Answer the phone, somebody!" Reluctantly Errol steps over, drying his hands on a dish towel, and after another ring, picks up the noisome thing.

"Yo, dude," comes the familiar, froggy greeting.

"Hey, Lou," mutters Errol, his spirit rising and falling in the same instant.

"What's the latest? You still bummed?"

"Clayton got released. He's home."

"All right! . . . That's cool. How is he? Okay?"

Errol inhales. ". . . Not great . . ."

"You talk to him?"

A painful topic. "Yeah . . . but he wanted to be alone."

"Also bummed, huh?"

"Yeah . . . Said he has a lawyer."

"Well that's good! Right? I mean now he can squeeze the city for its fuck-up." Lou reminds himself, however, that in some long drawn-out way this means spiriting even more tax money out of his own pocket. But hey, it's gonna go anyway, right? To one no-account fat cat or another wound into the system. So why not, once in a while, to the deserving, to some poor police victim? Lou recalls the faces at the precinct last night. Not your sympathetic crew, not your ideal public servants. Far from it. I mean where would this country be if George Washington and the boys behaved like that? Running rough-shod over everyone. Who woulda hung with *him* through thick and thin? "So Errol, my man, whassup? I'd say let's get a beer, but I'm dining with Reenie. Prelude to a little action, at long last. She loves playin' the prick-teaser."

Errol can barely attend. ". . . Yeah, well . . . good . . ."

"Hey . . . Moll and little Lilly musta had fun playin' wit' you in the snow, man."

Vaguely Errol remembers. "Yeah . . . It seems I do better with things like that."

"Oh come on, my man . . . You know what you need? . . . A boy, a kid you can play ball with."

Errol's mind stalls. "Not in the cards."

". . . What? Leslie don't want one?'

Errol breathes deeply. "Lilly was it. We're done . . . I had one of those—you know, procedures."

"You're kidding? . . . But what if . . . ?"

"What if what!?"

". . . I guess not . . . Still, I can't see myself doing it."

"You do it *after* the kids arrive, Lou-is."

". . . I guess . . . As a matter of fact, Reenie and I talked the whole shebang once; said she wants me ready, intact, just in case."

Errol's mind clouds. His thoughts fight for light but lose their way. Just then Leslie comes into the kitchen to start supper. She ignores Errol, who nonetheless feels uneasy about continuing the conversation. In a low voice, he tells Lou, "I may go see if Kenny needs something."

"Peace, man, is what he needs. I mean if he's got a lawyer."

"Yeah, well . . . call you tomorrow."

"Hey man, cheer up, the guy's out. Right? Maybe our efforts helped, helped speed the process. Maybe he'll get a couple a mil from the city, who knows?"

"Yeah, maybe . . . Talk to you."

They hang up. Errol, without a word to Leslie, leaves the pan and drifts out of the kitchen, toward the front door. From behind him, Lilly calls, "Dad! Look!"

Errol stops by the door and turns. Lilly and Molly, tied together by a sash, are both draped in white, angelic, gauzy things, carrying their dolls. They stop to show him, arms spread, dolls in hand, faces beaming.

"Isn't it pretty?" prompts Lilly.

"It is, Lil. You both look . . . like ballerinas." He smiles at them, wondering if he should go give them a hug, though Molly is not usually too receptive. But the girls are smiling back as together they negotiate a full circle, Lilly holding her skirt up like a little dancer. Errol wonders where she got that from. Maybe she'll do ballet one day. Now both girls wave and, wobbling on their toes, titter forward into the kitchen. Errol stares for a moment at the spot where they were, then turns again and steps out of the apartment, closing the door quietly behind.

Tip-toeing, he steals down to Clayton's bashed-in door. Listening for a moment, he leans and peers in. Clayton has returned to the living room, having showered and put on clean clothes, and is kneeling down by his desk rescuing negatives, filters, and other photographic equipment. Errol watches his hand move slowly, hovering over items, before picking them up and placing them in one of several boxes. Errol feels an unexpected sadness fill his chest. ". . . Clayton?"

Stiffly the other peers back over his shoulder. With his thoughts far away, it takes a moment to register just exactly who's calling. When he recognizes Errol, he waits to see what the guy wants.

Errol now steps around the corner, half-filling the door, swallowing his awkwardness, and asks, "Just wanted to see if you need anything . . . a hand or something."

Clayton feels himself carefully draw in a long, shallow breath within his aching ribs. He looks down over his still-strewn belongings. What's this guy want? Me to say everything's just fine? Okey-doke? I'm cool? Clayton's thoughts slide off, called by memories of the arrest: unable to get his footing, nothing covering him, dragged past pasty-faced Errol watching in his doorway. Then his mind falls further back, to his apartment before it was ransacked, to his so-called girl, Yvonne, some weeks ago, before things went bad, soured by her prima-donna expectations, detached, as they always were, from reality.

He shifts himself around on his knees so that he can see Errol more easily, remembering the few times they've spoken. Something a little sad about him. Said he writes plays, though I never hearda one, and said he teaches. Now there's two low-end, dead-end jobs for you. What's he thinkin'? . . . And his wife—I've passed her a few times, plastering that big, false, couldn't-care-less smile. Two losers for you, which is what I *don't* need right now.

He recalls a pair of cops, a few weeks back, in street clothes, had stopped him on the block one evening, asking him for I.D., telling him he looked like someone they were looking for. He didn't say a thing, just showed them his license and credit card, told them where he works. Betcha those motherfuckers sent a unit out anyway, just to shove their fuckin' power in my face. Show they can trash any damn place, particularly a brother's.

Clayton finds Errol again. The guy's just standing there, like a scarecrow, like he's got nothin' better to do. What's he want? What am I gonna say to him? "Hey man . . . you don't have to stand there 'n' watch. This is gonna take a long time."

Errol blinks as he nods. His mind scrambles for something to say, while his memory re-winds back through day and night. He half-steps back. But when Clayton sees he doesn't disappear, he asks, "You need something?"

Errol doesn't follow and shakes his head. "Just wanted to see if you . . . uh, need a hand."

Clayton studies him, muttering to himself, yeah, the guy seems lost, sad. Then one thing occurs to him. "Hey man, you know any cleaning services 'round here?"

Errol thinks. "I could look in the phone book . . ."

"I got a phone book. That's one thing they didn't rip."

They stare at one another. Clayton feels his impatience returning. "Listen, I got a lot to do. You mind grantin' me a little privacy, seein' as I don't have a door?"

Errol's mind somersaults back, away, and his body follows, retreating a step, until he remembers, "Hey, glad to be a witness . . . if your lawyer or you need one."

Clayton meets his gaze and nods in acceptance. Errol experiences a faint eddy of relief, before moving out of the other's sight, toward his apartment. Yet something's pressuring his skull. He brings both hands up to press back. Did I say something wrong? The guy's pissed, sure . . . Unfortunately this thick, gummed-up void I call my brain can't seem to figure any of it out.

Clayton, by himself again, looks down at the belongings he's trying to assemble. He searches for another box, thinking as he does that most of the white people he's met down in this building are, well . . . odd, lost types—something's off. Not like Mr. Park, my boss at the photo shop. Korean. All business, no patter, no questions, so long as I show up. Henry said he'd call him. Hope to God I still *have* my job. That's what I need, man. Second thing, what am I gonna do with this place? How am I gonna live here? The pigs' prints are everywhere, ripped open the mattress . . . ruined my negatives, all my chemicals gone . . . didn't even leave me a door.

*   *   *

Christine and Fin turn north up Broadway into a black-and-white-evening landscape resembling an Antarctic ice shelf, dotted with penguins rocking stiffly over the glassy sheets. Their minds skate quickly back through the recent encounters. Christine attempts to imagine the impact on Errol of the two less-than-appreciative responses to his efforts, and she wonders what series of disappointments could have closed off Leslie. Or has petulance long been her reaction to Errol's diffuse exertions?

Fin, in the course of trying to understand Kenny's despair, feels his jaw unexpectedly loosening, lubricated, perhaps, by the rush of images from the arrest and return. How could it happen that those cops bashed their way into Kenny's apartment and then compounded it by humiliating him? Could the gun explain it? And how alienating for Kenny to recognize that he alone in the building was victim of the cops' screw-up—a horror compounded by mounting disrespect, despite the array of modern tools and sensitivity training available to the department. Fin glances at the alert, Athena-like face next to him and tries to reconstruct the order of events that have brought her here. Did it flow from the cops' actions, or Errol's reaction, or her decisions and his? Is it possible to follow the threads, or are the strands too many? While he suspects she would be just as happy walking with Errol or Joseph, his own excitement soars above the skyline, propelled by his hope that their conversation will rise to a higher plane.

Curious about his silence, she slides her eyes over, only to encounter him studying her, whereupon he flushes—a side of him, she hasn't seen before. She wonders if he has so soon put aside Kenny's troubles and Errol's . . . though maybe it's healthier to move on, put things behind you. But she finds that she cannot. "Fin, I was thinking that if only someone could talk to Leslie, or suggest something to Errol—bring some help or intervention . . . Do you think he'd welcome that? . . . Would she? . . . What's your guess?"

Fin squints ahead into the darkness settling down over the glowing white, blurring boundaries and detail. Good night, Angelina, where is it you ride?—the plaintive tones and lyrics of a folk melody, conveying opacity between lovers, sound in his head . . . . Wonder if music moves her? Would she want to listen together sometime? . . . But then he remembers her query. "I suspect Errol would be taken aback . . . shocked, by our talking about him . . . baffled by our interest. How could we possibly know enough . . . about him or his marriage, when he may not himself? . . . I suspect he'd be horrified to learn we're thinking about him, and making judgements."

Closing her eyes, imagining dread eating into Errol's pale face, she allows that this may well be so, similar as it is to the dismay she experiences when men approach her without the slightest understanding of who she is. She releases an uneasy sigh, before resetting her thoughts. "Errol must think he's invisible . . . even to us."

Yes, grants Fin, but then who believes himself or herself to be clearly and completely seen? Now his attention shifts back to her, her generous nature, her noble profile, her clear eyes, which continue to avoid his . . . Good night, Angelina, where is it you go-o? My words of true love were whispered too lo-w . . . He assumes she carries burdens, as we all do, but what can they be? Nothing close to the ones borne by those they've just left. And what about the depth of his own concerns? . . . There are moments when he is not without charity . . . or is it a pose . . . to get into her pants? The truth, as ever, must lie somewhere in the murky middle, in the discomfiting, mysterious, murky middle.

Now she is wondering, "What could have attracted those two originally?" Not that she doesn't understand attractions radiate beyond the rational, when people are young and dreamy.

Head rolling, Fin's brain scrambles for an answer. "People change, right? Leslie may have been more accepting and fun and attractive when young, or maybe Errol was . . . or maybe it was a case of opposites attracting. I can see that living with Errol could be . . . bewildering, as he seems to get easily derailed and wanders off unable to quite get back on track." Fin winces at his slatternly cliché, but Christine isn't diverted. "And yet he's a good soul. I wonder if Leslie recognizes that." She thinks of Daniel and her own one or two truly close friends . . . What holds us together? . . .

As Fin walks, heart thumping, he feels the stiffness returning to his jaw. Angelina, Angelina, he silently cries, may I sing to you her-e? . . . But alas, undeniably his jaw has locked, frozen by the cold and his too-eager jawing—muscles turned to metal, lips glued by his own blood. He tries to pop them apart, but manages only to rip a strip of outer skin, freeing not words but an anguished cry, "Chris—stee-nn!"

"What?" Christine glances over. "You okay?" she asks, though her thoughts linger back with Errol and Leslie. "Despite everything, it seems Errol's a good dad to those little girls, each of whom is quite distinct and watches him so differently. I hope they sense his love. I found it painful to see the rift between the parents, for the unspoken sadness that clouded the girls' eyes." She looks over to see if he noticed.

With care he bows, picturing the two faces, even as his fingers lightly investigate his lower lip and his jaw, which is tender and burning. Somehow it all encircles him like a thick, cold fog: Errol's distress, the injustice done to Kenny, Leslie's discontent, the little girls' apprehension, and his own pain . . . So much desperation . . . nursed by no common tongue in time of one common cry, he recites from somewhere. And now, when finally the opportunity to talk with Christine has come, my mouth is clamped, welded, and the merry Fates laugh at me, taunt me, as maybe I deserve. He decides to make one last Samsonian effort, to force apart mandibles and lips, come-what-may. But his determination only tears more layers, strains tendons, shoots pain through skull and jaw, then down his neck . . . Yie! . . . What will men not do for forbidden love? he jeers to himself. Desperately he finds her eyes and tries: "Err-ol . . . 'ss so inn-no-sin . . . He be-leaves 'eople 'r' like him . . ."

"What?" asks Christine, not quite catching it. Throwing a closer glance his way, she sees that his lip has begun to bleed again, and she reaches for and takes back her scarf from his hand to gently wipe the blood where it has run along his chin and down his neck. His hairs stand up; his eyes widen, as intently he watches her ministrations, thinking he may burst. Angelina! Angel—lina! What is it you d-o? But then she is finished, and her hand, gone from the masthead, is pushing the scarf back into his. "There. I think the bleeding's stopped," she tells him, frowning at the raw lip. "Maybe keep still for a bit," she suggests, looking into his eyes to gauge the pain.

Aware that his sight and other senses are growing faint, he inhales rapidly. Above, birds flutter in the branches, and cymbals crash, it seems, while a white-hot snap of pain shoots out stars of excruciating beauty—as nearby, through his swaying, stuttering vision, he finds that she is close, yet absorbed in her own thoughts. Another muffled moan escapes his parted jaw, held in a mannequin's smile, as he struggles to maintain his balance along this electrifying mountain ridge, lest he trip again and tumble down the long slope into darkness.

With concern Christine takes his elbow, urging him to resume their walk, patting his upper arm, hoping he won't swoon into the snow, for how would she get him up? Her thoughts drift back to the group, wondering what holds it together—odd mixtures that we are. She checks Fin scuttling ahead, before her thoughts return to Errol, dear, earnest Errol. She wonders how deeply the incident will scar him, as it must Kenny. "Too bad, Fin, the two men won't talk, and exchange reactions to what happened," she says. "It's so outrageous of the police and city to allow this, and then not admit their error. How can they deny it or try to justify it? . . . I understand the cops have a tough job, but part of it is to defuse situations, not ignite new ones; to make things better in a community, not add to the problems. There must be a way to balance toughness and care." She stares down at the snow-covered walk over which she glides.

Fin nods in agreement, but fumes from his grinding cerebral gears are collecting and choking him, without the venting of speech. Twice today he has been blind-sided by wading unheedingly into the wrong place at the wrong moment, and now he is muzzled by the wounds. Groaning, he hurls his eyes upward, raking the now blank, gray sky and dark buildings. But as he does, he trips and stumbles ahead and partially into her, so that for a second time, she must catch and steady him. Halting, bending at the waist, placing hands on knees to regain balance and breath, he sucks in air and chagrin, then attempts to expel them, along with the pain and embarrassment. She, able to see only the top of his swaying head, urges, "Fin, maybe you should sit down for a minute."

Loathe to meet her eyes, he slurs, "Mm o-kay . . ." But she is recalling the policeman's punch cracking into his chin. "That cop really bashed you."

Gradually straightening, assisted by her sympathy, he wonders whether to relate the other incident back on Elizabeth Street, as he would very much like to, before he remembers he can't . . . not now, with his lips shellacked shut.

Watching creases of discomfort course up his face, she questions, "Fin, do you think you should see a doctor? Or go to an emergency room?"

His eyes leap back to sky, into which he wishes he could fly, recover, then land again next to her, reborn, able to talk. Instead he closes his eyes, shivers, and shakes his head. She tightens her hold on his elbow, to steady him, but he, wanting to show that he's strong and fit, pulls free and moves ahead a half-step as they push on. She follows, sticking close, holding his coat, fearful that he might slip or pass out.

And so for a time they proceed silently. In the evening light the streets have become dream-like, as the drifts harden into shining shapes, and pedestrians waltz and weave over the ice, all held in an envelope of eerie quiet. The cold and the quiet were good for writing today, she thinks, and wonders if Dan was successful. From just behind Fin's shoulder, she notices that he casts an odd, lumpy—lumpen—outline: tall and sturdy, yet bent, head tilted to one side, hair disheveled, both young and old. Of all the members of the group, he seems the least defined and settled, liable to lurch in any direction. If Dan has a quiet gravity and focus and thoughtfulness, Fin seems precariously poised at a moment when possibilities, and maybe temptations, remain open, before life-directing decisions are made—a time in life that has long intrigued her.

Unable to speak, Fin focuses his mind on the street ahead, trying to define its colors, its purples and grays, and watching the bundled passersby, round as snowmen. A shiver drops through him, and he realizes it's grown colder. Where's his body heat gone? Expended in confrontations, old stone? . . . Drawn off into the granite and mortar crumbling around him. Gravity grinding and settling—time's requiem . . . Of all of us in the group, Errol deserves better. Yet how to arrange it? . . . Therapy? . . . Doubtful . . . When the group first gathered, there had seemed to be hope that a successful play might somehow elevate Errol's life, broaden his world, bring in a little money, raise his stature in Leslie's eyes, but recently that has faded, and then, this afternoon, additional blows. Kenny, at least, from the little we know, has more flexibility, being younger, unattached, seemingly free to pursue his photography.

Fin turns partly back toward Christine, still at his shoulder, to mumble something of this, but her thoughts, too, have been racing, and seeking his eyes, she spills them out, "Fin, you know I was married before . . . but was lucky enough to get out of it, when I saw it wasn't working, with a minimum of acrimony and pain—whereas Errol probably doesn't have that option, with those two dear daughters and . . . I don't know how long they've been married. Do you?"

Fin twists more completely around to her, shaking his head, then studying her and considering her news. He hopes his surprise, at her marriage, does not show. Yet he feels it casts her in a different light . . . a little older . . . a woman of experience . . . But then he hears her continuing, "I found it unexpectedly chilling to come face to face with another's implacable views . . . One dimly recognizes that only through compromise can things thaw . . . but with Leslie that seems improbable. I may be wrong, but it appears her anger and frustration are so deeply rooted that there is little room to maneuver."

Fin, too, sees little hope, nodding heavily, heedfully, before he hears her add, "Yet it can't be easy with Errol. As you said, his emotions sweep him up so completely that there seems to be a certain obliviousness to the practical . . . which may be good for a playwright, but exasperating to those close."

The two ponder these thoughts as they reach Houston Street and stop to wait for the light. Carefully they take each other in, and Fin, feeling his pain easing a bit, is able to appreciate their exchange of observations and ideas—an exchange more prolonged and fluid than those with Sam, shared without emotionalism, egoism, or fear . . . At the same time, he becomes aware that something is rising into and filling his eyes. What? . . . Happiness? Have these blows and the misery he's encountered, loosened a screw, so that feelings flow at the slightest provocation? . . .

As they step out together to cross the street, Christine, too, realizes that she welcomes this opportunity to reflect on events, and welcomes the friendship they've found. She foresees possible exchanges around their work and craft—exchanges that Dan may well want to join.

Ahead lies snow-covered Washington Square Park, a writhing, hilly expanse glowing in the descending dark, as occasional gusts lift sparkling snow curtains off the tops of drifts, and, despite the hour, children play in its open spaces, their dark forms running, calling, and darting as they arc snowballs through the dark, purple sky. From the park, the friends' respective routes home will diverge, and so the two come to a halt.

"Fin," she begins, "could I show you a draft report on this incident, when I get a few interviews? . . . You've written on these issues, written well, I've thought."

He studies her, surprised by her compliment, for she has never really commented on his columns or reports before. For a moment, gazing at her, he loses her question . . . but then recovers, mumbling, "Ss-ur', luv ta."

She cannot help but smile at his restricted speech, assuming it will not hinder him long. "Thanks . . . I'm so sorry about your jaw and lip. Hope they'll heal soon, and I've enjoyed our talk and walk." She smiles again, recognizing that most of the talk has been hers. "Thanks . . . and good night."

The mention of night once more lifts his eyes to the now darker sky, where a soft gray haze sits above the expanse of the park, and wrings, yet again, faint moisture from his eyes. He *has* become maudlin, if the mere sky can summon this. It must be more than the sky . . . Yet to the west, above the buildings, two twilight cracks of blue rekindle the coals of his dreams, despite his body reminding him of its pain and fatigue. When he finds her again, she is waiting, apparently happily, and she extends her hand in 'good night.' He stares down at its gloved form, and quickly bends, bringing the supple calfskin to his lips and planting a kiss on its cold, pliable surface. She releases a final smile as she meets his eye, before reclaiming her hand, swinging around, and walking off.

He watches her go, wondering if she will look back. But then he remembers the bloodied scarf lent to him, stuffed in his pocket, and he dashes after her. Catching her midway across the park, near the fountain, he calls through his clenched jaw, "Cwis, Cwis . . ." She slows and turns, eyebrows rising.

"Y' scaff," he blurts, pulling it out. Only now does it occur to him that he should have it cleaned or that it may be ruined. Hesitantly, he holds it out halfway. "Sanks . . . bu . . . I shuh ge ih clean firs . . ."

With a laugh, she reaches and takes it back, murmuring through some distraction, "A token of the day." She looks at him. "It has been quite a night and day, hasn't it." He feels his cheeks burn again, and feels a painful twinge as a smile tries to stretch out from his eyes. But renewing his determination to repay her, he faintly grumbles, "Real . . . I c'd ge ih clea' f' you."

She shakes her head, her lively eyes laughing. "No, not necessary . . . Better to allot that time to our work." He studies her. She seems quite straight about this. This time it is he who extends a hand. "Sanks."

Quickly, lightly, she stretches forward and bestows a brief kiss near his swollen lip—quite surprising him in the gesture and in the resulting pain from his sudden recoil—a pain that suffuses his jaw and cheek, nearly blotting out his sight. Not quite knowing what he's doing, he reaches awkwardly for her shoulders to pull her to him, holding her against him for a brief eternity. For that split second, the lights do go out, and he is floating weightlessly above the park, picturing her face, feeling her lips painfully through his. But then he feels her fingers and hands prying and pushing herself out of his grasp—successfully with a shove and a cry—and both are falling back a step. He experiences, in the same instant, both thrill and horror at what he's done, as she wavers before him, regaining her balance, surveying him through flashing eyes. She seems about to say something—What was that?!—just as he is mentally cringing and asking himself the same. Now he can see that blood pressed from his lip has been dabbed along hers, and as he stares at it, she becomes aware of it herself and tries to wipe it away with a swipe of her gloved hand. This erases some but smears faint streaks over her chin and upper lip. Still stunned, she tries again to comprehend, examining him unhappily, uncertainly, with trembling disappointment . . . After all we talked about? . . . Or was it my fault? A profusion of thoughts rush and thrash through her mind. But wanting only to leave, she pulls herself around. Feeling her lips sticking, and trying to moisten and clean them, she strides, then runs off through the stinging air.

*   *   *

Off the phone with his friend and lawyer Arnie, Terry feels the incident draining out of him, not without regret. If things are beginning to feel resolved and cleared, so that he can get on with his own work, he also feels troubled, suspecting their efforts were in vain, for what really did they accomplish?

Gazing across the room as he picks up his pen, he sees that Viv is applying preliminary strokes, setting the scene on a new canvas. On the floor near her, the kids are coloring large sheets of brown wrapping paper, creating a snowscape dotted with hills and white trees and colorful childlike figures. Feeling love for his family, he steps over behind to look more closely. Viv's is an interior, the bar maybe, framed by walls of somber, shadowed yellow and the outlines of wooden chairs and tables. Ceiling lights cast faint halos above sketched, bent figures at the bar who seem to face past each other. Terry expels a breath, which Viv hears, and while she does not look back as she dabs the first strokes of figures seated around a table, she does ask, "What'd Arnie say?"

"He said fine, not unexpected that he has a lawyer. Said we did what we could."

Vivian puckers, not sold. "Probably it was Clayton's lawyer who got him released," she thinks aloud, now roughing in those seated patrons. Terry sucks his cheeks a bit, leafing back through the anxiety, the calls, the discussions. Much of her reaction arose, he knows, from the time when they were stopped. He expels another breath, turns, and pulls himself back to his desk, lowering himself onto his chair, trying to decide where to begin. Vaguely a dream from last night returns: a wounded figure, a wrecked apartment, shattered furniture. The figure extends a hand to touch the splintered chair arms and table legs . . . What connections do we seek from these things with which we live? Kinship? Emblems of ourselves? Affirmation? An enduring worth bestowed upon them, embodied in them, and reflected back upon ourselves? . . . If I can sort that out, I may try to render it . . . in my own expressionist style. His gaze returns to Viv, who, with lighter, quicker strokes, is outlining the juke box, doing so with what almost appears to be agitation, in the process of which she calls over, "One thing I know for sure . . . I'm not going back to the bar."

A dying cry falls through Terry's chest. His mind stops, then flails for explanation, "Why?" Yet he knows.

"What I said last night: too many of them make me uncomfortable." She glances down at the children, who don't appear to be listening, but probably are, at least to her tone. "They don't have a clue," she mutters. Terry feels his eyes fall to his work as he consciously avoids looking her way. He pictures the friends: some alert, aware, some more mature, some less . . . but over all, not bad-hearted. He struggles to formulate a preference, "I wouldn't want to . . . just abandon them."

"Don't! . . . Don't stop going for me. I'm just saying *I'm* not goin' back. I don't need to listen to their crap again. And we can save on sitters."

"I guess I'd wanta hear their thoughts, wanta discuss the whole thing," he confesses uneasily. "Get a sense of what everybody made of it . . . After that, I suppose, I could wrap it up, at some point . . ."

"Do what you need to do. I am."

Nodding to himself, he explains, "I felt that we made an attempt, to do something." His eyes rise to survey some of his paintings on the far wall. The good ones, the best, were conceived out of some emotion, some passionate thought, or feeling, or view of life. But he fears he's lost the ability to sense those things. He's grown too concerned with how his work will seem or fit in. Something has intervened between his emotions and his translation of them onto the canvas. He has long hoped that running the gallery, selling paintings for other artists, along with his own and Viv's, was something useful and noble, but the struggle of staying just ahead of bankruptcy has worn much of that away. The reality has become too apparent: that it's just selling, selling like any other selling—only with inflated expectations, and hype, on everybody's part. The people for whom they'd had hopes, turned out to be . . . well, all too human, whether the artists, the museum people, the customers and patrons, the landlord and suppliers. All squeezing or draining what they can, in their universal self-absorption. He pictures the best of his work, whose planes and patterns, shapes and colors somehow suggest relationships, connections, emotion . . . but those are a relative few, and he's sold only a handful. So what's the point? . . . His own satisfaction, which may be an illusion? . . . He would have thought that the scant attention his paintings have drawn should have long ago cleansed him of that vanity.

So what to do? Continue preparing the publicity for the next exhibition? . . . Or pull out the teaching applications he's collected? . . . Can't start a new picture today. Deliberately he draws in a deep breath, hoping his mind will clear and give birth to new ideas. Somewhere in the rotating haze of unformed notions, he hears the downstairs buzzer sound and stares over at it. None of the other three moves or seems to have heard. It may be a customer. He alone is holding the gallery together. Heavily he rises and scuffs to the door. It is, he hears, Joseph, with his son, Noah. He buzzes them in. Looking around, he meets Viv's none-too-happy gaze thrown back at him over her shoulder.

*   *   *

Heeling like an over-sheeted sloop, Fin veers with fatigue through his newspaper office, eyeing the lay line to his desk in a far corner. Only two others are in the half-dark place, and glancing up, they lazily salute Fin, who returns their greetings with a tuckered smile. On the surface all get along in the office, but of course below, it gets more complicated. Fin realizes that he never had lunch, which may partially explain why his legs are lead, and, oh yes, too little sleep as well. God . . . He drops into his chair, shivering from hunger, exhaustion, pain, and emotion cut short. Physical complaints clamor for attention: his stinging lip, his aching jaw, his tummy doing flips. And somewhere in his head, he's confusing what happened with Sam and with Christine, and Jesus, not to mention poor Kenny and Errol. Together it all but knocks him out as he tilts his head back and slides down in his chair, lifting his dead legs up onto his desk. His eyelids, once these improvements are complete, snap shut. Inside the black planetarium of his mind's eye, stars, comets, and planets, wanderers all, are moving every which way. His mind reaches up for one of them, but encounters something sharp, solid—a rocky planet maybe, or next week's column . . . Yes, write up Kenny's story, without comet or comment, just the bare facts, from the rocky Martian desert. Let this story, this miscarriage, this embarrassment stare the city in the face, this city which some believe to be the capital of the known world. Opening his eyes he lunges for a pen and pad, to begin jotting, but after a few desultory phrases, the pen slips from his fingers, and his eyes re-close. Sam, naked, is sliding up to him; he can almost reach her hip, and bottom. On the other side of him Christine is waiting, arms folded. She too may be naked, but now he can't find her. Instead the cop from Central Booking is seated there, facing him, watching him coolly, thinking, Fin suspects, that he's a lightweight, a flake. And Kenny too, looking none too happy—the three forming an isosceles triangle, Kenny reaching for the apex—a quake-quake-proof design, he's read. Then he notices that someone, bless him, is bringing dinner, steaming steaks—Peter, waiting tables tonight, glowering. Fin fears he will dump the entire steaming tray into his lap. He sits up, eyes batting open. Might as well go home 'n' crash . . . But oh . . . Sam . . . ? He pictures her face, the moods that flow across it. Then dials her office number. Unexpectedly she picks up, returning his hello with a limp, "Hi . . ." Something in her voice stirs apprehension. Warily he asks, "How ih go? . . . By d' way, Kenny was re-leese." His jaw has relaxed just enough to form a few simple syllables.

There's a pause, before a moan escapes, stretching over the line. "Kenny? . . . Well, good . . . I'm glad, glad for him . . ." She coughs, inhales, then in a low voice reveals, "Peter went nuts . . . hit me . . . destroyed everything of mine in the apartment."

"Wha? . . . Aie . . . yie yie . . ." Fin feels his head sway, his spirits fall back, plummeting down an elevator shaft. "You okay?"

"No . . . Didn't you hear what I said? He hit me . . . They had to call the police."

"Jee—zze . . . Well, I'll come uuhh . . ."

"You can't," her whisper warns. "The cops are still here."

". . . D' cops? . . ."

"They put him on notice—restraining order." She releases a long breath.

"Ho—ly . . ." Fin, wondering how much he's responsible, struggles to get past the pounding in his head. His chest, twisted tight, seems wound round by a major rubber band.

"You there?" she wonders, detecting a just-discernable rasp.

"Yesss . . ."

She inhales. "He destroyed all my stuff . . . all my family heirlooms." She cannot prevent a sob, which she hurriedly sniffs back. Fin attempts to picture this, though he's never been there, doesn't know what she had.

"Peter guessed about us, told the cops. Called me a 'fuck-around.'"

Fin sits up straight in his chair . . . wonders what to say, what to offer.

". . . Sorr . . . y"

"Don't be . . . It was my decision."

Was it? he wonders. Was it even a decision?

"A friend here has offered me a spare room," she tells him, "for as long as I need it."

"You . . . weh-come t' m' couch," he offers hastily, hesitantly. He hears a soft, nasal laugh. ". . . No . . . no thanks . . ."

"If you-rr suck."

"It's okay, Fin . . . Why are you talking funny?" But her need to draw in a deep breath pulls her mind elsewhere. "The whole thing is just . . . unreal . . ." she murmurs. "It's wiped out a part of me, part of my family . . . part of everything that meant anything . . . I didn't realize how vulnerable

I was, how brittle he is . . . how precarious it all is . . ." Fin hears another swallowed sob.

"But I'm going to make him pay," she says, her voice stronger, even as it's cracking. "I'm suing him, suing him good. A friend here knows a lawyer."

A lawyer? He feels annoyance at Peter, and anger at his weird behavior, at his violence toward her, for hitting her, for the destruction . . . Jee-z . . . His own contribution hovers in the air somewhere just outside his head, wings beating frantically.

"Fin?" she begins, her voice firmer now, "What were you thinking last night, while we were fucking?"

"Wha?" He panics. ". . . Sinking?" His mind flails for something, anything. He remembers her shadowy form, her softness, how good it felt. "Dunno . . . One min I wass slee'ing, d' nex . . . I wass . . . well . . . fel' so close . . ."

"Any closer and you'd be out the back door, as the line goes . . ." she half-laughs. "I mean was it just the sex, the thrill, or what?"

Fin scratches his scalp, rubs his eyes, feels the gears jam. "No . . . wass mor' . . . I 'ean . . . I' was . . . jus so nice, so . . ."

"Nice? . . . Henry James you're not."

"Brain's froze."

"Yeah. From hanging out in your living room." Sam remembers now that she arranged to meet her colleague, to see the apartment. "Fin, sometime I need to talk, but right now I've gotta run. Go see my temporary digs." But as she says this, the images of her shattered belongings lying on Peter's floors bring a convulsion, a cry, tears of rage. "He'd better not dump everything out on the street! Or I'll have him arrested! And tell every person working here, bosses included." She wipes her eyes, clears her head. "Fin, any chance I could get some help, moving?"

"'Courss. Lemme know. How 'uch you ga . . . ?"

The weight of it all presses down into her heart. ". . . I don't know . . . don't know what . . . how much, is left . . . Don't know . . . Don't know what I'm going to do." Her voice breaks. Before he can think of a supportive word, she throws a final, "Gotta run. Call you. Maybe you can meet me there." And she's gone.

Fin holds the phone not far from his ear. He can hear his own circulation pumping as he imagines climbing the stairs to Peter's. The pumping's growing louder. Hope Peter's away at work. Keep an eye out for . . . what? Booby traps? Shotguns triggered to go off when something's moved. Ka-boom! . . . Hey Mr. Sub-ma-rine man . . . feel guilty . . . and there ain't no place I'm go-in' to . . .

*   *   *

When Christine steps into her apartment, Daniel is there by the door, as if he'd been waiting. After she wrestles out of the raccoon, whose lining partially follows her, and she drapes the thing on a sturdy chair, they take in each other and lean into a forgiving embrace with more tenderness than passion.

He asks her how her day went. She looks at him, thinking back before turning away, shaking her head, emitting a half-laugh. "A frustrating day . . . a long winding road of a day." And she exhales something of its emotion as she heads to the stove to make tea, pressing her palms over her eyes and down her cheeks, bringing back all the faces. Unexpectedly, Fin's face is foremost, because, she hastily explains to herself, of their recent chat, and his behavior remaining something of a puzzle. Once again the sound of the cop's blow connecting with his jaw re-echoes, this time so vividly that she can almost feel it herself, or has her memory heightened the unexpected violence?—something her life has not brought her close to. But his weight falling onto her shoulder was immediate and visceral—so that now she consciously shifts her attention away to Kenny . . . coming down the hall slightly stooped, his anger swallowed yet darkly clouding his eyes. These recalled moments weigh so heavily within her that she realizes she needs to release some of their contained emotion. And so she swings around and faces Dan and begins to relate these fragments: the cops, Kenny, Errol, Leslie . . . the discussion with Fin. Dan's deepening frown reflects the impact he sees it all has had on her. In prior conversations, he has heard something of Errol's struggle to get a play produced, and now these sad stories.

Christine, however, suddenly remembers the blood dried on her face, and excuses herself to retreat to the bathroom. There, in the mirror, she watches her uncertain expression leaning close to find the faint, yet unmistakable traces. It's doubtful Daniel noticed in the dim light by the door, not that she would be averse to telling the story. But she thinks it will be simpler not to, as it was of little consequence. Now, thin smears can be seen on her chin and upper lip and in the corners of her mouth, sufficient to remain sticky. She tastes it with her tongue—sour, unpleasant, and yet eliciting a curious, if pointless, interest. She runs the hot water, but something holds her staring into the mirror. She feels almost reluctant to wipe away the blood . . . Why? . . . Some tangible connection to the strange, wrenching events? A reminder of the violation, and hurt, and physicality of it all? . . . Of the almost inexpressible range of emotions? . . . Was she wrong to kiss Fin, misleading him? Yet she feels protective of her freedom to do that, weightless though as it was. Which is more difficult to explain: that we can feel love for many, or that we don't feel it for more? She pictures a leaf in clear water drawn along, pulled and caught by a vortex stirred by her swimming legs. Was it Newton who proposed that every body, every particle, attracts every other, according to mass and distance? Does emotion increase mass, reduce distance? She shakes herself and tests the running water before taking some with her fingers to begin washing away the brownish blood, which requires surprising and repeated scrubbing, until her skin is irritated and pink.

She rejoins Daniel who has moved into the kitchen and is looking into the fridge for something to eat. When he hears her, he turns and sends over a smile, even as he seems to stare uncomfortably at her washed lips and cheek. Then he looks away, inhales, and tells her that he wants to apologize for being a little peevish over the previous twenty-four hours. He explains that probably it stemmed from his writing, which he has not been happy about lately. She knows that he is this way sometimes, that his writing often influences his mood, and she absolves him of any need to apologize. Rather she wonders if it is she who should apologize for getting so enrapt in the Kenny incident. Instead she launches into a further description of it, and the difficulties Errol labors under, and Kenny—after which they look blankly at each other, wondering where these concerns leave them.

Feeling residual cold returning, she again faces the counter and clicks on the electric kettle, then swings back to find him, and for a moment they take each other in. She tells him that the incident seems to have, "sent reactions through the group . . . changing things . . ."

Uncertainly he looks at her "How do you mean?"

As she searches for the answer, she remembers that Tom showed up, following her call to him, and she tells Dan that he sent his regards and would be writing up the story. Watching Dan, she feels that at this moment their closeness has diminished, or abruptly widened—he seems suddenly far away. But she knows it is not what she wants. It may only stem from the relatively small differences in their quiet writing lives, or from her witnessing those on the edge today. While she's hardly one to abandon commitments at the first unexpected novelty or bump, she does want to experience new things in a complete way, wants to respond to them and weave them into herself. Should she have upbraided Leslie as she might like to have done? Should she have joined the grappling with the cops shoving Errol? Should she have praised Errol in front of his kids and wife? Should she have kissed Fin fully—an impulsive lark, as she would have made clear to him? And while these actions are not really her . . . maybe she should have tried. They are part of her, some strand or corner. Are we not here to develop in ourselves all ways that we might? Slowly she moves over to Dan and puts out her arms. They embrace, with more feeling than before. He cannot know what she saw and what she went through today, any more than she can know the emotions and thoughts that arise in the course of his piecing poems together from his life. But they appreciate each other, respect each other, admire the work the other does, and even share aspects of that work, which is a great bond. She counsels herself not to allow little things to obscure it. She has seen enough misfortune today, and she imagines the cold steel of things-gone-wrong. But then she stops, having imagined enough for now, having heard and seen enough. Yes, it is a circus, a multi-ringed array of acts and talents, of misfortunes and mistakes, beyond what we can grasp. She pulls Daniel closer to her, noting that he is less hefty than Fin, more delicate and supple, as they squeeze, then kiss with suddenly released, stored-up feeling. As she does, she is conceding it's not easy—may be impossible—to live in all the ways we know, and may want to try.

*　　*　　*

Lilly and Molly have been tucked in and kissed on their soft cheeks and brows, and their covers pulled up to their dark eyes which close as they nestle into their pillows. Leslie has disappeared into the bath and bedroom, quite clearly avoiding him.

Errol wanders, hands in pockets, into the living room. Mind empty, his gaze bumps over the furniture and imitation Persian rug whose fringe is already fraying. Indeed all is wearing, aging: the green armchair with its threadbare arms and seat cushion, the fading red sofa, the lamps with tilted shades and the old, cracked white bowl with its spiraling blue arms that he long ago made and that only Terry has said he liked. He reaches into it and finds two green and brown marbles, jacks, dice, and a tiny doll. Maybe they *should* spend some of the money they've tried to save, because nothing here pleases Leslie . . . For him it's serviceable enough; it's not as though they do any entertaining: Lou and his girl several times; Terry once . . . some cousin of Leslie . . . She could use a bit of her money, if she chose to, but that goes for clothes and dance lessons, things for the girls, and God knows what.

Have I been a fool? he wonders. Not only with this incident, but with everything? . . . His mind wavers. The possibility of clarity recedes. He stands precariously in darkness, unable to gauge where he is or should be.

Before any elaboration, or explanation, can be summoned, he finds that he is walking out into the hall, lifting his heavy parka from its hook, and is slipping out the front door. Familiarity eases the way, speeds his descent, as he pulls on his parka, as his legs loosen up and his feet get the feel flapping down over the steps to the first floor, where he pushes through the front door. He'd been thinking that he would walk, but now he decides to sit and think, feeling the cold air awakening him and bringing the possibility of clouds slowly lifting.

Carefully he lowers himself onto the first cold granite step, waiting for the chill to strike up through his butt and back. But it's not so bad. He pulls at his collar, refastens the velcro, and closes his eyes. The perfect faces of Lilly and Molly appear, smiling, gazing up uncertainly. Molly, her mother's child, has her doubts about him, but Lilly holds him in her mind as her private friend, a sometimes secret ally . . . As for Leslie, she's lost hope. It's written in her face. She's living her own life, doing her own thing. They share an apartment; that's about it.

Behind him, he hears a noise. Someone's coming out. He slides against the low wall to make room as the person sidesteps by him. Errol glances up. The other, a man, steps down to the sidewalk, then turns back. It's Clayton, who grunts, "Hey, wha's happenin'?"

Errol, reluctant to look closer, mumbles, "Not much."

Clayton's eyes slide away, noting that it's gotten damn cold again. He clears his throat, and air mails phlegm into a snow drift. Then breathing freely, he declares, "My lawyer's gonna take it to the city, for that . . . for sendin' those cops in."

"Good," grunts Errol, his hopes rising but then falling nearly as quickly. He feels his thoughts circling and rearing up like a mounted knight, watching a portcullis clang down.

Clayton peers back at him, wondering about his attitude. "You saw them, right?"

The several encounters reappear, stutter, then freeze in Errol's mind. "I sure did."

Clayton's attention is drawn back to the street as an extra long semi rumbles past, shaking the sidewalk. "How can they think that's okay?" he asks, eyes moving up the dark building facing them.

Errol feels his head faintly wobbling in sympathy, "Don't know . . ."

Clayton's gaze returns to Errol, noting the guy seems dazed tonight, none too sharp. Won't begin speculating why, although what he's got to be sour about I don't know . . . It wasn't him who got pounded, kicked . . . all the rest. But enough . . . enough of all that. "'Preciate the help," he says, staring over the other's head. Just discernibly, he sees Errol nod. But Errol's not sure whether this refers to what they all did, or to his offer to testify in the future.

For a moment Clayton studies him, wondering about him, then murmurs, "Later," and pushes off toward Broadway. His mind turns to his grumbling stomach. After rejecting that vile institutional food they pushed my way, I'm starved, starved for something good . . . What's it been? Twenty-four hours, since I was just sitting down to eat?

Errol doesn't move as the other's dark form disappears down the block. His brain remembers it was going to sort some things, but now it feels locked—chest too—until he forces a breath, in and out. His mind searches for a thread, some explanation . . . something . . . Things aren't goin' too well . . . wrong road, wrong intuitions . . . somethin' wrong with me—an empty stage . . . No, gotta change, somehow . . . go somewhere, clear the soup . . . away from the noise and distractions . . . I'll explain it to little Lil; she can pass it on to Moll, who 'll tell Leslie . . . Yes . . . need to go figure . . . just what's goin' on, and why . . . and what should be . . .

VIII.

Wednesday Week

Tilting Terry takes in a cheekful. Swirling his Manhattan through his teeth, he bathes his tongue, swallows, and expels the heat. From his breast pocket, he pulls out a newspaper clipping from last Friday's Metro section and pushes it across to Joseph. The bar is quieter tonight, he notes. Fewer patrons, the light seems thicker, deeper, almost ochre, blurring the figures at the far end of the bar. Degas mixed with Max Beckmann, he thinks, then looks over at Joseph as Joseph lowers his head to read the clipping. Yes, Terry thinks, things not only feel different tonight . . . they are different, without Viv, and Peter, who, rumor has it, may not be back. It's early yet, of course, but something's off . . . Maybe only a question of critical mass, so when the others arrive, it will feel more familiar and alive. Or maybe it's that the rest of us feel chastened somehow. Before Sir Errol brought the incident to us, we shared easy friendship, easy banter, optimism . . . but how thin, shallow, easily shaken, how sadly fragile, quickly withered . . . leaving us silent . . . discouraged.

Fin, to Joseph's left, is also tipping down a good, long swallow of his second Sam Adams as he swings his tender jaw and pulsating eyes around to stare deeper into the long room, finding motion: patrons swaying, scissoring, breast-stroking to the syncopated rhythm of some seventies soul piece. His head begins bobbing, his lips protruding to shape the words and feel, if he could only remember them, the outlines of which hang in his backbrain, whispering, teasing his tongue. Now his head undulates back; his eyes climb over Joseph's arm encircling the clipping, which he tries to read, but can make

150

out only the headline: "Questionable Arrest." A full column tails down the page, into the past. He'll take a look when Joseph's done.

Joseph's reading is rapt. The images, shouts, and faces from last week rise around him, crowding in, as if buildings leaning over a sidewalk. Errol's words and his pain press at the margins. Colors: red, black, and yellow, sweep the scene like searchlights, illuminating, then bleaching out detail and arguments. The alternation of darkness and brightness interrupts his progress, forcing him to read and re-read. He tries to shake these distractions, but now other noises join the din: footsteps, the rustle of clothing, Terry calling out, "Christine!" And to his left, Fin is pushing back his chair, jarring the table, exploding upward, upsetting, then catching, the chair. Joseph hurries over the last lines; the police department has not issued a statement, hinting that something's wrong. Much, nearly everything crucial, remains unclear. Joseph twists his head around as he slowly rises.

Christine comes to a halt behind Fin's chair, unbuttoning her gray sheepskin, warmly greeting the three, "Hello, Terry; Hello, Joseph; Fin . . . hello."

For days Fin has played this moment in his head, by turns curious and apprehensive. Now his body is tense and trembling as he faces her, swinging too close, then falling back a half-step. "Sorry . . ." She studies him, faint lines playing in her brow. He swallows and asks, "D' you have your piece for me?"

Amusement shimmers in her cheeks; a mild chafing lifts her chin. She reaches into her coat pocket and pulls out a large white envelope, holding it for him. He takes it, eyes falling to it, where he discovers she has written his name with a fine flourish. Gazing at him, she notices, "Your lip, Fin, looks like it's healed."

As he finds her again, a wry smile is stretching the corners of her mouth—which sends a sharp twinge through his jaw, then skull, disconnecting thoughts. He manages to clear things in time to see her leaning to confer a sympathetic kiss to his cheek, and he, painfully perplexed, returns it, off target, lips popping emptily.

"Hope you'll give me your comments," she smiles, amused by his awkward effort, nodding to the envelope.

"Of course." Awake now to every detail, he rotates it in his hand, studying it, weighing it, then sets it on the table. Her eyes shine brightly above her cheeks which have grown gravely smooth, before she swings about to Joseph. Fin's lips part, waver, then close.

Joseph, who has been patiently waiting, lifts his spreading arms to claim his reward, taking her shoulders and offering a chivalrous, Continental kiss to each cheek. Guinevere returned and re-tuned, he thinks. "Glad you decided to come," she tells him intimately, meeting his gaze, as Fin and Terry watch motionlessly. Next she swings behind Joseph, a hand trailing across his shoulder and off, and moves on to Terry who pushes out his full lips to exchange brief taps. That done, she continues on, smiling at him over her shoulder, and choosing the chair next to him, across from Fin, removing her coat and settling in. The three men lower themselves carefully back into their seats.

Fin wonders that she sits so far away, that her eyes now avoid him. A message? Reality returning? . . . And yet, as easily no as yes, he hastily protests. As likely disguising her hidden attraction, as not . . . Or is he trampling on the truth? He lifts his stein for another hearty draught. Hey Mr. Sub-ma-rine man, I'm not drownin', but there is no place I'm goin' to. The parting waters ripple through his mind.

Joseph now slides the clipping across the table to Christine, who, glancing at it, tells them she read it last week, and pushes it on to Terry. But Fin raises a requesting hand, and Terry sends it on to him.

Staring at the moderately busy bar, Christine wonders what she wants to drink tonight. A beer for a change, she decides and begins selecting among brands, until her recollection of *The Times* report redirects her attention back to the men. "Unfortunately, I thought the report soft-pedaled the outrage. What did you think?"

Terry tips his head her way surprised. "Really?" She asks if he read it. "Certainly," he replies, covering mild annoyance with a twitching smile. Her chin drops a little. "And?" To which he explains, "I assumed the reporter wanted to present the facts, as they were then, if incompletely, known."

But Joseph, too, has found it inadequately conveyed the several outrages. "It certainly short-changed the violence, which is at the heart of the complaint."

Terry nods as his eyes escape to the bar, following the bartender in the smoky mirror, moving back and forth, carrying drinks, collecting money, back and forth. To the three, he repeats his belief that the department will argue that because the officers believed themselves threatened, their reactions were justifiable. And they may be able to make it stick.

A frown rumples Joseph's forehead, as Christine swallows, inhales, and expels her incredulity: "The police will be able to excuse their conduct?"

Twisting unhappily her way, Terry maintains this may be so. Christine closes down her eyes, dims her sight, and stares at her fingers which are reaching over the table's edge like spiders' legs.

Fin has finished the report and, blinking in reflection, looks across at her, thinking that the lawyer's statement lists, if it doesn't actually describe, the violence. But when he says as much into her clear-eyed intensity, she quickly counters, "But it doesn't *begin* to convey the severity of the beating . . . which required medical care and stitches. And then they sent him home in women's rags . . ." Irritation jerks her eyes away, briefly to the other tables, where she finds several men watching her. Did she dispute too loudly? Or not loudly enough? She feels her indignation swelling once more: "None of that was reported! And no mention of what they did to the apartment. I don't understand why Tom didn't include any of it!"

Straightening in his chair, prodded by sharpening thoughts, Fin replies, "He probably wanted corroboration, a second source . . . and so far as I know, the police have never issued a statement . . . leaving him with only one side of the story, however accurate it seems to be. But I assume this is only the initial report."

"But Tom was there in the hall when Kenny came back," Christine exclaims, her voice sliding between cry and control. "Tom saw his injured face, saw the apartment, heard what Errol witnessed . . . What about all of that?"

Silently, shrinking back, the others acknowledge her point, as they stare down at the creased clipping lying like an insect poised to spring away. Terry, however, shares Fin's caution, "But we don't know why things happened as they did—not yet anyway. And those actions don't necessarily condemn the police, who I'm sure will claim they were only reacting . . . Their continuing silence, however, suggests they do have a problem."

"*If* it's all not dismissed and forgotten," Christine groans. "If some other outrage doesn't bump it from the papers and the public's consciousness." Shaking her head, she stares at the table's ancient gougings, initials and symbols from the decades. Her anger has subdued the others. But then her features appear to soften, and her demeanor grows more conciliatory, "Maybe it's the headline . . . The emphasis on the arrest draws attention away from the mistreatment and abuse."

Nodding Terry takes her point, yet feels it's necessary to repeat his caveat, that all may turn on the issue of the gun, and first shot. And, as no one can predict how that will play out, the debate looses steam, leaving the four slouched in their chairs, until Christine submits one final thought: that several issues around the arrest need to be addressed and resolved by the city. And with this no one disagrees.

Christine now feels she wants her beer and excuses herself, rising and winding over to the bar. The others sit silently in their semi-circle, held by the manacle of the arrest, until Terry shakes himself and reaches for the clipping to safely pocket it, and Joseph asks no one in particular when a follow-up report might appear. But no one has an answer.

As Christine returns with her stein, she carries a new concern, Vivian's absence. When she first arrived, she had assumed that Viv was either late or in the loo, but as neither seems to be the case, she questions Terry about where she is and whether she's coming.

Within his helmet-like head Terry's eyes close to armored slits. A wince slices his cheek, as if cleaving copper, before a hand floats up to smooth it away. "No . . ." he confesses unhappily, "I'm afraid she's not . . . The incident revived her own memories of being stopped, left her tossing 'n' turning 'n' fuming all week. So for now, she says she just wants to stay home and be with the kids."

It takes a moment for the others to absorb this, and as they do, their eyes pinch in disappointment, at the desertion, and at the doubt cast upon their sincerity. Viv, it seems, found them wanting.

Hoping for explanation, Christine appeals to Terry, "But we need her, Terr . . . She's part of the group, and obviously we need to hear and understand what she was thinking." Yet Terry can offer only uncomfortable acknowledgement amid deepening lines of regret.

". . . Well, I feel bad," murmurs Christine, "that she was disappointed in us. Will you tell her, and ask her to reconsider?"

Shifting his weight, pulling his creaking chair, Terry agrees to do so. At the same time he counsels himself that he should try to soften the news, and he tells them that she decided, really, for her own reasons . . . and that she may, in time, change her mind and come back. "You never know . . ." But his eyes escape this unlikely reversal, sliding beyond to the bar and the heads of veterans there, talking in salvos, hunching close, bursting into laughter. He watches impassively, yet at his center feels shaken. When he dares to swing his attention back to his friends, he finds them deflated, adrift.

Christine, peering unobtrusively at Joseph, wonders if this will now be enough to tip him into quitting the group. Her eyes move next to Terry. Will he continue to come without Viv? Doubtful. And Fin? Has she unintentionally humiliated him, despite her affection for him? And if he does come, will he be ever watching her? Glued to her face? . . . Will our little group thus dissolve? She hopes not, as she recognizes that she somehow needs it, its other dimensions: its easy, accepting companionship, its banter and humor, its irreverence. Yet they need a quorum, and their numbers are fast falling. She pictures the round table empty in the yellow light, pictures other patrons moving past, wondering where those people went—imagines the ghosts of the group, bearded, in plated armor, hovering, conversing, speculating about their deeds, their doubts, their loves, their souls. She looks at the three men staring into their steins or glasses, turning, tilting or swirling their drinks. It reminds her that she's thirsty, with remorse, and so she lifts her glass to her lips and feels the effects of the alcohol spreading through her, easing her distress.

Fin too feels movement again, in his beery brain, in the floor, in the flow of thoughts and images from the still snow-splattered city. He's begun a column in which he's attempted to capture those twenty-four hours—all the events and images rolling together down a snow slope, binding and blurring together. If he were to claim that some good came out of it, would he also have to acknowledge the bad? Such as his own over-stepping? He glances at Christine, no doubt disgusted with him, designating him persona non grata . . . Just button the lip, float with the music, gaze at such dreams that come—first a medieval jester, bowing and laughing among St. Mary's tables, in his cheeky checks of yellow-brown and red, telling ribald jokes, reddening faces, collecting golden coins in his fool's cap.

As if a product of his fancy, a warmth envelops him, and then the table, and with it Sam arrives, a wary samurai hand at hip, coming to a halt behind him. Seeing her first, Terry calls, "Sam!" And the others twist around to greet her. Fin fights free of his reverie and springs up, smile reviving, while Sam, squinting under its shine, braces herself for come-what-may. The discretion Fin first thought politic to display is swept away by the sight of her sweet, sad face, and he spreads his wings to welcome and envelop her within his rustling feathers against his thumping heart—to which, after momentary reluctance, she yields. Within her opened coat, he feels her mounding warmth—an entire, exotic, Leda-like being—and then her wet lips, like rain, briefly running along his neck, inspiring him to tighten until she gasps a little and tickles him to release her.

The unexpected affection catches the others off-guard, briefly silencing their rising words of welcome, until slowly they too pull themselves up from their seats to offer their own greetings, each shuffling cautiously to her and opening their arms, Christine last, encircling Sam with lingering affection. As the two women release each other, all can see that Sam's forehead and cheeks are flushed, her eyes watery, and some notice a red blotch along her jaw. Terry lifts his coat from the chair between Joseph and himself to make room for Sam, and she, peeling back hers, drops into it, asking them as she does, "What had you in its grip when I first came in? You looked like you'd seen a ghost."

Uncomfortable glances pass among the others, before they look to Terry to tell the news, but prior instructions from Viv direct him to first pass on her praise of the recital. "Sam, Viv wanted me to report that Lizabeth and she were just purring and dancing when they got home; Viv was so thrilled it moved her to tears." And with darting glances at her shining eyes, he adds, "Wish I'd come, and brought little William. Viv said your voice was just lovely and full."

Once more Sam flushes. "That's very kind. I hope she didn't feel she had to say that."

"Viv?" questions Terry. "You know she says pretty much what she thinks."

"Hey!" interjects Fin. "I was there too, and I heard it, and it *was* lovely and moving." And although he sees her wary eyes are reddening, he cannot reign in his acclaim: "To hear the feeling, to see the effort performed so beautifully, to experience the emotion of the songs, was just . . . deeply stirring." His memory of her voice mingles with the emotion in her eyes, and evokes one last cri de coeur: "What, in our largely pedestrian world, expresses our hearts more deeply or moves us more?"

But Sam, watching him, fears his moony expression will give them away, and wonders at his words. Why, Fin, why are you piling it on? . . . While he had generously helped her move her stuff—the pieces that were left, the fragments swept into plastic garbage bags—he had then pressed her to make love again. Maybe it was just the moment, both laughing and panting together from the trips up and down the stairs, leaning against each other, alone in her friend's apartment. At first she hadn't really been in the mood, yet she had allowed it, partly in wanting, partly in payment, she had decided. Some of her reluctance, she had later come to realize, stemmed from her not having entirely released Peter from within her—the good things, that she knows will only slowly fall away.

Ruefully Joseph now breathes and confesses, "I'm sorry I couldn't make it . . . I guess I really missed something." Immediately, however, he regrets his surprise and choice of words, and swallowing hastily, explains, "Unfortunately I was just so far behind on everything, that I locked myself in my office all weekend to work."

Sam, off-balance from the rush of memories and unexpected praise, finds Terry again, "I'm sorry Viv isn't here . . . She mentioned, when we spoke for a moment at the recital, that she probably wouldn't be. But I guess I didn't believe her. I didn't understand how deeply both incidents affected her."

Terry nods, relieved not to have to explain, but then repeats to himself that it's disingenuous of him to continue to act as if her decision were temporary and did not reflect her deep hurt and anger. At the same time, withholding his own probable decision to pull out at some point, sends his eyes down to his drink which he restlessly swirls.

Sam, remembering the feeling that infused her singing at the recital, suspects that much of it was called up from the break with Peter. As she warily appraises the reactions of the others, she decides she wants to, indeed needs to, bring them in, and finding their eyes waiting for something, clears her throat and begins, "First Terry and Fin, thank you for your kind words . . ." Her light brown eyes run appreciatively over the two sets of darker eyes. "But unfortunately I have to announce that Peter and I have broken up—after last week's gathering, and journey down to the precinct, which he spurned . . . 'Breaking up' doesn't quite capture it . . . or maybe it does . . . Anyway, it has occurred to me that the recital may have been, in some way, our requiem, as it turned out . . . although, in the end, it was not so hard to let go."

Christine, uncertain that she has heard clearly, seeks confirmation in Sam's gaze straining to hold firm, and she murmurs her sympathy, "Oh Sam . . . I'm sorry . . . That's hard . . ." Terry is realizing that Sam's announcement confirms the hints he'd heard from Viv, and he also feels bad for her, and for Peter, whereas Joseph is attempting to grasp just exactly what he has heard, and what the implications are for Sam and the group.

Sam stares down at the table. "Peter, in his gentle way, got violent, attacked me, after smashing all my belongings. I had to call the cops . . ." Aware of the irony, she surveys the others to see if they share it, but finds only despondency. "I haven't spoken to him since . . . And knowing him as I do, I suspect we've seen the last of him . . . the lone exception being Terry . . . as Peter wants something from him."

At first Terry doesn't follow—has no idea what Sam is referring to, until slowly it dawns on him that Peter must hope for a show—which draws a moan from deep down and prompts him to anxiously wipe his chin at another suspicion confirmed. It leaves him feeling annoyed with Peter, and wanting to explain. "I'm afraid Peter never caught on to the realities of the art business. But I'm sorry to hear it ended . . . and ended this way." Sadly he seeks Sam's clouded face and imagines her hurt, before turning back to the others. "In the world of selling art, I'm afraid, while there are uplifting moments . . . mostly it's cold calculation, mostly un-adventurous and un-heroic."

"We needn't feel sorry for Peter . . ." she reassures them with a mordant tone. "He has the sangfroid and delusions a-plenty to survive."

Stilled by this cold assessment following her bleak story and Terry's, the friends shift and squirm in their seats. Just now another group of men and women files past them, trailing eddies of frigid air, anticipating warm toddies and Irish coffees, and carrying on about a laggard comrade—which temporarily diverts the friends, except for Christine, who, under the weight of Sam's news, studies Fin across the table. With his affection for Sam revealed, Christine wonders if he knew about the break with Peter, or had any role in it—an awkward intuition, from which she forces herself away, even as it occurs to her that Sam may actually be better off apart from Peter, with his slightly sinister undercurrents. An unbidden sigh escapes her.

Terry and Joseph send their murmured condolences to Sam, even as they are lamenting the loss of Peter's candor and caustic humor. And then once more silence drops over them all.

At length, Joseph is first to voice a recurring thought, "As I watched Peter last week growing increasingly impatient, even irritated, with the various opinions, I realized how little we know each other . . ."

Glancing among the sallow faces, and through the hazy bar, Sam feels it's unfortunately all too true. "It became sadly apparent for Peter and me . . . In some ways, it seems you don't know a person until you've been through a crisis together. In fact, we may not know ourselves."

"I suppose," continues Joseph, "as we've never really talked here about deeply personal things, it shouldn't be a surprise . . . although maybe we thought we had a clearer sense of things."

Christine, aware of some distress weighing her down, struggles to name it. "It's difficult to know when to ask or act or intervene . . . certainly in Errol's case . . ." Looking sadly at Sam, she reflects how little she in fact knew. "And with Peter, I assume we all noticed his edge . . . but . . . I guess we weren't in a position to ask . . . but perhaps we, or I, should have."

But Sam shakes her head. "It wasn't clear to *me*, before all of this."

Fidgeting between the two women, Terry is now concluding that he probably shouldn't have revealed Viv's views, as they've created more anxiety than understanding. And while the group should have been more sensitive to the racial traumas that Kenny's arrest released, he concedes, "Because Errol's so private and Peter so touchy, it's unlikely any of us could have helped."

And Joseph, twisting with frustration, nods in accord. "We have to admit that ours are mostly casual connections."

For a short time all reflect upon this, until Terry, the least comfortable with these speculations, and eager to return to the practical, asks if anyone's heard anything of Kenny over the week. "Is he back in his apartment, and at his job?" But when no one claims to know, Terry allows they'll have to wait until Errol shows. But Fin again, in recalling the encounter in the hallway that afternoon a week ago, warns it's unlikely Errol and Kenny would have spoken since, to any real extent, and he cautions Terry, "When Clayton came home, that late afternoon, it was far from a moment of triumph. I mean the two of them didn't just sit down and begin swapping war stories. Errol may have felt he was brushed off or received an unintentional slap in the face, as it seemed Kenny wanted to be by himself." Fin surveys the others before adding, "I guess we imagined that Kenny's return would be a big relief to all, but it kind of turned out to be a . . . sad mismatching of moods, and needs, and views . . ." To which Christine adds, "Clayton, I suspect, was just too tired and angry, and maybe embarrassed, to talk . . . and poor Errol, needing some acknowledgement, seemed to get caught in the crosscurrents."

"Unlucky soul," murmurs Sam, picturing Errol that night arriving at the bar. Terry, also thinking of Errol, recalls that a day or so after the incident he spoke to him on the phone and sensed he was unusually subdued . . . So why didn't I ask him about it? . . . Didn't want to intrude? . . . But if we don't, who will? . . . And now Terry sees more clearly that his quitting the group might well sound its death knell, and as he has no such wish, he decides to put it off. After all, they're not bad people. Sir Errol, in particular, doesn't deserve it. And the rest, myself included, are no worse than most: the usual self-involved, dimly aware bundle of concerns.

Fin, glancing across at Terry, notices his eyes partly closing, and wonders what thoughts drag them down. But then he notices Terry's eyes snap open and his head tip back in calling out, "Lou!" And the others turn to find Lou dragging toward them. In place of his usual edgy, opened-mouth readiness for come-what-may, his face appears jowly and tired, his body slumped and dispirited.

Terry repeats, "Lou! Howya doin'!" even as he, and everyone, can now see Lou's not doing good. Lou veers over to an empty chair between Joseph and Christine, extends his arms to its back and leans heavily, breathing and pressing his knuckles until they're squeezed translucent. As he begins to regain his breath, and as the warmth of the bar begins to dissolve away the cold, he takes in the others. But then his eyes sink, and he expels a long raspy breath. "Stopped by Errol's, to pick him up, bring him over, but . . ." Lou lifts his head, revealing that his eyes wander unfocused. ". . . he's not there . . ." The creases in his brow deepen as he draws in another lungful. "Leslie's there, with the girls. Tight-mouthed, tight-assed, unhappy as usual. The girls look like they've been cryin', poor things . . . Leslie stares at me, like I have some idea, like I'm the problem—though, obviously, I'm not, and she kinda hisses at me, her voice cut flat, 'Errol's gone, disappeared.'"

Lou finds and squints furtively at Christine and Fin, who he knows met Leslie. Then he wipes his mouth, shakes his head, as if it's still difficult for him to believe. "I'm standin' there wonderin' if I'm hearin' right . . . and I realize I'm feelin' suddenly a little dizzy. Maybe this bugs her into repeatin', 'That's right, gone—two days now. Not a single word—nothin'!'" Lou surveys the others, who once again appear stunned into stillness. He gathers himself once more. "I mean . . . I look at this woman, and I begin thinkin' okay, maybe I *am* hearin' correctly, and maybe I can understand why he might have done it, split. But then I look at the little girls, and . . . I tell myself whoa, somethin's gotta be way wrong here, for him to do this. If that's what went down." Lou stares at the table, at the gouged lines and letters, and then around at the scarred, cleaved faces of the knights and ladies, all watchin' 'n' waitin'. "Jesus," he mutters, "you never know what's goin' on with people." A swallowed cry catches in his chest, as now the table and the rest of St. Mary's seems to lift and cycle like a carrousel: lights 'n' shelves, steins, glasses and people, all circling within the walls with their crests and crowns . . . Jesus, maybe I'd better sit down—which he does, almost throwing himself sideways into the chair.

The others look confounded as the news sinks in, their eyelids fluttering or closing in disbelief. Yet there must be some explanation. Lou, glancing around unseeing, props himself up on an elbow, and stumbles on, "I begin wonderin' . . . where would he go? . . . What was he thinkin'? . . . Hope nothin's happened . . ."

Fin asks, "He have any family, or friends he could go to? Where do his parents live?"

Lou shakes his head. "Both gone, like mine." He inhales glumly, then blows it out. "As for friends beyond us, or cousins, uncles . . . I never heard him make any mention."

Christine feels herself resisting apocalyptic scenarios despite Lou's distress. Errol needed to clear his head, she reasons, after taking Clayton's arrest and return so hard, and then Leslie coming down on him in front of us . . . You can't pretend things are okay after that.

Terry tries to jog Lou's memory, "You know him, Lou; you're the closest. Where would he go?" But Lou can only shake his drooping head as he reaches back through past conversations, seeking some hint of something . . . and coming up blank. Instead he gropes back for his recollection of Leslie. "I tried to ask her, you know, prod her, when I collected my wits, but she was . . . either too upset or just plain p.o.'d . . ." He glances around, feeling lost himself. "She's not too fond of me to begin with, so when she's speakin' to me, she's sorta sendin' it up over my head, into the hall. Her eyes—under her eyes is all gray—so she says that two days ago he told little Lilly he was goin' on a trip, just for a while . . . And that was it. That was what she told her mom. And when I looked down at little Lilly, she nods, watchin' me with her little round eyes, very business-like . . . Of course, she has no idea. So I'm staring at the floor, wondering what to do, when Leslie starts up again, 'Isn't this great? He leaves his wife and daughters, for God knows how long, when *I've* gotta work, every day. So who's gonna take care of the girls after school? How am I gonna pay the bills and everything? I mean just *what* was he thinkin'? . . ."

"Well, as we know," says Lou, swallowing and looking around the table, "his problem is that he never *stops* thinkin' . . . And he *is* concerned with other people, unlike herself. So it's not real constructive of Leslie to dump it there, in front of the kids . . . So I, uh, just look down at the girls and say, really right to 'em: your dad's my best friend. To me he's a good, kind man. And he tried to help your neighbor down the hall, and he wants to do good for his students at his school. So . . . remember that . . . and I think he'll be back real soon . . .

"When I dare look back at Leslie, her eyes is all daggers. 'Maybe it's time for you to go,' she snaps. 'If you think you can explain away the fact that he's not here, and that he'll probably lose his job, well then, maybe it's an indication of where *you're* at, and it's probably a good thing you didn't mislead some woman into marrying you and starting a family. So, good night.'

"I try to send a smile down to the little girls, tryin' to reassure them, but Leslie's already shovin' the door in my face, closin' off those little ones . . . So I stand there for a moment, brain in the spin cycle. But then, realizing where I am, I take a few steps down the hall to what must be Kenny's apartment. It's got a door at least, second-hand, different colors . . . but that must be it, right? . . . Silence though, no one around, except me. So I head over here . . . . Feel bad for those girls. And for Errol . . . whatever sent him off." Lou again takes in the others, then half-rises, half-pivoting toward the bar. "I need a beer. Get anyone somethin'?"

"I'll take a Wicked Ale," calls Sam, as Lou, with difficulty, straightens up and drags himself away.

At the table, no one knows quite what to say. The bar seems to have grown quieter as some of the patrons have left. On the juke box in the back, Fin hears an old tune from The Band. Je-sus, he mutters, that reaches back. *The Night They Drove Old Dixie Down*. Where'd they dig that up? The fading tunes that connected a generation—the few who cared.

Lou brings back two steins, for Sam and himself, and settles down, taking a good, long swallow. The others sip or breathe back in the squeezed-out air, their unfocused gazes wandering here and there, alighting only on their companions' faces.

Christine's thoughts have turned for a moment away from Errol and his daughters to Sam, wondering about her breakup. Peter, she knew was no breeze, could be volatile, and now violent . . . . Yet a distant voice reminds her that Dan and she each have their firm ideas and occasional temptations, which often take time to understand, sort out, accept—with much laboring—Adam's curse. Now her mind circles back to Errol who seems to have hit a wall. Hope the girls are too young to really understand and long remember. She recalls his haggard face that late afternoon, that face which, in part, produced those little ones, and she recognizes that to hold back her gathering feeling—a wave of sadness for him and the girls, for Sam, for Kenny, and maybe for Dan and herself, and for the dwindling fellowship—to quell this undeniable upwelling, she must bite her lip inside, bite it nearly as hard as she can.

Joseph is thinking that no one round the table seems entirely exempt, from problems, issues—which confirms his view of life: wrought with imperfection . . . but still, it's unsettling how pervasive it is, and how it slams some hard, while passing more lightly over others . . . In the last week, he's gotten much of his work under control, gotten a portion of the screenplay out, all while Errol, apparently, was agonizing. It would be a blow to lose him, and these evenings . . . with the Lady Christine . . . Terry, Sam, even Fin, just when we were edging closer, shoved, hurled, by events, then parted by them, and maybe by insensitivity and betrayal.

Across from him, Fin's eyes are slowly circling the table, trying to see how each is taking it. Who's lettin' it in, who's holdin' it off, who's aligning it with his own, or her own, troubles, who's trying to understand why it happened as it did.

Emotions, breaches, mistakes . . . How to get a handle on . . . Christine, he sees, is feelin' it. Lou, of course. Joseph and Terry pondering. As for Sam, he remembers their surprising, thrilling closeness, even as they were breaking, he confesses, an unspoken code. He gazes at her while she's not looking. In some real, if indefinable, way, she's among the closest, sharing some implicit understanding. But then she gets clamped by consuming anger or disappointment, and he's not sure he's equipped to deal, not sure he can help. One hopes, he's come to see, to find someone with whom you can talk, throw it back and forth, the incoming and the off-loading—without the inner dome of heaven falling, and things tumbling away—the land where understanding dwells, with the like-minded, good-hearted other, in parallel universes, maybe—something that is possibly our modern Grail, the cup in which goodness and companionship await . . . And how empty to suddenly discover you've lost it, or it's cracked and drained, leaving you wandering out there directionless and alone, cut off from your hearth, or two tiny children, your insides pulled to the poles.

His eyes reach unrequested back to Christine, embodiment of an ideal . . . But whoa! What's he dreamin'? She's as human as the rest, and he's no less foolish. He watches her cupping her stein with two hands. What's tugging her? What is it that hits her deep? What has brought the glassiness he sees in her eyes? Tear ducts from the heart? What, in all this, moves her most? Wrings her good? He has some idea . . . But then his thoughts return to Errol. "Hey Lou? Shouldn't we go look for the crooked dude? Must be someplace."

Lou stares back, as at a blank wall. "But where? . . . Could be anywhere in the city, the state, the goddamned country? . . . Where to even begin?"

Terry too is thinking of Errol. Shoulda done something. I heard something was goin' on, when I called him. Viv would have known what to do. Would've been good for her to be here tonight, to see these other sides, that troubles are visited, to different degrees, but pretty much all around.

Lou's mind strains to picture Sir Errol's face, the features, the whole ball of wax. He's trying to see him that last evening as they pushed home through the storm—wearing that useless, old raincoat. Christ, Errol, I'll fuckin' buy you a new one. He tries to imagine just where his friend might be. Could be anywhere, anywhere in the Tri-state area—that old ra-di-o phrase, anywhere in the ra-di-o-listening area. Is that what defines us? Our world, the boundaries, the things we listen to and do—moving around, talking, buying—our passive living, seldom getting to the heart of things, life on the surface . . . Jeeze, Errol! You listening? . . . Where are you? What are you thinkin'? And what, what was it that pushed you? . . . And when you comin' back? What kind of place you stayin' in? What kind of place can you *afford*? . . . I mean, Jesus, Errol, just what the fuck are you doin', man?

THE END.

SLIPSHOD WATCHMAN

NEW YORK CITY

Late 1980's

I.

I am an actor . . . but then beyond that, don't quite know, now. Nor do I know where to begin this story. Or why I seem to want to go over it again. But guess I should, guess I must, if for no other reason than to shake myself out of this, and get on.

But begin where? Go back over everything? Every ornery thing in this turnturtle life? Or maybe only to my move down here, to the West Village, which I had been thinking about for so long. Maybe that makes more sense.

And yet how to tell it, if only to myself, when there are so many ways to see it? How to select among the inventive and the invective, the protective and the hectoring tongues, to somehow get at what really happened, and why. Or is this vanity too? After all, I've been around. Truth? In this relative, apparently pointless world. I don't know. I do know that I want to, need to, tell it, straighten it out, for myself anyway, and until I do, I will remain . . . troubled. Yes, as good a word as any, for now.

Standing there, at the periphery, is her presence, like the ghost at midnight, like noble Banquo. I know what I should do, what friends counsel: forget her, put her behind you, remember that she too was human, fallible. But having mourned, having washed it out, I thought it should be gone, over, carried away in the salty flood . . . but no, can't shake it, can't stop the leak in the heart.

Ironic no, for one who can detach and pull back from things so quickly and completely, who can put feelings on hold in order to take a look. The actor's training? Or why I became an actor? The buried heart . . . Or cart before the horse again? Actor, act or, char-act-or, chiaroscuro, shiftings and shadings, light and dark, flesh and bare bones.

Music I remember, from Giacomo, to reggae and Ludwig van, was the release, mon, openin' da gates, d' poilly gates, givin' you voice, drownin' y' pillow. You was wrung out, Rasta, entirely. Nothin' left but cavity and sinew and d' meditations of d' heart.

But there's something else, intertwined, which I hardly dare face . . . recoil at retelling . . . Their story, which is part of this, which makes me feel false, puny . . . worthless.

Yes, Anne made the right choice. I do not deserve her. No center here, only changing configurations, bubbles floating across the surface of time, an intelligence unanchored, a blip, while they were real and caring and, in that at least, connected; while I run from role to role (old jellyroll, old rocking chair). She had a sense of that, I thought, I treasured, of what was ultimately important, but ironically she used it to measure me and found me wanting. (Easy mon, easy. All d' lines 'n' cliches is crowdin' ya brain, and even I can't fends 'em all off.)

Then why bother, brother? Why do it to yourself? Because I must! . . . What else is there? Except to let all go, and start again, at the bottom, ". . . down where all the ladders start, in the foul rag and bone shop of the heart." . . . When did it start? Why did it happen? (Who is you, mon?) . . . Must answer these, before I go west; if I am to function at all on the next production; if I am not to remain wrapped in a shroud of preoccupation and self-pity.

Haven and heaven, it seemed, the shaded streets, the quiet and calm, where I ran ecstatic, having found at last, in this city of headlong, heedless, rootless, frenzied energy, something preserved, reaching up from the last century to bestow serenity, sanity, and a sense of proportion and limits. It would be, and for a while was, a place to work, to step back into, to think, surrounded by others doing the same, before venturing out again, into the life-giving and life-taking thoroughfares.

And yet it was here that the story begins, and ends, although the seeds had been planted before I arrived, for they were living here, and I had begun rehearsals at Circle in The Square.

Down from Inwood I came, down on the squealing Number 1, and out at 14th Street, then west, leaving the deadwood behind. Manhattan is an island of enclaves, ethnic and economic, and Inwood was certainly one, a world forgotten, when I was up there—a vestige of the fifties, a backwater, barely holding onto its order and peace in the face of the immigrant poor seeping in. And the price was a kind of stasis, which the Hudson's tides, sweeping by at its foundations, could not cleanse or release. Thinking of Inwood now, and of my drab if roomy apartment, to which few people came, so far away was it, I feel a chill, feel the goosebumps rise; for there was something deeply sad and vulnerable about living up there and about the people, mostly older, with a few, pale Irish and Eastern European kids lounging on the street corners, and yes some Spanish kids too, dark-eyed, furtive, yet still outwardly alive, still hopeful and hungry. The tragedy of the neighborhood lay in its lack of prospects. Or was it that those who found them soon left? (Like me? Yes, mon, like you.)

I feel for those people, though I never knew them, never did a damn thing for them, before leaving . . . What could I have done? . . . Something . . . But other things lifted me up and away too easily: my trade, my actor's life, moving on to the next scene, the next role. Yet I must have sensed that this is not enough for a full life. Something is missing, just as I distrust talking in this manner—too easy, too facile—transgressions confessed and dismissed.

But will I change? Chances are, not greatly. I might have, with her, with her help, and for her. But that's gone, and I, like old Willie Yeats, am left to enumerate old themes. Talk, yes, Hamlet's and the actor's disease, the either-oring anything to death . . . . And yet I must. Must try again to get to the heart.

Did try, before, with Peter, after the funeral. Sympathetic Peter, who listens well, who knew them all, and who tells me when I stink. Small dark and pale Peter, the earnest, honest craftsman, painstaking in all things. Yet if not for the ungovernable pain, I might have shrunk from telling him, despite my pride having been stripped away, and yes, bones laid bare.

But I'm running ahead. Must start at the beginning. (And maybe, mon, just maybe, you be d' wiser for it.) So, onward, Macbeth! Andiamo! A rut tah tah taahh!

> Down to the Village I came,
> a prince of the stage in debut,
> ready to deliver it from humdrum,
> ready to make it anew.

My hopes were spurred on by the good luck that awaited me in happening onto the Bank Street apartment, vacated by an actor leaving for the coast—preceding me, as it turns out. And how I loved it! An ample, furnished one-bedroom, with two great round bay windows and a palpable, brooding character, as if I were in London, in Sherlock's digs. Everything was evocative, cast a mood, transported one, from the arches in the hallway to the stone fireplace, and somber, heavy furniture, all with a simple, dark gravity. What better place for an actor in search of character and the right space to think? Small spaces, say the Chinese, focus the mind.

But now soon, I will be leaving it, though not relinquishing it—am only subletting it. Don't know when I'll be back, and wonder if I could bear living here, wonder if I'm brandishing all like a war wound, though it is through real tears. My deepest self knows this, even if other parts of me stand back aghast, smirking. I ignore them; other opinions are nothing to a shadow. Nada, mon, nada. The masks are off; your blankness is revealed.

I remember her (Yes mon, yes, forget yourself.) typing at the great, dark heavy desk, sitting in its half-moon slot so that it half-encircled her, her lovely, equally dark hair on her shoulders. I remember her reading, sunk down in one of the deep armchairs, wearing only her pearl silk robe open to the thigh. I could not believe my luck then—Belongs to me? No, could not believe, was utterly stunned, as I cannot now believe the end. The end? The mind reaches for . . . and falls short.

But damn it! Get on. Back to Bank Street, its shade evocative of simplicity, stateliness, and a bygone era. Yes, to the neighborhood, beautiful and orderly, the silent accomplice. Yet how I love walking through its streets in different seasons, love to see the low buildings letting in the light, the soft thin morning light of Spring, thickening into Summer and early Fall—the sharper light of Winter, its brilliant, crystal days heightening the colors of the houses: blue, gray, brown, beige, and all the reds and oranges. Once they were homes filled with families, rollicking—an image which turns the blade in my gut another twist—the cost of my hoping foolishly, prematurely, for children with her. Rooms we might have filled . . .

Someone said, you have your freedom at least. But to what avail? Don't they know the Gods are always paid? So here I am, amid the streets, Bank, Barrow, and Jane—as I would beg, borrow, or steal to get her back—amid Morton and Leroy, Perry and Charles, ghosts of the centuries, hues from the Civil War. I can almost hear the sounds, as I wander where the streets run crazy-quilt, where 4th runs north of 10th, on and on between the soft red-and-orange bricks. Horses' hooves clip-clop clip-clop, and my eyes, as from a carriage, run along the intricate black ironwork fences. I smile at gargoyles in friezes frozen under windows, follow steps ascending grandly, to front doors of heavy, deep-grained wood, leading into lives I'll never know. (Fortunately, mon, if yours is any telling.) The old Blue Mill. Commerce and Grove. Hand and glove. Anne and Grove Court, her home, a doll's house, near Bleeker and Bedford. Alleys of sunlight between stark, graphic lines cutting buildings three stories high, where the day-long Summer sun bakes the asphalt and stone, clearing the street, sending people quietly veering into the shadows—Hopper's world—leaving behind stillness and silence.

It was on a day like that, warm and still, a Spring afternoon, when I met Becky, or Rebeccah as she prefers. I was returning from a class with André, enjoying the short walk back from Bethune, when approaching my building, I saw a young black girl climbing over the railing and down into the space fronting the basement apartment. I remember first my surprise in seeing a black person at all, for I'd seen none living on our block; and next I remember wondering what she was doing—attempting a break-in? No, too young . . . and wearing a dress at that. How my first impulse shamed me, more deeply than I knew.

I stopped by the steps and waited, for she had not yet noticed me, and watched her bend to pick up something. Only at this point did she sense me, and her head snapped up in my direction. "'lo," she mumbled, then held up what she had retrieved. "Lost ma ball," she whispered, and she showed me her hard, red, rubber ball.

I felt bad that she believed she owed some explanation, and I smiled as plainly as possible and said, "Hello," while trying to think what else to say, for I couldn't help but notice that she had reached that perplexing pinnacle between girlhood and womanhood when no one quite knows who they are dealing with. I confess that so fresh did she seem that I tried to imagine the woman into whom she might grow, wondering if she must inevitably lose that disarming quality. Now, of course, I feel the choking truth.

As I stood there in awkward distraction, she attempted to climb up, but the stretch for her leg was too great, and the iron railing too high. About to go in, I realized that she couldn't get out, and so I stepped over to offer her a hand. At first, head down, she hesitated, but then realizing perhaps that there was no alternative, she extended one hand, the other clutching her ball. Quite easily—so light was she, a bird—I pulled her high enough for her to get a foothold, at which point she hastily extracted her hand from mine, gripped the iron railing, and stepped over. Although she didn't look back as she collected her school books and made her way between parked cars and then directly across the street, she did murmur, "Thank you."

Caught between idleness and curiosity, I watched her as she glided through the iron gate opposite my building and descended quickly into the whitewashed entrance of the basement apartment.

I might never have given it another thought if not for that evening, on the way to the theatre, when, as I bounded down the front steps, a voice addressed me, "Hello, sir?"

Turning, I discovered an African-American woman, perhaps in her mid-30's, wearing blue jeans and a white blouse, a woman at once graceful and worn, with deep circles under her eyes. She smiled no more than was necessary and said in a not unpleasant manner, "I heard you helped my daughter this afternoon. Thank you. Sorry she caused a problem."

Naturally I felt uneasy, and for some reason guilty. "Oh, no problem. I, uh, live here . . . was glad to give her a hand."

She nodded closing her eyes. "Well thank you, anyway . . . We live across the street." Motioning with her head, her face caught the street light, smoothing out her skin so that I could see fleetingly in it her daughter's features. "I tried to get her t' thank you herself, but she wouldn't. So I am . . . Her name's Rebeccah."

When our eyes met briefly, I sensed (alas with ambivalence) that kind of instant rapport one encounters from time to time. For me, it occurs most frequently when I meet warm brown eyes, shining and saying that there is not only a warm soul behind them, but one who thinks I am. A silent benediction.

For all the time I've spent seeking love and friendship, I now believe that the outcome rests not with me, but with 'chemistry,' with how he or she reacts to me; and usually the verdict is instant, leaving me helpless, passive and feeling very much a creature of fate, or the subconscious. In the few cases where I've tried to force things, the results have been disastrous. Any question why I've escaped into the world of the theatre?

And for all we did have, Anne and I never had that, that instinctive rapport. At first, it was the outer trappings—her grace and good looks, my gypsy career—which intrigued us, and thereafter, our imaginations took over, although I maintain and will forever, that if she'd been willing, it would have worked.

Anyway, Becky's mother and I . . . No, it was I alone, who glanced away, ill at ease, in some way unable to handle this fellow feeling. (I am trembling now, I know, from both stories.) When I looked back, I remember, she said, with more presence of mind, and yes, more courage too, "My name is Rachel."

Given enough time, enough rehearsal, I can recover. "I'm McKim. Mac." We both smiled. "By the way, I'm in a play, *Half Moon*, over at Circle Rep, on Seventh. If you two'd like to come, be glad to get you some tickets." (Why I blurted this out, I don't know. Perhaps it is my sole sense of identity, or all that I have to offer, or what I hide behind.)

She smiled, I recall, but said nothing as she began backing away. That was it, our first meeting. I spun around, trembling then too, no doubt, and hurried away to the theatre.

So what, in that simple encounter, was the big deal? Do you even remember, old sieve? Oh yes, it's there like a plunge into cold water, jolting, icy, crystalline. And from it unfolded the events that associate me—which tie me to her death . . . and in a sense, have initiated mine—my spiral into emptiness, driven by a guilt for which I can never atone. (The Catholic side of my heritage is not something I consciously subscribe to, but it plagues me like a stray dog who, once he's sniffed the encouragement of uncertainty, stays at your heels with quick-footed persistence.) . . . For oh, if I had done what I should have, could have, for them, things might have turned out far different . . . To even contemplate this is to step into the Hell I so richly deserve.

Yet I can't bring her back. Neither woman. (You see, mon, your mind mixes and messes them, though they are apples and oranges.) I don't know if Rebeccah blames me—probably not, but I know the facts. They fix their unwavering stare upon me, and I can neither duck nor dodge away. Nor wish to now.

I know the first thing I must do is get the story, the entire story, straight in my mind, and then, perhaps, the next step will be clearer. Telling myself even this much helps, takes a little of the weight off. And yet one thing rushes forth, will not wait. Did I hold back . . . betray her, because she was black? Despite our affinity? . . . I can hardly peel back the layers . . . Perhaps not 'because,' yet possibly, more easily let slide, turned my head away, again . . . How stark, how small . . . Yes, there are other things too, but they all turn back the blame onto me, because cutting through all of that was her reaching out, quietly, undeniably. Yet I denied her. Thrice.

Many times has my mind passed over this. But not until now have the words come, and on the backs of words, faces and events. My stomach turns and turns. Confession has been long in coming. Anne's been away; we've spoken only briefly on the phone. Peter is the only other.

II.

Peter the photographer, ever wearing his pressed and worn sepia and gray, sat there, deep in her favorite chair, staring down at his knees held close together, and then up at me, blinking as he does, before he murmured, "It *is* sad."

Which? All? I searched his face, only to find him searching mine.

"But you're being a little hard on yourself," he added more firmly, "if for understandable reasons."

Hard? "What should I be doing, Peter?" Inside, I felt the familiar tightening.

"I don't know. But in both cases, it seems to me, things were beyond your control. I mean, d' you think you could have changed either one?"

When I didn't respond, he stared at his bony fingers spread open on his thighs. "I suppose you could've called the police, or tried to speak to Tyrone. But then, you didn't know."

Hearing that name again twisted the knot. Rachel's friend, whom she had been trying to leave—his thick, short neck, body like a barrel. Even she wondered how he stayed in shape, for he neither worked nor worked out. Tyrone. Tyronosaurus Rex, king of his world, I cannot help thinking—an image which emerges from the slow stiffness with which he moved, and from his resemblance to the boxer, Tyson, turning slowly in the ring, staring out with malevolent eyes. What is he thinking now? What is in his heart, having done this? Does he, indeed like some brute, lack reflection? Or is he also in anguish? I picture his sullen face sliding behind the bars of Rikers Island. How does he see it all?

But Peter's question. "Yes, called the police, I guess . . . or tried to talk with him, though I know he wasn't too fond of me." Remembering Tyrone's glower once when we met, I imagined just to have appeared might have enraged him, and a voice warns: it might have been you, lying down on that floor. Had I considered that, then? . . . Don't honestly know.

"Mac," came Peter's voice, "you couldn't have known he would go that far."

Forcing myself, I found Peter's eyes, though his face was slightly averted, and I searched them, gray and delicate, trying to anticipate their reaction to the truth that I must tell him, which I then confessed: that Rachel knew, or suspected, and in her way asked for help.

When I had uttered this, Peter looked away. For some moments we were silent, until he peered cautiously back to clarify that this had indeed been earlier that fatal evening. I could only nod, my tongue being imprisoned by the stark encounter that Rachel must have foreseen. Again Peter withdrew into reflection, only to emerge to check that all this had happened after the performance—which it had, as my second, barely discernable nod conveyed.

Another pause preceded his asking, "Had you spoken to Anne?"

"No . . . I was sitting there trying to decide whether or not to call her. When the phone rang, I thought it might be her and was annoyed when it wasn't . . . I put Rachel off, saying I was busy, even though in the back of my mind, I understood, I think, what she was asking. But I chose to dismiss it, downplay it, ignore it."

His eyes moved over my face, then away into the room's dark corners. While he knew Anne had already pulled back, neither of us knew if it was final. Certainly it had not been something I was willing to concede.

Now his eyes returned to mine and seemed to widen with a thought, "Well . . . there was hope."

As I sensed Peter reading my face, I avoided those sorrowful and unintentionally penetrating eyes, and found I could only shrug and mutter to myself that I suppose there's always hope—foolish, baseless hope.

But now he wanted to know how long before the murder had Rachel called—the inevitable question, damning in its implication that there must have been time to recover and do something. And I had indeed figured, when talking afterward with the police, that there must have been an hour or so. And as I told him, I remember his face grew long, and his dark bangs hung out stiff in an arc from his forehead—a scythe. And with that, I felt compelled to explain that if Rachel had pressed me, it might have sunk in, and I might have acted. But she was so careful not to . . . and I chose not to hear, chose to turn away.

"Anne was on your mind," he offered, a bit too readily. For while it was true, what did it excuse? . . . But then I was surprised to hear him allow, "I, for one, can't claim I would have acted any differently."

Acted? . . . Glancing at him, I found his distress genuine, and was not a little pleased, deep inside, to hear it, until a more discerning inner voice asked: Pleased? That someone else might have turned his back too? Whereas Anne, I'm quite sure, would not have done so, would have set aside her own concerns and *done* something. (There! Is that not difference enough for her to have put it on hold . . . called it off?)

I imagined someone ignoring my plea for help. How devastating! How numbing . . . Could it be that Rachel had given up, after failing to enlist the one, close source of help she had? For though she was not a small or weak woman, Tyrone was so much stronger and had not hesitated in the past, apparently, to threaten. She had described his temper—as sudden as the Moor's . . . My God . . . had he acted out of jealousy? Had there been some Iago whispering? I had not considered this, but had assumed that their struggle had arisen out of her desire to be rid of him . . . as perhaps he'd learned of the fellow she'd met at work . . . Does this, in some measure, absolve me? . . .

Squirming in my involuntary attempt to reach for any exculpation, I glanced back at Peter and repeated, "But it was me she called, Peter . . . me."

He nodded hastily, as if to allay my anxiety, but then he wondered aloud why she had opened the door and let him in, why she hadn't called the police or relatives.

Her relatives, I said, live up in the Bronx, and she may have been reluctant to involve the police . . . Becky was probably already asleep . . . Tyrone may have had a key.

Peter looked down, dismay pulling at his pale features, a nineteenth century face, long and thoughtful, companion to Emerson or Thoreau, visibly and disconcertingly moral.

Watching him closely, I saw some weight sag his cheeks and felt it sink my heart, but Peter turned to sip some beer from his tall tapered glass, and I forlornly followed.

At some point I heard him mutter, "The funeral wasn't quite real to me. I couldn't believe it was happening."

Yes, I agreed. And how much more so for poor Becky . . . But this brought back the deed. The police told me that Becky had passed out during the attack and didn't remember much. Oddly, Rachel had once said that Tyrone liked Becky and had been concerned about her future. But then how could he take her mother's life? How? . . . I began to imagine what Becky must have seen that night: her mother attacked, strangled . . .

Staring into his glass and amber liquid, Peter now voiced the incomprehensible difficulty of living in such circumstances, where that kind of thing can happen, although we know it's possible anywhere. "What it must do to you!"

I told him it was why Rachel had moved here from Brownsville. But before he could stop himself, he noted, "Wasn't far enough, was it?" Then nervously he glanced at me . . . What could I do but agree, and mutter, "Across the street from unresponsive Schurtz." You see that Sherlock's colleague, having plied me with sympathy, now simply waited for it all to tumble out, aware that the guilty are often eager to confess.

Yet hearing my distress, kind Peter repeated that he would have acted no differently, had Anne been on his mind. Damn right! cried a voice inside. Not only was she exquisite, she was mine! Peter had seen it, had seen how good she was, how thoughtful, how high—in contrast to me, who's let slip the very things that were most important. A loser, a bloody loser! My body shuddered as if its inner walls had fallen.

Perhaps in response to these groans and tremors, he stared over with concern, and mumbled that I was assuming too much of the blame. "For one thing, Mac, love is what vanishes—I read somewhere." A shy smile stole across his face. "And as for the other, if Tyrone had been prevented that night, who's to say he wouldn't have succeeded another time?"

I groaned again, and perhaps he saw that this was lame. I presumed he'd said it for me, but the problem was that Rachel had seen the danger coming, had asked for help, and I failed her, dismissed her . . . because it was inconvenient, because I was preoccupied. "No wonder Anne left."

Sharply looking over, Peter frowned heavy-heartedly, so that I realized I had confused things, (mixed and messed), as Anne's decision had taken root before, when she may have sensed I was not the one. But needing Peter's objectivity, I watched his face floating pale above his muted clothing framed by the dark fabric of the heavy chair—a spirit, or father confessor. (My mother's Catholic imagery had long ago filled the vacuum left by my father's harsh Eastern European atheism, rising on the vapors of rejected Judaism. Oh yes, coming from that world, Pop's cynicism, like a scimitar, sent us scattering.)

And now, as my eyes wandered over the room's somber shapes, hanging like courtroom functionaries, Peter's voice came again: "Don't be too hard on yourself, Mac . . . Maybe by the same token, Anne failed you, in pulling away so quickly, with so little discussion . . . Although they say all is fair in love and war, shouldn't we really do better? All of us? . . . Of course, how to,

I realize, is the problem . . . Who has that strength?" With some uncertainty, he sought my response, but I could only flush and confess that yes, when the feeling goes, it takes with it all energy and patience. Naturally I wish she had explained more, more than my work in California must draw us apart. If I had been the right choice, some solution would have presented itself, and I wondered what I was lacking, what else she was seeking. I almost asked her, but then didn't, feeling like a worm. Feared she wouldn't tell me the truth, in any case, so as not to hurt me, further . . . On the other hand, is there any explanation accepted by a broken heart? . . . But then, next to poor Rachel, how small . . .

"Peter," I could not restrain myself from proclaiming, "we'd been so happy together, so good for each other, complementing one another . . . I had no idea, really, she was heading in the opposite direction, or at least I didn't choose to take in the signs." Had this further dismayed her? An actor lost without a script—as limited as some of the characters he's played.

But instead of consoling me, he breathed deeply, shifted in his chair, and chugged down the last of his beer, gah-glunk, gah-lunk, glunk. Aaahh. Only frogs need apply. "You know," he began in a dreamy, faintly elegiac tone, "Anne is really the most beautiful woman I've known . . . . Perhaps not purely physically, but she has a head on her shoulders, and she has a heart."

Thanks, Peter. I looked at him, taken aback a bit by the feeling which constricted his voice. But he, unaware, went on to exclaim that unlike so many other beautiful women, she'd been able to get past her beauty, which God knows isn't easy, so relentlessly do we men pursue it. Yet somehow she takes it as a lucky accident. And he gnawed lightly on his lip as he considered this. "Yes," he concluded, "she's genuine."

His eyes, I saw, had become slightly less clear, and I wondered if he was upset for himself, for us, or for unspoken reasons. As our gazes met, he smiled sheepishly, which quite changed his face, filling it out, lending a sheen. "I never told you, Mac, that I'd met her before you did. I did the photos for a story she was editing. We went out several times. It was nothing, but she was very . . . gracious, and fun to be with. Who would not have fallen for her?"

As surprise and humility once again swept through me, I saw Peter watching closely before he added, "You're lucky. Next to her, I'm no prince— for one thing, she's got several inches on me. But I was glad to see you get her, and am sad to see it end." Trying to smile through blinking eyes, he almost blithely pushed his hair away from his eyes. "I thought you two looked like a couple," he continued, "seemed made for each other, brought a lot of different things to each other."

"Thanks, Peter . . ." Different things? Like heartbreak and death? And yet were Peter and I now going to just sit there and weep like a like a coupla Sisters of the Poor? . . . No way! Screw her! . . . Yet part of me was smiling, because at least one other person in this Godforsaken world had seen us, and could confirm that 'we' had existed, 'for one brief shining moment.' Taa—DAAHHH! . . . Curtain.

I thought of hugging Peter, but managed only to say that I was sorry for him. And told him that maybe we should start a club—then wished I had a better line. A smile reappeared on his lips, parting them, before he denied his experience was in any way comparable. How small I felt, how pathetic, particularly as she, our esteemed creature, was winging willy-nilly into our pasts, without either of us having known her heart—a very private person, in contrast to me, who is quite ready to roll it all out, to any mildly interested ear—another major difference between us. I never met her father, whom she's visiting in San Francisco, never got a glimpse of the formative male image in her life. She likes him, I know, has a good relationship with him. A lawyer, strong and successful, no doubt; no equivocating thespian, borrower of all identities, owner of none . . . And I know that once harnessed into that Anglo sensibility, one does not burden an already over-burdened world with the personal and petty, when there are so many greater concerns. (And when, in any case, most of one's fellow citizens are all but beneath contempt.) . . . Very noble . . . from a distance. Damn her . . . Damn damn her! See if she ever finds 'life' again! Go nuzzle up to some clean whiteshirt. Go dry up in a proper, sterile, mapped-out life! Your proper Puritan manners, and judgement, amongst your proper Puritan sheep! (At least the English value their eccentrics; over here, it's only he with a dollar!)

"D' you have another beer?" Peter suddenly asked.

Startled out of myself, eager to repay him in any small way I could, I bounded up, to collect his dead Indian and repair to the war chest for another round. "So you've known her how long?" (You, who may still see and talk to her, you for whom she still exists.)

"A year last March. The Ides."

My God! . . . He's been counting? And loving her all this time? Recalling several evenings we three spent together, I wondered if unknowingly I had flaunted 'us,' rubbed it in his face . . . God, McKim, of what, beyond your own face, are you aware? . . . Still, he had come on his own, those times, freely, happily . . . to catch a glimpse, a word?

What is it all worth? When love so often means disappointing or hurting another? And for what? A few months of happiness, before drifting away, or leaping and forsaking? And for that matter, is my career so different? All this work to produce plays which too often are chosen to cuddle, coddle, or mildly titillate for two hours or so, a mostly comfortable audience? And where is it now I'm going? But to Hollywood.

All in contrast to Anne who not only did more for Rachel and Rebec, but who pursues her career with less desperate and more idealistic motives than I. It is by her own light that she steers, and draws the rest of us along after her. Perhaps that is one thing I've learned: that without worship, or transcendence, you shrink. Right, Equus? Is she not a far, far better person than any I've known before? A far, far better place than any I've . . . (Ei-yie, yie, mon. Easy, easy, mon.)

Given the flawed soul I am, perhaps a retreat into a monastery might be best. McKim of Mt. Athos. Get thee to a none-ery! Fox in the chicken coop. Mac the Knife . . . . Good God, Macbeth, how you ramble; how your brain, like clouds, blows hither and yon, taking one form, then another, decipherable only to witches . . .

As I slowly poured the amber beer (*New Amsterdam*, brewed 'round here, they say. All right! New Yawk's comin' back!) into Peter's glass and set the bottle down on the table next to him, the foaming suds harmonized with his quiet 'thanksss,' and with the shimmering penumbra her memory cast. The moment felt surprisingly and redemptively rich. Life, even with its ineluctable ups and downs, does have its moments . . . For a time, I had Anne. Can't knock fate; the opportunities have come; the fault, dear Brutus . . .

Looking over at Peter, I saw him delicately holding his refilled glass and carefully peering at the ascending bubbles as if into a stream of faces. "Perhaps, Peter—and I'll be quiet after this—perhaps we should both go to her, hats in hand, down on our knees, and plead that she take us back, in any role she can: friends, admirers, assistants, charity cases, brothers. Only don't leave us to wander through this lovelorn world without her! Tell her that goodness, meaning, life itself, depend on it. And that only she can forgive us, save us, and restore the original light!"

As Peter sipped his beer, I saw his thin, tolerant smile forming, and he raised his glass. "Yes, McKim, all Hail Mary full of grace, and bless this soul, this Schurtz, servant of God, potential idol of Tinseltown, once he's fixed his name and nose, for he has found, in lost love, none too early, but not too late, humility—scourge of all those trying to make it on the screen and stage."

What? Was that Peter?—Yet I exclaimed, "All right! All hail, Macbeth!" And I raised me own glass to me own fallen soul. "Does not the salvation of the world lie in commiseration? And does not the key to it ride these very suds we pour down our throats? God be praised, for he thinks of everything!" . . . Except for poor Rachel, I remembered once more, though I did not mention it to Peter, the fisherman, for it was too much, at that moment. Could only sink back into my chair and close my eyes.

Peter, however, not so encumbered, picked up the thread, reminding me that humor was not Anne's forté, so that if we came to her as I proposed, she might laugh a little, but underneath would likely grow uncomfortable, wondering if we fellows really were a bit too much. And he rendered her interior voice in his own high wee voice, "I believe that here, they've gone a bit too far, these chaps. Over the edge. Certifiable. For there are limits, must be limits.'"

And I told Peter that she would be right, about myself certainly—which I mention here as an example of my new humility.

A sly smile stole over his face, and he said he understood it cannot be easy for her to see nearly every male make an effort toward her, before they know the barest details of who she is. To which I sang, "Oh, too true, too true, any cock'll doodle do." And it was true; I'd seen it: those not-so-discreet double-takes, the attempts to impress her, date her, hook into her any way they could. I had done it, though fortunately for me, she had seen me first, at a rehearsal, and had heard a little gushing from director Derek, thus encouraging her own fantasy before she met me—a fantasy which only recently had come apart. (The words jolt like an electric shock. Apart? A part. All I seek and all I fear. Is not fair foul and foul fair?)

"You were lucky," Peter declared, "lucky to have had her for a while."

"Thank you, Peter . . .

> 'This thought is as a death,
> which cannot choose
> But weep to have that which it fears to lose.'"

I looked at him. "Shakespeare."

He looked offended.

But was I lucky? To have had her for any time at all? (Eden and maiden?) Is a happiness which does not last, no happiness at all? Three months of transcendent bliss; years of heartache and sorrow. (I know all the lines; they are what make up my simple heart.)

I knew that Peter was watching me, as I was myself, and I tried to hide from us both the water in my eye, for I saw that for all my efforts and awareness, and some little success, I am not much. Actor, act-or, shadow, Smoo . . . acting out his lines, suddenly come face to face with his own insignificance.

Yes this too will pass. Soon I will be in California, working in the sun . . . But toward what? . . . Aye, there's the rub; the thistle in the kiss, my love, eh Dylan? . . . For what is all this trained sensitivity? What purpose this maimed, or ill-formed, soul? Simply to give feigned feeling to lines read over and over, while around us our numbers are struck down one by one?

As I allowed these thoughts to gently crush my heart, my feelings began to change. I was growing tired of this mournful, injured attitude; anger and impatience were brewing. And Peter, too, was stirring. I heard him say that I should stop feigning this ineffectual pose, for in fact I'd given her things she hadn't had: a certain irreverence, a looseness, a little life. And that when he saw us together, she looked happy.

I bowed to him, even as we both knew this was a grievous, stinging balm. "She may recant," he added. "She may have already."

"Poop, Peter."

". . . The distance may help—help clarify things."

"Clarity was never her problem." I'd seen she always knew pretty much what she wanted, and how to get it. "So it is with her type, quiet and unobtrusive, but woe to him who stands in her way." This I delivered with a certain mixed satisfaction, and yes, with vindictive vehemence. Bitch! (But no, she's no bitch at all.) Yet I went on, snapping bitterly that, despite her frequently noble mien, she is not unsusceptible to power, prestige, and good looks.

"You mean she's human," Peter reasoned, eyes narrowing. "Well, you have your peculiar good looks, at least."

"Touché." But I could feel my cheeks crinkling and burning as we both laughed quietly, venting our beery camaraderie, fermenting here in Sherlock's den.

When it subsided, and we regained our breath, I corrected him, saying that in fact I didn't have the looks she liked, had too much of my father's ethnic features—his nose, as Peter noted. But Peter claimed that he thought we could almost be brother and sister, with dark hair and standing tall. I had to tell him she liked those fair-haired, ballet types, Martins, Baryshnikov, and described how I saw her eyes light up once when she met them at a benefit. Fortunately for me, they were both there, and she couldn't choose between the two.

"Still Mac, you're luckier than most . . ."

"Maybe. But what, then? Accept this death stoically?" And I asked him if he would want to go through it. Imagining it, perhaps, he didn't reply, and so I pointed out that luck, like beauty, lies in the eye of the beholder.

But he shook his head, saying, "No, I'm talking about fortune; the hand you're dealt. One man's as opposed to another's."

I suspected he was reflecting on how he'd never had a chance with her. "Okay, but Peter, would you trade lives with me?"

Looking away again, he pondered. "No . . . not if to work, I'd have to go to L.A."

We smiled at this easy joke, though the fact was we both liked moving around, and as we considered this, our minds for several moments wandered off, until he broke into our reveries, "But Mac, you entertained her, took her out of herself. She may see that one day, and come back."

"Oh Peter, don't . . . The spell is broken, the trust gone. How could I ever believe her again?" (A lie, probably, but I would not let my heart entertain anything else, so soon.) From the tone of my voice, if not from my words, Peter got the picture, shaking his head and saying he never pretended to understand these things, and for a time he looked away, focusing across the floor, before asking unexpectedly, "You have any pictures of her?"

". . . Pictures? You're the photographer! . . . What the hell were you doing?"

"Never took any. Never could think of an excuse to. Probably intentionally, as it would have brought her down with the rest, in my mind."

"Jesus, Peter, you had her propped up higher than I did." Irritated with my own idealization of her, I looked away as I sought some suitable image for my anger . . . Tyrone, fucking Tyrone. How could a person do that? Actually put his hands around someone's neck and . . . It's a frame of mind I never want to explore, acting and Stanislavsky aside.

(Or do I? . . . Do it to Anne? Rip her clothes off, run my hands over . . . A terribly powerful, twisted, sexual surge. Hips and breasts. Bloody creep, Macbeth! . . . Its force surprises me, frightens me . . . even as I've read it's about power . . . or its lack.)

"Like to see 'em sometime," came Peter's voice.

"What?!"

"The pictures, Mac."

". . . Oh . . . I guess took a few . . . You can have 'em."

"No, I didn't mean that."

"Well I do. I don't want 'em. Will never look at them again . . . I wish, though, I had one of Rachel . . . and Becky . . ." I wondered if Becky had even one of her mom. "Poor kid . . . I really should do something . . . though God knows what."

Out of the corner of my eye, I saw Peter thinking, his hands cast over his nose and mouth as if in prayer. "Maybe we could help her out with school? . . . That's one thing."

"From L.A.?"

"Before you leave . . . Or financially, for college . . . I don't know . . . must be something."

Something . . . I felt my spirit reach, then lunge. "Peter! . . . Yes, of course, that's it! . . ." Why I didn't think of this, I won't ask. "But have got to get her address up there . . . Suppose the precinct would have it . . . Not much time, before I leave."

I pulled myself forward in the great armchair, feeling like a besotted Watson stirred into action by a Holmesian revelation. But was I actually going to do this? . . . Yet I found myself standing, feet deploying. In fact I was moving. My God! Actually acting? Act-ing in something real . . . She would be proud of me . . . In truth, it was for her, that I was doing it . . . Anne . . . Becky . . . Rachel . . . someone . . .

III.

"Becky?"

I stared through the darkness, and thought I saw her form sit up upon the vague outline of a sofa along a wall. I had grown increasingly tentative coming up to her cousin's apartment in the Bronx, and now felt even more so. What could I bring her, but memories of the unspeakable event?

"Becky?"

The form now arose, one among several, which my adjusting eyes discovered in reclining variations around the room. But it did not approach, at first hovering, dark against dark, then fading away without apparent motion or noise. The hair stood up on my neck. A door creaked open, then closed.

"Rebeccah?"

Now from a different direction came a child's groan, and I took a step toward it, while from behind me, filling the hall from where I'd come, her cousin's voice intoned, "Re-bec-cah, child, get up. This man 's come all the way up here to see you. Comeon, now."

Embarrassment now joined my discomfort, rising and searing my face, making me thankful for the dark. What was I doing here?

This time, emerging like a phantom from between the arms of a large chair, I saw a third form hover and then float toward me. "Rebeccah? It's Mac." The form seemed to hesitate, quiver, then sink onto an ottoman. I stepped forward, bumping into a chair, edging around it, and sliding forward, arms out, until I could tell that indeed it was her, crouched fearfully, rubbing her not-fully-awakened eyes.

"Rebec . . . just wanted to talk with you for a minute. Is that okay? . . . Mm? . . . Hmn? . . . Okay if I sit down?"

No response, and so after a moment, I turned and pulled the chair I'd hit closer and descended onto its rim, to the relief of my shaking legs. "Rebec, I realize that no words are adequate . . . but I wanted to tell you that I admired your Mom. She was a wonderful woman. All of us did, and we—Peter, Anne, Maggie, John, Jillie and I—want to do what we can, want to do a little of what she would have done for you." I watched and listened for any reaction, but there was none. She moved not at all, head down, face averted. Was this yet another ordeal for her? Or was she merely sleepy, or depressed?

"Rebeccah, we thought that, as your mom would have done, we want to help you with school." Still she did not budge or respond. It was beginning to feel even tougher than I'd feared. "Unfortunately, I'll be away, for a while, but the others will be here, and we're all going to do what we can, to help with college, even though it's a few years off. Your Mom wanted very much for you to go, but it takes a lot of preparation, and money . . . She knew though, and we know, Rebec, you're a bright girl. And we want to do whatever it takes."

Still she had not moved. Was she asleep? I realized that I had no idea what she was thinking. "Rebec? Did you hear me at all?"

Silence. No movement, until finally, she raised her head.

"Have you thought about college at all? Rebec?"

She nodded once, but then her voice whispered, "No."

". . . Well . . . d' you think it would be a good idea?" Continued silence. (What did you expect, dick-head? This is hardly the time . . . . Although if not now, when?) "Rebec, it can give each of us a better chance to do what we might want to do in life. You know?" (Right, chump! Look at you, fine example, hiding on the stage.)

"Rebec, what we're going to do is put some money into an account for you, for college, with your name on it. To pay for college expenses . . . And, from time to time, we'll add to it, until you're ready." . . . Still nothing . . . What did you want? Grateful round eyes? Smiles, forgiveness? . . . I looked around, through the darkness. Did this mean anything to her?

Then I heard her whisper, "Thank you, Mac . . . Thank everybody . . ."

A bell! A veritable bell to me. My eyes burned, my heart sang. Through everything, she was still there . . . Moreover she did not blame me, or had forgiven me, and in this, gave me more than I can ever give her, dear God. "Thanks, Rebec," I managed to croak. "I'll tell them." I tried to find her eyes, but she was staring down at her toes. There in the dark, she seemed smaller, lost, and I tried to imagine what she must be feeling. But it was impossible and certainly too painful. "Rebec? Anything you need? Anything I can do for you?" (Now? cried a voice inside . . . Now?!) But this time she looked up at me through the dimness, with those round eyes I'd envisioned. I barely dared to look back. Had Rachel told her anything? . . . Carefully I inhaled. "You okay here? Your cousins nice?"

(What am I asking? And who am I to be doing so? P. Pilate of Bank Street?) Intensely uncomfortable, I stood up abruptly, not thinking, only to hear a cry and see her recoil, pressing herself onto her ottoman, covering her chest and head with her arms.

"Becky, Becky, it's okay, 's okay. Sorry, was just stretching." And I sat back down quickly. But she did not move, did not uncover herself.

"Rebec, sorry . . ." Though shaking, on I went, jabbering, "Bec, as long as I'm here, isn't there anything I could do for you? . . . Take you to a museum? A movie? Shop for school?" For an instant I glanced away, and when I looked back, I saw her roll off the ottoman and silently slip away into the darkness. The unseen door opened and closed.

"Rebec!?" I called, but half-heartedly, at half-volume, conscious that the cousin must be within earshot. And what, in any case, could I do? Run after her? . . . It was over. Jesus, what a jerk! How thick, how maladroit. Anne, Maggie, would have done better. At what are you good, Schurtz?

And so, I stood and turned away, consoling myself that Becky would have had eventually to leave Bank Street, to make her way through the world. Perhaps what we were offering would help her. What more could I do? . . . Yet must face the fact that I will never know what she thinks of it all, or of me.

Clamped by these thoughts, I staggered out of the room, and back down the endless corridor that the hall now seemed, to the front door where I again met the cousin, a heavyset woman, Rachel's age, whatever that was . . . She appeared calm and intelligent, but I fear that as I repeated our intentions, I saw a skeptical look in her eyes, particularly when I mentioned the money. But this didn't bother me. I don't mind having to prove myself to her, or anyone. I said that I would like to telephone regularly, to speak to Rebeccah. Was that all right? She agreed easily enough. In fact, she reacted to everything with remarkably little comment. A pipe dream, she was thinking, no doubt. Well, she'll see.

Said goodbye, went down the stairs and out, trying to be alert and look around, to get a sense of Rebeccah's new neighborhood, but . . . in fact my consciousness had withdrawn into a single, blinkered eye deep inside.

IV.

Nervous and couldn't concentrate, I remember, as I stood tapping my foot by the door of the slowly twisting No.2 snaking its way south over the rusted elevated tracks between the black, brown, and burned out, derelict buildings of the South Bronx. Undoubtedly agitated by my screw-up with Rebec, not to mention memories of Rachel, I was sighing and sweating and breathing irregularly—snorting and stamping like el toro—to judge from the stares of my few fellow midday passengers, their eyes wide and wary. A mad matador about to whip out his sword?

Fumbled again, really fucked up. Sent poor Becky fleeing, didn't sound sincere, wasn't relaxed, hadn't prepared enough. (You of all people!) Underestimated the care and tact required. Others have proclaimed that new beginnings are possible, and redemption too, if only one can find the conviction, and the guts.

Squinting, I looked down at the still-life streets, half sunlit, half shadowed. Groups of men had gathered around doorways, clutching brown-bagged bottles, as I lurched by above. A world of the dead, producing thousands of Tyrones, angry, frustrated, without the structures of hope—so far from Bank Street, where Rachel's hope had taken root . . .

And Schurtz? Marked for life, the real criminal on the cross, freed by dumb chance, while poor Becky must somehow find a way to live with her experience, of seeing her mother extinguished . . . How does one do that?

It occurred to me that Rachel never told me who Rebec's father was or what had become of him, and I wonder if Becky knows . . . I remember the traumatizing effects of growing up with troubled, ill-matched parents. How much worse had it been for her?

Is her only hope that her cousins will provide the necessary support? . . . And that our small efforts might, in some way, help?

When the train finally entered the dark, veiling tunnel, my thoughts fled back to the weeks following our first sidewalk meeting, when I would encounter Rebec in the afternoons, home from school, waiting for her mom's return from work. At first we didn't know what to say to each other, but slowly, as she became accustomed to me, she began to tell me about her days at school, describing what she was learning, her classmates, teachers, and thoughts. We would sit on the brown cement steps and let our minds go, or walk through the red blocks, turning and squeezing through the strands of people on the narrow sidewalks, to the cleaners, the grocery, or to John's Pizza on Bleeker.

Eventually it occurred to me to take her to the theatre, which, we discovered, delighted her, in no small measure because Maggie and John were so friendly and encouraging. And in time, she must have convinced Rachel to come to the play, one Sunday matinee.

It seemed they found something in it to enjoy, although their expressions afterward, backstage, were somewhat dazed, among the crew resetting for the evening performance. Becky stood there quite independently, eventually smiling and saying that she liked it. And I remember her staring at me in an unabashed, new way. Yet what could white, middle-class love problems have meant to her? Characters who expected to live in the sun's warmth, but who found themselves alone in the cold at midnight? Such stories are supposed to resonate, but whatever enjoyment those two found came from, I suspect, watching Maggie, John, and me wring our hands over imagined crises. And Rachel, I noticed, who could be candor itself, hung back reticent and still, as if she feared bruising our feelings.

I should have pressed them. Who knows? In hearing their reactions, I might have learned something. Certainly I might have better understood how Rachel saw her own situation—and thus might have been alert enough to help that night. How simple that extra step, how easily sloughed aside—adamantly fiddling while Rome burned. For all the accumulated wisdom in all these plays, I do not act with any more insight, nor do my habits reflect those lessons.

And that matinee was not the only opportunity. A week or so later, Rachel invited me to dinner. (Guess who's coming to dinner, Rebeccah?) It was the first time I had entered their basement home, and although I remember the air was heavy with cooking smells, it was quite cozy and neat, with most of the furniture newly arrived from Macy's.

They, understandably, were watching to see how I would react, just as I watched them after the play. But I had the easier task. Following a tentative few minutes, I soon found myself enchanted, charmed, and dinner, of pork chops, mashed potatoes, collared greens, and sweet potato pie was a treat, exotic to me in this nouvelle, Asian era—although with all our chatter I had little time to savor it.

The apartment itself was in blacks, browns, and whites, with perhaps more mirrors, shining surfaces, and leathery textures than I would have chosen. Mother and daughter had desks at opposite walls, on which to do homework, for Rachel was taking a night course at Macy's, for advancement within their accounting department. I wish I could have seen them once working back-to-back in their snug home.

The kitchen took up one side of the large, square room, and the bedroom and bath were down a short hall. Minimal but adequate, I thought. Yet how happy they seemed, and I decided this was all one really needed—though now I recall that Rachel was looking for a larger place, to accommodate the prospective husband she'd recently found.

As I think about it now, it was a dream-like evening, when I could have been in a different country, and where there was something magical, although perhaps it was only the warm light, simplicity, and closeness of we three sitting around the little dinner table.

When we finished eating, Becky, I remember, rose to retrieve a notebook from her desk and began reading stories about her classmates and visits to the Zoo, and about some of our neighborhood merchants whom she and I got to know in the course of our errands—all woven into a connected narrative that moved between experience and imagination so smoothly that I hardly noticed the leaps. Only as she finished, and inadvertently showed me the blank pages, did I see that she had made it all up on the spot. Was there a more joyous, observant, humorous playwright in the city? The endless range and variety of human creativity astonishes me as nothing short of miraculous.

Once Becky went off to brush her teeth, Rachel began telling me about her work at Macy's, and about her fellow, Robert, whom she'd met in the department, and who seemed to be very much what she was seeking, once he concluded a difficult divorce.

"You know, Mac, he's a good man, treats me nice, and you know, I like that. Don't know why I ever put up with anything else . . . 'Course I do know. And I know it helps that Robert's got a good job. Helps a whole lot."

Later, after Becky had said goodnight, she told me a little about Tyrone. She said she understood him and the difficulties he was encountering, adrift in Brooklyn where the opportunities were few and the perspectives limited. He was apparently somewhat younger, and she admitted her error in allowing an attachment to grow some time before, when she had turned to him in temporary need—for now she was having difficulty shaking him.

And then, while she didn't ask me directly for my story, she fell silent and waited, watching me quite placidly, so that I had to say something. Not that it was hard, for having only recently met Anne, I was only too happy to express my joy. And Rachel concurred, "The little I've seen of her—she seems real nice. 'Fact I sensed she and I could be friends, you know?"

While I nodded, I don't think I did know. I'd sensed something between the two of them, some vague something, but hadn't put it into words.

There was one other thing that night, however, which gnaws at the corners of my consciousness . . . As I began to leave, standing up and thanking her, she stretched back in her chair in a revealing way, watching me with what I thought were strangely open, smiling eyes. And although I almost immediately turned away, my eyes could hardly fail to run over her. Couldn't have avoided it. I felt a twinge, a mental gulp, as I wondered if this was unguarded on her part, or intentional . . . Certainly the moments after that were awkward, as something new had thrust its head between us, inappropriately, given everything. Yet fleetingly I wondered what her blackness might mean, what differences there might be. I felt surprisingly ham-fisted and slow, and she must have seen my face, must have read my every thought. Jesus!

As we reached the door, I blurted out several compliments, but I was nervous, and yes, divided, largely over what had to be my own imaginings. (I know I live this second, shadow life, which speeds ahead a thousand miles, while a simple smile is forming.) I remember her standing there watching me, quite self-possessed, as I was not. No doubt she saw into my awkwardness. Disconcerting to be so transparent.

I don't know—we'd both drunk enough—perhaps it was nothing, though this hurts my sense of an actor's perspicacity, something that any student of human nature prides himself in. I remember it took real willpower to find her eyes, though she was close. Christ, Mac, you're no prude, not fastidious, hardly pure! Why should others be any less human? Yet I expected her to be. Even now, my body is tense, and I cannot decide how much I've remembered or conjectured.

And so, at some point, it occurred to me I would have to either kiss her good night, or not. In most cases, it would have been automatic, and God knows if she were an actress it would have been pro forma, or performa. But as it was, it was something different . . . starkly real. I could feel her body heat as she waited before me smiling; could smell her perfume, alluring and slightly off-putting in its heavy sweetness. Abruptly, almost spasmodically, I took and shook her hand, whispered my thanks, spun around, and wrenched open the door—stepping out into the cool night. Thank God . . .

Not that I wouldn't have liked to embrace her . . . as a friend, woman, and yes, as an experience, I'm afraid. Yet if I had, what then? What would have followed? What? . . . And what's the lingering big deal that I didn't? . . . Perhaps part of it lies in the suspicion that if I hadn't held back then, I might have heard her that other night . . . and she might be here now . . .

As the memory of that evening returns in clearer detail, I see that several times earlier I had stared at—well, had taken in—her full cashmere sweater. Had I sent unintentional signals? Might this have been what she was reacting to? . . . And yet essentially it seems something more.

For someone living in these emancipated times, in this hip city, I am disappointingly slow. Or is it that I am obscuring things from myself, out of guilt? . . . Or is it merely time clouding? . . . Whatever the case, I suspect there are pieces missing. I imagine Rachel must have laughed at my bolting departure. Yet our friendship grew, because of our proximity, if nothing else. But no! There was chemistry, I need to declare. And warmth, and, yes, a kind of love . . . Though God knows it did her no good. And orphaned young Rebeccah Brown.

Too much? Is it an inconsequential story at the edge of the anthill? . . . I don't know. A person dies, is removed from the stream, like a fish caught, as we all will be sooner or later, and is quickly forgotten, with few exceptions. So naturally we hold on, to this, our only chance, for as long as we can, by whatever fumbling means we can. Yet I cannot shake my sense of failed responsibility, to Rachel, and yes, ultimately, to myself.

V.

Need a rest . . . but other memories are insinuating—flooding back actually.
"Excuse me, are you McKim Schurtz?"

Am I? The eternal question. When it was posed this time, I was standing alone on the stage, having been called to the theatre early that afternoon for an additional press session, following our unexpectedly successful opening of *Half Moon*. 'Successful' meaning that critics had been sufficiently inspired to spew bright streamers out upon the public, not only praising the play, but also one M. Schurtz, newcomer. (Yes, old 'Stuffy,' now having the last laugh on his myopic, bourgeois schoolmates who had so dubbed him.)

This is to say I was buoyant, jubilant, possibly giddy. And to set the stage more completely, I might just repeat some of those notices: "In the lead role, Schurtz brings just the right balance of intelligence and vulnerability, strength and obdurate blindness." "Breathes life into an otherwise too familiar role and story." "A middle-class Stanley Kowalski, this character, as played by Schurtz, fills the story with feeling and fire and a sense of something risked." (Not too bad, old man, and yet if these pundits were as discerning as they think they are, they would have attributed far more of the credit to playwright Peck.)

Nevertheless, feeling rather good and at peace, I was watching Derek, in the first row, deftly fending off the usual inane personal questions, when this voice, transporting its question as upon a gentle breeze, startled me from behind. "Excuse me, are you . . . ?"

Even before I turned, I remember thinking the voice was round and resonant, and aware. And then, there she was . . . dream of dreams, who I would conjure if conjure I could. I must have blushed, for she did, but then managed to introduce herself, explaining that she was from the magazine, and asking if I had time to chat about the play, and myself—the only two subjects, as luck would have it, with which I was then conversant. How long have I lived with this inexplicable, oil-and-water mixture of confidence and its abject absence?

But so stunning was she (Zow!) and so susceptible was I, from ingesting the play's dramatic situation, if not its wisdom, that I went spinning. "Chat?" I croaked, as she waited eager-eyed. "With Schurtz? You're sure? A conversing? Here and now?" (Oh fool! For the life of me, I could not stop—a chicken without its head.) "Talk? Why not?" (And here, God knows why, burst forth Peck's lines, his absurd ones from his play within a play.)

> My lady, if it's history you do seek,
> to the victors you must speak;
> while if it's insight you desire,
> to an outcast go inquire;
> but if you want mere opinion,
> why then, by all means, consult with any minion.

As she had not, at that point, seen the play, the lines came out of nowhere, and this may have accounted for her rather perplexed expression. For a moment neither of us moved—she, no doubt, awaiting my lead and return to intelligibility. But fortune was with me that day, try as I might to subvert it, and I was able to maintain a kind of distracted poker-face, whose silence and inscrutability, she told me later, intrigued her, poor girl.

Semi-conscious, I led her back among the sets, where by chance we sat down upon a bed, catching her off-guard, disarming her, being suggestive without being forward. But soon that didn't matter, nor did anything else, for we talked easily and for a long time about the play, acting, me, and finally her. I don't remember what was said, but at the end I asked her if she'd like to have lunch, and she said yes. Yes? . . . Yes!

Nor do I remember her leaving, for I was somewhere off the floor. My performance that evening was all over the place: too much here, nothing there; I forgot a line, several maybe. I didn't know a woman could do that to me, in real life. Maggie recognized it immediately and threw a cup of cold water into my face between acts, reviving me enough to apologize, as it had been her scenes that I had screwed up. And I couldn't sleep that night, as I haven't recently, these past few weeks, since it ended.

I don't know . . . before I go on . . . was it worth it? Would I do it again, knowing the inevitable, life-inverting pain? . . . And my turning off in Rachel's hour of need? . . .

Don't know that I can honestly lay this on the other, but Anne had pulled back; her specter hovered over me; I was coming apart. (A part? Actor, act or—all that again.) But would I? . . . The full force of my soul cries out, Yes! She was my chance, my life . . .

The restaurant she suggested was in midtown near her office. It was French, white décor, and elegant, of course, and I remember watching her wend her way between the tables, turning heads, largely female and older. I don't remember what she wore, though my sense of it is the usual: simple, black, expensive. But she was the same: direct and unaffected—superb. I'll never understand how all those things in her went together. In that sense, I guess, I never knew her.

After ordering shrimp-something which I hardly touched, we began talking, as plates came and went on flashing arms. We may as well have been in audience in the Vatican's inner sanctum, for all the world intruded. First, we turned to the theatre, to favorite plays and theorizing why so few good ones were being produced or even written these days, and then we moved on to her magazine. She had taken a job there, one of the newer woman's magazines, because someone she knew offered it to her, and she thought it would help her sort through the range of careers she'd been considering. Yet in the three years since, she'd found not only was she good, so that she was promoted to a department editor, but she enjoyed it, and now intended to stay in the field for a time.

"My one disappointment," I remember her saying and laughing (How quick a study I was with her lines!) "is that I'm not creative, at least in the way I would like to be. I can write, but not fiction; I'm not a story teller, though I wish I were. Oh, how much I would enjoy that! I envy novelists and playwrights who create worlds outside, who get beyond themselves. And actors too."—she remembered just in time.

Given the opening, I inserted my frequent observation, stumbled on years ago, that these worlds are seldom created from whole cloth; that they are usually life itself transplanted.

"Yes," she agreed, "but it's the telling and editing, the transforming, isn't it, that lifts it into something memorable, and provides the teller with a way out of her life, or his."

(This, as I sat there wishing to find a way into hers.)

Excuse me, but are you part French?" she suddenly asked.

". . . What? Schurtz? French?"

"Mother's side? . . . Polish, then?"

Lost, my face evidently went blank.

"Sorry," she said. "I thought I saw something, something of those faces of the Revolution, so pale and serious."

"Me? . . . So, behind your lovely, earnest face, you do have fantasies! Creative and didn't know it."

"I wish . . . Mac, do you have a chance to read fiction, or are you always studying parts and plays?"

A more penetrating question than she knew. As I groped, she mentioned Atwood, Yourcenar, Spark, Stegner, Updike, and wondered had I read any? Fortunately, when I hastily and dangerously nodded, she went on without asking which—a stroke of luck that won me time to rack my brain for the one title from among them I'd seen long ago, brandished in the hand of some friend—something about wife-swapping in suburbia.

"Updike, to consider one," she continued, "or Oopdike, as I call him, bless his seemingly conflicted soul, adoring women yet mostly appointing them supporting roles—this fine observer. Yet he's noted, in the world of writing, that whereas fiction and poetry are like sailing out onto the open ocean, with all the implied risks, delights, and freedoms . . . criticism, in contrast, leans upon the thoughts of others, and is thus a comparative hugging the shore . . . And all of this, dear Mac, is to say that what I admire is that sailing out . . . beyond the safety of the shore."

Out? If she wanted out, what hope the rest of us? What hope had I of possibly following? . . . I was about to note that fiction grows upon a bed of real corpses, but she appeared so much in earnest that all I could do was sympathize.

"Mac, I came to one of your rehearsals some weeks ago. Derek invited me, and I watched you all trying different things. At times just letting your imaginations go, particularly you two. I found it exhilarating, hilarious. I was captivated. In no way could I ever do that."

Ah hah! So that was it. But while I was not about to disabuse her of that misimpression, (this thought from such a beauty came, ne'er I the one to call it lame), in reality, what Derek and I had been doing was simply free-associating, pulling old tricks from out our hats, until something fit. "A kind of editing," I explained, "wading through a great deal of detritus and error."

Her smile, I saw, dismissed this as undue modesty, before she eagerly completed her thought. "Despite my handicap, or perhaps because of it, I have begun thinking that I might now want to eventually move into fiction editing with a trade publisher. I think I could be good at it; I'm sure I would enjoy it. In a sense, I seek to do what Derek does with you, helping to select, and encourage, and maybe slightly correct the course of those who sail out upon the sea."

Her own modesty, mixed with a strange urgency, surprised and puzzled me. "Have you written any fiction?"

She nodded quickly. "I've tried. Even took a course once, but it was embarrassing, revealing that what was in my head carried no grace or melody." And displaying her discouragement she shook her head.

For some reason, her confession had a sobering effect upon me—whose dreams, at least, had never acknowledged any such thwarting. I found it humbling as well, probably because I had never set my goals in terms of others, but in contrast, had spent the majority of my time focusing on, and trying to pin down, my protean self. Why some of us wounded turn inward, into the consuming dark, while others turn outward, to help the world, I don't know. How soon would she see I was mired in the first camp, and gracefully let me go?

But not that day. It was our beginning, and she was alight. "Mac, on the other hand, as OopDike and others have noted, the world is awash in fiction, more and more of which goes unread, so that I wonder if moving over to books might be like joining the church, arriving just as the congregation is slinking out the door."

"Sucked out, by the vacuum!" I snapped with unexpected vehemence. Not sure what I was thinking. The world is too complex, too multi-layered, for me to judge it. I can barely apprehend, much less comprehend, things which bump against my nose. Aware of this, I moved to safer ground. "Same thing, Anne, with the theatre: the audience for serious plays appears to dwindle, even in this jeweled seat of culture. But what really is it? . . . Fewer good plays, outrageous ticket prices, out-of-control production costs—the consequences of our acquisitive society, of every piggy one of us, all plucking at the golden goose. In fact, sometimes I think our civilization's death is near, with parts of it dying for much of our century. The old dust to dust . . . Eventually the theatre may come back, if we survive. But at best, I give the species two or three centuries, before annihilation quiets the raucous continents."

Anne, I found, was studying my face, her lovely dark eyes wide, ardent, and delicately defined. "I very much enjoy this kind of chat, Mac. I find it too seldom. However, I'm not as pessimistic as you. Look at the beginnings of this country, too often remembered as a time of peerless, moral leaders, yet it was full of contention, acrimony, back-stabbing, and terror so that the whole thing almost flew apart before it came together. Yet somehow, through all the wrenching crises and various horrors, it has provided many of its citizens with a good life. And you and I talking in this way fills me with delight and hope."

Really? . . . (Who she talkin' 'bout, mon? This abject oil-and-water mixture? Maybe if she take a closer look, mon, da sparkle fall from her eyes.) I inhaled. "I don't know . . . I'm afraid I find a certain satisfaction in making pronouncements about the demise of things which have disappointed me, even if that demise will drag me down with it. A fatalism born of impotence, probably."

"Maybe, McKim, you're too close to judge. Many people love the theatre, and although I agree we're not in one of its inspired periods, a revival can begin with one compelling work, or a single playwright, or actor," she added, with her sparkle.

"But commercialism, Anne, has infiltrated all the arts, driving out those with originality and vision, throughout the world, and certainly in movies. We've entered a becalmed Sargasso Sea." (I realized I was trying to remember her Cheever metaphor, or, oops, was it Updike's ocean?) Glancing over at her, I caught her hiding a smile—at me or my metaphor?

But then apparently reaching for gravity's rainbow, she said, "If we, who are fortunate, don't change things, who will? Individuals can make a difference, as I'm sure I don't have to tell you, with all the history you must have read and played."

Although she probably didn't intend it, a squeak of doubt escaped her voice, which my casual laugh tried mightily to assuage. "History? Of course, when I can. *Guns of August*, Vidal's *Lincoln*, to name just two recent ones." (If by recent you mean within memory at all.)

Her raised eyebrow may have conveyed almost anything. Perhaps she didn't cotton to calling Vidal's version 'history,' but believing I'd better beef up the list, I hastily added, "Not to mention: *Henry IV, A Man For All Seasons, Equus, Travesties, The Real Thing . . . Macbeth*?" The last I slipped in warily. "All histories are, in a sense, witness to their eras, to their behaviors, issues, conflicts . . . neuroses."

That seemed to please her, and she looked closely at me. "I understand you're working as a kind of 'big brother' in the neighborhood."

For a moment I couldn't fathom what she was alluding to, until it dawned on me—Rebeccah. The story must have been spread, and exaggerated, by ebullient Derek, tale teller and tweaker. "Well, that's not quite the case. There's a young teen who lives across the street, with whom I've become friends, along with her mom. I'm afraid it's no more than that. She often comes to the theatre with me because her mom works late. But . . . it does me more good than it does her."

Despite my honest disavowal, I could see that Anne had again found something admirable in it, evidence perhaps of a social conscience. Well, why not? If she could believe it, I might learn to. Has not truth out-stranged any fiction?

"By the way, where do you live?" she asked. "I'm not far from the theatre, just over in Grove Court."

"Really? How lucky! Hard to find a more charming place than that. And we're neighbors! I'm on Bank Street." When warmly she smiled, I felt as if it were Aphrodite blessing me, from no farther away than just across the table. With it, however, came remembrance of poor Paris, upon whom Aphrodite also smiled.

VI.

That's how it started, really, that lunch, although she told me that for her it had been the rehearsal, when she had been struck by our invention and pizzazz. A few nights later, she came to the play itself, and seemed excited afterward, seemed to have been absorbed by it. Certainly the fact that her magazine did a story on the importance of off-Broadway stages in bringing serious work to the public—a story which featured *Half Moon*—adduced her appreciation. But then that publicity helped swell a second wave of ticket buying and indirectly led to my leaving New York. Was there method to her kindness? Did she foresee that success would lift me up and away?

I wonder now if she ever really considered us long term. I asked her once, but somehow she avoided it—don't remember how—and I didn't press her, figuring there was time.

After the performance, I had invited her backstage, where Derek, who for some reason hung around that evening, was the first to rush up, arms and eyes fluttering, and, like some poodle marking territory, spray her with caresses and attention. Why, Derek, why the display? I was embarrassed for her, and annoyed at him. But she took it light-heartedly enough. Problem was that when she stepped back next to me, I felt compelled to reclaim her, and hence awkwardly hugged her, before I was ready, before we were. Had wanted it to be special, didn't want show-biz glibness.

But she appeared unaffected. She could be, I was learning, very smooth, much more so than I. And I liked that, though didn't quite trust it, just as I don't quite feel comfortable with this telling. Something's off, something's not quite right. Yet must go on, or flounder. Corrections to come.

I remember that merely seeing her, those first few times, took my breath away—part Anouk Aimée, part Garbo, very elegant in a simple way. Could hardly believe it. Always feared it would come apart, the whole thing, like a dream.

> . . . I don't fight it; my love is this fear.
> I nourish it, who can nourish nothing,
> love's slipshod watchman.

Yevtushenko. Russian gloom or romantic posture? Was I setting up a self-fulfilling prophecy? Or is there some independent, objective reality out there? And how does an ordinary man like me decide? I feel myself shaking, recoiling, as it comes back, like re-opening a wound, stitch by stitch. No, no, get on, just get on, and quickly through it all.

Eventually we extricated ourselves from the theatre, and went off alone for a late supper. Went to the Blue Mill, not far from her court. She told me what she thought of the play, and my performance. "McKim, you were good . . . real, truthful. I was held; it hit pretty close to the bone." And her tone, the real barometer, supported her assessment, while her other comments indicated that she hadn't missed much. She saw that the play's opening was stronger than its end; that my character's transformation must be taken on faith; and that Derek might have helped Maggie and John bring out their characters more by not rushing the early scenes—something that might have given everything more resonance in the final scene. Of course she'd heard our discussions at rehearsal, and I had mentioned some of this, but even allowing for that, no question, she'd observed closely.

Later, drifting the short distance to her door, we discovered how much we both loved the neighborhood, its trees and graceful steps and stoops, its intimacy and textures, its people and sense of community. And beyond that, the awareness that people were alive and trying things, even if vainglory underlay most of it.

This discovery moved me deeply, as if someone else was speaking my heart. Some of the joy, I recognized, came from its unexpectedness, for she very much fit the mold of an Upper Eastsider, someone a little less inclined to expose herself to the risks and openness of this world, and more important, not so likely to appreciate me. Yet not only was she open, but she listened closely, as our conversation leapt back and forth, eager to catch everything—lips slightly open, poised to speak. I felt encouraged, at last, to reveal my soul . . . Yes, so it was, for a time.

When we reached her door, I was sure we would see each other again, and my spirits were soaring. I decided this time I would just shake hands, and we did—four hands, warmly, whole-heartedly.

Walking home, up Hudson, I was caught between ecstasy and apostasy—
What was real, what was imagined? How to explain it? How had I deserved
it? Eh, McKim Schurtz? "Excuse me, *are you* McKim Schurtz?" Indeed!
Would a nose by any other name smell as sweetly? . . . Mother, poor woman
at sea, born a century too late, did you ever once imagine what it would
be like to live shackled to this moniker? Is it possible to conceive two less
compatible syllables? Did your choice reflect the incompatibility you had
by then discovered in your marriage? Or more probably, you were trying
to compensate for your husband's lack of grace and class, as you saw it, and
preserve your own family's former, and largely imagined, social status, and its
Catholicism, in the face of your husband's questionable, probably half-Jewish,
origins? But how did you expect your son, under such a yoke, and picking
up on your mixed signals, to take himself seriously?

And Father, mocking, if not denigrating, almost everything . . . calling
me, to needle your wife, Macbeth, MacDuff, and finally McMuffin. You too
could not take your son seriously. And so how could it surprise either of you
that he fled into the theatre and roles, where dissembling is commended?
And where many people find an otherwise missing sense of family . . . And
where I met Anne.

> Reflections are tricky, independent steeds
> that mirror past and present needs.
> Some silvery chimera passing?
> Some low and cunning ferret glancing,
> which cannot slough off its mortal coil?

Schurtz . . .

Summer was then in full bloom, settling over the West Village more
evocatively than I could have dreamed. In the warm night air and yellow
light, the streets took on, once the bustle of Seventh Ave. was left behind,
the stillness and heightened unreality of stage sets, each block with its own
lighting and character, which Anne and I would try to define and compare,
as we meandered through the streets.

Usually we saw each other only after the performance, once she had moved
her schedule, working late and going in late. Often we would join the others
for a meal or drink, gatherings which Anne said she looked forward to for
their warm, lively chatter and humor, and their sincere acceptance of her,
though I cannot imagine a group which would not accept her. She mixed in
easily; Maggie and she always found much to talk about, and Peter would

join us to see and be near her, I now realize. Derek, too, would come from time to time, and Karl, when the stage was put to bed. Even John, who was usually reserved, in his tall blonde way, would clear his throat, puff himself up into Falstaff's shape and frame of mind, and leaning next to her dark, delicate beauty, would whisper lewd suggestions of what might be done if she would but accompany him 'round the corner.

She would smile and give him a light elbowing, apparently unruffled by his ribbing her straitlaced manner . . . but I wonder if she may have been, underneath, put off, telling herself that while this was all new and fun for now, it would not make a life, not these theatre people, with their exposed members, membranes, and egos.

But maybe not. It lifted and freed her, she said. Was exotic, radiated joy and life in greater variety and profusion than she had known. "Mac, this has been a dream, getting to know you and your world. I'm so appreciative; I'm so happy. I love it."

And indeed it seemed she did . . . Yet alas, how could our first physical fusing live up to expectations? Fear, no doubt, was a problem; fear that such sensitized minds could not let go. She's not a sensual person but a cerebral one, whose antennae are ever on and waving. Nor was she a woman one fantasized about in certain ways. Not that this was necessary. Hardly a complaint, merely a difference. And yet it did happen, finally . . . I don't remember the details; I was so concerned about her reaction; I remember searching her eyes . . . It was in my large, wooden bed, where she may have wondered if it was not Holmes to whom she had given herself . . . Now, as I remember it, eventually we found smiles, even if neither of us had been swept away . . . And we did improve with, as she put it with uncharacteristic humor, rehearsal.

It was not until our third week that she told me she was recovering from a failed relationship.

"Who isn't?" I blurted out defensively.

Did that reaction disappoint her? Yet I did ask her about him, and could have predicted that he was the successful, big-firm lawyer, whom she soon after described. Everything she should have wanted, she said: smart, interested, kind, handsome. Yet the situation, more than the person, she explained, was just too predictable. She had seen her life unfolding ahead of them like a trip-tik, and that image had scared her. She could not go on, despite knowing it would hurt him terribly. (Is this the source of much of her humility?) Although he'd taken it, standing in front of her, courageously, unselfishly, even philosophically, she said—had been concerned about her—still, she could not change her mind. Maybe, she reflected, she wanted less perfection, a chink, passion, anger . . . humanness?

I could picture him: blonde-haired, good-looking, cleanly chiseled in that not-quite-real, not-quite-there, narcissistic Ivy League way. Can anyone ever overcome such advantages?

She had wondered also, she told me, if he could ever really see and react to a world outside his own—if indeed he would ever encounter one. The gold coast of Connecticut, the Nutmeg State, where both were born, she said, produces, in its pleasant climate and fortunate economic environment, train-loads of good, handsome, decent people. It was she, she said, who was the malcontent, a maverick from a troubled family, and fatally scratched by contact with California. "Life, Mac, is too short, too rich, too stirring, for me to settle into that world, never questioning or doubting, never journeying off the shore."

As I agreed, I wondered how she would react to the craziness I came from and must carry in my head. Eventually it would test her composure, and us. And for an instant, I think, I saw the sad reality ahead.

To her credit, I believe she sensed this and embraced me with feeling, matched only a few times subsequently . . . And what did I do? How did I respond? Trying to be like him, I played strong and cool, arms around her . . . while my heart pounded like the sea . . . yet felt prohibited from crying out . . . Oh Fool! Oh flawed temperament; timing ever off; opportunities, and time itself, slipping through my fingers . . .

VII.

Finally I did tell Pop about her, on one of my lunch excursions uptown to his real estate office. He looked at me with bored, heavy eyes from out his large, long head (What, if anything in this life, pleases that man?) and said nothing, turning instead to his business and then, as always, to the issue of how I might make a living. My contract with MGM has temporarily shut him up—actually made him cough, when he heard the figure, and break into a shit-eating grin, the bastard . . . And yet I cannot deny that the profits of his years of sweat have eased my way considerably . . . Old Pop, dear Pop, you never told me who you are and what you dream . . . if you know.

I haven't told him that it's over. Would he care, or have even seen that she is extraordinary, if they'd met? Doubt it. That kind of beauty means nothing to him; wouldn't notice if it passed before him. Has always been that way, so far as I know. His early life was too tough, probably: family decimated by war and hate . . . pieces scattered over countries. Little is certain; he's told us only an episode here and there. Why so silent?

But can't lead my life to please him, any more than he has reached out to us . . . And yet again where does this end? Who will say, I care?

She did, for a while. In so many ways, she was it. The right fit, in every way, even physically. Didn't have to bend to kiss her. Kissing in fact became something quite new and other for me, with her. And she smelled so great, just herself. And not small up top either; felt them when we pressed together, firm yet soft—right through her business suit. Yet what stood out was her aura of delicacy and self-possession, which it seems many beautiful women have. (Confidence, is it? Self-awareness?) When I would embrace her, her response was never needy or selfish, never awkward or purely physical, never just an embrace, but a bestowing and mutual nearing and touching, which grew from, I believe, her awareness of the other and of what she had to give—and from an awareness of the choice we had made and a respect for everything that contributed to that choice.

Alas I am not that way. No way, José! Except with her. No, I'm afraid it's: Hey yo, Proteus, Hamlet, Henry! All the Henrys. Anxious, insecure, hungry, lustful . . . desperate . . . perhaps as Pop is, in part, after all.

But with her, I was my best self. She made me so simply by being herself; nothing needed saying. And when she withdrew, so too did my good self, as Rachel so sadly was to discover. I have thought that the genius of a redeemer like Jesus Christ is that we can see ourselves in him, to some degree. (Something Mother might intuit but could never articulate.) We can see what might be humanly possible, what might help us do some good for our fellow man, our sisters and our brothers. That was her effect on me. My sensitivity to, and concern for, things outside myself expanded; I was a better person, for a time. In fact, I went so far as to offer to help Rebec with schoolwork, and she accepted, urged on by Rachel. It was something I enjoyed, actually, particularly Reading and Composition. (Whereas in Math, I was as hopeless with that new stuff, as she was good, fortunately.) Yet I know I did it to impress Anne, and one afternoon went so far to take Becky uptown to Anne's office, to show her the world of magazines and publishing. Anne was splendid: receptive, delighted, introduced Becky to everyone, as I stood there, feeling half-good, half-phony . . . And sadly perhaps, it worked; Anne was never again as pleased with me, or perhaps in love, as she was that afternoon and night.

Too hard on all? Expecting too much? More than humanly possible? . . . My concern for Becky was sincere; I was more than pleased to do it for her, but in my heart of hearts, it was not my thing. It did not provide the deep, inner engagement and fulfillment that acting does . . . Yet I feel this is wrong, feel that I am not loving my neighbor as myself . . . and suspect it is because I have not the wholeness, certainly not Anne's goodness, in me . . . Cannot fulfill this moral cornerstone of our culture, and it wears on me, like the sea . . . even as my heart stands stony, a promontory against the waves.

Too clearly now, I see that I am but another in a line of conflicted generations, following my father who had sacrificed to support us, yet who would spit on the Bible and spurn most of his fellow men, including sometimes his son, and following my mother too, this lady who complains, from her court-won palace, she's never gained the comforts she needs, yet who would sink down upon her knees, hands upraised, if He appeared.

Anne is not conventionally religious, though on occasion she goes to church, Episcopalian if there's a choice. But very clearly, there is a spiritual side to her, and quite consciously she tries to be a good person, so that one small fear I harbor, under my own ache, is that whoever she hooks up with next will not appreciate her goodness, beyond possibly attributing it to expected female compassion.

God knows, however, it's not her about whom I must worry; she will do fine. Rather it is this untethered thespian who needs attention. Adrift, rudderless, the works. His heart lies in Grove Court, that off-bounds bower of bliss.

Never could decide how I felt about her home, a small duplex, a houselet, into which she invited me, the crossbreed, at the end of our second week. A museum, early American, or maybe Louis XVI, before he lost his lease.

She had taste, God knows, and must've had a maid, along with her Vassar legacy, which I've dubbed the Seven Sisters Syndrome: ne'er a one of them who doesn't love antiques. What their forebears did when there was nothing but antiques, I don't know. Anyway, lots of white and wheat—purity, maybe? Wool this, wool that; lambs lambent in everything.

I saw right there that I'd have to clean up a bit before I let her near my place. Heave the empty six-packs building toward the ceiling, and the sports sections collecting near the fridge, a season's worth. Projects Peter, John, and I had been working on, a kind of archival tribute to male bonding.

Her front door was miles from the quiet street; left along the stone path and through the white arch—secluded, decor by Disney. Yet, "Oh wow!" I exclaimed. "Isn't this a work of art!" And it was. But not to live in, not for me. Impossible. To actually sleep in that quaint New England bed? So small, unrumpled, pristine. Or actually use the bathroom, with its cream towels and cream rug, poised and perfect. Mom would've swooned. I would have left fingerprints. No way!

Nor were Anne's tastes cheap. That alone would have disqualified me, ultimately, I suspect. I mean the stereo was major bucks; likewise her desk, computer, and all the kitchen stuff. Compute it, shred it, nuke it; never need to actually touch it, the cutting edge of civilization, under the patina of old New England. Beats me . . .

How, I wondered at first, does one ever embrace such a woman, without soiling or mussing something, some priceless heirloom? . . . But no, she was fine, right there, calm, attentive, caring. And it was I, natch, who was shaking. What do I have to offer someone like this? Nothing came to mind.

Following the tour, like those at the Met, past the roped-off old rooms— Hester Prynne slept here—we sat down in her living room and talked, lubricated, if I may speak for myself, by some excellent red Burgundy in wonderfully large elegant glasses, which I kept pinging (nerves, nerves,) as I held mine in one hand, then two, then one. Ping!

Perhaps out of my fatalism, or desperation, I asked her how she would react to messy digs, such as actors often keep.

"Oh, it doesn't bother me how my friends live. I just like my own place clean. A little obsessive maybe, but not the worst, and after all these years, I'm not likely to change, right away." And she smiled.

"Yes, you are getting on. What, almost twenty-eight?"

A second deeper smile swept away her first.

"You have a cleaning service?" I pressed, glancing around.

Now she blushed. "No. Does it seem that way?"

You rat, Schurtz! Taking advantage of her sincerity; pushing her into apology. (Your dramaturgy has taught you shamelessly how to make the innocent squirm.) But here guilt rushed in. "Sorry. No, not at all. I'm afraid I was merely feeling uncomfortable about my place, which isn't quite up to this."

Whatever irritation or disappointment she felt was dismissed. Glancing around, she said, "Usually this place is in chaos," apparently satisfied that now it was not.

Chaos? Pillow creased? Papers on the desk? I could teach her a thing or two about chaos. Bubble, bubble, toil and trouble; actors play on piles of rubble.

But we got on, fortunately, past these things. In fact, we could talk on and on, effortlessly. She loved to hear stories of the theatre, and there at least, I did not fail her. That first evening at her place, we must have chattered on till three. I loved her laugh, when she finally relaxed; it was so unexpected and unrestrained. I tried to think of funny things, anecdotes, just to hear it tumble out. I remember watching her when she got up for another bottle of wine—so graceful, so very much a woman. And I remember thinking that I wanted to be right next to her, with nothing separating us, nothing, so that I could hear, and feel, every thought and sensation . . . Extreme, I guess. Life, people, aren't like that—couldn't be sustained. Wasn't.

Who are you, old McKim, forever walking yourself out into the rain? And why? . . . The product of your early, unpopularity? The result of your pudgy, bruised, and conflicted mix? Aberrant or mutant, who discovered that attention could be won by self-deprecating humor, later refocused on others? Certainly not athletic, not early on anyway, nor a brain. Not much of anything, and haven't really recovered, even with this modest success.

Nor had home been a refuge. As adolescence came on, things grew unhappy between Mom and Pop, with their views diverging, and with them all too clearly avoiding each other, long before they split. Was better, I discovered, to make up the world, as I began to see Becky doing at the theatre. For with Rachel increasingly busy in the evenings with work and her new man, Becky, I dimly recognized, was alone. Why it didn't penetrate more quickly, why I didn't do something more, I don't know. Too wrapped up in my own stuff . . . that "stuff" being Anne—the heights, I now know, and knew then, too.

Leaving Anne that night, I remember wanting to preserve our harmony, and so again I shook her hand and began to turn away, but saw her leaning, an arm reaching, and I turned back, embraced her, pulled her to me, held her tight—one of those few sublime moments, probably *the* moment . . . For a long, long time, we stood, arms wrapped 'round each other. Don't remember how it slipped into a kiss—oh deepest of kisses! Yet I remember telling myself that one cannot kiss a dream and keep it still a dream . . . . Jesus! Put too much on that poor woman's shoulders, and when the trap-door opened, there was nothing there, nothing close . . . Oh, there's work, California, things to do . . . but little purpose; just keeping busy, playing out the game.

Yet I've run ahead. There were good moments, wonderful moments, many. When she finally came over to my place, after I'd spent an afternoon cleaning it, she seemed delighted—she could be very gracious, as Peter said. And I had a bottle of Chateauneuf over which I told her the story of old Dave MacAleer, an actor who lives above me, whom she eventually met. Though in his sixties now, he still works when he can, but otherwise lives on next to nothing. Our landlord has been a saint and no longer raises his rent. How many guys would do that in this sweet city? Pop included. ("Do you know the taxes I pay on that shithouse?" he would cry at me.)

Pacing the floor above me, I hear David's footsteps slow and solitary, as if they are my own, years from now . . . He thinks there's something wrong with me, that I could not keep her . . . and sneered at me, when I agreed.

Anyway, I told her the story of how he'd had some success on Broadway, and television, in the fifties and early sixties, and I repeated some of the sketches he'd described to me. It had been an exciting period, he'd told me, riding the new prosperity after the war, and television was finding itself, trying things, experimenting. There were surprises then, he said, unlike now. But the poignant story was about his wife, and son. It may explain why he reacted to my loss the way he did. After the war, he'd come from Massachusetts, in his mid-twenties, with his newly-wed wife whom he described as beautiful and sweet. He showed me a picture, and so she seemed. He was quick, sharp-witted, cutting sometimes, in a Yankee way, and eventually landed several parts. And then not altogether intentionally, they had a child, a son. In short, things seemed to be going along just fine, until his wife, possibly from neglect, fell in love with another actor, a friend, his best friend . . .

No saint himself—he doesn't believe in them, and of course now he's pretty philosophical about it—yet it crushed him, just took the life out of him, he said. The purpose, everything. Didn't act again for years. I don't know, waited tables, drove a cab, something. Eventually he found out that his friend and wife had split up, and that she had moved west, to Oregon maybe, with his son, who was by that time almost three. When he'd first lost her, the shock had been so great he'd merely wanted to get away from anything to do with her, and then, when he'd finally recovered enough to want to see his son, they were gone; he had no idea where. He's confided in me that now he would very much like to meet his son, to know him as a friend, and he wonders if the son knows about him, even wonders if he's alive. He feels that some part of himself has disappeared, just vanished.

He suspects something must have happened to his wife, for he can't believe she wouldn't have contacted him all this time, or had their son do so. "No, something musta happened to her. She wasn't a bad girl. Maybe, as I said, I drove her to it."

Anne reacted as I had, with dismay, "How can people run so carelessly and roughshod over each other, when we know better? And when most of us aren't in such desperate straits that we need be compelled?" And she suggested that we invite him to dinner sometime. Then she asked me why I'd told her the story, to which I replied, honestly I believe, that I like the old fellow, feel sorry for him, wish there was something I could do (my refrain) . . . and fear following in his, and my father's, footsteps—fear it might become my story.

Looking at me somberly, she confessed, "It reminds me of my separation from . . . Ted, which I handled so badly."

I remember frowning and beginning to ask what else she might have done, when she rushed on, "I tried to be sensitive to him, but it felt too confining and prescribed, with no place for change or spontaneity. I didn't have the necessary strength to handle it well. I cut off conversations several times. When he wanted to meet, to show me how he'd opened up, I rejected it, not believing him, and hung up—fearing all would be too superficial and painful."

Listening to her, I became aware of a contradiction: that we want to be swept away by love, while at the same time maintaining control over our lives . . . I also wondered if her story revealed that she had loved him more than she ever could me, as in many cases those first loves reach deep.

Yet, if in telling those sad stories that night there was a silver lining, it was that we sat holding each other long into the night. In some ways—emotionally, consciously—it was as close as we ever got . . . But then . . . what is revealed by all of this? . . . Don't know, though I feel slightly better for it. A few words in memoriam, a proper burial. Sic transit gloria. "All things fall and are built again . . ." Yes, all that.

In compensation, perhaps, for life's battering, there does seem to be a balancing. Silver linings do appear. Or maybe it's just chance evening out, or the laws of nature exerting themselves: for every action, a reaction; what goes up, must come down; the bee fertilizes the flower it robs. I remember that the night following our sober talk was our first rendezvous between the sheets, and while I express it inelegantly, it was . . . sublime.

Nonetheless, how quickly it all slips away, mercifully, on the one hand—so diminishing on the other. And while I remember her as someone quite extraordinary, she cannot remember me on that same elevated plane, quite rightly. She deserves a fine man, as good-hearted and aware as she is, though that may take some searching.

As for me, despite all the great ideas carried in the lines of playwrights, which I've swallowed and can regurgitate, how disappointing that I remain mired in the muck, waist-deep, with the worms. No cygnet here among the downy ducks. There's a line Dysart speaks in *Equus* . . . something to the effect that no one can shrink your life for you. You do it to yourself. Lyrics, lines, and voices. All is told. I repeat them well enough, yet stand in steadfast freeze.

> "I could accuse me of such things
> that it were better my mother had not
> borne me." Eh, McHamlet?

Inside, there needs be something more, yet I know not what it is. Even when called to my most meaningful role, I answered not, but turned away, denied that person . . . and Anne must've noticed this weakest link . . . and might've told me, had I asked her.

VIII.

Problem was that things were converging, but I didn't see it. (No, mon, dey never does.) In my darkened Bank Street confessional, I remember one night, when I was ready for love, and Anne was halfway there, in her underwear, our conversation inexplicably drifted back to the two across the street, mother and daughter, whom we'd left a while before. Increasingly we were shepherding Becky home after the show, as Rachel's returns grew later and later. Fortunately, in the warm Summer's evenings we could sit comfortably on the stoop, we three, chatting happily enough, until without sound or warning Rachel would appear before us, apparently pleased to find us waiting but also puzzled that we all got on so well together.

"Mac, no child," said Annie, "should see her mother so little, particularly when that mother is her sole, close relative and friend, and when adolescence is taking hold."

"Unless that mother is mine," said I.

She seemed to smile, though didn't otherwise react, and after a moment continued, "It may be even more crucial for a girl."

Of course! cried an interior voice. Girls and their mothers! What man can wrap his mind around that? Instead, I embraced Anne from behind and held up and together her breasts, assisting her soft, see-through bra. (All the metamorphoses females go through! Little girls, lovers, mothers.)

But Anne was not to be wooed away yet. "On one hand, Becky seems to be doing well enough in school and is certainly open and interested with us, but she seems to have no friends her own age. And clearly she needs a family."

I told her that Rachel had mentioned some family members somewhere in the city, but seemed to seldom see them. "Maybe I could encourage Rebec to bring some of her school chums to the theatre, after school."

214

Without looking around at me, Anne nodded and took one of my hands away to kiss it and hold it silently for a time, until finally she said, "McKim, you're showing her that a man can be interested in her as a person."

With this, my lingering, malingering, hand felt as if caught in a cookie jar. But then its brother freed itself from her's and returned to her bosom and pulled her back into my lap. "Whereas with you, my dear, I want nothing but your body." And I twisted around to kiss her hard, I remember, and she seemed to like it, for a moment, then struggled to get free again, having not yet finished her thought. "Wait McKim. You know it's sad that Becky's one of the lucky ones. She, thanks to her mom, has gotten out . . ."

For a moment we were silent, until I spoke the name that evidently was lurking in our minds. "Unlike Tyrone."

She looked back at me sharply, then nodded, and picked up her wine glass, staring into it, and swirling it around.

"Seeking the future?" I inquired.

She shook her head. "I don't understand why Rachel puts up with him, lets him come around."

Nor did I. And although I remember, in one early encounter in the company of Rachel, he had appeared amicable enough, he had stared strangely, almost dourly, at me. And when we all parted, both Anne and I noticed Becky instantly became subdued and lagged behind, a Nilotic outline of reluctance, as they crossed the street and descended into the apartment.

Now, with both of my hands having retreated to Anne's shoulders, I wondered if Tyrone, on those occasions, had felt as if he'd stumbled into a small, rural town here, where everyone seemed to know everyone else's business.

"At the same time," she said quietly, "I can see she wouldn't want to anger him."

"No . . ."

"But there must be some way Rachel could handle it . . . I wonder what he thinks of our chaperoning Becky. There's something going on in him, some undercurrent."

"Did you see him stare at me, Annie, that time?"

"Yes." And she glanced around at me, before lowering her voice to add, "And I noticed Becky looked very ill at ease . . ."

I nodded, as evidently we both sensed something uncomfortable about the whole thing. But surprisingly Anne now found my hand with hers and returned it to her breast.

"Mac, we seem to be peering out at things through the same lens. I appreciate that. I love it."

I kissed her hair.

At that moment, dear Annie, you were in my arms, and the world be damned. But there were hints the world was edging in. Some clear-eyed, sharp-eared person might have seen or heard them, but I was more than happy to slip away from the world, into your soft inner sanctum.

So, predictably to some, it didn't last. Everything blew apart. Everything . . . Anne knows; her office telephoned her in San Francisco, and later she called, but it was brief and pained, and we didn't talk about us. She's still out there, with her dad.

Old Tyrone. Ty-rone, ty-rant . . . . Or victim? Who knows? (Who even cares? Which may be a root of the problem.) He did it up, did it up royally.

Of course I've wondered what role I played, even before that night. Did he resent me? . . . I suppose if I'd thought about it, I'd have seen: how could he not? . . . And yet will any of us ever know? . . . So, I must tell what I do know, or what I let myself know. (Onward, mon, and jus' d' facts, mon, jus' d' facts.)

A few days after her death—I don't remember how many—I was asked to go down to the D.A.'s office, for an interview. Was still in shock, in a fog, vision blurred, unable to freely breathe, barely noticed where I was or the young ADA across the desk.

"Let's see, ah Mr. Schurtz, what's the spelling on that? S-h . . . ?"

"S-C-H."

"I-R or U-R?"

"U-R-T-Z."

"Ah! German, is it?"

Though he found my unhappy stare, I allowed him to interpret it as he would.

Distantly I was wondering how he would effect the end of this sad story. I remember gazing around at the austere, little office, with iron shelves rising to the ceiling, clamping law volumes so thick that once wedged in no one could ever pry them free.

"Now, excuse me, Sir, . . . you knew the deceased?"

Deceased? . . . Rachel? My mind stumbled, as her face, so vibrant and determined, and at times so close, came back.

"Sir?"

". . . Yes?"

"You knew the deceased?"

"Rachel?"

He checked his clipboard. "Yes."

Although Rachel's face hung before me, eye to eye, I managed to respond, "Yes. We were neighbors. I live across the street."

A flash from his scribbling golden pen momentarily disoriented me as I watched his left hand wiggling furiously in its hooked labor. "That was it? Neighbors?"

"Friends." More than kin, less than kind. All.

"Nothing more?"

I shook my head, barely attending to him, although I remember I did hear him inhale under the strain of slow progress. Now he checked his notes. "Forgive me, Sir, but the defendant claims that you were having relations with the deceased."

"What?" That woke me up. "With the deceased?!"

"Excuse me. With Ms. Brown, before the . . ."

Pulling myself up straight, I searched for his eyes, and found their focus narrowing in on me. "Not that we subscribe to his story, but that may well be his defense, that she was double-dealing him."

Quite against my will, I felt my blood stirring, rising into my temples, felt my brow tightening, knew my face was reddening. "Nonsense, a pure lie," I spit out, then found I was eager to add, "For one thing, I was involved, and as a matter of fact, so was she."

Scanning a page, he nodded. "You with a Miss Anne Farraday, is it?"

The mention of her name, here, made me feel indignant, though I realized that there could be any number of ways it could have been introduced. Reluctantly, I nodded.

"If you'll excuse me again, Mr. Schurtz, the defendant claims he was dating her, Ms. Farraday, and that she told him all about Ms. Brown and you."

Some loud crash resounded through the room as I shot up, knocking over my chair.

"What? . . . Bullshit!" . . . Poor Gertler. (For that, I now remember, was his name.) He pushed himself back, as if he feared I might leap at him. Did he see my hands clenching? Fists forming? Did someone tell him my favorite role is Macbeth? Turn, hellhound, turn! "That's a fucking lie!"

"Yes, Sir. We will be interviewing her, as well, as soon as she returns." As he pulled himself back to his desk, straightening his tie and wire-rimmed glasses, I turned to pick up my chair. Tyrone, the bastard . . . plotting his revenge, willing to take it anywhere. A beast . . . a human beast . . .

Sitting again, and finding Gertler, I growled. He waited to see what might follow, but I inhaled and calmed myself, and he dove back into his notes.

"So, well . . . then there was nothing going on between you and Ms. Brown that could have aroused Mr. Brown's concern, or jealousy?"

I stared at him. "Brown? That's his name?"

He checked his sheet. "Yes."

"Same as hers?"

"Yes . . ."

"They were married?"

". . . Common-law, I believe." Checking his notes, he confirmed, "Yes." He studied me with unabashed curiosity. "She never told you?"

I couldn't move at first, couldn't speak, until slowly it settled through me, leaving me limp, empty. After several moments, I recovered enough to indicate, no, she hadn't . . .

What, I wondered unsteadily, to make of this? I had no idea. Was Becky his? She seemed too old. Couldn't be. I heard Gertler clearing his throat.

"Just to complicate things further, we received a call from a Mr. Robert Gibson, who works at Macy's, who apparently worked with her. Said they were good friends, or more than that, actually. Said although he's in the middle of a divorce, they'd made plans, marriage plans. You know anything about that?"

I nodded. "She talked about him several times."

"Did Tyrone know?"

I looked at Gertler through some haze. "I don't know . . ."

Gertler appeared to be weighing the same conclusion I was: that maybe this was what had incited Tyrone. "So, how many times would you say you saw Tyrone?"

As Tyrone's sullen image floated before me, I tried to recall. "A few times; three or four."

"Did she tell you how long they had known each other?"

"Not specifically. For a while, I guess. Several years."

Head down, pencil twitching, Gertler mumbled, "Brown of Brownsville . . . . I assume that it's through you that Miss Farraday knows Mr. Brown?"

I bowed slightly, then recognized I needed to quell a sudden nausea. (Or is it now, in remembering?)

"Did she give him her work address?" continued Gertler methodically.

"Not that I was aware of."

". . . Would Ms. Brown have done so?"

"I don't know. Any of us might have mentioned the magazine where Anne works. I took Becky there once; she may have told him."

"Okay . . . Now, did the deceased ever express any concern about the defendant? Did she ever say he was dangerous, in any way?"

"She said that she wanted to get away from him, and that she was having trouble doing so."

"How was that? Was he persistent? Or was she ambivalent? Or what?"

"She didn't elaborate. I guess I assumed that he was being persistent."

"That's a guess? Or are you fairly sure?"

I looked at Gertler with some annoyance. What was he trying to squeeze out of me? "I said . . . that she didn't go into it, in any detail." (And yet, Macbeth, you knew, somehow; you had your suspicions.)

"Never explained why she didn't stop seeing him?"

Even as I shook my head, my mind was replaying that last conversation with her; and I wondered if Gertler could read my thoughts.

"So there is really no light you can shed on why the defendant attacked her?" Gertler, I saw, had suddenly changed. Like a pointer, he'd grown intent on his quarry, focused and absolutely still. Probably no more than doing his job, yet why did I feel so uncomfortable? No, I indicated, nothing, even as I sensed something else coming.

"We understand that she made a call to you that evening, maybe an hour or so before she was murdered. Is that the case?"

Murdered? . . . The term turns the knife. Caught. ("Whence is that knocking? How is't with me, when every noise appalls me?") They know! I had not thought they would know . . . I must look white with guilt. Or red with telltale blood.

"Sir? Are you all right? . . . Like some coffee?" His lumpy, legal face tilted to one side as his eyes held their stare.

". . . Yes . . ."

"Yes, what, Sir? . . . Coffee?"

"She did call."

"That night, before the . . . ?"

"Yes."

"And what did she want?"

. . . Yes, what did she want, McKim? . . . Help, friendship . . . protection? Yes, you knew, even if she didn't say as much . . . You knew . . . But, concerned with Anne, you could have cared less. Admit it. The world could have been calling and you wouldn't have been home, would have turned a deaf ear . . . closed your heart. "Don't know . . ."

"Don't know what, Mr. Schurtz?"

The name chills me. My name. Me . . . and father's name too. I imagine his storming out of our suburban family home, his untold wanderings across chaotic, war-ravaged Eastern Europe. A fogged dream . . . One that I fear I am repeating—his emotional detachment . . . Get a hold of yourself! . . . And yet, how to both remember his past and free myself from it? ". . . Don't know what she wanted, when she called . . . I mean she said she wanted to talk, but that was all . . . Never said about what." (Oh McSchurtz, you had a pretty good idea.) "You see, things were falling apart with my friend, Anne." Suddenly seeking Gertler's reaction, I found pain and distaste etched into his mouth and cheeks. "And I was trying to decide whether or not to call her, to ask her if she would talk . . . so that I didn't want to talk with Rachel, or with anyone else . . . You see?"

Poor Gertler, how could he understand? It must have sounded pathetic. Guess it was. I remember he shook his head. And for a short time we were both silent.

But eventually, he had to resume. "So she never mentioned what she wanted to talk about?"

"She asked me, that is, hinted that she wanted me to come over, to talk, I think. Wanted 'company,' was the way she put it."

Gertler paused for a second, studying me. "She didn't mention Mr. Brown?"

". . . No . . ."

". . . Why do you hesitate?"

". . . I guess . . ." (Guess I must confess.) "that something in her voice . . . It occurred to me that it might be something to do with him."

Gertler waited, suspecting the rest might come out. Our eyes met briefly, before mine lowered to gaze at the desk. "I never believed it would lead to that."

He began writing for a bit, and my mind went blank, thankfully. Then he asked, "She ever mention drugs to you?"

"Drugs?" I felt my skull squeeze my brain. She had been so hard-working, a concerned, loving mother . . . What to say? . . ."No . . . never mentioned them."

Gertler couldn't restrain a slightly superior, skeptical look, as he paused again, waiting. But I held my tongue, and position, even as my mind fled back to a conversation with Anne touching on this, and to signs I'd seen in Rachel when once she had suddenly sped up, talking rapidly of everything she wanted in her life. But maybe it was simply enthusiasm, or maybe it had been the wine . . . How could I be sure?

"You looked as if you were thinking of something," Gertler said.

"I was trying to remember . . . but I can't honestly say I saw any signs."

Apparently he accepted this, before he told me, "The autopsy revealed a level of cocaine. And he tested positive as well . . . . He, incidentally, had a wad from her cashed paycheck on him, when he was picked up . . . . Any thoughts? Anything coming back yet?"

I glanced at him, feeling foolish indeed, but more than that, suddenly and in a new way, sad for Rachel. And Becky.

"So, Mr. Schurtz, you had no idea they were into that?"

No, my head indicated, shaking slowly, steadily, or maybe uncertainly, even as my mind was leafing sadly through the moments . . . and thinking, too, that drugs don't necessarily lead to problems . . .

"But if you did, at some point, notice something suspicious, you never imagined it could lead to, or be a sign of, trouble?"

I could only stare at him haplessly, and answer, "No . . . not trouble like that."

"No idea that Mr. Brown's behavior could place her, and her daughter, in danger?"

". . . Not like that . . ."

"Would it be fair to conclude that you really didn't know her very well at all?"

I looked at him, annoyed, but also contrite. In some ways so it seemed. Yet this was someone into who eyes I had gazed a number of times, with whom I thought I had shared a rapport and had shared, to some extent, souls, and in whose daughter we had all seen the joyful embodiment of the new life she'd been working for so hard. Something was not computing, something was missing, and yet what could I say but, "Guess not."

I think I saw Gertler wince at this, but I didn't attempt to go any further.

"One final thing, Mr. Schurtz. Did Ms. Farraday ever tell you she met with Mr. Brown?"

What is this foreboding, I wondered, as I replied, ". . . Not outside her office."

Gertler waited to see if I had more, before he revealed, "The guy maintains—and I repeat his credibility is all but nil—that not only did she see him several times but that he supplied her with cocaine."

Already stunned, I could only sit there clenched and drowning in this absurdity.

"Was that a possibility, Mr. Schurtz?"

Although I looked in Gertler's direction, I didn't see him. ". . . What? . . . No . . . no way. Never."

"Why would he bring it up?"

Absurdity upon absurdity. "Who knows? . . . Trying to spread the web of guilt . . ."

Gertler was squinting again, evaluating my guess.

"You don't believe him, do you?" I asked. He pushed his lips out into a doubting expression. "You haven't spoken to her yet," I blurted, "but when you do, you'll see what a crock it is."

"And yet he did get in to see her in her office," Gertler noted, glancing down at his sheet. "Twice, her secretary told us."

The idea of Tyrone gaining entrance to her office, on the pretext of seeking work, had filled me with doubt when Anne told me, and now with revulsion. And yet, before the crime, we had all been pulling for him. "Yes, Anne was trying to help him, find a path, a job . . . in part to help Rachel get free of him." Although it had occurred to me that Tyrone may have reacted to my visits with Rachel as I had to his with Anne, of course it wasn't the same at all. I was a neighbor and friend. "As for the coke—it's nonsense. Anne has never done drugs at all, that I've seen. Life is her high. The guy's desperate, grasping at straws."

Yet before I was done speaking, I saw Gertler's attention turning away, and, with increasing intensity, he began to explain that one of the things they were trying to determine was whether or not this was a premeditated crime, possibly connected to drugs. Or was it one of passion, or was it merely a crime of opportunity? And for the first time, I saw that this question fully engaged him and enlivened him. No longer was he the functionary sitting dutifully, going through the check list, but was leaning into each possible avenue of motivation, his eyes shifting sharply from me to his notes and back, eager to explore. And his conclusion, delivered in low, measured tones, was that given Tyrone's visits to Anne's office, it is probable that he had been plotting something for awhile. On the other hand, it is plausible that he may have simply needed cash that night, and Rachel wasn't forthcoming.

I felt anger collecting and compacting, anger at Tyrone and even Gertler. I recognized that it suffused and cloaked my brain, confusing the various strands and theories. Maybe Gertler saw this; my anger and swirling emotions couldn't have been hard to detect. In any case, I saw him pushing back his chair, standing, and explaining that if there was a trial, I might be summoned back from California.

I felt myself staring blankly at him. Was that it? He slid his hands into his pocket and regarded me with something less than admiration. And while, to me, it seemed too abrupt, I realized that Gertler had gotten what he needed.

As I made my way unsteadily through the dim halls, I felt confused, even a little dizzy. And in the course of this I began to worry that the legal system would be too soft on Tyrone. If called back from California, I vowed to make clear to the prosecutor, to Gertler, to the jury, what a loss, what a monstrosity he had perpetrated: (that strange word,) erasing our dear . . . dear friend . . . and leaving Becky a motherless child.

Anxiously I walked over to Peter's loft on Mercer—dashing across the streets, so eager was I to get his reading of it. When I'd told him the story, he turned off the print dryer he'd been feeding and stared at the floor. "Tyrone visited her office twice?" It seemed to perplex him.

"Under the pretense of wanting a job," I mumbled.

Peter avoided my eyes. "Seems odd. What could she offer *him*?"

I shook my head. "And can you believe that business about the coke?"

But gazing at the floor again, he didn't immediately respond.

"Makes me squirm, Peter." I wondered if I should explain how it did, but found him studying me, before he looked away without comment. Recalling it, I have this sense he was withholding something, but I have no idea of what . . . Instead he veered off to something else, asking, "How'd it go with Becky?"

Thanks Peter. I turned away and found a chair, lowering myself into it slowly. "I handled that with my usual aplomb . . . But that aside, I think she was still in shock."

"How's the cousin? Will Bec be okay up there?"

"Think so. The cousin seemed . . . I don't know, okay. But Peter, I screwed up, sent poor Becky fleeing from the room, at the end, with some obtuse comment."

Peter seemed to want to ask what or why, but didn't. Instead, he turned away, his brow wrinkling as he moved into shadow.

"Pedro . . . It's so horrible to imagine her being ripped from her cozy home with her mom—her mom gone, and herself thrust into that largely unknown world. I think the cousin seemed . . . sensitive, but I have no idea." Peter's eyes flicked my way, then down, before he faintly nodded. I breathed and desperately sought some other subject. "Have you spoken to Anne?"

Not expecting this, he sent a sharp glance over, lined by irritation, then after a moment, he stammered, "You, you mean . . . in Cali-California?" But before I could respond, he replied, "Yeah, she called once, after she'd heard, after you two had talked."

"How'd she seem; how'd she sound?"

Uncomfortably Peter searched for the answer, pushing his dark bangs back with a swipe of his hand. "Stunned . . . her voice weak, creaky . . . She must have been crying before . . . She blurted out, painfully, that it was her fault."

"What? . . ." My dizziness returned. "That makes no sense, Peter."

"As you know, Mac, she liked Rachel. She respected her struggle to get control of her life and re-direct it. Indeed she encouraged it. But she said she felt that she gave Tyrone the wrong signals . . . She seemed particularly remorseful about that."

This too made no sense. Indeed I could barely process the words.

"And she feels she deserted you, at a tough time."

I looked up, aware of thumps and things contracting inside. I saw Peter blink in sympathy—or was it discomfort? He looked away and added, "I think she may have feared holding you back, once you went out there. I think she thought you ought to be free."

"Oh Peter . . . come on." I dismissed this instantly, as it seemed wrong, off. Now I found I was reluctant to look at him, was increasingly reluctant to consider what he'd said. No way she could have meant it, right?

"Mac, you should go see her, when she gets back. Press her a bit. She's not so absolutely set on all this, as you seem to think. You two had something pretty good, something that shouldn't be abandoned so easily."

I felt myself flush at his selfless encouragement, and I allowed myself to wonder if there were any truth to it . . . I know I'd asked myself why I hadn't questioned her harder . . . but then, I knew the answer: because I respected her so much, and had figured her conclusion was clearly and carefully arrived at. It was also because of the shock, the unexpectedness of it, and the trust broken . . . And faced with that, I had retreated immediately into myself, protectively, to avoid rejection from the one person to whom I had given my heart and soul . . . And finally, there must have been pride, too. If she didn't see my worth, far be it from me to present advertisements for myself . . . Maybe it was a mixture of fatalism and self-punishment, a sense that it had been, from the beginning, too good to be true—something I didn't deserve . . .

And on the one night I had been prepared to put all of this aside and call her, to urge that we meet and talk, Rachel called first . . . And while I had side-stepped her quiet request, I never regained the determination to call Anne . . . And then Rachel was gone . . . And Anne too, to California . . .

"Go see her, Mac," he repeated, perhaps seeing that I was lost in the coils of explanation. And with that, he pulled himself around, almost angrily. In fact he scowled, expelling his heat. But then, looking back, his eyes softened. "Yes, damn it! Try it, Schurtz. For God's sake try it. You owe it to yourself, for your peace of mind. Not to mention that we all want to find out what was going on with Tyrone. Did she see any hint of his anger, or craziness?"

Yes . . . so be it. I would! I stood up, went over to him and squeezed his arm. "Thanks, Pedro."

Fortunately he didn't look up into my leaking eyes. Instead I heard him grumble, "Sometimes, Mac, I wonder how you act in those plays as well as you do. I mean, you're so fucking dense, myopic, blind! My God, Schurtz, you need direction!"

Okay, so who doesn't, Peter? Who doesn't need a little direction now and then?

Descending the iron stairway from his studio, each step a dull knell, I found that while I was moved by his concern, I was also hurt by his anger. Not that I couldn't understand it. If he were me, he'd have been fighting every which way to keep her—no temporizing, no feeling sorry for himself, just keeping his eyes on the prize.

Okay. Fine. But he's not me. He's not stuck with this odd configuration, deceptively designated: M.S. or H.M.S. or MSG. Sounds innocuous, but problems lurk. Luckier than most, Peter? Maybe, but there's no single arbiter. And don't for a second think the blessing isn't mixed. Whom the Gods would destroy, they first make mad with power.

Go see her? . . . Okay, yes, when she gets back . . . But optimistic? . . . Can't pretend. Can't shut my eyes to the reality out there . . . It isn't a question of debating points, but rather some core which finally came into play . . . Not that she doesn't have a romantic side to her. I don't think she'll make the mistake that Catherine Earnshaw made, forsaking her soul for whatever . . . No, but then I can't honestly say that her soul found its mate in mine, even if mine found its in hers . . . Yet I will try. Give it one more shot. Though seldom have I convinced anyone of anything, outside the theatre.

That first rehearsal she saw, when I helped Derek out of a bind, was me at my best. It's my strength, coming up with alternative lines and readings, but we both forgot it wasn't real, was not of this world, the world where Rachel lived.

Circles, mon? Is all connected? Sometime so it seem—or is it only in my mind? Is there some objective reality out there? Laws of science that pertain?

Circles carry me back to my family, whose patterns I fear repeating. Patterns in which each of us, each in his own way, has felt wounded and betrayed by life. (Even my brother, Whale, must've felt this—he who I usually refuse to acknowledge, despite his massive girth—as for several reasons we've long been divided: as bitter rivals for the scraps of parental attention; later, and by our vastly different values and life styles.)

Yet among all of us, it was Pop who unquestionably bore the heaviest burden: a youth and early adulthood raked over by the williwaws of World War II, uprooted and hurled first one way, then another; his mother and father taken off; she, it is thought, to a death camp. We believe she was Jewish, though Pop remains determinedly silent on this, as well as on his father, German, probably dragooned into the Wehrmacht to be blown away, obliterated over the Russian steppe. All roots extinguished, while Pop dodged and wove across the ravaged landscape, trying merely to stay alive for four long years, until somehow he was finally cast up on these shores.

Sometime ago, I left my parents' worlds behind, burned my bridges, and joined the ambulatory, emotionally-wounded. Yet Pop, unlike me, carries with him a story he feels he can never replay, never dare sort out, and can only release, or in some measure reflect, in his sudden rages. Oh, impossible burden! What guilt to have even survived! And at what cost? I tremble to imagine what might have been necessary for him, as I replay my own expediencies. Oh poor, tormented soul!

I have tried to draw him out, but he won't be—absolutely refuses. Must be so firmly and deeply cemented that to reach that inner vault, one would have to destroy the entire edifice. And how little use he has for his fellow men: no friends to speak of; a wife with whom he probably replayed, ironically, the cultural chasm of his own parents, and who withdrew emotionally from him years ago, for all-too-easily understandable reasons. And a son who has become an actor, a Hamlet, temporizing while around him murder rages, as

> ". . . all the drop-scenes drop at once
> Upon a hundred thousand stages, . . ."

So much breast-beating, mon? What purpose do it serve? What good do it do? You not change, mon. That's the wager; that's where the smart money lies, all d' words aside. D' mills 'a' God grind slowly, mon, but dey grind exceedingly small. The sweep of words carry me; unnamed forces lead me. Though you know all d' lines, d' question is: What you gonna make of them, mon? What you gonna do?

IX.

For some reason, an evening with Maggie comes back. Must have been after a performance, and quite some time before things fell apart. Anne, I believe, was away in Connecticut visiting relatives, and so Maggie and I wandered over to a Soho café near where she lives. The place was a student hangout, with a few artists and lawyers interspersed along the bar. Its size and high ceiling absorbed the sound, so that while it was crowded, it was incongruously quiet, with the bent bodies and clay-red walls evoking, again, Hopper's world.

Oddly, being temporarily free of Anne provided me with a little spark of excitement, which, joined to Maggie's normal inclination, left us both brimming with chatter. She began with stories, calamitous and funny, from friends in other productions, and I found myself studying her face under her tightly curled brown hair. Her skin appeared almost translucent around her cheek bones, and I was struck, as I had never been before, by the vivid differences between Anne and her, almost as if from different species. Where Anne, and Rachel too, were serene and graceful, Maggie was bird-like, her eyes and hands fluttering around her nest-like hair, her attention darting off to the people coming and going in the café, only to alight back on me, to read my face, with an urgency that Anne never displayed. What did this suggest? Less confidence, less-formidable defenses, unbridled curiosity? I wish I knew.

At some point, I recall, she sighed rather deeply and observed, "Not the liveliest of audiences tonight, were they, Mac?"

"No, Mags. Had to look out several times to see if they were there at all."

"Was it us?"

"Didn't think so."

"It was good that you picked up the pace. Otherwise none of us would have lasted through the third act."

I realized suddenly the warmth I felt for Miss Maggie. Not as whole or powerful as that I felt for Anne certainly, yet surprising and stirring. Of course, in the theatre, it's not unusual, given the circumstances, but nonetheless it's gratifying—being as it is my family now, and what sustains me. And I told Mags what a delight she was and how much I'd enjoyed playing opposite her. "You listen, you hear, and pick up any variation. Your integrity keeps us all alive and on our toes. You're the cat's meow."

Purring, she looked down, then up again and began returning the compliment, saying that the cast seem particularly harmonious. "Hey, old man, you've pulled this thing together as much as Derek has. And you give a lot, Mac, unselfishly, which is not so easy to find in this realm."

"Quite an admiration society. If only we could write each other's reviews."

". . . Do you think you'll take that film offer?" she asked, her voice suddenly nosing lower. (And now I realize that this evening pre-dated my signing.)

"Yes, I think so . . . Wouldn't you?"

As she weighed this, her lips pinched together before her eyes searched mine.

"Most likely. But what will happen to Anne and you?"

Although I had thought of this after my agent called, I'd decided it was not a serious obstacle. In fact, I'd thought it might strengthen Anne's belief in me. But now, Maggie's concern sent cold doubt plummeting down my spine. "We'd still see each other, Mags. Aeroplanes, zeppelins, xeroxes—send replicas."

But this did not draw a smile from her, probably because she, too, was looking ahead more clearly than I. "You love her, Mac. It's not very hard to see. And who wouldn't?" As Maggie attempted again to read my true feelings, I wondered how difficult it had been for her to say this. I knew that she had not been in a consuming relationship for a while. "But she's got her career, too, Mac . . . I don't know how you guys are going to manage it. The odds can't be good."

I looked around the warmly murmuring café, at young men and women, faces close together; arms draped over one another—simple lines, muted colors, living sculptures. Intimacy. But how deep, how strong, how lasting? . . . And me? Lose the one in the world I love without question? For what? . . .

"Give it up, you're saying? Don't sign? . . . I thought she'd be proud of me. Makin' some money for once."

Maggie nodded. "I know the dilemma . . . Have you two . . . broached the awful subject of marriage? That might be the glue you need."

Marriage? That once and future concept? Not distasteful, but simply beyond the horizon. And yet I felt my heart leap, even as I knew that this would not be Anne's reaction. "Don't know, Mags, something tells me she's not ready. Might send her running."

Again Maggie nodded knowingly. "Yes, she's got a lot of things she wants to do, most definitely." We looked at one another closely, and I thought I saw sympathy in Maggie's eyes, and a sincere, shadowy sadness. And so I asked, "You think going will kill it?"

"Who can predict? But I suspect that the strains over the great and growing distances would be great, might be more than weekends flying back and forth could hold together." I nodded as I attempted to imagine this. How long would the energy last? Then I heard her ask, "What if you get another part out there?"

"I won't take it; I'll come back."

Tilting her head down, Maggie gave me another sad, doubtful look. "Over your agent's dead body . . . It almost makes me want to cry."

"Oh Mags . . ." And I reached for her hand and held it.

When she quieted her emotion, she allowed that Anne, like me perhaps, has a restless side, and she may be sifting for the right career opportunity. "I hate saying this—I may be way off—but I don't want to see you take a fall, Mac."

I imagined myself tumbling into darkness, then pulling myself back out by the heels. Regaining my breath, I asked her, "So what would you do?"

"I don't know . . . If I met someone as good-hearted as she? . . . Somehow I don't see it happening. Doubt I'll ever have to sort that one out, sorry to say."

I felt for her. "Nothing developing with John?"

She grimaced staring across the room. "John is an enigma, most particularly to himself." Now, as her focus retreated inward, I observed how the light blue of her eyes was echoed faintly in her temples and cheeks, like the horizon touching the sea. I felt my heart beating for her, in hope that she might find someone.

"You know, Mac, I think I'd tell a producer to forget it, if I found someone comparable to her. Screw the stage. What does the world care if there's one less actress, more or less, short of a Streep or Garbo?"

I considered this. "But Mags, it may be different for a guy." When I saw her begin to frown, I urged, "No, wait . . . Most women I've known want, or need, a man who's doing something, achieving something; whereas men don't necessarily need that in a woman. Do you think Anne would have been interested in me without my so-called success?"

"If she has a heart . . . But how different is it for you? You want someone who's attuned to many of the things you are. Or how will you talk to each other? You wouldn't want a couch potato cutting coupons? Even if she's gorgeous . . . would you?"

"How gorgeous?"

Unhappy eyes appealed to some naiad by the ceiling, and she began shaking her head, until I appeased her indignation with a wave of my hand. "But I'm talking about professional accomplishment. I don't require professional accomplishment."

"But that interest and energy has to be fed by something! Has to come from some experience!"

"Yes but Mags, that could be anything. Past or present, professional or not."

"Well Mac, there are financial realities . . ."

"Yes! . . . And social realities, too. Anne 's not going to stick with some struggling, unknown actor."

"Okay . . ." (Perhaps she saw I was mixing two points.) "But what I'm saying is that much of what we all find interesting about Anne comes as a result of her work."

"I'm just saying it's not a requirement, that it come from work."

She looked away for a moment, a pulse beating faintly in her cheeks, before she sighed, "What do I know? Maybe it *is* because she's gorgeous. I'm the last one to be giving advice. Anyway, old Sigmund said there's none to give, on love."

Studying her, I wanted to help her in some way; her heart was good, even if our conclusions didn't coincide. When she met my gaze again, she muttered, "Sorry . . . I was just trying to . . . I don't know. Love is so hard these days. So hard to find, and keep." She looked away again, bringing one hand across her eyes, to clear her mind it seemed.

Once more I reached for and squeezed her hand.

She looked back. "And Mac, . . . what's going to happen to Becky if you go?"

Her light blue eyes now looked cellular, biological, as they held on me. Somehow they conveyed feeling as well as insight. How is it that mere cells, connected by tiny wires, do this? . . . "Who's going to be her friend, tutor, and caretaker, Mac?" she reminded me. "And what's going on with her mother?"

I tried to explain the things Rachel was attempting to juggle, and then suggested that maybe Becky should come regularly to the theatre after school. She knows the group. Someone might even have a job for her.

Mags twisted her mouth and frowned. "Mac, I've asked her about her school friends, but she never gives me a straight answer. Does she have any real friends there?"

"I think so. She's told me about some, but it's true, they don't seem to extend beyond school."

Maggie looked down at her hand around her drink. "That's not good, not healthy."

I agreed, though no solution came to mind.

"Mac, somebody's got to speak to Rachel, for one thing. She's gotta get her act together, get involved, go see Becky's teachers."

"She works."

"So?"

I promised to speak to Rachel, but realize I never did, never made the time.

As Maggie looked around for our waiter to order another drink, she said, "I've got to hand it to Anne; she quite genuinely cares for them; and she's earnest about helping Rachel get somewhere. Downright intent, in fact."

I'd seen it too, of course. But Rachel was pretty savvy and could take care of herself. It was Rebec I worried about.

"Anne told me that Rachel's having trouble ditching a former boyfriend or someone, some unsavory member of the unemployed. Anne said she'd try to help Rachel by helping him find a job, although from what she described, I wish her luck."

While Annie and I had certainly discussed Rachel and Tyrone, I don't remember when she decided to seriously help him.

"I mean if the guy's not dumb," Maggie continued, "and I assume Rachel wouldn't pick a dumb one, what's he been doing all this time? Maybe someone should ask him whether he wants work?"

This seemed a tad harsh, I remember, for we knew so little about him. On the other hand, we probably should have been able to piece a bit more together. Mags and I sat there silently for some time watching other couples and groups of students, none of whom appeared to be gripped by burning issues, even though love, sadness, and loss would, most likely, eventually overtake them all. So . . . what? Eat, live, and be merry? Are we all not balancing precariously in our chairs, until the crash occurs? . . . Part of life, is it? So the playwrights tell us. Only, that evening, it never occurred to me it would befall me so soon.

"Look at these kids here, Mags: aspiring actors, artists, yuppies, so young and hopeful. At barely past thirty, I thought I was young, but they make me feel old. How will they survive the bumps? They look so soft, look as if they have no idea . . . how life can grind you down, like poor David, my neighbor, alone in a room."

"They're not oblivious, old man. They may not have the labels yet, but they have their own sense of it. Different senses than we do, probably, but no less compelling. Don't you remember? You've told me about how strange your family seems to you." She was right, and for a moment I recalled the one ironic line my father would sometimes speak, 'One must laugh not to leap.' . . . But what does it imply? Find laughter where one can on this earth? In illusion, ridicule, inebriation?

"What are you looking glum about, McKim?" she suddenly asked, reversing her mood. "You're sitting on top of the world."

Caught somewhere between astonishment and amusement, I stared at her, but saw her mood was shifting yet again. "You know, however, one day you *will* fall off, down with the rest of us, old man." I continued to stare at her, unable to follow these swings, as she, following some inner compulsion, swung back once more. "Sorry. I guess misery loves company . . . . I don't know how men like John get through life, so narrowly focused in on themselves that they never notice a thing. Part of it, I know, is that he's got a crush on your fucking girlfriend, McKim. If you'd stop bringing her around, I might have a chance!"

I felt myself recoil. "Are you serious?"

She looked at me with a certain disgust, then rolled her eyes away. "Where's the damn waiter? . . . He's evidently as blind as the rest of you."

My gaze moved away from her, now that her bitter humor had returned. Yet I could recall John playfully pawing Anne on several occasions. I had thought it innocuous. We all did it to each other, but then Mags knew John better than I did.

She shook her head and again searched the room, before adding with a croak, "The deck is stacked, Schurtz, stacked!" And she turned her grim gaze down into her empty glass. "Where's the fucking waiter? Any waiter."

X.

Yes, waiting for the waiter. As the world slips and turns on its head . . .
I think I shall always remember Maggie's face that evening, so mercurial, so
alert to different rhythms, seeking them out, in fact, and warning me that
Anne was too. On one level, I had always known this, and if I had been able
to take a step back, I would have seen it more clearly. There were signs . . .
semiotics and women noticing the things. Men love it half the time—are
perplexed, exasperated the other half, wishing women, those communal
animals, weren't quite so, before thanking heaven for them. But we evolved
for different roles, different tasks, and weren't designed to spend all day
together. Work is changing things, nonetheless maybe the wonder is that we
get along as well as we do.

One evening, some weeks later, as I was in our dressing room awaiting
the performance, toying with my makeup, Anne called to say that she wanted
to stay home, rather than join the usual crew. When I said fine, I'd see her
later, she hesitated, even though we'd been spending every night together. I
heard it and asked if 'later' was okay, then waited for the expected approval.
It came, but following another hesitation, and without much enthusiasm. I
didn't have time or the inclination to analyze it, and yet I had not forgotten
it, when I arrived at her place later.

I know I watched her as she brought her feet up under her on her couch
and her arms around herself, dressed in her pearl nightgown and robe, and I
could see that she was unusually subdued. In response, I think, I did a rather
odd thing for me: fixed myself some tea—hardly ever drink the stuff, certainly
not in Summer, but maybe I needed the warmth, or clarity, or saw that I
would be carrying the conversation. I told her about the performance, how
John made a wrong entrance, and how we'd all just managed to keep from
breaking up, in an emotional scene. And then, probably self-destructively,

despite sensing I shouldn't, I told her about progress with the movie contract. Only a point or two to resolve. She listened without stirring.

After that I tried a story, or two, before it became too much. Had to ask, "So Annie, what's wrong?"

"Nothing," she said, shaking her head, looking down.

Yet I saw, and heard, it wasn't so, and, as I studied her, she avoided my gaze.

One impulse, to accept this and let it go, wrestled unsuccessfully with another which urged me press on. "But Annie, your voice is telling me something else. Any Anniething you want to tell me?"

When she looked over at me, the expression around her green eyes wavered between sadness and annoyance, and even accusation, before she quietly said, "It's nothing."

Well. I sat down at the other end of the couch. Playwright Peck observed that if psychology has provided the tools for better understanding, it has also given us so much more to consider, complicating the wheat-chaff problem, making it easy to miss the forest for the trees, or forget that half a moon is a most lovely jewel in itself. It may be old Nature maintaining her balance: the more we learn, the more we need to, just to keep abreast, so to speak. Wanted to say all this to her, but didn't. Didn't know if it would make sense, or maybe feared she wouldn't be receptive. Guess eventually I did ask, "Can I give you a hug?"

". . . Not right now. Do you mind?" she pleaded softly, not insensitively.

"Want to be alone?"

"Mac . . . could we just talk about something else?"

"Sure . . ." As I'd already tried the theatre—"Mets lost tonight. But hell, they'd won eight outta nine, even though whatshisname's arm still isn't right."

I don't think she even heard me. Some people, and she's one, can really get into themselves. I mean seriously. Considered asking her about Rachel's problems, but suspected that would lead to more frustration. Instead asked if she knew anyone at the magazine for Maggie. Wrong question. More frowning. "You know the situation there, Mac." But at least her expression softened.

"Okay, how about the mayor? How's he doin'? What d'ya think?"

A hint of her famous sense of humor flickered in her eyes for a second, then snuffed out. "I think I just want to go to bed."

I could get next to that. But should've known: soon as I closed my eyes, she began talking. And not about us, which would've awakened me, but about abstractions: life-plans and how to balance desire for travel and career with those for family and think-time. (Think-time? What's goin' on when it's *not* think-time?) She told me that Camus wrote her, or maybe it was just wrote: Time to think is the most valuable thing in life.

Okay, for a writer maybe. But not in place of sleep, not after a long day, not when sugar plum fairies had come out of the wings and begun their routine. She must have thought I'd fallen asleep, for she nudged my shoulder, but I was there, right there, and kissed her and told her that she, and not Camus's thinking, was the most valuable thing in my life, hands down.

Maybe I'm just not profound enough . . . or not serious enough . . . although I'm dead serious about my work. Maybe I'm too narrowly focused for her, or maybe just not mensch enough . . . These judgements, tastes, choices can be a little capricious, I know. At the same time, I'm aware I have a little devil-may-care streak in me. I mean I knew she would have appreciated a serious chat, there in bed, in place of humoring her, but I guess I was a little irritated that earlier, when I was ready, she was silent . . . Destructive, I know, but it shouldn't have been that destructive. Something was off from the outset, and she probably filed away my responses as evidence for the prosecution of, for the dismissal of, one M. Schurtz . . .

Excuse me, are you . . . ?

If I could have seen where things were headed, I might've snapped out of it, rallied, had a real heart-to-heart, but basically I was blind during most of it, head drowned out by some tune in my heart—some cello playing high then low, some cellist really digging in.

Not that there had been any dearth of chatter lately. We had yacked about many things, frequently the future. At one point we actually talked about children: she thought I'd make a good dad, judging by my interaction with Becky. And she asked me if I thought she would be a good mom, as she pursued her career. Instead of answering directly, I asked if she thought she'd be like Rachel—busy, to put it simply. We both paused, before I told her I wasn't the best judge of 'good' mothers, having had no experience, but I told her that in my book she'd be good at whatever she undertook. I know I imagined her pregnant, tummy and breasts swollen up. Could have worked up some real maudlin stuff, if I hadn't controlled myself and cut it short. But maybe it was already too late.

Now that she's gone, I tend to remember the endearing moments . . . even the contradictions. For instance, though she never talked about her beauty, she could be a little sticky getting dressed to go somewhere, or in front of a camera—say when I got my polaroid loaded. Wouldn't let me click off a single exposure until every hair was in place—took forever, and then she never really liked any of them. The ones I gave her disappeared; the rest I hid; thought of submitting them to Vogue, or the S.I.'s swimsuit issue. "A little vain, Jane?" I teased her. She attempted to change the subject, wouldn't face me, was abashed and dashed away. Had to chase her around the apartment and hold her down until she admitted it. Embarrassed, Annie? Why? She wouldn't say. And yet her eyes were investigating me, taking me in. But alas it didn't register.

I can picture her lovely, rich, chestnut hair, slightly cropped, and picture her coolly elegant in her business suits, going off to the office. I wanted to go with her, be her secretary, bring her coffee, jump on her . . . God . . .

One last story, one funny-odd episode. She had her heroines, as I'd had baseball cards in middle school. Hers were not the Olympians like Eleanor Roosevelt, Joan of Arc, Catherine The Great . . . Helen Hayes, or O'Keeffe, but Jackie 0., Katherine Hepburn, Streep, Maria Callas and even Cher and Elizabeth Taylor. I was flummoxed, tried to seal my lips, hold my cheeks in, especially when I saw how religiously she pursued it, reading whatever she found, then filing it! Filing it, Annie? Really? . . . Why? Her expression wavered before she looked away.

"You measuring your life by them?" I pressed.

A little color rose in her cheeks. Facing away, she explained, "It's just a mindless pastime, like following sports. I started as a kid, and have kept up. Now it's changed, though, for it reminds me of the realities behind the glitter, the struggles, the ups and downs, that things are seldom what they seem."

It had taken, I could see, a supreme effort for her to reveal this, and my heart went out to her. I embraced her, even as I wondered what exactly she felt she had to protect. As I held her, I felt her slowly relax in my arms. Of course, now as I think of it, there are actors I look up to, watch, read about, even if I haven't been so interested in their personal lives, in part because most of what's written has been pretty thin. I know a bit about Olivier, Gielgud, Brando, Hoffman, Daniel Day. Maybe this was Annie's means of getting out of herself, forgetting herself. One thing I did notice, when I read some of those profiles, was that each of those women had long, dedicated careers. Had she, too, made this association? Maybe, without being completely aware, or maybe she was absolutely clear.

(Yeah, mon, all d' 'maybes' pile up, and though d' Lord he smile upon you, he do so for a time, and den he go away. Same for all da folk . . . Dats d' balance, mon. Law o' da universe. Havin' had d' gold early, mon, you is in for a spare time, sorry t' say.)

Once when we were wandering through the Met, I turned and looked at her from a little distance. At that moment, she was like a painting, composed, elegant, in the faintly golden light of a Rembrandt, and yet her eyes were sad, as in one of his self-portraits, while otherwise she was as cool and poised as his Polish Rider . . . searching past me, into the distance.

I can begin to see that one problem with reaching for objectivity in this remembrance is that I don't *want* to let go, don't want to lose what I thought was there . . . May never want to. Dream for a lifetime. The promised land.

These days, it's embarrassing to catch the expressions in friends' eyes, as they imagine the sadness I'm feeling. Yet Time, I suppose, will do its thing . . . And maybe she was wrong for me. Which of us would have sacrificed a career? Maybe what I need, and may end up with, is some naive but devoted little dumpling from Queens who thinks, for longer than Anne did, that I am the Sun and the Moon, or that at least I occasionally reflect their brilliance . . . Maybe it's what I need, or the price of doing business in the theatre, something that comes with the territory.

XI.

Odd what comes back and what does not. Cannot explain the rhymes or reasons, although I've noticed that different moods sire recollections which reflect them. The present lends its lens, o'erlays the past, even as the past is prologue; a wheel proceeds by circling.

In these weeks, so many unexpected things befell me that I should not have been surprised by one more. Befell, beguiled, beseeched, befuddled, bewailed, beheaded. Being is a multifarious art.

Got a call from an attorney who claimed to represent Tyrone. (Tyrone? Oh groan, that name again, returning like an albatross.) Said he would appreciate it if I could come to his office. Wasn't thrilled; know I hesitated on the phone. Help Tyrone? Free Capone? No way. Help execute maybe; man the guillotine. But help? . . . Rachel's executioner? He who tried to ensnare Anne? Surely the fellow must be kidding . . . But after a short pause, he gently pointed out that he could subpoena me for the trial. Trial? If I'd only been more alert, I'd have foreseen that a plea was much more likely. But my mind was not bent that way, nor did the guy sound unreasonable, and when I couldn't quickly think of an excuse—one problem with no day job—I ended up taking the walk.

Not a long walk, but one into another time and world, as the ambience of the area south of Canal, along Broadway, is not fully of the 20th century. Boss Tweed or Hurstwood can be glimpsed disappearing around the next corner. K-Mart shoppers, with faces and attire reminiscent of the 19th century, hang out there, waiting for a special in aisle C . . . . What is this? My own ambivalence? Fear that I was slipping into that world? Walking over there, I know, I could not quite believe that it was happening, that I was going quite against any interest I had, almost against my will.

Like much of the neighborhood, the law office's interior had never made renovation's acquaintance, nor had the building's linoleum floors. Not a single picture graced the office walls; the furniture must have come from a school-board auction. Depressing, with a capital D. Or perhaps my recollection has darkened it, after sitting in the empty, magazine-less waiting room for nearly thirty minutes, across from a lone, taciturn secretary who did nothing but work on her nails, as single mindedly as if they were prison bars. And nary another soul passed that way . . . Felt Lost. Capital L.

Finally, when called in, I was surprised by the fellow, despite having no particular image in mind. He was a slight, light-skinned black, conservatively, and not inexpensively dressed in a dark suit. He wore round, tortoise-shell glasses, and spoke quietly and carefully. His face reminded me of a more intellectual-looking, less-angry, Malcolm X.

"Thad Bettors, Mr. Schurtz. Thank you for coming. And I apologize for keeping you. I'm afraid a client called with an emergency just before you arrived. It was something I couldn't duck . . . . Sorry."

Duck? Quack quack. Annoyed though I was, I waved off the need for apology, shook hands, and sat down. Peering across his large, old, uncharacteristically uncluttered desk, I noticed that there was about him an air of ill health or convalescence, which, to my consternation, evoked some sympathy. Unnecessary, as it turned out.

He began by telling me how much he liked the theatre, though he seldom had time to go, and that he admired actors, putting themselves out there for the world to see. On guard already, this really zinged my antenna.

He asked me about the play, how it was going and so forth, but I'm afraid I answered rather tersely, unsure how sincere he was. Attempting to loosen me up? And yet his persona and attitude were so understated, so non-threatening, almost frail, that I tried to keep an open mind.

"So now, Mr. Schurtz, I understand that you've already spoken to my friend, Philip Gertler, an extremely promising assistant prosecutor, just getting his feet wet, so I hope you will excuse my retracing some of that ground. In any case, I'm sure you understand the adversarial nature of our judicial system, where we believe the truth has the best chance of surfacing when opposing sides are allowed to make their cases to a jury. I would imagine that in your already-impressive career, you've been in a courtroom drama or two."

Yes yes. More quackery. Did he really think all these honeyed words would have some favorable effect?

"Now, in this case, I'm afraid a man has been charged with the murder of a woman, a woman with whom he'd been very close."

"Had been," I emphasized, barely containing my annoyance.

"They saw each other regularly."

"She was trying to end it, end all contact."

"Surely if that were the case, she could have done so."

I felt myself grimace as I looked away. I was tempted to lay out the steps Rachel had taken, but then decided to let him reveal what he knew.

"So if I may continue," he resumed carefully, "we know neither the immediate circumstances surrounding the unfortunate event, nor the causes leading to it. Nor can we be sure we will ever learn them . . . There may be a court-admissible witness; there may not be. It's not clear at this point, for that one potential witness is the woman's teenage daughter, a minor, who has suffered a great deal . . . Is that your understanding of it, Mr. Schurtz?"

I stared at him. "It seems to me that you're temporizing about a murder, Mr. Bettors. Are you implying that there could have been some circumstances that would have justified your client's act?" Trembling, I recognized that inside I was raging over his blithe minimizing of Tyrone's crime. Should I bring up the issues of drugs and money, or, again, let him introduce them? I watched him closely as he in turn studied me. I wondered if he found me as inscrutable as I did him. Probably not. If life has revealed anything to me, it is that my face is a Rosetta stone upon which, apparently, all the world can find the key to my thoughts.

"I'm not sure either of us was in a position to know, but in any case, Mr. Schurtz, under the principle of presumed innocence, and for the purposes of argument, it is conceivable that our client did not initiate but acted in self-defense."

"Strangled her? . . . You must be kidding!"

His face gave away nothing. "I'm sure, if you think about it for a moment, you might easily imagine a situation where it might be the only recourse."

I almost sneered, then cleared my throat. His credibility had all but disappeared. Yet, as this was not the trial and there was no jury to play to, I did not want to reveal my hand, but wanted only to get through it and out.

"You live on Bank Street, directly across from the apartment where the incident took place?"

"Incident? Please, Mr. Bettors."

"Where the woman lived."

And died. I nodded, hiding, I hoped, a shiver elicited by the images forming in my head.

"And how long had you known the deceased, Mr. Schurtz?"

"Since April."

"Nearly five months, am I correct?"

"Excellent, Mr. Bettors, excellent."

"And you saw Ms. McPherson frequently during that period?"

"McPherson? . . ." Clumsy confusion, or trick?

With unflappable calm he checked the sheet before him. "Excuse me. McPherson was her maiden name, I suppose you could say, though they were never legally married."

A little strange, as Gertler had accepted their common-law status. I tried to remember the name on Rachel's mailbox. Was it not Brown?

"You saw them frequently, during that period?" he asked.

"Regularly. Rebeccah in particular, once the school year ended."

"And you visited their apartment, and they yours?"

Ah hah. So this was it. "Yes. We became friends. They had me to dinner several times . . . Twice." I watched him write this down, then pause thinking, maybe imagining how he might construe this. I found it almost amusing.

"And you returned the hospitality?"

"Only meagerly, as alas I'm no cook."

"But they did visit?"

"Also twice."

"Mother and daughter?"

"Yes . . . or Rebeccah only once."

Again he paused, this time watching me without expression, but with, apparently, inexhaustible patience.

"Is this questioning leading somewhere?" I asked, with just the right proportion of innocence, even as I was feeling slightly uneasy in trying to remember what had brought Rachel alone one evening—possibly some question she had . . . I know it was a short visit. We chatted; she left, but nothing of what his expression was insinuating occurred. Maybe kissed her goodnight. Crossed that threshold, but none other.

"Mr. Schurtz?"

"Yes?"

"You looked like something was troubling you."

I put on my patient, dubious expression, head tilting down a bit.

"Was there?"

"Something troubling me? No."

A faint smile rose and fell across his face. ". . . Now, from what I understand, Rachel was an attractive woman? Was that your estimation?"

"Ms. McPherson?" I asked. He nodded, and I replied, "Well yes, but what . . ."

"If you'll just allow me to complete the thought . . ."

Okay, plod on, if you must. Meet you at the finish.

"So, she was attractive to men, and was available despite her situation. She invited you to dinner; presumably her daughter retired early; she visited your apartment once . . . Please allow me, Mr. Schurtz . . . . Thank you. In the majority of cases, would it not be normal for a man and a woman in such circumstances to have relations? Is that not a reasonable supposition?"

"Ah, Mr. Bettors, just for starters, I was in a relationship, was involved with another woman."

"Yes, Ms. Farraday. That right? But she, as I understand it, had left you."

Thank you. The guy was a real sweetheart. Turn the screw. ". . . It was not quite final." Although I'd corrected his leading, underhanded misimpression, I could feel my face burning, and felt it intensify as he studied me.

"Whatever the case, Mr. Schurtz, I know losing love is painful."

Although clearly he was awaiting a reaction to this, I'd regained control and watched him impassively.

"While I recognize that it's of no consolation now, perhaps this experience could be useful to you someday, as something you may draw on for a role. No? . . . Sorry, just a thought."

I found myself blinking and looking closer at him, wondering if there was any tack he might not try. Yet I found myself wondering if Tyrone had thought he'd been able to exert some influence over Anne—a fear which I quickly quashed. Across the desk, it seemed to me, this impish lawyer suddenly shrank, and his expression took on a satanic leer—until I blinked again, returning him to his original size and physiognomy.

"Yet your relationship with Ms. Farraday did not prevent you from spending time with Rachel, it appears . . . In no way, mind you, am I casting judgment on this. Merely trying to establish what happened."

"We were friends, pure and simple, Mr. Bettors. That was the extent of it."

"It is not for me to question your story, Mr. Schurtz. That is for the jury. But I hope you will agree that your friendship went further than most between men and women."

"Hardly . . . Not at all . . ."

"But, Mr. Schurtz, you might understand that this could cause some misgivings on the part of my client."

"She had left him, Mr. Bettors, had moved out of Brooklyn, to try to start a new life for herself and her daughter."

"I'm merely trying to establish the facts, some of which tell us that you two spent several evenings together."

"I have a number of women friends, Mr. Bettors. It's not at all unusual in the theatre."

"Okay. Well, allow me this, if you would. Just reverse the situation. Suppose Mr. Brown had been invited to visit, for whatever reasons, Ms. Farraday, and he spent several evenings with her, and suppose then that she visited him, in his apartment, placing them alone together, several times. How would you look upon that? And would you expect nothing of an intimate nature to take place? In this day and age? Would it not be reasonable for him to presume that she had come . . . for something?"

This was outrageous! And Bettors knew it, stretching things beyond the pale—indeed it was so absurd that I felt it beneath my dignity to reply. Yet at the same time, I felt strangely immobilized by the innuendo, which slithered through me uninvited . . . What, I wondered, was that? . . . Did this boil down to a contest of wills? A contest playing itself out in sexual terms? Was he attempting to foment and then play on my jealousy? Or was this only in my mind? Whatever the case, it disgusted me, so that I wanted to hurl the entire thing away . . . I wondered if Bettors could see this struggle, in my protruding jaw and unhappy eyes. I stared at him through occluded sight.

"I gather I have made my point, Mr. Schurtz."

"To the contrary, I know what you're trying to do, and it's transparent, and a little pathetic. Your hypothetical is nonsense, fits none of the realities. The situations are not comparable. You're trying to establish something that never happened."

"And yet it is my understanding that Ms. Farraday did see Mr. Brown several times."

"In her office, to try to help him find employment."

"I have information that it went beyond that."

Plainly this was a bluff, and I know I stared him down, a disparaging twist in my lips, until he felt compelled to justify himself. "I'm simply trying to find out what happened, Mr. Schurtz."

My turn to display a dubious smile, bounteous patience.

"Okay, Mr. Schurtz, perhaps you will now see that just as the possibility of my client having relations with Ms. Farraday is not to your liking, sticks in your craw, if you will, so you might acknowledge a similar effect of your spending time with Ms. McPherson on Mr. Brown."

Still pushing it? Well, I had explained, and saw no reason to repeat it. What I did replay, quite calmly, was my disdain for his tactics.

But he went on. "From my experience, I believe a jury will find your friendship a recognizable threat to their relationship. And as we do not know what transpired on that fatal evening, it is not unreasonable to suppose some argument or fight erupted over your relations with Rachel, and it is certainly not beyond a reasonable doubt that her death could well have been the accidental result of such a fight."

"You should write plays, Mr. Bettors, or better yet, soaps."

He smiled a little. "I've certainly encountered enough raw material for them . . . but if I might continue, it is rather curious that she called you that evening."

As he paused to see if this last shot produced any effect on me, I heard an internal voice asking: How is it that everyone comes around to this? Seems the whole world knows . . . Does this constitute my penance? . . . Am I deserving of it? . . . Maybe . . . but his insinuations show he lacks integrity.

"Mr. Schurtz? . . . You drifted off again."

As I refocused on him, I wondered why I simply did not get up and walk out. Why not?

"Why was it she called that evening?" he asked more pointedly.

Although I saw his face, the voice seemed miles away. I leaned forward, to be sure he would hear. "Because, Mr. Bettors, I was a friend and lived across the street."

"But why did she want to talk to you?"

". . . I'm not certain. Possibly she feared that your client was going to show up."

"Why should she fear that, if there was nothing to hide? They had been together some time. Why the sudden change?"

With some exasperation, and sadness, I wondered: should I now go into the whole thing, the escape from him and his world, the fellow at Macy's, the drugs, the money? . . ."You know, Mr. Bettors, Rachel was a fine woman, trying, and succeeding in making a new life. And you, simply to try to slide your unfortunate client out between the bars of justice, have been dragging her down to his level . . . Well that's sad; and it won't work. Too many people know the kind of woman Rachel was; too many people will see his heinous murder for what it was. The whole business about the drugs and money will come out. Come to think of it, Mr. Bettors, you'd better hope there is no trial . . . Probably I've been slow in seeing this, that you've been simply looking for a bargaining chip. Well, there aren't any. Your guy took a life, a good, courageous life, and I hope to God he pays."

I saw Bettors look down for a moment; there was a brief frown, and then he recomposed himself. "I don't condone what happened, Mr. Schurtz. And I can understand how you see Tyrone . . . But while the fellow may've been making a living selling drugs, he'd never killed anyone before, had never come close . . . And he did care for her, and Rebeccah, in a way that his world allowed. And so what I've wanted to find out, Mr. Schurtz, is why now? What suddenly set him off? Something did. What? . . . And the fact that he was trying to get to your friend suggests to me he was trying to get at you, because he thought you were touching his woman."

As the emotions of our statements rolled over us, as we held each other in sight, perhaps we both saw anew the two sides of this sad tragedy. At least I believed I did. And I wanted now to make sure things were clear. "Yes, Mr. Bettors, Rachel and I liked each other," I began; "yes, there was some fellow-feeling there and yes, she was attractive to me, but she'd found a new fellow at Macy's, Robert somebody, whom she hoped to hook up with. It wasn't me. And frankly, all other men aside, she simply wanted to get away from Tyrone . . . and that life. Your harping on their relationship is a sham . . . As for me, I was just a neighbor, not at all central to where her life was going."

I think Bettors heard the truth in this, although he maintained his poker face. After a period of silence, I saw no further reason to stay, and so stood up to leave. But as I did, he too stood and asked, "Explain one thing to me, Mr. Schurtz. Why after spending all that time with them, especially with the daughter—and I admit at first I thought you were just trying to get to Rachel through her—why did you not go to her that night?"

Standing face to face, I was surprised by my own calm. "I have no satisfactory answer . . . other than I had been thinking of calling Anne, to plead with her. I was thinking that it was her, when Rachel called, and was disappointed, irritated, that it wasn't . . . I heard Rachel's request, her need, I believe, but I put it out of my mind . . . Sounds weak, sad . . . and I'm afraid it is. But that's the case." What I couldn't add—saw no reason to—was the soul-rending tear, the foot in the heart, that Anne's leaving had left me with . . . this and the omnipresence of Rachel's eyes looking into me, which made me wary . . . fearful of my own inclinations. Maybe, to some degree, I was afraid to go to her because of my attraction . . . and possibly because I had no interest in coming face to face with Tyrone . . . Those reasons—all wound together . . . I cannot weigh their relative influence. Each alone might have been sufficient to cause me to turn away. It may never come completely clear. I do remember, earlier that fatal evening, before Rachel called, while walking home from the theatre, I paused under a large dead tree, distinct from all the other trees which lay leaved in summer fullness, and I stared up at its dark, bare branches reaching to heaven, and asked . . . cried to God, as those branches seemed to be crying, for another chance, with Anne.

Suddenly remembering where I was, I found Bettors watching me in a distracted manner. I nodded to him. I don't believe he responded, or if he did, I don't recall how, before I turned to the door. Don't remember the walk home, though I know I sank into the chair that had been Anne's favorite and didn't rise until it was time for the show.

XII.

I have come not to bury Schurtz, nor to praise him, but to appraise him. He's still young, everyone tells him, and has much to look forward to, meaning a promising career that will take him to the coast and celebrity . . . Celebrity? That plastic wrap of achievement; that adornment that is somehow diminishing—though people will think I'm being disingenuous. Yet I witness that nearly any public mention will do these days—exposure over substance. Even before its arrival, I was wary, of the word itself. My agent, however, reminds me that my career depends upon it. Without it, he tells me, I would live in noble obscurity—a stagehand.

Sometimes it seems that everything about the theatre, in this country at least, carries the seeds of its own corruption. Whatever idealistic notions the playwrights harbor, the producers, or maybe the so-called market forces, soon limit. Or maybe it's that the audiences really want soothing, familiar tales, and stars. Or maybe it's the ever-escalating production costs, in a world where everyone wants to partake of the riches. Celebrity becomes the measure of a production's worth . . . I wonder if I will buy into this in California . . . Maybe celibacy would be more truly honest, fecund, and faithful.

Or am I being naive again? After all, the theatre is a most human institution. And should I quibble when my success has pleased Pop, and brought me Anne? Small matter that it has also permitted me to avoid resolving certain personal issues. Oh yes, I have confronted Macbeth's ambition, Anne's charity and beauty, Hamlet's equivocation, but not my own issues, despite knowing that I must, if I am to become the actor, and person, I wish. I have told myself that I was waiting for the perfect situation, and companion. However when both appeared, I turned aside . . . Why? . . . The same question asked and asked again, with the slow motion of my self-awareness, until that motion itself becomes an issue. Together, all weighs me down—a chain around my neck.

And making it all the more uncomfortable is this fact that I am considered a success in this business where many equally good, or better, actors could bring what I bring, and more—raising the question: Why me? . . . Ah, but Schurtz, none of this is new; people have wrestled with this since the dawn.

Yes, but this is my life!

And then I remember Rachel . . . and am silenced. Or should be. By what measure, dear God, have I complaint with this life? . . . The encounter with Bettors has called her back. I cannot help but imagine her last moments: her neck caught in those furious hands—conscious, as she must have been, of what was happening—watching one's very life growing dark . . . God! I cannot . . . I feel as if I, too, am dying. Or should have, in her place . . . Why did she not call her friend, Robert? Or her cousin in the Bronx? Or the police? Why did she stop with me? Me, sitting sullenly bent over myself in my bower, wondering how to breathe life into a lifeless love. Oh sad creature. Even my meager renown fills not this emptiness. Why did she not simply flee, lift up Becky and together run into the street? Why, as it appears, did she lose hope, after so long and seemingly successful a struggle? Why suddenly give in? Was my denial the straw that broke her back? The fatal, weakest link? . . . Or was I only a disappointing rustle in the leaves as night came on?

Why can I not put her out of my mind? Why does my own explanation not sit well with me? The answer, alas, is simple and long recognized by me: she asked. Not many people do—yet when she did, I answered not.

Another explanation (not an excusing) fights its way into my consciousness, a variation, that I have mentioned: that I could not handle the intimacy of her eyes, even now staring into me, reaching in, with their dark steadiness, their open warmth. What did she see? Why was I examined with such open caring? Why did she expose that part of herself to me? For me to act upon . . . to act? . . . Whereas Anne, and I, can be guarded, or worse . . . Was not that last evening a double horror for Rachel?

I have not been a bad person over the years. There is evidence that I can summon a few of the better behaviors—consideration, occasionally—and yet this is not sufficient. And as I've said, my punishment is that now I must live with the recognition—I who am, at least, alive. (Hey mon, d' guilt hang upon you in tatters, an old coat from d' shoulder. Beyond, a shadow's watchin'. Dese tings linger in your heart fo'ever.)

No, no more explanations are necessary. One way or another we must live with our hearts, into which we alone can see. Yet now what sweeps back, on Bettors' innuendo, is the evening she visited me alone. Must've been a Monday night, when the theatre was dark. Don't remember where Anne was.

Working late? A trip? Think I was watching Mets-Dodgers from Shea, the crowd roar all but drowning out the announcers.

The buzzer gave me a start, and her voice over the intercom a second one. As I waited for her to climb the few stairs, I felt a little strange at her coming over. Or is it that I feel it now?

At my front door, she asked if she could come in for just a minute, had a couple of things she needed to speak about. I stepped back and welcomed her. As she moved past me I noticed her perfume followed her like a spectral cape. Inside, she swung in a tight circle, taking in the place, which Anne had helped me straighten and enliven a bit. She, I noticed, seemed buoyant and bright, in tight jeans and an elegant, open raspberry shirt over a white, sleeveless undershirt. As she had since meeting Robert, she looked pretty sharp.

She didn't want to sit, she said, and I could see that she was up, way up. "Mac, I was with Robert earlier, and we were talkin' 'bout all sorts of things." She gave me one of her self-contained, magnetic smiles, and when I offered her a beer, she declined with another, as if to say: Me? Don't need a thing.

"Mac, he thinks I have a voice, a real singing voice. He sings in a choir uptown, and he told me I oughta invest in some lessons, so I could join his choir, or at the very least it'd help my career, if I developed my voice and so forth." And her eyes flashed more radiantly than her smile.

As happy as I was for her, I couldn't help but wonder if she was on something, but then told myself it was probably just him—his encouragement.

"Mac, you must know a good voice teacher, who wouldn't charge an arm 'n' a leg, and who'd take on an ole black girl like me?"

Her self-definition startled me, but I told her, sure, I knew several.

"Would you give me their names, honey? Write 'em down for me? And can I tell 'em you sent me?"

As I left her for a moment to fish around for my book and something to write with, she hummed a little, then softly sang, "The first time ever I saw his face," just loud enough to hear, and it sounded clear and good. God knows I've been to enough auditions.

In the instant after I'd given her the names, she leapt unexpectedly to quite another subject, heralded only by a narrowing of her eyes. "Mac . . . you know Anne's been a real friend to me, regarding my career and this course I'm taking, and what I might do in the long run . . . but I . . . I don't know how to put this . . . . I don't think she has to go so far as to help Tyrone . . . find employment, I mean." To emphasize her point, her eyes bore into mine. But then astonishingly, I swear, she nearly burst out laughing, was just able to contain it, her sides quaking. "It's not that I don't appreciate it, and Lord knows, he may even . . . but I don't think it's a good idea . . . . I've told you I'm trying to get away from him, and this is probably givin' him the wrong idea."

Maybe she saw that I wasn't quite grasping it. "He . . . I don't think he's taking her efforts seriously," she said. "Fact, I'm sure he's not. Probably thinks it's somethin' else. You know what I mean?"

Though I was beginning to, I was reluctant to articulate it for myself.

"He could become a problem, for everyone. You know? . . ." As Rachel watched my face grow long, she nodded in confirmation. But then once again, I saw the ripples of another suppressed laugh roll up her throat to her mouth and cheeks, only to disappear behind a sudden frown. "Whatever it is he's thinking, it's not about jobs. Will you tell her, Mac?" I indicated I would.

"Most likely has something to do with me, but I can't stop and wait till he faces the music . . . By the way, this voice lesson business is something Anne also suggested. I hope you'll tell her about that too, if I don't get to her first. It's been so busy at work."

Just then, Carter or Strawberry must have hit a homerun because the TV exploded with sixty thousand cheers, and I spun away, relieved to do so, hurrying to turn down the sound. Returning, I saw that she now leaned against a book shelf near the door and was idly peering through a pile of polaroids left there. As I approached, she looked up with an amused smile, reminding me that the pile included poses of both Annie and me, some of which were nude, I'm afraid.

"Aren't you two a handsome couple."

I'm sure I flushed as she gazed at them. I remember feeling the blood rise, as I hoped she would quickly return the photos to the shelf. But no, she brought them closer, studying them, and then, with an ambivalent smile, looked up to say, "Underneath her very proper strait-lace, that lady's lookin' for a way to break out, isn't she?"

Although she had caught something of the truth there, I didn't think it was quite in the way she was implying. Awkwardly I managed to blurt only that, "They weren't for public consumption."

Chewing the inside of her lower lip, Rachel glanced at them again, before asking, "Her father a priest or something?"

"A lawyer."

"Same difference," she mumbled, nodding to herself, then stared down at the floor. After a moment or so, she found me again and appeared to be waiting for something from me. With growing discomfort I put out my hand for the photos, but she seemed not to notice. Instead she drew herself in to speak.

"You know, Mac, you're like my friend, Rob, at Macy's. You two like women. I can see it in these pictures of Anne. They're sexy but in a considerate way. You don't make her look foolish. Rob's like that; he takes pictures too. You're both . . . respectful . . . . Whereas Tyrone is not. He doesn't like women . . . which is something I want Anne to know. He's out for anything and everything he can get. And I mean it. Don't give him an inch . . ."

Nodding, I wanted to ask her why she continued to see him at all, but I didn't. I also wanted to get those pictures from her, although the urgency seemed to have abated.

"You're a nice man, Mac. Nice lookin', too," she said glancing back at the pictures with a distracted smile. "But I wanted to ask you about Becky; she's been acting listless lately . . ." and she gave me another once-over, "but I'll save it for another time. You're probably thinking I want you to take pictures of me now." And she slapped the polaroids into my hand with a punctuating smile.

Taking a step back toward the door, she thanked me for the names. I told her it was nothing, and if none were to her liking, I'd see who else I could find, or could even help her a little myself.

She paused, looking through me this time, then said with some intensity, "You're a strange one, too, you know? . . . I wonder if you even know what you're doin' . . . . You have to be a little careful with us girls, particularly my age. We can be a little too eager to hear things, in certain ways . . . and I can't believe Anne would be pleased to have you spendin' time with another woman . . . And, Mac, don't go takin' her for granted. Spend time with her—a lotta pitfalls out there, a lotta wolves . . . . Sometimes I don't know whether you're an innocent, or that's just your game."

As she watched me closely, I felt uneasy, and to an extent revealed. But my self-protective faculties, having been summoned by the ring in her voice, proceeded to lay down an emotional smokescreen, to hide me from myself, even if I knew, somewhere inside, that she had said something to me that no one else had.

"Well goodnight," I heard her say, "and thanks." I heard her step toward the door, then pause once more, glancing back at me. I don't recall exactly why, but I reached for and grasped her hand. Part of it was a surge of appreciation . . . part was our rapport, and a sense that she was someone I cared for, however ill-defined that was . . . I don't remember the next moment—maybe she moved, maybe I did—but somehow we embraced each other, lightly, cheek on cheek, and lingered . . . I was surprised how soft she felt; I could feel her body against mine, and I reacted with a powerful tremor. As she began to pull away, I quickly kissed her. Almost automatically, it seemed, our lips brushed, and for an instant I felt another current snap through me, followed by, I remember, cool air, as I saw her moving away, through the door. I heard her footsteps on the stairs, as I reached out for the molding to steady myself, as I closed the door.

In time, I turned and drifted back across the room, to where the silent screen was sweeping over faces of fans cheering, hoisting beers and turning to each other, waving fists and pennants, and of ballplayers slapping backs and shoulders . . . even as I knew I was shaking, under my calm, shaking with conflicted feelings, with electricity and confusion. I slumped down into a chair and let my eyes lock onto the screen—its reds and greens, blues and oranges, silver and whites—a fuzzy, summertime, multi-colored Christmas tree, its branches waving gaily in the breeze.

I don't know, there is something very seductive about being in the presence of one who looks into you so deeply, who seems to see as much as you see yourself—the photos, her eyes and voice—seeing me all draped out like that, looking outside and in . . . With Anne it was never quite like that . . . The fact that she was almost a work of art gave it quite another dimension: excitement yes, awe yes, but distance, too. Much between us we left implicit, although maybe we wanted to hear it nonetheless. With Rachel it seemed her eyes reached in, so that it felt as if all my vessels and sinews and feelings were seen, accepted, and drawn out, with the result that everything felt excited, felt like a kind of surrender, a lowering of the screen.

For all the vast differences in circumstances and fortune, it appears that I am in danger of repeating the failings of my father, as he replayed his, perhaps. Desperately we thrash about and reach for some envisioned connection, only to shove aside life's many other offerings. Although I see this, I remain locked in habit . . . and so I will go out to California, without the necessary changes having been made. Non mutatis mutandis. All the many plays tell me a man has only his integrity. A man gaineth nothing, if he sell his soul. Mine is strongly eroded. Perhaps there was never any hope for a hybrid like me, with elements so crazily mixed . . . And what purpose going on with this story, when it only sinks and sinks again? . . . Yet, it is my only hope, and only story, and, given my weaknesses, perhaps it is fortunate that the specters of Rachel and Anne call me after them.

XIII.

Steam and smoke billow along Seventh Avenue as I walk south. It's rush hour and trucks and cabs shake, rattle, 'n' roll for every foot forward. I'm in a cartoon, pulsating like Felix the Cat, strutting with Travolta, flowing in a fog with other footsteps, energized by the crowd and its commotion, yet going nowhere.

Today was our last at Circle. Following the final performance, we cleared out our dressing rooms, and though most of us will continue to see each other—in fact I'm having dinner again with Mags day after tomorrow—we exchanged fond goodbyes through smiles and hugs. Over most of us, however, hung the shroud of Rachel's death . . . and Anne's withdrawal from our group. Some had suggested a party, but few of us had the spirit for one.

Together, over the course of our run, we had ascended to giddy heights, balancing on the unsteady legs of good reviews, largely responsive audiences, the resonant script (which sadly presaged events, for some of us) and our warm friendships, including three special outsiders. But now, all's dissolved, almost as if it hadn't happened—except for the lingering pain. Pain is, evidently, to remind you.

Now, as I walk, forms float along the sidewalk into my vision, materializing out of the sun, a procession endless and astonishing, lifting me away from myself. Here comes a kerchiefed old woman in black, from a Sicilian village, rocking under her weighty sack of laundry, her face a stony apex to her squat, triangular form. And there a dapper anglophile, all tweed and leather, brisk and supercilious. And now a punk couple in black and pink, expressions sliding between disdain and distress. Which of the two shaved heads belongs to the female is only hinted at by a faint bulging of the thorax. (A distinction irrelevant to them perhaps.) Next I pass a Latino 'super,' grim and grimy from wrestling with a furnace, whose parts lie like machetied limbs randomly strewn along the sidewalk, his olive overalls blackened by swaths of oil and soot, his eyes never rising to where he might encounter others—not now, not like this. And there a seated Korean, upon a box, slicing fruit, performing, without expression, an age-old task; while a Pakistani from within his cave of magazines gazes out, irony deepening the lines in his brow, as he reviews the hopeless parade. And here a ballerina bobbing by, Polish possibly, from her profile and pale coloring; the thinness of her face accentuated by her dirty-blonde hair pulled back tightly into a single braid, feet out unapologetically, her face plainly, almost defiantly open. She, at least, has found the way . . . And a beggar so dirty and wrapped 'round with rags that one cannot find his face, nor tell his race, his silent empty cup held out beyond his mumbled syllables. Oh most miserable soul—yet I do not give, tightening the cord around my heart. What good would it do? I ask myself. Change nothing . . . except my own soul. ("Theft never enriches; alms never impoverish." All the lines . . .)

Several students hoot cryptic cries of joy and self-definition, grinning at the sky and passersby to see if they are noticed. The salt of the earth, and its cream, all flowing down these streets, day and night. And who among them would know of *Half Moon* or M. Schurtz, or even Circle Rep, though they pass it daily? Our small company has secretly believed that we, in our work, are speaking essentials to the world, but in fact, it is to a pitifully small few—a circle indeed.

And though praises have I sung of our West Village community, it, too, is but a small, essentially closed circle, occasionally reaching through to the outside, while it swallows those outsiders it lures in—our genius fly-trap. Quite unlike a real village, where tinker, tailor, and candlestick maker know and depend upon each other, our lives are almost collegiate, that is, abstract, and in preparation for some ascension. It is the life of the future, of advanced civilizations, alas unrooted, and we are but spirits who leave no trace—as Anne and I will not. We bloomed, then abruptly wilted, quickly, quietly, cleanly . . . Oh, if only we'd produced something together, something which could be held . . . a child or even some joint work . . . but no, she wasn't ready, at least not for me . . . Nor was I, possibly. After all, I didn't really fight. This, as much as the loss itself, may be what troubles me, that I let it slip away, so easily.

But no! When she returns, I will go see her! Have it out, give it my all, or die trying. Oh . . . poor choice of words.

Strange, as I think of it, that even at the height of our love, the hours Anne and I spent together filled but a small part of our days, weekends excepted.

Four hours maybe, breakfast and post theatre. Otherwise she was at work, while I divided my time between *Half Moon*, classes with André, auditions, Rebec, and miscellaneous. Friends outside the theatre kid me about this soft life, dismissing my protestations that there are emotional costs, as well as those of poverty. But I don't know why I bother. It's one of the reasons we actors stick together.

And despite her sensitivity, Anne, I think, never truly understood. Once, I remember, when I bared my soul about acting, she responded by asking, "Did you ever consider directing? . . . I think you'd be quite good." The pitch of her voice, I suspected, carried the underlying message: that perhaps I'd better turn to directing, as acting may not provide me with a living.

"Would you prefer, Annie, that I direct?"

Instead of the expected disavowal, she studied me before replying, "It's not for me to decide. I thought only that you might be an excellent director." Not the sort of thing an actor wants to hear on the verge of his first movie part, despite her sincerity.

I remember that this exchange followed her attendance at a party where she met Kevin Kline, Malkovich, and Duvall, and from which she returned aglow. Next to those immortals, what chance had I? Her question, stemming from that experience, I suppose, was natural. And one more thing: her invitation to that party arose out of the article she did on the theatre, through which we had met, and now, increasingly, her job was taking her to the watering holes of the movers and shakers . . . and then she would go home to her obscure little actor. Our relationship was born in fantasy and now was dying from it. The Circle Rep may send up candidates for kingship, but cannot crown them.

She, however, was born among the Eastern elite, and while she had moved away for a time, to California, she returned for college, and now, in natural progression, was moving up the mainstream ladder to a rung where her opinion was read and courted. Goodbye Schurtz. I'm sure I'd recognized this inevitability, but had somehow managed to deny it. Why? . . . Something called love.

Well, I'll show her! Like Heathcliff, I'll disappear west for a time, and then return incredibly successful, irresistibly handsome, pushing past her conventional husband, to sweep her up into my arms, and let her cry out her love for me, before she expires from her broken heart, despite the rain of my restoring kisses . . . Yes, Schurtz, righting the balance. (Eye for an eye, Mon. So be it.)

Indeed as I look back on the period following that party, there was a perceptible cooling. And I hated it in her, even as I could understand it.

How could she, an ardent, dynamic soul, not warm to those fellows? They can stir even me. And while some people have compared me to Kevin Kline, I have not his insouciance and range . . . nor, face it old toad, his skill . . . . One day, perhaps . . . But at present, I am, at best, closer to Decline than to K. Kline, and my stature is as if seen through the wrong end of a telescope. While our silhouettes may look similar, noses excepted, up close my persona is riddled with holes.

That's not to say it all fell apart immediately. Things went on for a while; we still had moments . . . I remember a hot Sunday morning at her place; we were slicing fruit for a salad, seated on either side of her kitchen counter. The lemon I was cutting spurted out, sprinkling her chin and throat. For a moment she looked at me with annoyance, at my clumsiness, before wiping it off and continuing her slicing. Taken aback, not entirely in control, I squeezed the lemon, deliberately, spraying her face and white cotton nightgown. We studied each other quite seriously, searching for different things of course, and finding, perhaps, sides of the other previously unknown. Then she laughed to herself, shook her head, and resumed.

Wanting anything but to be ignored, I squeezed it firmly once more, near her, until lemon beads collected on her neck and collar bone and ran down inside her gown. But instead of leaping away, she held herself there, trembling, with great will. Certainly I was struck by this—how odd it seemed—nonetheless I went heedlessly on, standing up, stepping around the counter, where I took her shoulders to turn her toward me. Now finally she sprang up and pulled away, yet did not run off, so that I could reach again for her and hold her shoulders, before taking the lemon wedge and running it up her neck and around to her jaw, cheek and lips. And she allowed me to tilt her head back against my shoulder where I could see, as her dark hair swung back, that a strange, mingled expression spread over her face. And so I ran the lemon down to the open neckline of her gown, and inside, along her shoulders and down over her breasts. I felt her shiver powerfully, although I didn't know if this was from the cool lemon, from pleasure, or from her exertion of will. And as I paused over this, she brought her hand to mine, to urge it continue, and it did, while the other hand unbuttoned the hindering clasps to her nightgown and slid it off.

Holding her, however, I remember, what struck me more than the excitement was simply the sight of the tiny goosebumps on her skin so white, marmoreal, in contrast to her dark lovely hair. It took my breath away . . . I'm not sure why, after our months together. Perhaps it was because she seemed so forbidden moments before. Perhaps it was because she was not normally a sensuous person . . . or perhaps it was because she was behaving so differently, almost passively—quite unlike any other time—It threw me. And its mystery supplants the memory of our subsequent love-making.

I did ask her about it, later, in bed, but, returning my gaze, she simply kissed me once lightly and rolled over—at which I almost laughed. Who was this?

The next morning, I remember, I asked her again, but she pleaded no time, before work, and I guess we never did get back to it, as with too many other things. For increasingly, other things interfered: those work-related dinners and parties, so that frequently when we met after the show, she wanted only to go to bed, sometimes with hardly a word.

It worried me; I knew we had to deal with it, but at the same time, I didn't want to sound confining or possessive, with California closing in, and I figured that at best we would have to learn to cope with long separations, would have to cultivate independence . . . . Guess my heart never acknowledged the possibility that it would end.

XIV.

Haunting me now, as I move from memory to memory, is the sense that I am omitting things, either because I've forgotten or because part of me doesn't wish to face them. And though this gnaws at me, I fear, at the same time, that going back, fine-combing will stall me, will sap the will to reach the end.

I do remember, however, that the terrible prospect of separation crashed through finally, unexpectedly, during an otherwise innocent moment. Although to be honest, it could've come at any moment; the circumstances were ripe.

One evening I waited for her at the theatre, long after the others had left. It was unlike her to be late, and when she arrived by cab, she apologized as she slipped her arm through mine and turned us breathlessly homeward. She began recounting the dinner conversation she'd just had with two women colleagues, now friends, about their lives—surprisingly enough, I might have interjected. What suddenly struck the three of them, at almost the same time, was the recognition that, while they'd all been groaning and grumbling about the impossibility of balancing everything in life, it was probably more feasible and desirable to pursue various interests not all at once, but over different periods in their lives. While this didn't seem quite the thunderbolt to me that it did to them, I acknowledged the practicality, and possibly the wisdom, of it. I confess that what I'd thought I would do after acting had never occurred to me in the slightest. Nonetheless she went on about how healthy and indeed rejuvenating this would be for our population that is living so much longer these days, and in her enthusiasm, she kissed me as we turned onto her street, and I could feel the excitement in her lips and arms. Of course I was also wondering if there would be an 'us' in her life's next segment, and unfortunately quipped, "So then, California *does* lie ahead in your future, after all."

Immediately I saw that this was a mistake. Even in the street light, I could see her face fall, and her voice too, ". . . Oh Mac . . ." She was silent until we reached her gate, where she picked it up, "Mac, you of all people—you who are about to go off to a brave new experience—you should understand what we were talking about."

"Sorry. I just wanted to know where that left us. I don't think it's worth losing you."

She glanced at me, and I saw her disappointment contract into worry, distracted only by the need to fish for her apartment keys. Inside, our conversation was put on hold until she'd poured us some wine. God, tired and soon to be besotted. Not the ideal state in which to discuss our fate. Anyway, wine in hand, down we sat, and she resumed: "Mac . . . dear Mac . . . you're not about to deny that acting is the first priority in your life, are you?"

"Of course not, Annie, after it's understood that you *are* my life."

From her slightly vexed expression, it was clear that she did not wish to hear this. "McKim, you'd give up a relationship before you would your career."

"But I just stated the opposite. You don't believe me?"

With a searching, troubled look, she studied me. "I believe that *you* believe that, now, at this moment. But if you stayed, after a month or two, you'd grow frustrated and unhappy."

"Try me, Annie."

An almost imperceptible squirming preceded her absorbing this truth— perhaps for the first time, and a faint, gray sadness spread across her face. "But Mac, we both know how important the movie is for your work."

". . . Maybe . . . but what will happen to us?" She opened her mouth to reply, then closed it, and my heart sank. "Do you see, Annie, my going west as a graceful way out?"

She did not look at me.

"Or do you see us holding together, somehow over all those miles?"

In a low voice she said, "I'm not sure what I've thought."

"Doesn't sound like you, Annie."

". . . I think at different times I've imagined both: that we would remain together, or that we would simply dissolve, drift apart." Her expression, as she forced herself to carefully take me in, slid between sadness and accusation, defiance and hopelessness. Or so I interpreted it—after which I looked away, until she murmured, "In many ways it makes no sense."

"What?" Though I knew.

"To try to hold on."

I felt dizzy. (As I do now.) The mirror and paintings in her living room undulated at the edges of my sight. "But Annie, are you so ready to throw away everything we have shared? Does that make sense? . . . And what is 'sense' anyway, in this life? . . . Tell me what is objectively sensible. Tell me what we're each doing that is so important outside of 'us'. Tell me that it is not true that when each of us drops dead, most of us will be forgotten in less time than it takes to tell about it. And, as a consequence, isn't *love* the only thing that matters in this world?—where indeed the physical matter that matters most, light, is not even matter, but a particular wave of electromagnetic radiation . . . And thus, isn't the only thing we need to decide whether we still care enough to want to be together?!—All the other discussion, about work and careers, being just so much claptrap."

She continued to watch me sadly, then her eyes fell.

I studied her face, now shadowed and long. "But what? . . . You're not sure about this? . . . That you care enough?"

When she didn't deny this, I could feel that old numbness set in. She looked away to the side and sighed, "I'm afraid, Mac, it isn't clear to me."

As I heard this, I felt I was being torn away slowly from her, limb by limb. She must have glanced over and saw the need to explain. "It would be difficult, Mac . . . So much of our focus, and energies, will be elsewhere."

"But what's the alternative?"

Staring into her wine, she shook her head, and for a time we sat there silently—I nursing my drink with self-consoling sips. After that, we went to bed, without speaking. I know I didn't sleep, and she, I remember, turned frequently, tugging the sheet over her, then throwing it off, throughout the night.

In the morning, there was no time to talk, and we parted politely on the sidewalk, she going east to work, and I west. But it was a lost day, and I have no memory of the performance that evening.

I tried to reach her by phone, but, as she was continually in meetings, her secretary finally gave me a message that she would see me at my place around ten-thirty or eleven. I remember when I got home from the show, I tried to read, watch the news, but couldn't concentrate. I attempted a little cleaning, but could hardly push the vacuum. When, at almost midnight, she arrived, she came in rather cautiously, apologizing, but I remember that behind the fatigue in her face I saw a distant glow, about which she soon told me. She'd been to a book party where she'd met a number of interesting people, including a senior editor who had all but offered her a job when she'd expressed interest in making the switch to books. I guess I tried to look interested, supportive, but she must have sensed the truth. And yet probably to avoid talking about our situation, both of us kept batting this balloon up into the air. She wondered if the timing was right for leaving the magazine, and I pointed out that working as this fellow's assistant would be a step down from running her own department. Yes, she agreed, but still, at some point, it was a move she wanted to make.

"Was it a firm offer, Annie? Or was it only an offer to shoot the breeze?"

She looked at me solemnly. "He was serious. I don't think he's the type to make idle proposals, and I think it would be even less likely for him to do so with someone in my position."

I wasn't sure her position was as sacrosanct as she thought, but generally her judgement was keen in these things. "So what's the next step?"

"Lunch, Friday, and he'll show me around and introduce me to the department."

"How old is he?"

Her sagging expression signaled that she found this gratuitous. "I don't know . . . Why?"

"Just curious." I could see she wasn't pleased with my inference, but of course I'm always aware that few men would *not* react to her as a woman. Bloody Helen of Troy. Sack the whole department for her, the bastard.

She asked if I had any red wine. Of course I did; I knew she was coming. As I opened the bottle and poured, an unhappy quiet filled the room, until she moved and sank down into the armchair, and I was left on the couch to sit alone. Yet she raised her glass. "To our new endeavors, or at least to yours."

I think I chugged my wine, for its veritas soon flowed forth, "Annie, doesn't this new possibility further complicate what we were talking about last night?"

She appeared caught off guard. "No. Why? . . . I don't know how quickly, if at all, it will happen. And if it does, my schedule certainly will not be any more full than it is now."

Oh no? That's not what I'd heard about fiction editing. I think probably we gazed rather helplessly at each other, unsure where to go, until I felt compelled to ask, "Annie, do you still love me?"

I saw her wince a little and inhale guardedly. "Yes, Mac . . . but holding onto all that we have will be very difficult. For one thing, we don't know how long you're going to be out there."

"It won't be forever . . . and isn't that secondary?"

"It's a crucial time, Mac, for both of us. If it were simple, we wouldn't be having this discussion."

"Well let's start at the center of it."

As she looked at me, her face seemed to darken with sadness, before she said, "I can't see it in isolation. Perhaps I'm too practical, in that."

When I heard this, her tone, even more than her words, froze my heart.

"McKim, I'm not taking this lightly, not at all. You must know that . . . Forgive me, but it's beginning to feel like a repetition of my earlier relationship, which makes it all the more painful."

"Annie, you said you got out of that because it was too predictable, and yet here, when the first ripples of uncertainty and difficulty appear, you start lookin' for the exit."

She frowned. "No, Mac, that's not the case, not at all. Please don't think that."

Maybe I'd sensed this was wrong, off, and I apologized. But then almost immediately asked, "Haven't we got so many things going for us, so many things we can share? Where are we going to find that again, Annie?"

Hopelessly, it seemed, she glanced at me, before answering, "But how much are we going to share three thousand miles apart? We can't fly every weekend; it's too much."

"So move out with me. Wayne Gretsky made the move; it can't be all bad."

A little smile, at least, appeared, giving me hope, until I realized that she had taken it solely as a joke, whereas I had been more than half-serious.

"Timing is against us, Mac. I know it's a cliché, but in this case it's true. If we were ten years older, or even five, and we knew what we were doing, we might see everything differently."

"So let's look ahead, realizing that."

"But my soul rebels. It's not ready. It wants and needs to experience things . . . The only way I can explain it is that I've had it too good, too insulated, so far. You know? I feel like I've lived in a convent, sun-shiny and protected . . . I'm sorry, but I can't get around that; I just can't put it aside."

"But does that prohibit us from staying together?"

"We will be split, geographically. And we have only so much time and so much energy."

"And you don't feel it's worth it?"

". . . I wouldn't put it like that, Mac." I saw the struggle move over her face, and then I saw her face harden with decision. "Let me say that I know there's a part of me that wants to go wherever things take me. You've already had that, through your acting and plays, each one a new world, a new persona. I haven't."

"I'll stay . . . and you can explore, and try that new job."

"Mac, staying wouldn't be good for you. It wouldn't work. You'd be kicking yourself."

Alas, it was partially true, although voices in me didn't think it should be. Is not much of this career-climbing simply vanity? And yet I doubted I could convince her of this—and was not really certain I could convince myself.

Her following silence felt like a mercy killing. I knew that her perspective on all of this must be growing clearer. I reached for arguments, answers, but sensed it was all slipping away. Maybe I was tired, maybe it was the wine, or maybe it was a moment of hopelessness, or reality, but at some point I asked, "So . . . well . . . what would that mean? . . . Just split? Allow our careers to decide for us? Is that what you want?"

Again I could see the turmoil working beneath her skin. "Maybe, Mac . . . Maybe we should try a separation, a trial one, before you leave? See how we handle it? See if it feels right, or wrong? See if all the strain of holding together seems better?"

"I don't need a trial, Annie. I know what I want."

"Well then . . . maybe I'm less clear about what I do." And she sent me a chilling look I'll never forget: as dark and determined as I'd ever seen. She'd made her decision, right there, resolutely, if sadly. And now she watched and waited, feeling perhaps she'd chosen her way and said her piece.

After that, time seemed to hurl through the night. I kept my eyes to the floor as everything swirled above me.

Eventually she said she ought to go home. My heart had slowed, but with careful, deep breaths, I managed, step by step, to slide forward, straighten, and rise, as I saw her moving toward the door. Somehow I got over there and out, and we walked together, yet apart, over to her place, at which point all grew dark. I don't remember saying goodnight; I don't remember walking back alone. I only remember pushing under the covers, hiding my eyes, burying away. Unable to sleep, I remember trying to say lines, consider roles, take my mind away. I know I told myself that if an acting career required this, mine would be short. As Maggie said, Who needs it? I didn't sleep that night or the next. Her face hung above me, over the bed, as it still does; and if the building had caught fire, I wouldn't have moved; if MGM canceled the picture, I wouldn't have cared—their loss; not mine. I'd already lost all I could.

Thinking back over this, I find it more painful now, for then I was in a kind of shock. Still, I've wondered why I didn't press Anne for all I was worth. Get down on my knees, show her the depth of my feeling . . . But just as that question lingers, so does its answer. I knew she knew her own mind . . . And yet who's to say she might not have been moved by an ardent heart-pouring such as she'd never heard before?

Read a little history once, back in the indeterminate past. Yes, some little tidbit that slips out from the vault, the story of Montezuma and an Aztec myth, a myth which predicted that gods, or powerful beings, from the east would someday come to vanquish and subjugate the Aztecs. And thus when Cortez and his handful of conquistadors appeared, driving toward the capital, Montezuma was torn between opposing them and bowing to the inevitable. Uncertain, he wavered, fatally, and his empire fell.

And you, Macbeth? Oppose what you'd long foreseen? That we would not last; that it was from the beginning too good to be true; that life is not like that . . . Why waste effort fighting the inevitable, straining after the unattainable? . . . Now however I see it would have been better to have done all I could, come what may. (Easy to say, Mon. So difficult to do.)

At some point, the following morning, I realized that I would have to rouse myself from the stupor in which I had lain for hours. But then what? (Out d' window, mon? A graceful swan?) Unable to laugh, my choice was to leap. Subway it up to Broadway, climb the Panasonic sign, dive down onto the concrete. I imagined people gathering round the down-faced corpse, murmuring: Who's that? Some actor, some jilted lover. Don't nobody turn him over . . . . Oou . . . Oh dear . . . Actors, dey say, is high-strung, go off at any little thing . . . . Alas, poor Yorick. Who indeed knew him well?

At the theatre, I decided not to say a word, but Maggie noticed something.

"Ptomaine for lunch, Mac? You look sick. Your cheeks've become jowls; you've got wattles, old man."

When I didn't smile, or do much of anything, she suspected it was something serious. "Aw-oh. What now? Film canceled? . . . Can't be girl-trouble, can it? . . . Not you two?"

Although I said nothing, my eyes gave it away.

"Oh, McKim . . . you two? . . . You who are examples to us all? You guys have a fight?"

"No."

"Worse?" . . . . She saw it was so. "Oh dear . . . No wonder you don't look good. You want to take the night off? We've got whatshisname."

I didn't. Worse to be home alone.

She put a hand on my shoulder. "Hey, you need a shoulder, McKim? You're looking tragic."

I guess I smiled a bit and put my arms around her. Nice to have a second pair of arms, a second heart.

"How bad is it, Mac?" she asked as we stood together.

"Don't know, Mags."

"Have to do with California?"

". . . In part."

"It's not definitely kaput?"

"Don't know . . . Not good . . . She wants time to think, some time apart." ·

"Anne? I'm surprised. It's not like her. But hey, who knows these days? . . . Don't count her out; maybe she really does need time, time at a crossroads, you know? . . . Check with me before you throw in the towel, okay?"

I kissed her forehead. "You're a sweetheart."

"Hey, don't get me excited . . . You know, damn it, I'm always '*a* sweetheart;' never '*the* sweetheart.'"

"Soon. It'll happen soon. I'm betting the farm."

"Which farm is that, Mac? Save your money. Buy her flowers. Blood roses."

The image stayed in my mind. After the show, I was reluctant to join Mags and the others. Wouldn't be good company, for one thing. Also was not sure I could take their, or anybody's, sympathy. Didn't mind it from Mags and John, but the others? Too intimate for their scrutiny, or lack of it. And I hoped Peter wouldn't show up, to see Anne. He didn't, but I ended up going with them, anyway. Force of habit, I guess. Or abject loneliness.

Inevitably, it was mentioned. Karl appeared stunned, saying that we seemed so close, so right, such a solid couple . . . Yeah, Karl, I thought so too, and Jillie, our tech director urged, "Courage, Mac. She'll come around. Who could throw away our leading man? He of the silver tongue, and heart of gold." There was a little ambiguity there, but that's okay. I knew none of them had an inkling of the real story. It was elusive enough for me.

"It's the times," exclaimed Mags.

Maybe, but what does that mean? That no one's responsible?

Karl called, "You should've married her."

My heart missed a beat. "Thanks, Karl."

Maggie alone saw the pain. "Enough, guys. *Que sera sera.* Cool it. Let's move on."

I was thinking I should've taken Anne to a taxidermist and had her done. And looking over at the oblivious Karl, I told him silently, hold onto yours—you never know. And, as if he'd somehow heard, Karl glanced at

Soukie, his longtime girl, sitting by his shoulder talking with Mags, then draped an arm around her.

Later, Mags gave me a squeeze and said, "Ya know, Mac, some people just don't know how good they have it." She said it loud enough for John to hear, which he did, but took pains not to acknowledge. And so she turned back to me and said earnestly, "You know, there is something about her . . . something determined, steel-like, that won't be denied. I've seen it . . . It's great for her career, but for love, Mac? I'm not so sure."

"Sure, kid," I replied in my best Bogart voice, "I know. Just as I know that everything we do in this mixed-up, crazy world don't amount to a hill of beans."

"I'm serious, Humphrey."

So am I.

"McKim, you said it's a trial separation, right?"

"Yeah . . . but I suspect that was to let me down easy."

"Mm, could be. I know that once she's set, she's set."

Although I attempted to draw in some oxygen, I couldn't quite get enough. As I tried again, hoping to avoid attention, Maggie watched frowning, then swung her gaze to John. "You too, Falstaff. She's a loss for us all. Maybe we should have a moment of silence, a prayer, that our lost friend be returned to us, that she be forgiven, as we women eternally forgive our male members, if you will, folks."

Quips and smirks circled among them before they fell silent, sending fleeting assessments my way. I was embarrassed. Was it growing mawkish? And yet who has not gone through some variation of this? And in some of their faces, I did detect hints of loss or sadness. She was a brightness gone from our group. She had often lifted the level of conversation, lifted us out of ourselves, and now, without her, we appeared susceptible to preoccupation and gloom.

Maggie again tried to shake us, "Hey guys, wake up," as she shouldered into me. "Hey, we're all still here, still alive; life goes on . . . We'll all find love—and probably treat it as badly again. But you especially, Schurtz, will find other women, particularly out there in Lalaland . . . I can't vouch they'll be like your Princess SummerFall WinterSpring, but hang in there and keep your head up; you've got work to do."

To which John added, "Yeah, Mac, hold on. Give her time. A little pain, a wounded heart, will do you good. Wear them well, and they'll become you, adding the heft and depth an ambitious actor needs—all at the relatively cheap price of a little damage to the resilient, indeed irrepressible, ego. And

McKim, look at it this way: you'll always remember her in the flowering of her womanhood. No slow, sad falling off, weakening into apathy, where you take each other for granite—sic—Instead, immortal images for the ages."

I think we all stared at him. I was going to sling something back, but held it in. And John, perhaps feeling a little uneasy under the array of strange looks, decided evidently, that the only graceful exit was to press on. "Seriously, Schurtz, seize the opportunity to enrich your emotional reservoir, you dog. Take it where it will go. Fight for the glory that life offers, fight for it on the beaches, in the fields, in the cities and the mountains. Glory in the blood, sweat, and tears, and never *ever* give up until victory is yours!" He had thrust out his Churchillian jaw, and when our eyes met, we stretched across the table to slap high-fives. But I didn't tell him I'd already professed my undying love to her, and what had it brought me but unbearable loss.

Now I noticed Maggie's eyes flashing at John, apparently unhappy with his not-dispassionate advice. Round and round it goes. Makes you wonder if evolution got it wrong. Shouldn't have placed self-consciousness so solidly in the genes. (What do it do for ya, Mon, besides twist ya up? Heap bad medicine, oh father in the sky.)

XV.

All that was not so long ago, and the pain has hardly diminished, despite the jumble of memories and feelings. I suppose I've spent too much time lying here on my bed staring at the ceiling and into the heavy shadows. But what else? My attention finds nothing of interest. My energy has emigrated.

Of course I tried to call her after a while, but got only her machine or secretary, neither of which sounded friendly. And she didn't return my calls.

On the other hand, although I was not aware of it, my performances at the end of our run with *Half Moon* improved. Or so Derek announced one evening after having been away. He stuck his head into our dressing room one night as John and I were wiping off our makeup.

"Hey McKim! . . . That was marvelous! A revelation!" So quickly did he sweep toward me that I leaned away to avoid his embrace, but he stopped, thrust out a hand and firmly shook my hesitant one. "Amazed, Schurtz! Simply amazed with what you've done! Am I not right, John?" John may have agreed, or may never have heard—though neither Derek nor I checked in the split second Derek paused before rushing onward.

"D' you see the audience, Mac? Spellbound. You've filled out every inch of Jacob's skin. Watching, I felt that he saw now everything that was going on, and that his inability to react was clearly from some early wound that refused to heal, that wanted compensation. His, and your own, internal tension welled up, spread out, over the audience so that not one of them moved, or even coughed. It was astonishing, and thrilling!"

Wincing, and not a little dubious, I was also cautiously pleased. Some directors work by cheerleading and Derek is one. Still, it was nice to hear something positive, even if substantial discounting was required.

When Derek exited, I found John smiling in a sardonic way. "What'd I tell you, Schurtz? Gotta bleed a little first, in this business."

"You bleed, John. I don't want it that much."

"Right. That's why you're leavin' your queen for California."

"Got it flipped, John, backward. Guess you didn't attend to the gossip too closely." Consumed by himself, more than most of us, he could be a pain.

"Whatever," he conceded dismissively. "It's probably the right thing for you to do, however, for as great as she may be, there must be, will be, others."

Really? I very much doubted that, too. And then recognized another reason I was annoyed with his careless misinterpretations and behavior. "Is that why, John, you keep Miss Maggie on a string?"

He turned away to resume checking his face in the mirror. I saw, however, that this had reached him, nettled him. But after a moment or so he recovered. "Good point. She's a charm, all right . . . for the right guy. Guess I should make that clear . . . As for me, I'm waiting for one like Anne, at least something close. The type that would send you walking off a roof, a heart-wrencher, a home run . . . a knock-out. You know what I mean; I'm sure you'd do it all over again. And who knows? Maybe she'll give you the chance. Though old man Peck warns us, doesn't he, not to wait for those all-consuming illusions."

Yes, Peck warns us that the excessive value too many of us put on beauty is a yearning for the magnificence prior generations found in God. But coming from John, this seemed to me just so much noise, so much rant, reflecting his conflicted self-loathing. But then, who doesn't own a share? Maybe what I had briefly gained from her was a boost to the ego, some uplift . . . proximity to the exalted . . . I don't know . . . At that moment I had no real interest in reasoning it through. I also felt detached from the person up on the stage that Derek was praising. Just another actor fixed in the spotlight—burned, for a time.

Of course eventually she did call, naturally when I was least expecting it. Was in the bathroom, about to brush my teeth, when I set out after a great water bug that had scrambled out of the tub and across the floor, and so let the phone ring until I got the bastard with my shoe, banging everything in sight. By the time I answered it, I suspected it might be her. Who else would call that late?

To my hello came a distant but heart-stopping, "Mac?"

". . . Anne?"

". . . Hi. How are you?"

The truth or something sanitized? "Okay." My heart was making it hard to hear.

"Sorry I've been slow getting back to you," she said.

I wanted to snap off something wounding and bitter, but nothing came, and I swallowed the urge.

"It's not too late, is it?"

"For what?"

"Were you turning in?"

"Into what? . . . a roach?" . . . . But I relented, "No, I just whacked a huge water bug, the size of my big toe. It's prime hunting time for all of us alpha-males over here. What's up?"

"How's the play going?"

"Fine. Better, they tell me.

"Good."

"Any new thoughts about us, Annie?"

". . . No . . . Sorry, I need more time."

". . . More?"

". . . I know, Mac. I know it's . . ."

"It's goddamned difficult . . ."

". . . For us both . . . Mac, if you have a moment, could I ask you about something?"

"A moment? I have the next sixty years, Annie."

". . . I'm sorry, Mac. Really I am. It's not easy."

"Okay, what?"

"Mac, have you seen Rachel lately?"

"Only briefly at the theatre, when she's picked up Rebec."

"Well you know I've talked with her about work and about getting free from Tyrone, possibly by finding him a job."

"Mm, yes . . ." (Not the subject I'd have chosen tonight.)

"Well, I've become a little doubtful about how serious he is, and I wanted to speak with her, but I haven't been able to reach her."

"You tried her at home?"

"Yes, and I've left messages at work, but she hasn't called back."

Deciding not to note the irony, I told her, "Annie, she asked me to warn you to be careful with him."

"Yes . . . well, I will be . . . but I suspect she should be, too . . . and I hate to see Becky exposed to that."

"To what?"

"I don't know, it seems he's involved in drugs."

"Wonderful." Not exactly a surprise, as my mind turned back to several instances when Rachel hinted at this, or might have been high herself.

". . . There's something else, Mac . . . Tyrone thinks you have a thing for her."

"Great . . . I hope you straightened him out."

"Of course, but he thinks I'm naive, or am protecting you, or myself."

"So Rachel hasn't told him about her Macy's fellow?"

"Apparently not."

"Terrific." Although I could understand why not.

"If you see her, would you ask her to call me?"

"I will."

"Oh, and one more thing . . . she wouldn't have told him where I live, would she?"

"Wouldn't think so. Why?"

"Someone, a man, sounding like him, came to my door while I was out, rang the bell and waited for a while—a neighbor told me."

I felt annoyed. My concern hit the wall. "You know Annie, I would cut out the social worker bit, if I were you." There was no way she could miss my peevishness, but she didn't respond to it. And so I asked, "Can we set a time to talk about us?"

". . . Mac, I'm not trying to be difficult, but I've barely had any time for myself."

"Time is what vanishes, they say. Or is that love?"

". . . Another few days, Mac, at least . . . I'm sorry, I'm exhausted . . ."

What could I say? She sounded sincere.

"Please try to understand, McKim."

"Okay . . . actors are supposed to excel at that. Hope you get some rest."

"And you too."

"Rest? Oh no, I'm on patrol, hunting the invaders in the night, anything that slithers or crawls. If I don't, there goes the neighborhood."

"Good night."

"Dream a little dream . . . for me."

Churned up when I got off the phone, didn't watch where I was going, and stepped on the goddamned oozing water bug carcass with my bare foot. Really pissed me off. Then scalded myself stepping into the shower to wash it off. Somebody trying to tell me something? . . . Call Rachel? You call Rachel. She's right there at Macy's!

Yet I did try her there the next day, but she wasn't at her desk. No one's ever at their desk; their desk is where they ain't. Left a message. Think she got my machine once . . . but I certainly wasn't staying home alone, if I could help it. Next time she tried was that evening . . .

XVI.

Done! Out! Have flushed the bulk of it . . . Undoubtedly I'm forgetting stuff. There is at least one other incident I'll get to next. But the overriding, essential reality for me is that Anne and I are abruptly . . . nothing, not a pair, not close, not really even speaking, now that she's in California. Shows you the chasm . . . No other way to describe it.

She didn't tell me she was going to San Francisco. Guess it was sudden. I didn't learn until after the murder, when she called from out there, after her office informed her.

I think of the hours I sat by the phone that day and fateful night, on the verge of calling her, and that next day she wasn't even there. Maybe that sums it up.

As for Rachel, I hadn't seen her much either, after Anne and I separated. Guess she was following her heart too—Robert. Where the hell is he? Why doesn't he check on Rebec?—The fact is, though, after her last visit to my place—seeking voice teachers, followed by our brief embrace—something had changed between us. We couldn't quite relax with each other, couldn't look comfortably into each other's eyes . . . Part of it may've come as a result of my separation from Anne—that relationship having stood as a clear barrier between Rachel and me . . . I don't know. Part of it may have been her own, or my own, turmoil. You sense things, but how often do you really know? . . . On the phone the last time, Rachel's voice seemed more like it had—warm, sensitive . . . and yet there was something she wanted . . . and held back.

And then afterward, there was an incident at the courthouse, when I was asked by Gertler to come down a second time, for possible consultation during a pre-trial conference with the judge and Bettors. Gertler told me it looked like Bettors would probably accept a plea, something in the neighborhood of twenty-five years, with parole after ten to fifteen. I remember wondering how one even begins to weigh a life . . . thought the sentence seemed a little light.

Anyway, I was making my way through the halls there, feeling uneasy to begin with, when I sensed something rushing toward me. I sort of bent away, trying to see, just as a figure lunged at me. I threw up my arms and fell back a step as Tyrone's leering face arced past mine. His handcuffs slashed at and dug into my forearms, despite efforts by two deputies to hold him back. His sweating face hissed at me, "Yeah, baby, you'd better be afraid. 'Cause I'm gonna get you, gonna get you good. It's you I shoulda done, anyway."

I stood frozen against the marble wall. And, as they tried to pull him away, as other guards ran up, his leer snapped into a vengeful grin, hissing, "But your friend, she was lookin' for it; she wanted it, baby. You ask her about it. She was go-od. She was aching for her Tyrone. You ask her, boy. She liked it! . . ."

Finally they managed to pull him back and began to drag him off, but straining around, he called back, "But you, baby, you're dead! Dead, you hear!"

It was grotesque. I remember the cold of the marble coming through my shirt; my hands sweating, heart and head thumping . . . What did he mean? . . . Just taunting me, trying to rile me? . . . Didn't even want to think about it . . . No way! Wouldn't give him the satisfaction.

Suddenly another face floated before me, as I leaned back trying to regain my breath . . . Bettors, curious, yet placid. "You okay, Mr. Schurtz?" he asked, his expression, behind his glasses, showing first concern, then perplexity and pity.

I remember he looked other-worldly, like a choir boy . . . but all together it was too disorienting. The images Tyrone had implanted tried to worm their way back in . . . those and visions of Rachel's last moments. I couldn't speak. Wanted to ask Bettors why he hadn't told his client about the other guy, Robert, but instead could only nod, yes, okay.

For an eternity, it seemed, he studied me, his large eyes moving over my face, so that soon I began to wish he would go. And ultimately, with a brief parting smile, he did, leaving me alone with the heaving, leering image of Tyrone's face, and his deed.

I tried to push both from my mind, heave them from me, before I could straighten up and move unsteadily to the door. But even outside, I had to pause against one of the great granite pillars.

Never did meet with Gertler, or the judge. Assume the plea was accepted. Since then, I have doggedly avoided these latest memories, which summon a twisted feeling . . . nauseating and perverse . . . I know I must marshal all my will . . . Can't let him get to me, get the better of me.

It was the evening after the murder that Anne called, from out there, sounding devastated . . . We spoke of little else . . . Didn't understand— neither of us. She kept implying that she was guilty . . . I tried to correct her, that I was. But she didn't hear, it seemed, even when I cried out . . .

The only thing that lifted us past this was our concern for Becky, the scarred survivor, who must somehow pick herself up and go on. We couldn't help remarking that if she were white and middle class, she could look forward to years of therapy. But as it was, we hoped that she'd be able to forget, move on somehow, and that her cousins would help her find her way back to life . . .

XVII.

Better today. Have gotten out of the apartment, and to this restaurant at least, where I feel as near to peace as I've been for a while . . . Have always liked this place, with its sky-lit airiness and space between tables . . . Am also picturing Maggie's shining face, soon to appear. We'll have a meal together, console each other, maybe share the evening. Who knows? . . . Can feel my body sagging, as its skeleton of woes dissolves . . . Hard to believe it's all happened this way. Think I got everything out, and yet now, still, I don't quite trust myself; events ever run one step ahead of me . . . Had so much, and just let it slip and slide away.

Ah! Here she comes! . . . But with Peter . . . Well well . . . They're almost the same height. Never noticed. "Miss Maggie!"

"McKim!"

As I push myself up, feeling unexpectedly heavy, her sweet, scrubbed face glides toward me, and we embrace. Could hang here all night. "Easy, old man," I hear her warble somewhere below her soft bird's-nest hair, reminding me to remember Peter.

"Pierre." And we shake hands, before all sink into chairs around the small table.

Leaning back, studying me, Maggie narrows her eyes. "Mac? You look like you've aged ten years. Haven't you been sleeping?"

Uncertainly I seek Peter's less scrutinizing face, and find it watching hers, while below, their hands grope for and hold each other's.

"And not shaving either? This for the movie, or are you really feeling down and out?"

Turning to her and encountering her shining, sky-blue eyes, I feel my burden lighten. "I'm okay, now. It's good to see you two, looking so . . . like two flower children. When did this start?"

Shyly Peter smiles and looks down, while Miss Maggie defiantly flings out her reply, "And why not, McKim? We're tired of others having all the fun."

"And all the problems," adds Peter with a shudder, before he flushes, fearing I suspect, that he may have insulted both of us. But me? I'm beyond offense, am happy for the empathy, if that's what it was. "Courage, you two!" And I hoist my beer in salute. "To you both! May you love wisely and long."

"Good God, McKim!" she exclaims. "Don't drop that on us. That's one of *your* hang-ups! And may I have a sip of that?"

I slide her my beer, and she takes a long swallow, wipes her lips, and exhales, "I'll have one of those! Waiter!" Her hand shoots up, and a waiter appears to take their orders, as I study her closely, looking for her secret. But as I watch her, I see her expression grow sober, and Peter's too. His small gray eyes dart from Maggie to me before he speaks.

"This may not be the best time to bring it up, but then, as you're leaving soon . . . Mags and I were thinking *we* ought to do something for Becky as well."

"Yes, Schurtz, that was good of you to go up and see her, and set up that college account. Good going, old man."

"It was Peter's idea," I mumble, pretty sure I don't want to get into this.

"In addition to all of us contributing," Peter begins carefully, "we thought we should invite her down to the studio."

"And take her back to Circle to see Karl and the crew; show her we're all, or mostly, still here," adds Maggie. "The poor girl's world was yanked out from under her; she really only had her mom, right? So far as we know. Was there anyone else close, McKim?"

Emptily I shake my head, indicating that I don't know. Uncomfortably my mind is snaking back to that unfortunate meeting in the Bronx, in which I performed so abysmally. "Not that I think it's a bad idea, but what exactly do you feel a trip down here would do for her?"

"We're not starting from scratch, Mac," she replies, "we're friends, she and I, anyway, and we can show her that not everything disappears, that some things are solid, that there is some continuity, and caring, in this city."

I nod as I reflect upon this. "Sounds good, but . . ."

"It's a start," she cries softly.

My eyes fall to the table. "Well . . . you'll certainly do better than I did."

"Oh give us a break. Haven't you had enough self-flagellation, Mac? Besides, you brought her to us! You weren't required to do anything before, but you chose to help her with her school work. Pierre, tell him he's being a boob."

Peter waits until my eyes reluctantly find his before he does. Yet as I look away, I'm sure Peter understands my problem. But what Peter cannot know is how haunting it is, replaying, as it does, my family betrayals—all of us recoiling, retreating from each other. Somewhere long ago, I had promised myself the one thing I would never do is betray . . .

"Mac, stop," I hear Peter urging, "stop your silent breast-beating . . . What could you have done? At best, you could have put it off . . . As for Becky, you've done a lot more than most people would."

I look into their concerned faces, but they do not convince me. Indeed I decide that I must tell them. "There's something else. It may have been me who incited Tyrone . . ."

"Mac?" comes Maggie's familiar incredulity, "Come on, I can't believe you're still saying that, still heaping all that on yourself! It's delusions of grandeur, old man . . . More likely, Rachel finally told Tyrone to take a hike. And they were on coke, right? So who knows how their minds were working. But two things you can bet on: he needed her money, and his touchy male ego wasn't going to take rejection—No way, man."

"So why did he go to all the trouble of luring Anne in?" I ask. "Apparently going to her apartment?"

Their faces, I watch, go round with revelation. "You're kidding," expels a startled Mags. Confirming with my dead-serious stare, I ask, "Why would he do that, if not to get at me?"

They glance at each other.

"I knew," Peter mumbles, "Anne was trying to help him."

"All bullshit, apparently, on his part. All manipulation," I conclude for him.

Maggie shakes her head. "She kept mentioning him. I couldn't understand it—why she spent any time at all with that creep."

"Probably for Rachel," I explain. "Trying to help wean him away from her."

With evident skepticism, Maggie reflects on this, "Do you think she was that naïve, that she believed she could change someone like Tyrone? . . . Maybe she was interested in him for a story?"

I'm a little surprised at her hard attitude. "Mags, the fact is we didn't know what was going on with him, how things were affecting him . . . and we were aware of no reason for Anne not to try . . . before Rachel's warning."

She frowns at me. "Come on, McKim, a little white girl is going to reverse the damage of a lifetime with a chat or two? What's that?"

I glance at Peter who appears to be caught between these views and plainly puzzled. As for me, it summons once more the leering face at the courthouse.

"The question is, Mac, why you?" Maggie resumes. "Why was he angry at you?"

This brings the blood back, burning my brow, so that I must force myself to meet her gaze. "He knew that Rachel and I, and Becky, were friends, liked each other." (But hey Mon, was there not a little something more?)

"Maggie," rescues Peter, "I wouldn't be surprised if Tyrone was jealous of what we were all doing for Becky. It was certainly more than he was doing."

She gives him a disappointed look, mingled with irritation. "Well, there's no way we can *know* what was going on in his head, but I'd still bet we're giving him way too much credit. He's only a guy, after all, and apparently not one of the good guys."

Peter and I glance at each other with surprise and veiled amusement, not sure in which camp she's placed *us*, but when I look back at Mags, it's me she's studying. "I'll say this, McKim, even at the theatre, there were whispers about the way Rachel looked at you."

"Oh come on, Mags."

Maggie tilts her head and shrugs, as if to say, ignore it if you want, it happened nonetheless. "If people thought they saw something there, who knows what Tyrone imagined. Maybe Rachel taunted him? Or spoke warmly of you?"

And Peter notes, "Obviously Becky liked you. Maybe that pissed him off?"

"So he strangled Rachel?"

"No . . . but something set him after Anne."

I look away uncomfortably, and yes, guiltily, remembering Rachel looking into my eyes, as I was into hers . . . But that needn't be sexual, right? I mean it can just be fellow feeling, right? . . . I find and study my two friends. Their expressions convey the sad futility in trying to understand it all.

At some point Peter asks when Anne will return from California. I tell them it's supposed to be tomorrow, and I see their hope that she will shed some light on part of this. The waiter arrives with their drinks, and they begin preoccupied sipping.

Tired of all this, I try to redirect my thoughts . . . but find them slipping back. Can't seem to let it go . . . Maybe don't want to.

Peter, sensing something of this, concludes we'll probably never know what set it all in motion. "I felt bad at the funeral, as an outsider, watching awkwardly and not saying what I would have liked to."

Our minds wander in and out of all this, as we attend to our drinks, but then I hear Miss Mags cutting through, "Listen, McKim, don't waste you're time on the futile, not to say fatal. Anne is where you should put your energy, even though it may be a little late."

I indicate I've heard, then feel myself wanly smile, thinking I've lived with my family wounds so long—the feeling and the burden—that maybe I need the periodic infusion of pain or angst just to feel whole. But when I emerge from this latest vipers' nest, I find that my two friends have begun to peruse the menu, amid their own murmured conversation. Together they seem almost angelic . . . diminutive, diaphanous, good. And so it should be. And why should they dwell on my problems, when it is I alone who knows their intricacies, and it is I alone who could have acted, and still can? Following their lead, I stare dully at the menu. But what appetite do I have? Yet somewhere I know I will need energy to confront Anne when she returns. So I sit staring at the dinner items, listening to silverware clinking against plates, chairs scraping and creaking, footsteps and music, and above it all, the voices and conversations—sounds of city life through the centuries.

When I look over once more, and find them leaning close, talking together, I can only contrast how I sit hunched, oversized, rough-hewn, and rotten . . . while other citizens sitting or striding around us, drift or sweep, half-seeing into the future.

Thus has it been; so shall it be. But I fear for the delicacy of my two friends, fear that accident or darkness will overwhelm them, fear that they, and many like them, will not be able to withstand the horrors stalking at the edges . . . and that it may be only a matter of time.

XVIII.

The day has come, and the hour too. Busied myself packing and have gotten through most of the day, somehow, after speaking to her on the phone. And she? Cordial, business-like, friendly enough, despite people nearby in her office. Yet revealed nothing. No hints. Decided to meet at the White Horse, neutral ground, but then she called back to ask if we could do it at her place.

Now it's time to go. Judgement Day. What does it mean that she's switched our meeting to her place? Private pain? Turn in circles by my door, wondering, fearing, imagining where it will go.

Outside, I lock both locks. Have, at times, just walked away forgetting. Luckily no one discovered and stepped in. But now I hear footsteps approaching behind. Head jerks around. Only David, climbing homeward. "Evening, Mac. Thought you'd gone."

"This weekend."

"Then it's still on?"

"Well yes." Was he hoping it wasn't?

"Hey, I landed a commercial next week."

"Good, David. Who's the sponsor?"

"Some bank, wooing senior citizens. Would you believe? Me, their long-time adversary . . . Well, at least it pays. Have to accept the necessities at my age; screw the principle, gain some principal—the devil's compact . . . Always costs. Yet I hope it plays, could use the residuals, you know? . . . You okay? You look a little drawn."

"Just tired."

"What are you doing with your apartment?"

"Subletting it to someone at Circle."

"So you'll be back?"

"Hope so."

". . . I spoke to the super across the street. Said they're going to rent Rachel's apartment again, but he suspects it'll have to be to someone from outside the neighborhood, so many here have heard about the murder . . . I'd consider it; it's even a bit cheaper than mine, but I don't know . . . not much light."

Feeling anxious, impatient, chest tightening, I interject, "David, I'm sorry, I've gotta run."

"Yes, okay. Good luck. Drop me a postcard, if you think of it."

"Sure, I will . . . Fact is I'm going to see Anne."

"Oh? Well, why didn't you say so? I thought you two were incommunicado. But good luck; lay it on the line with her, Mac. Show her what you feel. You'll regret it if you don't. Take it from me . . . See you." And with a wave and a flash of ancient regret, he turns away quickly. To appear no less busy than me?

I bemoan my impatience and distraction, but perhaps he understands. In any case, I find that I'm trembling and that everything in me is leaning, straining, toward her. I push through twilight's slanted glow, as through a dream. Dark figures pass, but I cannot see their faces. It is unusually quiet, like memory, or premonition. I hurry over the pavement, south on Hudson, head down, feeling, I realize, cold.

"Schurtz! . . . Mac?"

Jeeze . . . someone else calling me? Not now, can't concentrate, even as I find myself turning, looking.

Derek hurries up. "Hi. Thought you'd gone."

What's this? Everyone has me gone. "Sunday."

"A real New Yorker—won't leave until he absolutely has to. How are you? You must be excited."

Thrusting my hands into pockets, I nod, glancing for escape routes.

"You're shivering," he notices.

Am I? So noticeably? Cast a glance down, while he waits and shifts, silently studying me, before remembering, "Hey, just met with a real dynamic group that's got a fine script and money. Can you believe?" He lifts the script he's carrying. "Reading it tonight, get back to them tomorrow, and we'll see. Otherwise it's *The Seagull*, over at the Cherry Lane."

"Not bad. I've always liked Eric, or is it Jonathan Livingston?"

He tries to hide his distaste, then rushes on, "Chekhov's always satisfying . . . Your friend Anne has a little of Nina in her. Not so young, of course, but . . . how is she, by the way? What's the story with you two?"

My eyes reach up for the land beyond the Moon, then fall back to him. "Funny, Derek, you should ask. I'm just going to see her."

"You're back together?"

Feel my face burn—sun flaring in polished bronze. "I'll find out."

"Oh . . . ? Well, good luck. But with you heading west, what will you do? That film, Mac, is the chance of a lifetime. I hope you give it all your energies, and think about what brought out your best in *Half Moon*. Which is not to dismiss your relationship with her. She's a remarkable lady." He shakes his head. "Hey, what's happened to poor Rebeccah? Do you know?"

"Thanks, Derek; you're hitting all the buttons."

"Sorry. Won't see you for a while."

I understand, but still . . . . "Becky's up in the Bronx, living with cousins."

Under his wrinkling brow, he reflects, then asks, "How's it going? At least she has that. Could be worse . . . It's a shame; she was just blossoming, gaining confidence around us . . . Horrible . . . something like that, out of the blue; two lives just . . . fsst! Makes you feel pretty vulnerable; could happen to anyone, anytime."

While I agree generally, I'm too keenly aware that it didn't happen just out of the blue and is more likely for some. "I should've seen it coming, Derek . . ."

"Think so? . . . But who knows what's going on between couples? . . . Did you know the guy?"

I look at him. Someone put him up to this? "They weren't really a couple; she was trying to get away. I saw him a few times. Anne was trying to help him find a job."

"Really? . . . That was generous. I guess she's lucky he didn't take out whatever it was on her."

I look down, feeling my body shudder, hearing something growl inside.

"Well, good luck with her, and the movie. Call if you need anything, even just to consult on your character. You have my number."

"Thanks, Derek. I'll probably take you up on that." Indeed, I see myself in panic crying out, back to distant New York. But then our eyes are casting a last look over the other, hands are shaking, waving, and we are backing away into the semi-darkness.

Still trembling, I strike off again, but feel no better as I reach her street, enter her gate, and cross the courtyard to her door, and knock too hard, slicing the fingers of my fist. A drop of black blood pushes out—the devil's flow. Lick it, take it back into myself. Awaken, McKim. Compose yourself, prepare, for this is your act of a lifetime, your most important interview. Snap to, old man. I wonder what her face will say. Glad to see you? Mac, I've made a mistake . . . Will she want an embrace, a kiss? . . . Nothing? . . . The door opens. Her silhouette hangs motionless just inside. "Mac . . . hello . . . Come in."

I do, stepping up and past her, and only inside do I turn to look. She is watching me. "Hello," she repeats. At once it seems terribly familiar and natural . . . and sad and distant. I feel I should embrace her, but something holds me back. She is trying to smile, putting on a friendly facsimile. Bittersweet.

"Hi, Anne . . ." For perhaps the only time I've witnessed, she doesn't quite know what to say, and as I wait, I notice that her hair is shorter—too short. But hush, Schurtz. And also for the first time, she wears no make-up. In fact her face appears slightly puffy, so that within her shapeless, beige dress, she looks spare, almost ascetic. "Did you take vows out there, Annie?"

"What? . . . I'm sorry, what?"

"Nothing . . . It's been . . . a bad time . . ." I say inadequately, as I try to hold back rising emotion.

"Yes . . ." She allows, then turns to close the door. "Can I offer you some wine or coffee or something, Mac?"

"Wine? . . . Wine not?" By all means, employ the truth serum—the enduring ritual.

She ponders for a moment, then glides away to her kitchen. Only when we are seated, wine in hand, at opposite ends of her couch, do we relax enough to begin to collect what we must say.

So here it is. Here *she* is, who was my love. Yes, I remember her well . . . Begin to feel smitten once more. It's hard to believe this moment has come, but movement, her hand bringing her glass to her lips, and her faint scent tell me it is so. I see her draw herself in, to speak. "Mac, the news about Rachel just devastated me." She looks away. "You, of course, were the only person I could really speak to about it, to any extent. It's been bottled up. I spoke to Peter, a little, and Maggie, but they weren't as involved as you and I."

I feel my eyes close. Things go dark for several moments, before I blurt, "No . . . but it was me she called that night . . . Do you remember? . . . Didn't I make that clear to you on the phone?" I feel myself shaking as I put down my wine, as her lips push out a little and her face falls into dismay. But then she attempts to re-gather her own sense of it all. "She did? . . . I guess I'd forgotten . . . That night?"

Surprised, reluctant, I confirm with a bitter frown. But then I realize I'm not entirely clear how I put it when she called from California . . . How is it, though, she'd forgotten entirely? Hadn't I clearly confessed?

Now looking more closely at me, she asks, "*Why* did she call?"

Still trembling, I search her eyes, vowing this time I need to make it very clear. "Anne, she said she needed to talk . . . wanted company, wanted support . . . Wanted me to come over, I think . . . But I didn't go."

She swallows carefully but remains silent as her eyes fall from mine. I see that she's grown noticeably more pale. It feels like an axe falling. Her bewilderment bows her head, her shoulders, and then mine too, pressing all down; both bodies curling inward, where I feel systems clot and curdle, so that I need to say something—explain, although I know there is no real explanation. Weakly I mumble, "I told you on the phone I was thinking of calling you that night, was wrestling with it, when she called. But I didn't want to talk to, much less see, anybody else."

Lines of remorse slowly work into her brow. She finds her glass and stares into it, as her eyes widen to absorb my confession.

"I don't say this to excuse myself. I should have gone; I might have saved her . . ."

Her features grow taut, then lined, until finally she shakes her head and murmurs, "God forgive me."

"You, Annie? It's me I'm talking about! I was the one who was there!"

She doesn't move—a bowed statue—until carefully, head rising, shoulders straightening, she looks at me, through me, for some moments. Then her eyes drop again, and she inhales. "There's something I have to tell you, Mac. Something else, that only you will understand . . . . Do you mind? May I?"

"About us?"

"Not directly."

I feel my hope tumble. What else? Though anxious, impatient, all I can do is wait silently, as with visible effort, she sends her thoughts back. "I'm afraid it concerns Tyrone."

"Tyrone? . . ."

"I'm afraid I *must* tell you . . . I've told no one else . . . no one . . . I hope you'll forgive me, Mac."

"Forgive *you*? That's my line. That's one reason why I came. To ask it of you."

Our eyes meet, but though she has heard, she is gripped by her own story.

"He had come, as you know, to my office to talk about jobs. Twice."

I indicate I remember.

She breathes. "When I mentioned the idea to Rachel, she was a little skeptical, but I'm afraid I was slow . . . naïve. I should have seen, guessed . . . But Mac, will you listen to this story, and then give me your honest-to-God reaction?"

As my mind skitters across possible scenarios, I'm aware of reasons why I might not, but I tell her, "Of course."

"You're the only one, McKim, I've told . . . besides the police . . . and the D.A."

As I wonder where it will lead, I'm also wishing I were the only one, period.

"Tyrone, I believe, had come by here before, as I think I mentioned. Anyway, this time, when someone knocked, I asked through the door who it was, and Tyrone announced that he needed to talk . . . about Rachel." She searches me for tell-tale tremors, as I do her, but our gazes hold steady.

"I really didn't want to. It was late; I had enough doubts about him, but then I thought I ought to hear what he had to say. It might help her. Possibly I could explain to him that she wanted, needed, to live a different life now."

"Did you know that they were married? Common-law, anyway."

Sadly, with heavy eyes, she looks at me. "Gertler told me, on the phone." Her head sinks slowly. "And there I was, thinking I knew enough to help."

I wipe my sweating hands on my trousers. She glances over at me disheartened, uncertain. ". . . Well, fool that I was, I opened the door . . . Fortunately, I didn't take the chain off; I don't know why . . . Maybe because I was in my robe and p.j.'s. I'd changed out of my work clothes, taken a shower, was going to eat and turn in." She shakes her head. "I asked him through the cracked door what he needed to tell me. He said he was upset about Rachel and wanted to ask me about her. But he claimed he felt awkward talking like this, outside, and would I let him in? . . . I felt so befuddled . . . I managed to tell him that I needed to rest—an important day lay ahead. He said it was early, and that he'd wait while I got dressed. I explained that I was heading to bed. He appeared annoyed, then leaned closer, nose in the opening, saying he was embarrassed to tell anyone, but he thought Rachel was two-timing him, and wondered if I knew anything.

"I didn't know what to say. I didn't want to mention Robert, if Rachel hadn't. He whispered he thought he knew who it was, and he mumbled a name."

Listening to Annie I feel my throat constricting. I try to swallow, but Annie is too deep in her story to notice.

"I couldn't hear him, Mac, and asked him again. He whispered something again, even lower . . . I brought my ear closer, then suddenly his hand pushed through the opening and grabbed my neck . . . I was . . . I tried to pull away, but couldn't. It was crushing me, my vocal cords, my breathing. He began shouldering against the door, trying to break the chain. I couldn't speak or cry out. I was afraid the chain would snap. I tried to use my arms and legs to pull away, but his grip was digging into my throat, and then somehow he got his other hand through and was pulling my robe, holding me there. I don't know; I felt faint; the pain was so sharp, beyond belief; I thought I might pass out—almost wished I would. He was crashing against the door and chain. I was sure it would break. I didn't know how long I could last . . . At some point I remembered, as he was jamming me up against the opening, that I often left a pen on the table by the door. Somehow I reached it and began jabbing his hands. I heard him grunt, swear; his second hand let go, but the other, around my neck tightened, gouging, feeling as if it would completely crush my neck. Things were growing dark . . . Then suddenly his hand was gone . . . . Released, I fell back onto the floor. I think I heard words outside. Evidently someone had come by. Eventually someone—I never saw who—called in through the partly open door to see if I was all right, but I couldn't speak. Maybe this person saw me on the floor. I don't know."

My own hand is crawling over my brow and eyes. I slide forward to the edge of the couch. "Annie . . . Anne . . . how horrible! . . . Are you all right?"

She opens her eyes and looks at me with a gaunt, haunted expression. "Now I am . . . but then, I just lay there . . . . After some time, I realized I was lucky to be . . . okay."

We look at each other. I want to offer something—to hold her—but I see that she isn't finished, now staring over at the floor where she had fallen. "For a long time, I couldn't move. I don't know how long. Eventually I saw a flashlight and heard other voices. A policeman called in, asking if anyone was home. I struggled up and over to the door. He asked me through the crack if something had happened. I said I could barely speak, had a throat cold—I was reluctant to mention Tyrone, until I spoke to Rachel first. The cop asked if I wanted to report anything, because they had received a call that someone had been trying to gain access to my house. I told him, as best I could, that I was all right. He asked if I'd seen anything or anyone, and again I said I hadn't—thinking that if Rachel wanted me to, I could call the cops back."

In silence, Anne and I sit there, going over this, replaying the horror. Time stutters and slows, until I hear Anne breathe, hear her voice creak, "A-alone, when the cop left . . . I began to feel sick . . . I staggered to the bath, just made it to the john, collapsing onto my knees . . . It felt as if my very insides were torn out . . .

"When it had passed, I was able to pull myself up again, and, as I stood swaying and trying to regain my breath, I saw myself in the mirror. I didn't recognize . . . me . . . My neck was raked and bruised, my chin sliced somehow, my face white . . . It all stung, hurt . . . I had come so close . . . to God-knows-what . . . It made me cry, Mac—this pathetic sight—I really cried . . . Had it really happened?

We look at each other through disbelief and pain.

"It's okay, Mac. I'm okay . . . Eventually I took a shower . . . for an hour it seemed . . . washing the cuts and bruises. I took several aspirin . . . I've never felt so sore or so alone . . . And then suddenly I remembered Rachel . . . and realized I should call and warn her, although I imagined she was probably with Robert. I tried, though I could barely put words together coherently. I got her machine and repeated and repeated: call me, call me . . . That was all I could manage."

Anne closes her eyes and rubs her brow, and for the first time, I notice bruises on her chin and neck. I slide over along the couch and touch her arm. She takes my hand in hers. "Really, I'm all right, Mac. Thanks . . . It's such a relief to tell someone; I've been dwelling on it, replaying it. I couldn't tell Dad, or my friend out there, or Peter or Maggie . . . not after what happened to Rachel . . . I minimized it to Gertler."

"God, Annie, I'm sorry . . . I can't believe that he would . . . the fiend!" Other figures and forms of fury rumble through my brain. Wish I had a gun.

"Thank you, McKim . . . Even though I was very sore and really couldn't speak for a while, for a matter of days, I knew that I had been lucky. Particularly in light of what followed."

I indicate that I understand. But her mind was moving on. "And so later that night, he went to her, and for some sad, sad reason she had never gotten, or listened to, my message." She glances with pain and fear at me. "I should have gone over there, and warned her . . . but I didn't know when, or if, she'd be back . . . At some point since, I realized that Becky must have been there, and I wondered if *she'd* heard my message . . . But I should have gone, and told her . . . or told the cops."

Hearing this unleashes an imagined fear: what if Tyrone had caught both women there? . . . What then? . . . But I can't allow myself to complete it. And instead return to my own role: that I had been right across the street, after the theatre, sitting by the phone. Once more I feel it all pressing down upon me, until I hear Anne continue, "But wait, McKim. You said she called you that evening . . . So she *was* there . . . at some point. She wouldn't have called from Robert's; she was there, just not answering . . . and was probably unable to understand my urgency . . ."

This falls on me like an avalanche, a suffocating, white weight. If I had gone to Rachel, she or I might have responded in some way to Anne's call and have been warned. We might have done something . . . God . . . I realize, too, that Anne is realizing this, and I cannot look at her. I cannot help imagining that while I was thinking of calling Anne, Rachel may have been in Tyrone's grip . . . I see it all, light and dark—a fury writhing before my eyes . . . But Anne, I hear, is moving on, back to other implications. "McKim, if I had returned your calls, it might have freed you to respond to her, and she to me . . . All of us might have understood what Tyrone was up to."

While I understand what she is inferring, I find that I cannot honestly connect these strands. "Anne, there is no way to be certain about that. What is certain is that, when Rachel called me, I could have gone; I should have gone; I was right there."

"McKim . . . later that evening, when I found I really couldn't speak, and wouldn't be able to go to work, and foresaw that I would have to retell this tale over and over in the coming week, and didn't want to, couldn't bear to . . . I booked a flight to San Francisco and in the morning took it and stayed with my father . . . but never told him, even after I learned . . . Said I had a throat infection . . . It was the next afternoon, out there, that I received the call, about Rachel, from the office . . . Fortunately, Dad was at work. When I heard, I sank into bed and stayed there for a day, then another." Anne looks at me, her features sagging, her eyes heavy, moist.

Her confession makes mine more urgent, to allay her self-blame. "Annie, I can understand how you feel, but I think you're being unduly hard on yourself, when in fact, you had been trying to help. I was the one who ignored her plea."

Her eyes find mine, seemingly unaffected by what I'd said. "At some point, Mac, it occurred to me that he might come after you . . . But when I called the next morning, before I left, and reached only your machine, I wanted to scream . . . but, at the same time, not wanting to bother, or further upset you, I decided not to leave a message . . ." Anne's eyes drop away from mine and grope along the floor and carpet, before they pause and slowly close. For some moments we are motionless, our minds re-weaving these strands. But then she looks up at me and stumbles ahead, "McKim, after the office called, sometime later in the afternoon—I guess it was night back here—a detective called to say they had caught Tyrone and to ask what I knew and whether I would be willing to make a statement. I said I would. And he asked about a suspected attack, or assault, on me, and I confirmed it, but explained that I had been saved by the door chain and by some neighbor. He asked if I would be willing to press charges, and I decided that after what he did to her, I would."

Though we gaze at one another, we do not speak, until her remorse wells up again. "I've agonized over my part in this, over not reaching her, booking the flight instead . . . Can you imagine? . . . I don't know how I'll live with it . . . All I can say, in my defense, is that realistically, I was in no shape to go over there, to her place—and yet I could have . . . But never did I imagine he would go that far. I guess I thought he needed her . . . but I should have warned the police, much as you say you should have . . . but there again . . . you see, Mac, I should have had a better sense of how he saw things and what he was trying to do. What he was saying didn't make much sense. And after the attack on me, I should have told the police . . . or done something."

We sit there mute, stunned. When that subsides a little, anger bulls in to take its place. I find my hands forming fists, however inadequate they might have been. And then I hear Annie reflecting, "I've been wondering just how far I would be prepared to go. Yes, call the police. But what else? . . . If I had a gun, say—though I'm strongly against them—but if somehow one came into my possession—I can't believe I'm saying this—but if it meant a life saved? . . . What then? . . . If faced with that, that choice? . . . Emotions unleash horrible reactions . . . And how often are guns taken away to be turned on the owner . . . To even contemplate all of this sends a powerful revulsion through me. How easily restraint vanishes . . . and yet, if it could have saved her? . . . There is no good answer . . . Maybe only the police . . . I don't know, Mac, I don't know . . . It's distressing—so internally tearing, to have these completely contradictory notions inside yourself."

I acknowledge with a helpless nodding . . . Yes, a gun . . . that saving tool and national epidemic . . . and yet I feel I need to tell her: "Probably, Annie, one notable difference between us is that I've lived with such conflicting notions for as long as I can remember, and I think I could have more easily accepted the ramifications, the consequences of a gun . . . even as I sidestepped the chance to act."

She studies me, perhaps trying to understand this, but as she does, she grows more calm, and her eyes clear. I, too, pull myself away a bit, away from the emotion of it. When she speaks, her voice is closer to the one I know. "Mac, it's so hard to believe this whole thing happened . . . that Rachel is no longer alive . . . It's beyond my understanding . . . that it was done, and how it was done . . . and I am ashamed . . ."

As she watches me, her eyes seem to be weighing the extent to which I've grasped her story. I try to show her that I have heard and appreciated it, just as I would like to ask her if she, in turn, has heard mine. But I don't. Probably it's unnecessary. And so, for some short time, we sit there, waiting for the rest to drain away. Or maybe hoping for some final insight which might explain it all. Or maybe we're beyond that now.

But then something in her eyes suggests that her thoughts have turned back to us. "Mac, I know that underneath all of this, our situation has gotten buried."

Buried? Images, sliding like grains down a sand dune, threaten to engulf my mind. The fate of all things. Abruptly I am in Montezuma's eyes, staring at the face of cold inevitability. There are many things that I could say to her, but I fear words cannot make the difference now . . . But then, what else is there? "Anne . . . we don't have to decide tonight . . . but I'm still hoping we can find some way of working it out."

Heavily, unhappily, she takes me in.

"Problem is," I add, "there's not much time. I leave on Sunday."

She absorbs this, looking back down at the floor. I see the corner of her mouth waver, begin to open, before slowly she shakes her head.

What does this mean? . . . I flee the possibilities. "Anne, do you agree, about the time?" And yet, I'm fearful of her answer, that her mind is made up. It is what I fear I read crawling over her face, as she continues to stare at the floor.

Impulsively I reach for her hand and hold it in mine. "We have too much, to just abandon, Annie . . . You're the person closest to me, in this crazy world . . . my mate, my anchor, my everything." But she, I see, is staring at my hands imprisoning hers. She tries to pull it from me, but I want some response first, and desperate to keep our connection, I hold it tight, even as she begins to tremble. I see her look up at me with unhappiness and apprehension. Then sharply, unexpectedly, she yanks her hand free and turns her head away. Her mottled face, I see, as I lean around her, is darkening. Overwhelming any appreciation of what she is feeling, though, is my own fear, my own wound widening—the mirror image of her deepening concern—and in my head I hear a rising plea, hear my voice echoing it: "Annie, don't let this drive us apart. What we have is unique, like nothing else . . . Don't take the easy road, the road that everybody takes, and just cast it off into the sea." But it is anger, now, I see furrowing her brow, and I see she wants to escape, and so, quite outside any rationality, I lean toward her, take hold of her arm and shoulder, and attempt to kiss her. And for a moment I feel her smooth, warm cheek as I slide toward her lips. But then I realize she is pushing and shoving my shoulder, and wrenching herself from me, and once free, she bursts upward, standing and twisting away, crying out, "Mac?! . . . Mac, how could you?! After all this? . . . How could you?" At first she doesn't look around, but when she does, I see that her face is gray with disbelief. She takes a few rapid steps away, and I—confused, lost—push up after her, merely to close the distance. But seeing this, she moves farther away, shouting, "Mac, I can't believe . . . Maybe you'd better go, Mac, right away! Do you hear me?! . . . Please go!"

I freeze. Incredulity, sliding into horror, locks me to the spot. What have I done?

"Mac, do you hear? This is not what I need! . . . I don't understand . . . after telling you my story, after everything that's happened . . . Do you even realize what you just did?!"

"But Annie, we haven't talked, about us. We need to resolve things, make a plan, ensure that we don't simply drift apart. We can't let this other tragedy . . . and mere distance cut us off from each other . . . We need each other, Annie!" I realize I'm saying this because I must, but also to avoid acknowledging her order to leave.

"McKim, I'm serious. I think you'd better go . . . right away! I want you out!"

"But Annie, you said that you realized these events have buried us, buried our discussion. And we can't just leave things at that. We need to talk . . . You *promised* to talk . . . I'm sorry that I . . ."

But she doesn't reply. Instead she is spinning around and running to the phone, where she snatches up the receiver as she looks back at me. "Mac . . . if you don't leave, I'm going to call the police!"

"I love you, Anne."

She begins dialing but then swipes at her phone book, sending it spinning across the floor, before she slams down the receiver. "McKim! . . . I can't believe you're pressing this, particularly tonight, after I thought I explained . . . And as for us, we *have* talked . . . It can't be the same; we can't go on as we were. In that sense, it's over; I've explained again and again, but you don't seem to get it. And now I've had it! Do you hear?! I want you out!"

Imagining leaving, tail between my legs, heart halved and left behind, I cannot. Would hate myself for the rest of my life. To never see her again? "No, can't, Annie. Go ahead and call the police. I don't care. I have nowhere else I want to go. I will stake my life on talking to you."

With this Annie lets loose a chilling, high-pitched scream, and wrenches herself around, her cry descending into a fierce growl, turning until once again she's facing the phone. She glowers at it for a moment, then grabs and jerks the entire thing up and heaves it generally in my direction, where it lands with a loud, ringing crash.

"Anne?"

But she, trembling, moves away a few more steps and does not look in my direction.

"Anne?" Still no response. "Annie . . ." She will not look. "Well . . . thank you for using AT&T." . . . (What else?) . . . Suspended between life and death, an actor without an audience, ineffective, impotent, I stand, legs shaking, brain empty, heart holed and pouring blood. Looking again, I see her facing partly away, arms crossed, staring at a wall. I ask myself how this happened, how it came to this? . . . I rub my eyes, then cover them, escaping into darkness. All around me a pounding increases, in my ears and brain and heart—so loud, so insistent, I fear all will burst. In my burrowing darkness, I hear her footsteps walk, then run swiftly across the floor and upstairs to her bedroom, where the door is slammed. But for a time, it is my throbbing, arhythmic body that worries me. Calm yourself, Schurtz . . . Could you walk home if you had to? . . . Not at the moment, could barely make a block . . . Then wait . . . Everything is aching. Signs of a system at risk.

But slowly my body regains its equilibrium; its functions resume their normal, unnoticed pace, so that I can begin to think . . . and understand her reaction . . . even as I hoped she'd understand mine . . . But leave or stay, now? Will she come down if I wait?

. . . Minutes drift away in the silence . . . Finally I decide I must do something. Call up the stairs to her, jump start the dialogue . . . but as I take a step, dizziness returns, and I must lean on the couch's arm, then sink and squat, waiting for the spell—panic, is it?—to pass . . . Eventually it does, and I rise and drag myself over to the stairs, where I lift a foot, but again my body resists, slowing, wobbling, telling me it's not up to the climb. I turn and lower myself onto the first step and hold my useless head.

Eventually, I hear her voice. "Mac?" I think it's in my mind, but it comes again, and with effort, I look up just enough to find her dark outline at the top of the stairs, head tilted down toward me. "Are you all right?" she asks.

I reach out to the banister to try to pull myself up, but realize I'm not ready, and so I crane my head back toward her in darkness. Am I? Everything seems labored, heavy.

"Mac? . . ."

Reflex prompts me to respond, "I'm okay . . . Sorry . . ."

I hear her breathe, hear the floor creak under her shifting feet. "Do you want me to call you a cab?"

My mind is crawling. "A cab? . . ." My neck is stiff; it hurts to hold up the heavy, useless orb. I test it, rotating one way, then the other. What's wrong? A flu come on? I hear her expel exasperation. Join the club.

"You should go home, if you can . . ." she repeats.

Yes, I think, I suppose I should. But . . . I feel strange. My heart feels sticky, despondent. I place a finger on my wrist to feel my pulse, but find no reassuring throb. Hmm, what does this mean? . . . With some urgency, my finger searches for any palpation and eventually detects a weak little thump. Normally this should be gratifying, but now I hear some doctor telling me to go home, take an aspirin, lie down, rest. Break-ups are stressful, young man . . . Jesus, such a delicate little thing.

But then I remember why I've come. "Anne . . . how can we resolve this?"

Once more I hear her inhale. "Mac, if something's wrong, maybe you should get some medical attention."

". . . I'm not dead yet . . ." Around me, however, the walls, and lights, and shadows slowly spin. I detect snickers at my denial. But oddly, having said that, I feel slightly better, and twist myself around to try to find her. Up there, I hear her stir and see her dark form settle onto the top step. I look away. Whether a minute passes, or an hour, before I hear her speak, I cannot tell, but she is saying, ". . . I know I promised to talk, but . . . I needed, we needed, to speak about Rachel and . . . and then to have you try to force . . ."

Yes, I understand her point, but *my* problem is time. "Anne, time is what we no longer have . . . and you have a hold of my heart."

I hear her groan.

How to respond? There must be some way. "Anne, I'm sorry; I guess it was desperation." I look up. Her head is averted. "Can you understand?"

She breathes. "But . . . all these events, including what just happened, have pushed me further into doubt. I can't pretend that I feel as I did before, about us."

A cold blade slices through me. "But how does it vanish so quickly?"

"It hasn't been so quickly."

Another blade, colder. I knew she had been questioning, pulling back; I recall the hints, the moments . . ."But Anne, for me, attachments last, are not so easily swept away."

I listen for her breathing, a sigh, a sign, anything. The silence unnerves me. "Anne, everyone has their ups and downs."

". . . I'm afraid I cannot ignore that things have changed, in me."

I hear but cannot completely process. "But we knew change was coming, knew we were both moving onto new things. But let's not discard it all, the entire carcass." An unfortunate choice.

"Mac . . ."

"It cannot be so easily replaced . . . Not replaced at all, actually."

"McKim, I hope that this won't seem cold or cruel, but I know I didn't enter into our relationship with the idea that it was permanent. For one thing, as you know, I was recovering . . ."

"Yes, but look at what we unexpectedly discovered. Wouldn't it be foolish to toss it all away, just chuck it over the transom?"

"I'm saying that at the outset, there were long-term limitations, which I brought."

"But things developed, far beyond what we, at first, anticipated."

"But I guess what I'm trying to find a way to say is, Mac, that I was not, and am not, ready . . . to make it permanent, to give up all other possibilities."

My brain warps under this cold blast—although I've long sensed that she looks ahead more clearly, more sharply, than I. Glancing up, I see that she sits with both arms wrapped around herself, her chin resting on her knees, her form, in silhouette, somehow feline. "Mac, I don't think you're being realistic about the distance. It was a long flight out to my father, and back."

Bravely, foolishly, forlornly, I ask, "Well then . . . shall we do it, get hitched? . . . Married?" And yet I know, as I say it, it feels wrong, even to me. She looks up, over her arms. Her mouth is parted in disbelief, as if asking, haven't you heard me? Am I not getting through?

". . . I can't bear the idea of you slipping away. There must be some solution."

For a moment she reflects, before confessing, "But Mac, after all of this, all of this around Rachel, things couldn't go on as before, even if you were staying here . . . I need some time to reflect, and adjust . . . Don't you understand?"

Do I? . . . My understanding of things in general seems to be lacking. I hear her add, "And with us so far apart, I don't see how we could work things out." Her coldness surprises me, as it sinks in, leaving my lungs frosted, unable to inhale or exhale, and without oxygen, my thoughts fall flat, slip to the floor. I can only mutter to myself, "I can't believe you're saying this . . ." But she doesn't hear. And I am reflecting back over many of the plays, wondering if any of their wisdom has sunk in, wondering if I remain as blind as their characters. A new appreciation of the adjustment Jacob must make in *Half Moon* slowly knifes in—his rather painful sacrifice of some essential part of him. If I weren't so desperate to see her, I might close my eyes, float up into the night sky, and think anew upon that sacrifice. But right now that sounds too much like death and capitulation.

"It makes me sad, McKim . . . I wish I had something encouraging to say."

"Our minds, and hearts, are not so far apart, Annie," I maintain weakly, and looking up through the darkness, I see her nod faintly, surprisingly, but then hear her explain, "I've been thinking that my own expectations have been unrealistic—maybe I've already said this—I think I was hoping for some insight from Rachel, some simple truth, some sense of more direct, essential living, which I felt I'd lost, distracted by the materialism in our lives and by so much rushing around . . . And maybe I thought Tyrone might offer an example of that, too. I hope that doesn't sound condescending, and maybe ridiculous . . . although maybe it is. In any case it was certainly wrong-headed . . . But I needed something, some fresh perspective, Mac, particularly in the world of work, where things have probably come too easily to me, beyond what I feel I've earned. People have long sung my praises, as you have, and as my father has always done, excessively . . . exceeding what I've deserved. For a long time I wanted to believe it all. It was seductive, but then I began to feel it was wrong and *un*earned. And I found that dismaying and confusing . . . I saw how hard Rachel had to work for every foot forward . . . but then I woefully misread that situation . . . Can you follow that, Mac? . . . I can't be sure it's clear, or makes sense."

"I hear you, Annie . . ."

"Now, having both imposed myself mistakenly and then reacted selfishly, I believe I've gotten burnt, deservedly."

Wanting to dispute this at first, I, instead, find myself agreeing, that it's pretty much true for both of us.

"McKim, all of this has contributed to sending me in a new direction—something I'd been thinking about, as you know, but not something I'd decided on . . . But now however, I see a way ahead, and believe I need to hold to it. Indeed, already I feel bound to it, so that I would not *want* to leave it, unless I see with my whole soul that it's wrong for me . . . And I suspect that you are similarly held, bound to that movie. And thus committed here, I could not go with you; I would burst, even though I cannot be certain the things holding me here are right . . . Maybe it's only misguided ambition, playing to my vanity, but I have to try. The opportunity may not come again."

"We may not meet again, Anne."

For some moments she does not respond, and I wonder if this is contrition. Probably not. Finally she turns and looks down at me. "Mac, I recognize this . . . but at this point, and particularly after these sad events, that part of me, the relationship part, is just not ready to . . . embrace anything in a serious way . . . I need time, to try, and to sort out . . . Part of me would like to hold you and love you, but I have too many other things tugging at me, right now."

Holding my own reaction at arm's length, I marvel at her gentle clarity . . . and in it hear the ring of finality. ". . . So Annie . . . I guess I'm not your guy."

"You are, Mac, in many ways. You're risking a lot, a lot that I wouldn't."

"But what? We're suddenly on different tracks?"

I hear no reply, and so, after a time supply my own, "I understand, Anne, what you said . . . It's just that I keep thinking that if you loved me, then all this other business, as powerful as it is, wouldn't divide us."

". . . I think we allow ourselves to fall in love, and right now I'm not free to feel love, even the love I know I have for you."

Resounding through my head, I hear the iron door clang shut. So, indeed, this is it. "Anne . . . if I had stayed in the city, do you think we would have found a way? That is, would you have looked for one?"

"Right now, I need time to restore myself. I don't mean to sound self-absorbed, but . . . I was wrong in looking outside myself . . . and maybe I was wrong in staying at the magazine as long as I have, with its emphasis on marketing and packaging and hype—and because I feel I made those mistakes, I think I need to start again, with a clean slate. In some way, I feel empty."

"You're being too hard on yourself."

"Possibly . . . but it's where I am."

I ask myself how I am going to accept where *I* am. It, too, feels empty. My eyes wander around through the darkness as I feel my brain grasping for something. "Annie . . . if we stay in touch . . . is it conceivable that you might change your mind, at some point?"

"Mac, I hope we stay in touch, but who can predict the future? Can you?"

"Actually, I can. I predicted this."

But she barely moves, and makes no reply, does not appear to appreciate the irony. (Ah Schurtz, d' chickens've come home to roost, and you is caught in the hen house, eh mon.) Yet part of me feels relief, for at least I see the wall, and road, ahead. As for my culpability, I have paid the highest price I could—perhaps more than my life itself . . . an atonement, through which, I may learn and grow . . . and some day possibly be a better person. Yeah, all of that, again. Or I may simply grow bitter . . .

But now what? Just arise and go, heroically, stoically, out, without comment, or tears? . . . Or stay here until she changes her mind and embraces me? But I always forget the other; that she has her own plan, and feelings, which need attending to . . . (No, mon, you must face d' facts: dat dis part o' your life is over, and dere's nuttin' you can do, but get on, on to California and a new chapter, and who knows.)

There will be much to remember, much to cherish—a great deal to regret. You, who have tried to arrange your life to avoid these holes, have simply opened more. So much for insurance . . . Maybe we will actually stay in touch. Stranger things have happened.

"Mac?"

I look up, but can't quite see her face between her hands.

"Are you feeling okay?"

I nod. I don't know why I am, but I am. Given the circumstances, near-death is probably okay.

"Mac, I don't know what else there is to say, right now . . . I'm pretty tired . . . . Thank you for letting me unburden myself."

"Annie . . . if my heart weren't breaking, I'd say something like, that's what friends are for."

"I'm sorry, McKim."

"I am too . . ." I breathe and look around. "So . . . we'll stay in touch?"

"Yes."

Confusion mixes with the rain inside—producing a wintry mix. Well . . ."I can't quite believe it, Annie." When I hear no reply, I look up. She has not moved, staring at the wall.

"The dreams we each had, Mac, were fairly simple, and yet because we didn't see clearly . . . look at the tragedy and sadness that has resulted . . . There is something wrong, Mac, that so much misery could come from such . . . simple things."

My mind begins to list several explanations, such as: things were not quite so simple. But then I let it go . . ."Will you write me, Annie, if I do?"

"Happily."

"And if I call you?"

"Of course. I hope you will."

"Don't say 'of course' to a heart that has lost its very reason for beating."

She is silent.

Well, it's time to go . . . Not unlike some earlier moment, I find myself pushing myself up, incredulously. Actor acting? On stage or off? . . . No lines . . . . Do you have the courage or resolve? "Good night, Annie."

She stands. "Wait." She comes slowly down the stairs. "A hug?"

We do . . . For a lifetime. Could stay here forever. Could, but can't . . .

A final kiss, two taps, two cheeks. Afraid to really look, but then force myself, to take in, one last time, this face burned into my heart—her eyes, their feeling, this entwining that, for a time, was one . . . And then I am squeezing her hand, and her other hand is touching my arm; then I am parting, making my way across the room, opening the door, looking back. She stands in the shadow of the stairs; I wonder what she is feeling; she has been through a lot, too—more—I wave and, incredibly, automatically, as if taking my mark, step through and out.

Suspended from life, or anything I can feel, I make my unsteady way back to Hudson, then north. Am thinking that I am in a play, playing my part . . . but have run off the end of the script, off the stage, am suddenly out the back door, floating, without lines or direction.

A few people along Hudson notice my impassive face, facing into the wind, impervious, pale, bloodless. But in New York these are only details in the passing parade. Forcing one leg in front of the other, a proud strut, goose-stepping, unaffected by the vagaries of this world, intent on my part, if only I could remember it. Listening for some sense of my role on-going and the one left behind.

I want the audience to know, far back in the cheap seats, want them to feel that this character, Schurtz, has lost his life, and yet goes on, unbowed. Hero . . . And though he cannot see where he goes, through the ocular dew, he knows his marks, knows how to improvise. God! Does he! Can get through anything, until the curtain falls.

My street. All the dark buildings stately and maintained. But to the left, murder . . . and to the right, betrayal; and behind nearly every door, love lost. The human story. So it goes. How, from these thrashing creatures, does this architectural perfection arise? How misleading . . . . McKim, Hamlet, and Macbeth . . . poetic names that lead to death.

At last, my building. But I can hardly make it to the stoop. A heaviness from behind descends, impedes my climb. I turn and face their building—Rachel and Rebeccah—feel myself sinking onto my cold slab. Dimly I see in those murderous windows across the street the outlines of this poor story . . . Yet to what avail? I thought that my re-telling would remove the shroud, but some details remain elusive, receding into the night as others come forward into focus. This much I *can* conclude: that for the first time, in place of pain and mist, I can name my transgression—for me, no inconsequential step. I know now that in reaching for an ideal, I ignored too much voices of the heart, in them, in me; voices spoken often through the eyes, which nonetheless reached deep within . . . That much do I grant.

There are, no doubt, numerous factors that kept, and would keep, Anne and Rachel and me apart—the small and mighty differences—but I should have spoken to each, that is, spoken my heart, as Rachel evidently thought I could. Certainly that evening I should have. Should have put Anne aside for the moment and asked, what do you want, Rachel? Why are you calling this evening, what do you need?

But I didn't.

And that I didn't shouldn't have been a surprise. My training from early on has been to adopt other identities in order to evade my own. My deepest feelings, amidst the clamor, remained difficult to hear—in part a family weakness, of course, but in part a coward's fear to look. One might argue that we are who we are, each his or her peculiar mix, each wound around with our individual ribbon of woe. Yet I was aware enough to choose . . . but held back . . . . Weakness, human weakness here has won . . . Sadly I'm not alone, I know . . . Rachel, Tyrone . . . and even Anne have some share of it. I know each struggled with one issue or another. And Becky, I fear, must as well . . . I can only hope our little effort will help: a little money, Maggie and Peter keeping up the contact . . . as I leave them all behind.

Years of practice have sharpened my ear for mimicry, at the expense of that for integrity. Little chance, then, that I will make the right choice, until I learn to listen—an actor's first lesson, ironically . . . But without this receptivity, when emotions and truths are not heard, or are denied, other forces step in, impulses resound beguilingly. I can only hope, can only vow, that the cowardly impulses will not predominate when I fly west to my next life. Ingrained habits are not shaken in a single mourning. Indeed it might be better if I sit here on these cold steps through the night, having nowhere I need go. Better perhaps that I talk to those two women across the street, whisper what only eyes have said . . . Not sure I could rise if I wanted to, as all of this, and something more, some second, seasoned body, weighs me down. Now that I can no longer play the victim—truth having made its guest appearance and changed the lines—I fear the next act is beginning, and I must face it, stepping back out upon the stage, bearing my recently acknowledged, horn-headed, tail-twitching twin, my own Macbeth, who sits upon my shoulders as we battle for a throne.

THE END.